THE RED HILL

DAVID PENNY

River Tree Print

River Tree Print

Publisher's Note: This is a work of fiction. Names, characters, places, and incidents are a product of the author's imagination. Locales and public names are sometimes used for atmospheric purposes. Any resemblance to actual people, living or dead, or to businesses, companies, events, institutions, or locales is completely coincidental.
Book Layout ©2014 BookDesignTemplates.com
Editor: Roz Morris
Cover Design: Damonza

The Red Hill / David Penny -- 1st ed.
ISBN 978-1499669763

For Megan
who has shown great patience

ONE

Three men lay tumbled in the bed of the cart but only one of them would live. Thomas Berrington had saved a score like these today and knew more waited his judgement. He lifted the head of the first and stared into blank eyes. Gone. The next... possible. The last had acquired a wound to his stomach, another to his chest. Blood frothed at a gaping hole each time he exhaled.

The dying man's eyes searched the pale sky, flicking left, right, as if seeking something to latch onto, each laboured breath an agony. Eventually the man recognised the figure leaning over him and Thomas watched a slow resignation fill his eyes.

Thomas leaned in and whispered, "You fought bravely. You're a hero." He had no idea if he spoke the truth or not.

Nothing in the man's eyes offered a clue. Instead he began to struggle. He might die within minutes, or draw this torture out for hours. Thomas had seen men cling to the tatters of hope long after they should have let go. He leaned close, his left hand closing around the man's right arm, just in case, his right reaching down to the weapons belt. He withdrew the knife. Without needing to look, without hesitation, Thomas slipped it between the man's ribs to pierce his heart.

For a moment the soldier's eyes widened, but already life was fleeing—then gone. Thomas closed the man's eyes and straightened to find the cart driver watching, his face expressionless.

"There's a place for the dead over there."

Thomas turned away to the last man, the one who might be saved. He dragged him clear, caught the stained body easily as it rolled free.

Behind him the pale walls of the city of Gharnatah rose, the eastern gate thrown wide to welcome the returning victors. Thomas had been born in a land a thousand miles to the north but considered this city home now.

He carried the man towards the infirmary tent set hard against the wall, screams and stench greeting him as he drew near. Hell enfolded him as he entered—hell in all aspects but one. Many of these men would return to fight again. No free table remained but Thomas saw the occupant of one no longer had need of it. He tipped him off with his leg and laid his new patient down.

"Ahmad!" Thomas shouted as one of the boys fetching and carrying ran past. "Drag this corpse out of my way and put it with the others. And fetch my instruments."

He leaned over, pulling aside the man's leather jerkin. This one had found a home for a musket round. It was lodged in his shoulder. Thomas dug with his fingers, searching for the object, causing the man to groan and rouse.

"Don't touch me!" The man swung a blow with his uninjured arm, but Thomas blocked it easily.

The musket ball was too deep to reach without cutting. "Do you want to live, or shall I tip you onto the pile with the rest?"

"I want a real surgeon." The man's voice was slurred, brains scrambled from loss of blood and pain.

"I am a real surgeon."

"You're *ajami*. I want a Moorish doctor."

"Want all you like, it's me you've got."

Ahmad returned with the box of instruments. Most seemed almost clean. Thomas rummaged through, picking out what he needed, a hooked blade and small forceps.

"Bring me poppy liquor."

"I don't need—"

Thomas smiled at the wounded soldier. It was not a reassuring expression. "You'll thank me when I start. Did we win?"

"A great victory."

"Aren't they all? Now lie still and shut up, I need to speak with a colleague." Thomas turned away. Stopped. "And don't run off or I'll drag you back and start without the poppy."

Da'ud al-Baitar glanced up as Thomas approached.

"Help me here a moment." On the table lay a pale figure, a slash to the man's side half repaired. "This one doesn't know how close to death he is."

Thomas put his hands on the man's shoulders and pinned him down while al-Baitar worked quickly. The stitching wasn't pretty, but soldiers boasted of their scars, each one testament to their courage—or foolishness.

"I need you to assist when you're done here," Thomas said.

"A few minutes. You can leave if you want, I can attend to him on my own. Go back to that pretty wife of yours."

"I'll stay." Thomas was unwilling to face the barely understood reasons behind his reluctance to return home. Most men would be only too willing to rush back to Helena, more than content to have been made the gift of a concubine from the Sultan's harem.

Instead Thomas watched his friend work. Al-Baitar's movements were sure, confident—but too gentle for this place. It was why Thomas was the one standing outside deciding who to bring in for treatment, the one offering solace to those who would die in agony without his mercy. He knew why the man lying on his own table didn't want him. Not because he was a foreigner, *ajami,* but for his other name—*qassab.* So be it. Thomas had been called far worse, and this butcher saved lives as well as took them.

Thomas spat in an attempt to clear the bitter taste from his mouth and drew the long tail of his tagelmust across his face. Dust coated his skin, gathered in the three day stubble on his cheeks. His wish for a quiet life had been thwarted once more. If only people would stop trying to kill each other. He had saved the man in the cart but wondered why—in a month the soldier would return to fight again. All Thomas had done was delay an inevitable fate.

Cart wheels raised more dust from the bone dry earth. A gust of wind brought the scent and sound of water from the Hadarro which ran close by, its flow hidden behind trees, water running out through a grill embedded in the city walls. The sun touched the tops of the Elvira hills and soon Thomas would follow the soldiers' footsteps and pass through the western gate into the city. Once he had completed his work.

He watched the passing soldiers with emotionless eyes. Those who caught his gaze looked away, uneasy at the coldness of his stare. Thomas was trying not to think of the time he had been like these men. A time richly coloured in his mind—that colour mostly red.

He shifted his attention from the men in front as feeble cheering came, followed by the rapid clatter of a horse in full gallop. Someone came fast alongside the slowly moving line. As they passed men raised tired arms and hoarse voices to a figure they recognised. Thomas narrowed his eyes, shook his head when he saw who it was.

Yusuf, the Sultan's youngest son, reined his horse hard and jumped to the ground even before it had come fully to a halt. A slack body lay draped across the beast, wedged between saddle and shoulder. Blood streaked the horse's flank.

"Save him, Thomas," Yusuf said. "I would have you save him. He's not dead yet, I think. You saved me, you can save him."

Thomas went to the figure and grabbed a handful of hair, lifted the head. He leaned close. The boy still breathed.

"Why this one?"

"Because you can." Yusuf's voice was stern and Thomas almost smiled.

He turned back to the horse and tugged at the unconscious boy's belt, caught him as he fell. The movement aggravated the wound. The boy's eyes opened and he started to fight.

"I know you." The boy's voice barely rose above a whisper.

"Good for you."

"You are the Sultan's pet." The expression of distaste on his young face reflected his feelings.

Thomas was used to such judgement. He glanced at Yusuf to see if there was any reaction to the mention of his father, but the young prince, already skilled in diplomacy, gave no sign of having heard.

"Can you walk or do I have to carry you?" The boy swayed, but appeared to be getting stronger all the while.

"I'm going nowhere."

"Then you can die where you stand." Thomas turned away.

"No," Yusuf said. "I promised you would save him."

"I save those who want to be saved, not fools."

"I order it!"

This time Thomas did smile, drawing his tagelmust across to hide the expression.

"Oh, I see. In that case..." Thomas grasped the boy's arm, but he pulled away and started shouting, calling on the passing soldiers to save him from the butcher.

Thomas grabbed him again, but already five men had stepped from the line and formed a barrier between him and the tent.

Yusuf moved to stand between Thomas and the men, believing his position as the Sultan's son protection enough. "Let them pass."

"The boy doesn't want to go," one said.

"Let him loose," said another.

There was no leader here, Thomas saw, only soldiers protecting one of their own. All five were scarred, stone-faced, experienced in battle, their tunics stained with blood and worse. Thomas had seen their kind many times over the years, grown up alongside them in a distant land he no longer called home. He wasn't afraid. There were only five of them. He took a step forwards, dragging the boy alongside.

Two of the soldiers blocked the way, jostling against him. One of them tried to remove his grip on the boy but failed. Thomas was stronger than he looked, and didn't plan on releasing this prize. He knew where Yusuf stood. If any of the men drew their swords he could step back and pull the prince's weapon. Yusuf himself would be no use—Thomas had treated his shoulder a year earlier and the right arm remained weak. The prince pretended he could fight with his left, but it was a poor substitute. It was fortunate he was the younger son and had no need to rule.

Thomas pushed.

Behind the two blocking him someone drew a sword.

Thomas released his grip on the boy and stepped back. The man on his right grinned, seeing only weakness. Thomas stepped back again and his hand found the hilt of Yusuf's sword, drawing it fast before the prince knew what was happening.

Now they were grinning, as if they hadn't seen enough fighting already today. But these were hardened troops—killing is what they did, and a chance to kill the foreigner was too good an opportunity to pass over.

"Stop this now!" Yusuf stepped between them. Thomas grabbed the prince's robe and tossed him aside. The boy he had been trying to save swayed and his legs went. He sat hard on the ground, head hanging down.

Thomas decided the first would be the one to his right. A fast thrust to the thigh, then a backswing to disable the other before stepping past them to the last three. He expected them to run, but sometimes he was surprised. He didn't want to kill anyone who had no need to die.

Other soldiers stopped to watch the entertainment, forming a barrier around which some passed and some stuck to the edges like flowing blood to a scab.

Thomas relaxed, his mind stilling. It was time.

"What the fuck is going on here?"

Or not time. Not today. Not here. But he knew these men would remember him.

Olaf Torvaldsson sat astride a small Arabian horse, his bulk making it look like a mule. The Sultan's general wore chain armour, marking him as someone of importance, but unlike that of his master, it was workmanlike, unpolished, nicked here and there from a hundred battles.

"Our friend doesn't want to go with the *qassab*."

"This is Thomas Berrington. He will not harm the boy."

"I know who he is."

Olaf dismounted and bullied his way between Thomas and the soldiers.

"And you know who I am."

The speaker nodded. Of course he did.

"I order you to let them pass."

"He's—"

"Let. Them. Pass," Olaf repeated, each word spoken slowly, each word accented and thick against his tongue.

Thomas reached back and handed Yusuf his sword. There was no need of it now. Already his thoughts had turned from the soldiers to the injured boy.

Thomas left the boy with al-Baitar and escorted Yusuf outside to his horse. The sky had leached itself of light while they were inside the tent, both from the setting sun but also from clouds that gathered above the Sholayr, dark and threatening. Occasional flashes of lightning played, distant for the moment, followed a long time later by soft thunder.

Beyond the tent the line of returning men moved slower, the last gasp of returning victors, their weary steps leading them into the city. The knot of onlookers had dispersed but Olaf remained, talking to a group of well-dressed men. Thomas knew he couldn't simply ignore the old soldier. They had a link of blood now.

"Where is your father?" Thomas asked Yusuf.

"He's coming. You know he always wants to be last through the gate. And there is entertainment planned."

"In that case I think I'll leave." Thomas could guess the manner of the entertainment and wanted nothing to do with it. "Stay with Olaf until he comes."

"I don't need protecting," Yusuf said.

"Of course not. Stay with him all the same, to please me."
Thomas knew how the young prince felt about him even as he
wished it were not so, but saving the boy's life couldn't be taken
back.

"You are eager to return to your wife," Yusuf said. Fourteen
was old enough to know of such things, particularly if you were
a member of the royal household and had lived within the harem most of your life.

"Not my wife..." Thomas started to object then gave up,
knowing it was useless.

"She has been with you half a year now," Yusuf said. "Isn't it
time you made her your wife?"

"I don't need a wife."

"Then throw her out."

Thomas shook his head. He couldn't do that.

"You can't leave yet," Yusuf said, forgetting about Thomas's
companion. "Father wants to see you."

"Then I have stayed too long."

A fresh wave of cheers sounded, some almost enthusiastic, and
Thomas raised his eyes as Yusuf's father approached, surrounded by the usual entourage of guards and hangers-on. It was a
large group, swelled by several members of Gharnatah's elite.
Yusuf's older brother Muhammed rode beside his father.

"I see you are repairing the dead again, my friend." Abu
al-Hasan Ali, Sultan of Gharnatah, ruler of the remaining ter-
ritories of al-Andalus not yet taken by the Spanish, pulled his
stallion to a halt and dismounted.

"Malik." Thomas used the usual honorific given to the Sultan
as he bowed from the waist, making ornate gestures with his
hands. "Congratulations on a magnificent victory. Allah has
been kind."

"Stand straight, surgeon. You have no need to bend your
knee in my presence."

Thomas straightened, but his gaze remained lowered.

The Sultan clapped Thomas on the shoulder. He was a little

shorter than Thomas, who bent his knees to offer the man an advantage. Abu al-Hasan tossed his reins aside. Someone would be there to lead his mount into the city.

"I need to talk with you, but first there is a matter of honour to attend to."

Thomas had seen the two men tied back to back on a single horse, but could not summon enough curiosity to wonder what crime they had committed.

"You're going to the bathhouse, Malik? I will find you there later." It was a tradition for the victorious Sultan to make himself seen among the common soldiers at the baths below the Albayzin, where many of those soldiers maintained houses and families.

The Sultan put a hand on Thomas's shoulder to prevent him moving away. "Stay. We might have need of you." He turned and raised a hand. "Untie them. Form a circle."

Thomas knew his hoped for escape was no longer possible. Around him soldiers laughed and cheered, moving out to leave an open space. The Sultan moved with them, stood at the front of the crowd as they gathered. Returning men slowed and stopped, the crowd growing, noise rising. Men started laying bets even before they saw who was fighting.

"What did they do?" Thomas asked, knowing there would be little logic behind whatever answer came.

"The short one accused the taller of cowardice. The tall one accused the shorter of killing men without need."

"It doesn't seem much."

"It's enough," the Sultan said.

The men were dragged to the middle of the circle and their ropes cut.

"Give them each a sword," the Sultan said, his voice commanding, carrying to everyone gathered.

Two blades were tossed into the ring. The short man picked his up. The tall one remained where he was.

"See, a coward," the Sultan said to Thomas, then more loudly, "Someone give him the sword."

A soldier darted in, picked up the weapon and pressed it into the hand of the tall man.

The Sultan raised his arm once more, his voice rising with it. "These men accuse each other on the field of battle. Let Allah decide the truth through trial by combat." His arm came down. The crowd roared as the short man rushed in, his sword flashing.

The tall man turned at the last moment, deflecting the blow. He stepped back, reluctant to fight, doing the minimum to protect himself as an attack came again. The noise ratcheted higher. Wagers were offered and accepted. The crowd pressed forward, those at the front struggling to hold position.

"Yes, Thomas, come find me at the baths," the Sultan said. "We must talk. I have another favour to ask of you."

Thomas wondered what it would be this time, still unsure of the value of the gift the Sultan had made after his last request. He wished he had never been offered the friendship of this man, but knew it was not something that could be refused.

The clash of blades rang in his head, raising memories he didn't welcome. At least it looked as though the contest would be over quickly. The tall man moved backwards, circling the arena, only using his sword to deflect the other's blows. The crowd began to hoot and chant, the noise rising to a crescendo as they grew restless. Thomas glanced at the Sultan, wondering if he would intervene before one of the audience took matters into their own hands, but the man's eyes were fixed on the combat, a tight smile on his face. The setting sun painted the killing ground red, as though ushering in the inevitable gift of blood.

It ended quickly, but not as expected.

The short man came in fast, a dervish, his sword a crimson arc. The tall man fell back and suddenly went to one knee.

Sensing an advantage his protagonist attacked, using both hands on his sword.

The tall man moved fast, reaching down to his boot, pulling a dagger. As the short one loomed over him his hand darted out, the knife embedding itself in flesh.

The crowd hushed.

The short man swayed, staggered back, not yet aware he was dead. Thomas saw it before anyone else. The knife had pierced his liver. Blood gushed along his side, started to pool around his feet as he trod the fluid into the dry ground. He swayed again then went to his knees. For a moment he tried to raise his sword arm before toppling sideways.

The silence continued a moment longer, then uproar. Soldiers arguing over their bets, haranguing the victor for losing them money.

The Sultan stepped forward, waiting for quiet to resume.

He moved to the centre of the ring, turned, surveying the crowd. His eyes found Thomas and hesitated, a smile coming to his lips before moving on.

"I declare this man the winner," he said. "But he remains a coward, and won the contest by foul means. Take his head."

He stepped back as a soldier came from the crowd, a heavy scimitar already in his hands.

"Malik—" The tall man, still on his knees, started to object, but before the first word was barely out his head had been severed. It bounced away and rolled to a halt, the eyes blinking once, twice, before going still. His body fell backwards, spouting a thick arc of blood.

The Sultan stepped delicately around the carnage and returned to Thomas's side as thunder sounded, closer now.

"Does that mean Allah is pleased with the result?" he said.

"It's a storm, nothing more." Thomas made no effort to disguise his lack of faith or his disgust at the outcome.

"I hate a cheat," the Sultan said, his voice soft, reasonable, as though he had not deliberately caused the deaths of two men. And deliberate it had been.

The Sultan patted Thomas on the shoulder. "Don't forget to come to the baths, will you."

Two

Within the palace the air is cool after the heat of the plain. Sweat hangs clammy against the soldier's skin as he makes his way to his target. His flight here has been rushed, impatient to return to this place before any others. The chill is nothing to him and he dismisses it, as he has dismissed all discomfort and worse. He has experienced the agony of a blade, the crushing blow of a hundred fists. All can be ignored when the target is clear.

In his mind's eye he pictures how it will be. A flash of steel. A fountain of blood. Exultation filling his body because this time, it will be right.

He stops at a place where he can view the inhabitants of this fantasy world and looks onto fabulous luxury. He inhales deeply, drawing in the scents: perfume, incense, oils and lotions and soaps. And women. The scent of many women. Women so beautiful that merely to look upon them might send a man mad.

He knows his way around this place now, far better than when first he entered its world. There had been mistakes then, of course, but he believes he has made up for them since, honing his skills, practicing on those who will not be missed.

It excites him knowing he is invisible to those he observes. He stops at a familiar place, small stones grating beneath the soles of his sandals. From the new vantage point he feels as if he is amongst the women. Some partly clothed, a small number barely clothed at all. Most are young, some very young: the servants, but also a few of the wives.

These women possess bodies and skin so perfect they are almost unreal. He has watched them at play and in conversation, watched as they are soaped and cleansed, watched the hair plucked from their bodies and their skin scrubbed until it is as smooth as the finest silk. And watched as the Sultan makes his infrequent visits to take one or more to a sleeping chamber. He knows all the places he can observe from now. Nowhere is hidden from him.

A man enters the room where a woman lies on a couch, her arm raised while a servant carefully removes all trace of hair beneath. The man is tall, his head bald, a strong body covered in rich silks. The woman is pregnant, her stomach heavy with an exquisite beauty, her breasts swollen into new glory.

"What is it, Jorge?" She is untroubled by the new arrival in this place where men are rare. The observer has seen this one before, this eunuch, and is not concerned; the man is no threat. At one time the watcher feigned friendship so he could find out the information he needed. Although the man looks broad across the shoulders and strong in the stomach, his skin is soft and his face weak—too pretty. And there is no fire in his eyes.

"The Sultan has sent a message. He will call on you this evening." There is no hint of a question, or that a refusal might be considered.

"Then I will bathe when I am finished here. Ask someone to come and play for me. And return, too. Amuse me with conversation and make me laugh."

"Do you need anything else, Safya?"

"I am Sultana to you, eunuch." There is amusement in her voice. "And yes, that is all. My husband comes to me soon, fresh from battle. I have no need of you this day."

The creature laughs. The watcher cannot think of him as one like himself. He lacks that which makes a man.

When the woman is alone with her servants once more the watcher reaches beneath his robe and grips his manhood. He is as hard as the stone that protects his back. Even with the coolness inside the palace walls blood runs hot through his veins.

He waits, preparing, knowing his chance will come to make amends, to please his master. Not yet, not tonight, but soon, when he is sure of success. Another failure will mean more than punishment. His master was angry when he failed before, injured the wrong girl. But his forgiveness is divine.

The man stays hidden, watching as musicians enter and play—the sound too refined for his desert ears—as the eunuch returns and makes the woman laugh.

Finally the one named Safya rises and walks from the chamber, her gait more laboured than when he first watched her. He scurries after her, making no noise, not wanting to be heard by anyone but needing to reach the bathing chamber before she arrives.

In places he is forced to take alternate routes where others might see him, and always he waits to cross a passageway unobserved. He missed the palace when he was sent away, but now he has returned and its familiarity soothes him. There will be no more mistakes; he has proven that.

He finds Safya again in the bath-chamber. Three girls attend her, their flesh the colour of honey. There is no sign of the eunuch, which will make his task easier when the time comes.

Safya extends her arms, a hand held on either side as she steps beneath hot water gushing from a pipe set high in the wall. She allows the water to fall across her head, her skin, then lifts her gaze and stares directly into the eyes of the hidden man.

Does she see me? No, she cannot, it is impossible. She merely looks this way, interested in the pattern on the tile.

She stands unmoving for an age, as though deliberately posing for him, displaying herself, and his hand burrows beneath his robe once more, gripping himself so tightly it is almost painful. He finds the deep swell of her pregnant belly the most erotic thing he has ever seen, and despite his best efforts a groan escapes clenched teeth and all at once he grunts as seed spills from him.

This is the one, he thinks. *No more mistakes.* He doesn't always understand his master's wishes, but that doesn't matter. His role is to obey without question.

He remains cloaked from view, watching the naked girls soap Safya's perfect body, until at last she steps from beneath the heated water and allows the servants to pat her dry, to anoint her with perfume. Only when the women have departed and the bathing chamber is empty, when the water slows and stops, when only a drip-drip-drip breaks the silence, does he reveal himself. In the middle of the chamber the scent of the women is strong and he breathes it in, savouring the lingering taste against his tongue.

He stands a moment, eyes closed, then moves fast, a dark blur leaping forward, hand going to the hilt of his sword, drawing it and swinging down hard on empty air, his imagination filling in the missing figure. He performs the movements again, again, again. He is hard once more inside the silken robes as he thinks of the next time, when he will go beyond rehearsal.

When he hears voices he slips back the way he came, leaving no trace of his presence other than a faint disturbance of the air and a single wet footprint on the stone floor.

THREE

As Thomas made his way through the streets of Gharnatah the melee of returning soldiers and hangers-on drifted away into side streets. Others moved alongside him where the Hadarro flowed between the precipitous red hill of the palace and, almost as steep, a jumble of shacks and houses making up the Albayzin on the opposite bank. It was where Thomas had his house, as did many of the soldiers with families. Many knew him but none called out. The mood in the city was exultant. Once more Abu al-Hasan Ali had brought them victory, expelling the Spanish from the town of Tajar. A small town, and a small victory, but victory all the same.

Thomas was detached from the atmosphere of celebration; tired, feet stumbling, head swimming from too many hours of duty, with yet one more duty remaining, one he could not avoid. It was impossible the Sultan had forgotten his invitation. The temptation to return home was strong, almost too strong to resist. Being a friend to the most powerful man in al-Andalus was not the blessing most considered it to be.

Alongside the river, raised above all but the worst floods, the pathways were laid of stone and the houses large and prosperous. Every small square—and there were many—held a fountain or pool, water a constant presence in the city. It was one Thomas welcomed. Unlike the Spanish beyond the borders of al-Andalus, who prided themselves on a lack of even basic hygiene, he had grown to love the act of bathing once so alien to him. To them, cleanliness was an affectation only the heathen Moors lowered themselves to. At one time Thomas shared their view, but no longer.

A knot of hangers-on milled around the street doorway to the Hammam baths, and Thomas almost allowed himself to be discouraged from entering. His small, neat house was nearby, and the last climb through the alleyways of the Albayzin would be a welcome distraction, as would the presence of Helena when he arrived. He was starting to turn away when a young voice called out.

"Thomas—I waited in case you got lost. Come inside, father will want to reward you."

Thomas pushed through the crowd, Yusuf slipping an arm through his as they entered the bathhouse. Inside, the normal hush and calm had been replaced with noise and confusion. Soldiers guarded the entrance to the main baths, but Yusuf was recognised and allowed through into a large room filled with steam, the scent of oils, and noise. In more normal times the aromas would have eased Thomas's mind, but not tonight. The usual attendants had been added to with many others. Young men and women, some barely clothed, strolled around the steaming pool or stood beside the elite group of bathers. The view no longer shocked Thomas as it once had, but was one of the reasons he had wanted to avoid the Sultan's summons.

"I don't see your father."

"He won't be here, but someone will show us where."

"Not us. He will want to see me alone."

Yusuf ignored Thomas, leading him along the edge of the main pool. The real cleansing took place against the walls where hot water streamed from pipes. The pool was for those who wanted to see and be seen.

"Ho, surgeon, come here."

Faris al-Rashid, one of the men Thomas had managed to avoid earlier outside the city walls, lounged at the poolside sur-rounded by a dozen hangers on. Most were members of noble families, rich men who mined or farmed or traded—except not one of them undertook any real work; there were servants for that. Faris was a notional leader to these men, his wealth ru-moured to exceed even that of the Sultan's. He was also con-sidered by some to possess more power. Thomas knew him, as he did many of the others lounging around, their arms draped over the shoulders of young women and men.

Once Abu al-Hasan Ali had picked him out as his surgeon

many others demanded his services. Thomas made sure he charged an extortionate fee, but knew his bill meant little to men such as these.

Aware he couldn't ignore Faris he changed direction, Yusuf trailing along behind. The boy slipped into the warm water, while Thomas crouched on the edge of the bath.

Faris reclined against the tiled margin, arms stretched out, pressed on each side by two young women, their bodies wet and slippery with soap.

"Here, surgeon, why not come into the water and have one of these girls. Are they not delightful?"

They were indeed, both beautiful, both nubile, the skin of one the colour of ebony, the other a northerner as pale as her companion was dark, her blonde hair reminding Thomas he had a woman of his own waiting at home.

"I'm too tired to do either justice, lord."

Faris laughed. "You need do nothing at all. They will do everything, anything you ask."

"I thank you, but I must wash myself first."

"As you wish. Yusuf, take this Nubian, she is almost an age for you."

"I am looking for the Sultan," Thomas said as the girl wrapped her legs around Yusuf's waist. The prince might be young, but he knew how to deal with her perfectly well, grasping the cheeks of her arse and lifting her against him.

Faris waved a hand vaguely towards the rear of the bathhouse, his attention distracted by the blonde. "He is somewhere that way, with Muhammed. What do you want with him?"

"He asked to speak with me on some matter." Thomas began to move away, trying to avoid staring at the sights all around.

"About what?" Faris's voice was casual, uninterested.

"I will know that when I see him."

With Faris and Yusuf distracted Thomas drifted towards the far side of the pool, ignoring those around him, hoping he could slip away once he had spoken with the Sultan. But before his escape he needed to cleanse the stink of surgery from his body, and his bones ached with a deep weariness he doubted even expert hands could banish.

"Thomas!"

The raucous bathhouse lay behind as he wound his way through narrow passages off which lay private rooms. He stopped, knowing it was impossible to pretend he had not heard.

"My Prince." Thomas bowed. He called Yusuf, the Sultan's younger son, by his given name, but knew not to attempt such an air of familiarity with Muhammed. This one had ambition to rule one day, despite rumours his father might be plotting otherwise.

"I wanted to thank you for your work today." Muhammed lay on his belly as two women kneaded the knotted muscle along his back. The young man was broad, strong. Thomas had witnessed him in battle and knew one day he would be as great a warrior as his father. The puckered skin of a scar ran across his shoulder. Thomas remembered treating him after a battle at Malaka when the Spanish attacked from the sea.

"I was only doing my duty."

"A duty no-one else does so well. Don't underestimate your skills."

"My skills are your father's to command. Yours too, Prince."

"We should talk soon, Thomas. You are someone I can trust, as my father does, and there are few enough like you in this city. When are you visiting the palace next? You attend Safya, I hear. She is due soon?"

"Weeks at most. The baby will arrive before the next full moon."

"Another son, I trust."

"It will be as God wishes." Thomas could spout religion if need be, and knew Muhammed was devout.

"Allah be praised. But a boy will be good. Can you not tell, Thomas? The women of the harem say she is bigger on the right side so it must be a boy. Is it true you can tell from such signs?"

Thomas smiled. "There are a million ways women will determine such things, but it is all superstition. No-one can tell the sex of a child until it slips from its mother's womb."

Muhammed rolled onto his back and the women began to knead his thighs. Thomas had lost his Anglo-Saxon prudishness a long time ago, but he preferred not to witness what might come next. He knew he would have welcomed such attention himself once—before Helena came to his house.

"Has someone offered you a girl?" Muhammed stretched his arms above his head, arching his back.

"I have a woman of my own, Prince."

Muhammed laughed. "Of course. One of my father's cast-offs. Such a shame—she was a pretty thing once. Did father speak to you on the matter he wished to discuss?"

"He speaks to me of many things, including how proud he is of his children."

"Yes—he says that all the time. Sometimes I think he might even believe it. I meant this other matter, the killings."

"Killings?"

Muhammed sat up and pushed the girls servicing him to one side. "He seeks your help, although I told him it was a matter for the big northman. What use is a surgeon in such matters?"

"Without knowing more, Prince, I cannot to say."

Muhammed shook his head, lay back and waved at the girls to continue their ministrations. "He seems to have faith in you. I have no idea why. As far as I can tell you do your duty, as we all do."

Thomas agreed, but said nothing.

He found Abu al-Hasan Ali in another private chamber some distance away. No women pleasured him. Instead a strong Berber worked on the wiry muscles along his back. The Sultan looked up as Thomas stepped into the room, squinting a little. His sight wasn't good. Thomas had offered to remove the cataracts plaguing him, but knew the man would not agree until he could no longer see his hand in front of his face.

"Did you have difficulty finding me?" There was no trace of reproach but Thomas heard it anyway.

"Only in avoiding others." Thomas sat on a stone bench, cupped hot water from a running channel and sluiced it across his head. A moment of bliss.

"People know I confide in you. Everyone wants influence, one way or another. You must be weary, shall I call for someone to massage you?"

"My day has been nothing compared to yours, Malik."

The Sultan smiled. "I do little fighting these days, I am not so stupid. But yes, it was a long day, and hard."

"Do you want to tell me why you asked to see me, then we can both ease our tired bones. Your son said something about killings."

"So he was one of these others, was he? Did he say anything more?"

"I didn't ask. I knew you wanted to speak with me directly. Although I am puzzled why you choose me to tell about such events. Muhammed suggested you consult Olaf Torvaldsson."

"He was the first I thought of, but he is not a subtle man, and I believe these are subtle affairs. You are someone I trust not to broadcast what he discovers throughout the city." The Sultan pulled a face as the Berber dug fingers in along his spine.

"What has happened?"

"There have been attacks on servants inside the palace. Inside the harem. Two dead I know of, but others have lived."

"And you thought to seek my assistance?"

"You are one who understands death, are you not?"

"Not this form of death."

"I have seen you on the battlefield, Thomas. You deal with this manner of death all the time. And I ask it of you. Demand it of you."

It always came to this. A polite request followed by an order. Such were the ways of power. Thomas bowed his head, accepting whatever the task might be, despite a deep reluctance.

"Exactly what is it you want me to do?"

"Investigate, of course. Find out who the killer is and bring him to me so I can take his head."

The Sultan, Thomas knew, was fond of taking heads, as had been demonstrated less than an hour earlier. He stared at the Berber as he pummelled the Sultan's back and shoulders. At least he was being allowed a moment to consider the request, even though they both knew only one answer could be given.

Thomas nodded. "As you wish, Malik. I will have to speak with people, and some will no doubt talk in turn. It will be impossible to keep the matter quiet."

"The facts are known within the palace. Such barbarity cannot remain secret long."

"I have some concerns," Thomas said.

"Ask then. We are both only men here at this moment."

From a demand to a pretence of friendship within a minute. Thomas smiled. "Why me? I'm a physician. I deal in healing bodies and, failing that, easing their passing from this world to the next. There are many you could choose before me."

The Sultan sat up, shooing the Berber away. When they were alone he swung his legs over the side of the wooden bench and stared hard at Thomas.

"I considered Olaf first, of course. He is a good man, but not an intelligent one, and this matter needs a sharp mind. There are others close to me I might have entrusted with the task, but..." The Sultan hesitated, then dropped from the table and came to sit beside Thomas. "A man in my position has many enemies. A man in my position is not always sure whom to trust. There may be only one I can trust completely." He slapped his hand down on Thomas's leg, leaving it there, an uncomfortably familiar gesture.

"And when Olaf refused you thought of me?"

The Sultan put his head back and laughed, slapping Thomas's leg again. "This is why I love you, Thomas Berrington. No-one else dare speak to me as you do. I am surrounded by flattery and greed. Everyone wants something from me. Everyone except you. You will do this for me?" The Sultan stared into Thomas's eyes, his own clouded.

"With what little ability I possess. But this isn't something I am familiar with. You must know I might fail."

"No-one else would admit that to me, either. Do what you can."

"Who has been killed?"

"Serving girls. No-one of importance, but that doesn't matter. I will not have murder done in my palace."

He doesn't even know what he says, and why should he? This man leads a life unrecognisable to the rest of us.

"When?"

"The second a week ago. The first two months before."

"You believe the events are connected?"

"Two servants killed in the same place? How could they not be?"

"The same place? Where?"

"A bathing chamber. And no, not the *same* place, but the same kind of place. Different chambers. Both killed in the same way, with a sword. A powerful blow, struck by someone who knew what he was doing."

"You saw the bodies?"

The Sultan turned to Thomas. "Of course not, but I spoke with those who did. I went to Tahir al-Ifriqi first. When he failed to discover anything I thought again of asking Olaf, but magnificent general that he is, he lacks imagination."

"And I don't."

"No, you do not. Will you do as I ask and put me further in your debt?"

"A Sultan owes no debt to a man such as me, Malik."

The Sultan smiled. "Tell that to my treasurer, he will beg to differ. And you know I owe you a debt no man can ever repay."

"I was doing my duty."

"You saved Yusuf. You likely saved Muhammed, too. No other man could have done what you did."

"Any competent surgeon would have saved them."

"Others have told me different. And you are intelligent as well as imaginative. Too intelligent to underestimate yourself. We both know without your presence Yusuf would have died that day on the battlefield. But you distract me from the answer I need. You will do this, Thomas?"

I have a choice?

"I can talk with anyone I want?"

"Agreed."

"Members of your family, those within the palace walls? Even within the harem?"

"You are no stranger to the palace. When do you visit Safya? She is close, surely."

"I come within a week. She is not as close as that."

"Come tomorrow. This matter can't wait a week. Do what you must to find this man before others are killed, before he turns his attention to someone more important than serving girls."

FOUR

Thomas expected Helena to be asleep when he returned to his house in the Albayzin. As he climbed the hillside the sound of revellers faded. The night grew warmer, and occasional thunder sounded, closer now than when he had stood with the Sultan on the plain.

It had taken the half year she had lived under his roof to begin to feel comfortable with her presence. He had been too long alone, grown too used to his own company to find it easy, but he was slowly growing accustomed to sharing his life with another person. There was the guilt, too, at accepting the gift, as if she was some kind of slave, although he tried never to treat her as such. And then there was the ease with which he had accepted her into his bed, and how swiftly that had happened.

He had not wanted the gift even though it was impossible to refuse. Helena had joined the Sultan's harem as a concubine at fifteen and left after seven pampered years when she was attacked and disfigured. The harem was no place for a scarred concubine. Thomas knew the new domestic arrangements must be far harder on her than they were on him.

The house was quiet as he entered, a single lamp burning in the hallway as it always did. Thomas hung his cloak on a peg, unwound the long folds of his tagelmust and put it next to the cloak, where it draped to the ground. He climbed the stairs silently and removed his clothing with as little noise as he could.

The bedchamber was small, dim, a faint illumination coming from beyond the door. Helena's scent filled the small space, her body curled away from him on her side of the bed.

We have sides to the bed now, Thomas thought, smiling. *How like a married couple we have become.* And then, because he didn't want to think of marriage, he pushed the thought aside. He slid beneath the cotton sheet and lay on his back, staring at the rough ceiling as Helena rolled over, not asleep after all.

"You're late. And you smell good." Her hand reached out to rest against his face. "And your chin is smooth." She kissed him. "You know I like it when your face isn't rough." She ran her fingertip across his features, from forehead to mouth, brushing hair aside where it fell across his face. She traced dark eyebrows, the bones of his cheeks and chin, the fullness of his lips and the width of his mouth.

"The Sultan insisted I go to the baths." Thomas closed his eyes, enjoying Helena's touch, feeling himself stir. He spoke for the sake of it, his words meaning nothing. "He wanted to celebrate his victory."

"So it was a victory?" Her fingers moved to his chest, tracing old scars that crossed his skin. She seemed fascinated by them, perhaps seeing there some reflection of her own mutilation. Despite only faint illumination from the hallway she kept her head to one side, her face in shadow.

"Victory of a sort, but a small one. Too many dead, even more injured."

"You did your duty, I am sure." Her fingers moved from his chest, searching for something of more interest. Thomas hated the way his body reacted to her, as if he was some youth instead of a man of forty years, but knew he couldn't resist. "As I wish to do mine." She came across him, her mouth kissing his, then his neck. "Your skin is soft and you smell so good."

"Aamir massaged me."

Her breasts pressed against his stomach, her body lissom across his. She kissed the scars on his chest, moved lower. Thomas groaned, knowing what was to come, no longer shocked by the wantonness displayed by this woman.

Afterwards—and it had taken hardly any time at all—she lay close, her fingers once more tracing the raised marks on his body, and said, "Have you given thought to what I asked?"

"You ask many things. Which was I meant to think on?"

"You know which one. Lubna. Have you made a decision?"

"I can't see there's room in this house for another person."

"We could make room, surely. And if you say no I fear what might become of her. She's my sister, and I do love her, even if we don't share a mother." It was so like Helena to qualify everything. "And she would be useful to me." Now they were getting closer to the truth.

"I need more time," Thomas said.

Helena kissed his earlobe, the side of his mouth, her breath sweet against his face as her hand moved once more beneath the covers.

"Don't take too long, or she'll be despatched somewhere awful." Her hand found its target.

"I'm tired," Thomas said.

"And I'm not finished."

"I can't get hard again so soon."

Helena laughed. "You underestimate me, Thomas Berrington."

And he had.

Thomas woke to the sound of rain, confused, unsure where he was. Heavy, persistent, the storm beyond the mountains had finally arrived. He sat on the edge of the bed as thunder shook the tiles above his head. Beside him Helena stirred, mumbled and drifted back into sleep. Despite his exhaustion he knew his own sleep would elude him while the storm lasted. He rose and pulled on a robe, descended the stairs and opened the back door.

Rain fell. Heavy drops bounced from the paving stones to cast a shimmering mist above the narrow rill which ran the width of the courtyard. He stepped outside, sheltering beneath the balcony that ran from the kitchen to his workshop. Rain sheeted from the roof and fell vertically onto the slabs. It was as though Thomas was trapped behind a waterfall. A wooden bench stood hard up against the wall and he sat, his bare feet speckled with back-splashes of water.

He was hungry, but for the moment remained content to sit

and watch the rain as his mind slowly turned over the Sultan's request. He didn't understand why he had been asked. It made no sense.

Thomas knew he could provide more help than the Sultan suspected, possessing skills which would be useful, abilities the Sultan knew nothing of. Abilities Thomas made sure to keep secret from everyone—even himself. His life before he become a surgeon was one he would rather forget. His real life had not begun until he almost died. And now he was being asked to resurrect what he had fought so long to suppress.

He sat forward, arms on knees. Could he turn the Sultan down?

No—refusal wasn't an option.

Then pretend to undertake an investigation before reporting he had discovered nothing?

His tired mind buzzed with silent argument. He didn't want this task, couldn't refuse it, knew he was incapable of pretence if he took it.

So can I say no—regardless of the consequences?

The sound of a door catching against stone made Thomas lift his gaze from the mesmerising fall of water to find Helena standing under the balcony. She had pulled on a white linen robe to cover her nakedness.

"There you are," she said, her accent coloured like his, but the colouring different. "I woke and you were gone."

"I couldn't sleep, didn't want to wake you."

"I wouldn't have minded. I'm awake now, anyway. I notice when you're not there." She dipped her head, pale hair falling across one side of her face.

Thomas wished she wouldn't do that. The scar didn't bother him. He thought she was beautiful anyway. "Aren't you tired?"

Helena smiled, the movement misshapen, her mouth lifting more on the left, and once more she brushed her hair to cover her face.

Thomas started to speak, stopped.

Helena turned from the rain to look at him. "What did you

say?"

"Nothing."

She continued to stare, her gaze impossible to break. "Say it, Thomas." She straightened her shoulders, as if defying both him and herself, and tossed her head back to reveal the full beauty and terror of her face.

"You have no need to hide yourself here," he said. "You know I think you beautiful. I always have."

"Even this?" She lifted a hand and traced the line of puckered skin with her finger.

"Even that. It is nothing to me."

"No. But to me... to me it is everything. I'm grateful to you, Thomas, but don't pretend this is nothing."

Thomas sighed. "I'm sorry if life here is a disappointment to you."

Helena looked away, shook her head. "This is my life now. It is the life I lead, and I am pleased to be here. You know it's true, Thomas. I am happy you let me share your bed, to be here with you, but I can never forget what I have lost."

Thomas wanted to tell her she had lived a lie, feted, protected, but knew his words would fall on ears that refused to hear. Helena's entire life had been one of unashamed luxury and indulgence.

He recalled the first time he saw her, face torn open by a madman. She had been Hulyah then, still using the Moorish name she was given on entering the harem. She had only reverted to Helena after she left the hill.

Thomas had been called in the dead of night, a summons he couldn't refuse, as he couldn't refuse this last one. And then, after he had repaired as best he could the awful damage done to her beauty, there had come a conversation with the Sultan. An offer. As though Helena was nothing more than a trinket that could be passed on now its beauty was tarnished.

Thomas knew he should have refused. Dreaded what might become of her if he did. So he had said yes.

He glanced at her now, knowing what she was thinking.

"The scar is young," he said. "It will heal. It's already better than it was."

"But it will never heal completely, will it?"

"No, not completely." Thomas couldn't lie. Sometimes he considered it a weakness in his chosen profession. There were occasions telling a man he was going to die might be handled better than with the truth, but he left such pretence to others. "One day, not too far from now, you will barely notice it." This was the truth as well.

"I will always notice."

"We'll see. I'll remind you of your words in a year."

"A year? As long as a year?"

Thomas smiled. "Perhaps less."

"By summer?"

"Perhaps by summer. I have a formula for a salve al-Baitar gave me. He claims it has a great power for healing. I will make some up for you." He glanced at the falling torrent. The sound filled the courtyard. The rain wouldn't last. In this land it never did.

Thomas had made a decision but had no idea how or why or even when. Sometime as they spoke was all he knew.

"I need to visit the palace."

"Now?"

"In the morning."

"Then I'll come with you."

"As you wish. Will you be made welcome?" He couldn't recall the last time Helena had accompanied him to the hill.

"I expect there are a few friends who will still be pleased to see me."

FIVE

As they climbed to the palace Helena stopped where the trees opened out to catch her breath. The rain had scrubbed the air clean and the view spread out across the fertile plain to distant hills glittering with a rare clarity.

"Lubna will be no trouble, Thomas."

He walked on. He knew Helena would raise the matter again, and yet again, until she got her own way. It was how she achieved her aims. Except in this instance he was reluctant to agree to the request. There truly was no space. He was only now getting used to the presence of one woman in the house and didn't welcome a second. And there was the Sultan's request. There would be little enough time for domestic matters until that was concluded.

"She is small," Helena said, as though she could read his mind. "There is space above your workshop. No-one needs a roof as high as you have there. You could build a small platform, somewhere she could sleep. And she will help me clean and cook. She is quiet. Very quiet."

Thomas plodded on. They had ascended two-thirds of the slope, the Albayzin on the opposite hillside seeming almost close enough to touch.

"I have no time to build a platform."

"I didn't mean for you to do it." A look of almost horror crossed her face. "There are people. You have had them do much work to the house since I came."

"She calls herself Lubna. Why a Moorish name? You gave yours up, why not her?"

"She wants to be a Moor like her mother." Helena shook her head as though not understanding such a thing. Sunlight caught

33

against golden feathers of hair fallen loose from her headscarf. "She believes she belongs in this land."

"And you don't? Hasn't this land been good to your father, good to you?"

"It gave me this." Helena drew the scarf aside to reveal her scar. "This is being good to me?"

"A madman gave you that. And you enjoyed a wonderful life before then. Do I treat you so badly?"

"Of course not. I am grateful for all you have done. If not for you I fear what would have become of me."

"The Sultan would not have seen you destitute."

"Which is why he offered me to you."

Something in Helena's tone caused Thomas's steps to slow. He knew the life she led now was nothing compared to the one she had experienced before, but a scarred concubine had no place in the harem. Thomas might not agree with the sentiment but he understood it. He barely noticed the scar anymore.

"I'll always be grateful to him for that," Thomas said. He wanted a change of subject. "Are you planning to visit anyone special?"

"No-one in particular."

"I'm sure you could visit without me if you wished."

"Perhaps. Although the harem may not want reminding of how fleeting their comforts are. Besides, with you I have an excuse. Everyone respects Thomas Berrington."

"The soldiers hate me. You know what they call me."

"Believe what you will." Helena raised a hand in greeting to a dark skinned Berber guarding a little used entrance to the palace. A narrow doorway was set deep into thick walls on the side of the hill. Inside were more steps to climb, but the ascent was almost done. Helena emerged first, as ever unable to follow protocol. Thomas followed into a shaded courtyard. Water ran silently along a straight rill from one side to the other. Flowering trees and palms shaded the flagstones. Swallows cried as they chased insects in and out of sunlight. It was difficult to believe violent death had invaded this place, and there was no sign it ever had. The palace held its secrets close.

As they moved deeper they passed more guards, servants, those who lived permanently within the walls. None showed the slightest interest in the new arrivals. Thomas was known, and whoever accompanied him was always welcome. The harem was situated at the far end of the palace and Helena stepped ahead, eager to see old friends.

Thomas knew she missed this life, would still be enjoying it had someone not taken a blade to her face half a year before. As the months passed the outward scar improved, but other secret scars darkened her soul, scars beyond his skill to heal.

Thomas found Jorge sitting in the courtyard of lions, as still as the statues guarding the area. Helena had gone to find whoever she was so keen to visit, and Thomas entered slowly, enchanted as always at the beauty and opulence of the Sultan's palace. Tall trees in large earthenware pots decorated with passages from the Qu'ran offered shade as well as refuge for small birds.

Jorge was sitting in a splash of sunlight, his smooth head uncovered, handsome face turned up to the warmth. Thomas stood in the entrance, unwilling to disturb the man he had known since a boy, the man he had turned into what he now was—a palace eunuch.

Only when he sat beside him did Jorge open his eyes.

"Is Safya well?" Thomas asked.

Jorge lifted a shoulder. "She is expecting a baby. How am I supposed to be able to tell? That's your job."

Thomas started to rise. "Is she ready?"

Jorge laid a hand on Thomas's wrist, drawing him back to the stone bench. "Not yet. A little more time is required. A Sultan's wife cannot be rushed." He smiled. A knowing smile. "I believe she wants to look her best for you."

"One day you'll go too far and they'll ask me to finish the job and take your cock as well as your balls."

Jorge sighed. "A man needs some amusement, otherwise life becomes far too dull."

"I believe you get plenty of amusement. More amusement than is seemly."

"The Sultan loves me, as he loves you. Are we not among the blessed of this city."

There was always cynicism masked within Jorge's words, and many times Thomas had little idea how seriously to take them. Often cynicism could mask a deeper truth.

Jorge was dressed in loose robes of fine silk, delicate slippers, his bare head shaved to the skin. It was either an affectation or a demand of his profession, because Thomas knew the man could grow a full head of hair and beard if he wished.

"Yes, we are blessed, I suppose," Thomas said.

"How is that new wife of yours? Behaving herself?"

"I haven't taken her as a wife…" Thomas left the end of the sentence hanging, knowing Jorge would find it impossible not to respond.

"Yet? But you will, won't you?"

"I'm not sure I like sharing my house with someone else. And now she's asking if her sister can move in."

Jorge laughed, the sound soft, as if raucousness was out of place in this courtyard. From beyond a curtained doorway Thomas heard female laughter mirroring that of the eunuch but responding to some other, secret amusement.

"You do fuck her, don't you? You have to—it's what she was made for."

"What we do is none of your business."

"You're a prim bastard sometimes. She was born to give pleasure. As I was born to serve, and you to heal, so Hulyah was made to give pleasure to others. I don't mean to denigrate her. We are the people we are given to be."

"She was made what she is just as much as you." As always Thomas felt a need to protect. He knew Jorge taunted on purpose, enjoying the reaction his words brought. "And she calls herself Helena now, her born name. Doesn't that tell you she recognises her old life as false?"

Jorge shook his head and smiled. "False perhaps, but a life

she threw herself into body and soul. Hulyah... sorry, Helena, was an enthusiastic concubine. You can't make someone love their job as much as she did. That has to come from in here." Jorge patted his chest. "Although perhaps people can change."

"As have you?"

Jorge laughed, the sound still barely audible, years of training behind every mannerism he showed, every sound he uttered. "If you hadn't taken my balls I would be dead by now. Or living in some back street of Qurtuba thieving and selling my body for my next meal."

"You could have died."

"Oh, of course, remind me of how much I owe the great Thomas Berrington."

"I didn't mean it that way." Which was the truth, but Thomas understood Jorge's reaction. He had been one of Thomas's first surgeries, and he meant what he said, that Jorge would likely have died if someone else had carried it out. The making of eunuchs was not a subtle art, not then, involving much blood, hot coals and searing agony. Before Thomas's time less than one in nine survived. Since then he had not lost a single patient, using gentler techniques to unman each boy that was sent to him. It wasn't something he was proud of. He would have preferred not to perform the procedure at all, but knew the alternative was worse. Far worse.

"You may not," Jorge said, "but it's what I heard."

"Then listen more carefully." Thomas allowed his irritation to show, as controlled in his own way as the eunuch, but the irritation wasn't with this man. "I don't need thanks, but I do need your help."

"Now there's a first. How can a humble creature such as I myself give aid to an exalted servant of the Sultan?"

"Sarcasm doesn't become you."

Jorge smiled, waiting.

"I must attend Safya, and then I need you to take me to some people." Thomas stood and walked to the edge of the rill. The water was almost perfectly still, moving only slowly, the better to reflect the beauty of heaven.

"What people?"

"Have you heard anything of deaths within the palace?"

Jorge shrugged. "Many people live here. They come, they go. People die all the time. Because they are old, because they are ill."

"These weren't natural deaths."

"You mean the girls in the bathing chambers."

"So you do know."

"Everyone knows."

"Are they afraid?"

"A little, but more puzzled I think. No-one understands why those two were chosen."

"When I return I want to speak with everyone who has first hand knowledge of—" Thomas broke off as a slender woman entered through an archway, but she hadn't come for him. She walked across the courtyard, her steps elegant, slow. She nodded towards Jorge and Thomas, smiled, went on. A moment later her scent drifted to them on the breeze and Thomas breathed it in.

Jorge closed his eyes a moment. "Why would you want to do such a thing? You are a physician, not a law keeper."

Thomas turned and looked down at Jorge. "I don't want to—I have been asked."

Jorge's face reflected his puzzlement, but before he could delve further three young women emerged from behind a silk drape, and this time they had come for Thomas.

"She is ready for you, physician," said one, while a second giggled into her hand.

Thomas nodded and started towards the doorway. "I'll find you when I'm finished," he said, and Jorge nodded, his gaze distant as though examining some memory.

SIX

Safya was waiting for Thomas in a nook at the far end of the harem, making him walk the length of the chamber, as though she had positioned herself deliberately. Thomas suspected this was the truth. The Sultan's wives and concubines were prone to teasing those few men who were allowed access to their chambers. Jorge lived here permanently, and often passed on tales he hoped would shock, but Thomas had stories of his own, too, and those he never told. Although the lives of these women were pampered, they were more than mere playthings for the most powerful man in al-Andalus. These women read widely, spoke of politics and history and culture, listened to and made music, created works of art through their weaving and needlework, and even greater works of art through attention to their bodies.

"How are you, highness? Do you have any discomfort?"

"Can't you call me by my name, Thomas? You have seen me as only one other man has. And of course I have discomfort."

"If you would relax and allow me to examine you, highness?" Thomas stepped back, waiting for Safya. She glanced at him, a teasing look which was wasted. Eventually recognising her body was no more than another task to the surgeon she allowed her outer robe to fall away, her modesty maintained with a simple silk cover. Thomas indicated the waiting couch and she sat, reclining slowly.

Thomas touched her neck, feeling for signs of the pulse. It was raised a little, but that might be nervousness. Despite her casual air Thomas knew this must be difficult for her. Custom and society dictated no man who was not family could lay sight on a member of the harem without the Sultan present. And a near naked wife reclining on a couch was certainly well beyond convention.

"I will listen, if I may?"

Safya assented with a movement of her head, lay back and closed her eyes.

Thomas put his ear against her swollen belly, moved in one direction, another, finally finding the soft murmur of a foetal heartbeat within, almost too faint to detect. Thomas knew many physicians would be unable to find this sign of life, but he had always possessed acute hearing, and at times it was almost as if it wasn't his ears doing the hearing, but something else which sensed the presence of a second life nestled within the first. He registered the softness of the silk against Safya's skin, the scent of her body, the rise and fall of her belly against his cheek, but it was nothing more than distraction from what he sought.

He lifted his head and laid a palm against her belly. His fingers moved, pressing, tracing the shape of the infant, building its contours in his mind. As if sensing his presence it moved, rolled, and he felt a leg, a foot.

Safya laughed. "I think he wants to play."

Thomas ran his fingers along her legs, testing her ankles, pleased to find no swelling.

"I need to examine you more intimately now, highness."

"Then you will *have* to call me Safya, won't you?"

Thomas removed a bottle of oil from his bag and poured a little on his hands. As he examined her he felt nothing other than confirmation of the child's health. When he was done he rose and turned to the window, wiping his hands on a linen cloth.

"I am finished, highness."

He heard Safya sigh. She had given up on him.

Thomas moved to the window to allow her privacy, staring down on the pathway that led from the main palace to the Sultan's chambers, a deep ravine separating them. A narrow rope bridge ran between the two so that travelling between would not mean a long descent and climb.

A female figure emerged from a doorway on the far side and moved towards the bridge before stopping and turning back. A second figure had called to her.

"How is my son, Thomas?" Safya joined him at the window. "Isn't that Hulyah?"

"I think it may be. Your child is well, highness." Thomas couldn't see who Helena was speaking to, the other person cloaked by the shadow within the doorway. All he could tell was it belonged to a man, tall, broad shouldered. Possibly a guard. Their conversation ended and Helena walked back out across the bridge.

"Has she been visiting friends in the palace?" Safya said. "Hulyah is still well loved on the hill. We miss her a great deal. You're a lucky man, Thomas. When?"

"I know I am. Within a month, highness, likely sooner."

"Allah be praised. Will there be pain?"

"Some. The gift of life doesn't come without a price, but I can help ease that if you wish."

"You'll come when you're called?"

"Of course."

"I would rather you were closer. I know my husband has offered you a house in the Alkazaba."

"He is generous. But my place is across the river with my people."

Safya laughed. "Your people? Your people are many miles from here."

"No longer. My people are all around me."

Thomas wished Safya would go to bathe. She made him uneasy with this pretence at equality; and her presence now he no longer looked on her as a patient unsettled him. He didn't know how Jorge lived among these women and remained sane. Thomas knew he was unable to move away until Safya did and so waited, staring out over the valley of the Hadarro to the jumbled white and terracotta houses dimpling the far hillside. He tried to make out his own house, knowing he could see the palace from his courtyard, but looking from this side every-thing appeared different.

"Perhaps for me, when my time is near, you will weaken and move closer?"

"I'll consider your request."

Thomas's answer appeared to be enough because Safya moved away. Once alone he turned to retrieve his bag, a leather satchel containing instruments he hadn't needed but without which he felt naked.

"You're all done here, I take it?" Jorge's voice was close and Thomas looked up from where he knelt. He hadn't heard the eunuch approach. For such a large man Jorge moved surprisingly quietly. "I have found someone you can speak with."

"I'm finished." Thomas rose to his feet and fell into step beside Jorge.

"Safya is healthy? The baby, too?"

"They're both well, but she's convinced it's going to be a boy. What will she do if it turns out to be a girl?"

Jorge laughed. "She'll try again. And girls are loved, too. There are many girls here. Personally I prefer them to boys."

"That's because, despite your protests, your heart is as soft as your head is hard. Where are you taking me?"

"To talk with someone who really know what goes on with-in these walls."

Thomas remembered his surprise, almost twenty years before, when he first visited al-Hamra, expecting it to be similar to the large houses he had known in England, France, and other parts of Spain. In those places servants were kept at a distance, generally ignored so long as they stayed in their place. In al-Andalus—at least the part Thomas lived in—there was less differentiation. The palace was not like any he had known before. It didn't house the Sultan, who preferred to spend his time in the surrounding hills, living like the nomad people his ancestors had left behind centuries before. The main purpose of the palace was to house the harem.

Surrounding the enclosing walls was the Alkazaba, another town almost as large as the city of Gharnatah itself, and it was here most of the servants lived and worked. It was to one part of this sprawl close by the rear palace walls that Jorge led them.

He was greeted in a way Thomas had not witnessed before. Within the harem Jorge was treated with respect, even a little deference, as though it was he and not the Sultan's wives who possessed the power. Now as they entered a large kitchen rich with the smells of baking, cooked meats and the tang of oranges and limes, the mostly young women working stopped to greet him. Embraces were exchanged with kisses to both cheeks. Jorge introduced Thomas but made no explanation regarding who he was or why he was with him.

He led the way through the kitchen, stealing a fresh roll, tossing another to Thomas, then on into a wide corridor. More servants moved here, carrying, talking, a constant motion, all with some purpose Thomas couldn't discern.

A short way along the corridor a wider doorway stood open and it was here that Jorge entered. A large woman sat behind a fittingly large table covered with papers and scrolls, small plates of food resting on some, carved boxes of cedar and pine hiding whatever lay within. Thomas was surprised to see the walls lined with shelves containing many books. He wanted to explore, but knew now was not the time.

"Jorge! You incorrigible rogue." The voice was as large as the woman's frame, rich with laughter. "Have you come to service me as you used to as a youth?"

"I fear I would only disappoint now. You are far more of a woman than ever you were before."

"Are you calling me fat?"

"Of course not." Jorge went around the table as she rose and they embraced. Jorge held her face in his large hands, staring into her eyes, something close to love in his own, then he kissed her full on the mouth. "You are as beautiful as ever, Bazzu. Even more so."

"Of course I am." She glanced at Thomas. "Who is this other

handsome man? Not a Moor, but no Spaniard either."

"This is Thomas Berrington. Thomas, this is Bazzu. What she doesn't know isn't worth the knowing."

"At last—I get to meet the famous surgeon the Sultan favours." Bazzu came around the table, moving delicately for such a large woman. She took Thomas's hands in both of hers and stared into his eyes. "I had started to believe you didn't exist. I'm relieved to find you here before me."

"You are unwell?"

She laughed, the sound rotund and salacious. "I have never been ill a day in my life. I have long wanted to meet you because you intrigue me. I hear much about you in the palace. You are the Englishman, no?"

"I am."

"Such a long way from your homeland. Do you not miss it?"

Thomas smiled, enchanted by the woman. "It's nothing to be missed. Cold and wet and grey. I belong here, where the sun shines and a man can pick fruit from the trees."

Bazzu glanced at Jorge and winked. "And such a sweet tongue on him. No wonder old Abu al-Hasan puts his trust in this man. Is that why you're here to see me?"

"Why doesn't it surprise me you already know what we are seeking?" Jorge said.

"I am the spider in the middle of this web they call the palace. I know everything." Bazzu sighed and returned to her seat. "And so, if you're not here to ravish me within an inch of my life, what is it I can do for you until that moment arrives?" She rested her elbows on the table, chin on her hands, and stared at them, dark eyes sparkling.

There were no other chairs in the room, so they stood.

She glanced from one to the other. Thomas realised the silence was stretching uncomfortably and stepped forward when he saw Jorge was not about to speak.

"If you are the spider, as you claim, then you know about the girls who were killed."

"Of course. But they were servants. Why are important men

like you asking me such questions?"

"Because I have been asked. And because I care." Thomas glanced at Jorge, who had moved some papers and now perched on the edge of the table, eating the warm bread roll he had stolen, tearing small morsels off before slipping them between his lips. "I want to speak with everyone who knew them, everyone they worked alongside, and in particular anyone who was close when they were killed."

Bazzu sat up and blew her cheeks out. "That's a lot of people. Practically the whole of the palace. Can't you come up with a shorter list?"

"We can start with those who were close when they died."

Bazzu rubbed a hand across her belly, a slow, sensuous movement she seemed completely unaware of.

"That would prove simpler, certainly."

"I have the dates when they were—"

She shook her head. "I remember each day like it was yesterday. These were my girls, physician—did you think I wouldn't?"

"You cared for them," Thomas said.

"I care for everyone here, but yes, those two perhaps a little more than others." Bazzu offered no reason.

Thomas wished he could start over. "Tell me where the attacks took place."

"You don't know?" Bazzu appeared surprised and a little disappointed in him. "Both were killed in bathing chambers."

"Didn't you think it strange their deaths weren't investigated at the time?"

"But they were. Surely Jorge told you?" She glanced at the eunuch, who shrugged. "At times he's less useful than he looks. The Vizier's men investigated their deaths. Fairly thoroughly, too, I believe. Isn't that right, Jorge?"

"So I understand."

"And these investigators," Thomas said, "did they come to any conclusion?"

"That wouldn't be for the likes of me to hear."

Thomas smiled and waited.

"I believe—and understand this is rumour only, and may bear no grain of truth—that it was decided their deaths were due to jealousy."

"Jealousy?" Thomas couldn't hide his astonishment.

"Their places were much sought after. The women in the bath chambers are closer to the harem than others. Closer to the Sultan's wives and hence to power and influence."

"And this is fought over? To the death?"

"Ask your friend," Bazzu said, indicating Jorge, who had listened to the exchange in silence, as though uninterested.

"Oh, I have several things to ask him."

Jorge glanced up, unconcerned. "We should speak with whoever carried out these investigations and find out what they already know."

"You know who they are?"

"Of course. They spoke with me too, but I was of no help to them. I knew nothing. They were Tahir al-Ifriqi's men. Scribes mostly, but clever men, and methodical."

A slip of a girl came to the door. "They need you to decide on the dinner menu, Bazzu."

She rose from behind her desk, trailing her hand across Jorge's shoulders as she passed. "You must excuse me, I have duties to attend to."

"A moment," Thomas said, and Bazzu stopped in the doorway. "If you think of anyone else we should talk with, those who were close to these two girls, will you let me know? Anyone who might shed some light on what happened."

Bazzu glanced down at the waif standing at her side. "Go ahead, Prea, tell them I'll be there in a moment." She turned to Thomas. "I thought this matter was settled. Why is it being dug over again now?"

Why indeed, Thomas thought, and when he made no reply Bazzu shook her head and left.

SEVEN

He catches a glimpse of the surgeon walking with the dissolute one at the end of the corridor before he slips across and ducks into a narrow entrance, satisfied they do not see him. Within moments he is hidden, stripping out of his normal clothing, reaching up to a high shelf and taking down the exquisite robe he has been given, together with specific instructions. The robe must be worn each time he makes these forays. Why, his master has not told him, but he has his own theory. He is a soldier, so believes the most obvious, which is that his own clothes must never be tainted. There is little likelihood a speck of blood will give him away, for a soldier's clothing is often stained, but he understands the need and follows the instruction. Besides, the robe is of the finest silk and caresses his skin like a courtesan's fingers. Already it makes him hard. The silk, and the thought of what he is about to do, make him harder still.

He moves silently as he makes his way to the place he can watch from, and soon the scent of oils and perfume reach him. He quickens his pace, eagerness making him careless and the tip of his scimitar catches on the stone wall, striking a spark as he hurries.

"When were you going to tell me you already knew everything?" Thomas strode along the corridor beside Jorge.

"Not everything, and I would have told you when I found an opportunity. But you came to me less than two hours ago, and for most of that time you were with Safya. When did I have a chance?" Jorge continued walking, turning and turning again. Thomas believed he knew his way around the palace but Jorge was confusing him.

"Tell me now."

"We're almost at the bathing chambers. We'll find women there who knew the dead girls. We can talk later when there's more time."

"We should speak with the scribes, too," Thomas said. "They'll have made a record of all the information they found. It's somewhere to start."

"They were sent to cover things up."

"You know this?"

"It was obvious from the start. They asked all the wrong questions. No-one wanted the story to get out. Murders within the palace walls? People would start asking why—if the Sultan can't control his own palace, how can he control a city? The men were the Vizier's, and he will want palace secrets kept where they belong."

Thomas shook his head. The air in the corridor had changed, growing warmer, humid, scented. "So why did the Sultan ask me to look into this again? What does he gain?"

"That puzzles me, too. There..." Jorge pointed to the end of the corridor where a slight figure dressed in a flimsy dress crossed from one side to the other carrying some kind of pot. "That's Alisha, she'll know both the girls." He raised his voice. "Hey, Alisha, I need you."

At first Thomas thought the girl hadn't heard, but after a moment she re-appeared from around the corner.

"I'm going to Safya," the girl said as they approached.

"How long will you be?"

"As long as I'm needed. She's ready to bathe, and she'll scold me if I'm late."

"I need to ask you questions."

"Then find me later. Much later." The girl sprinted away.

"Can we talk to Tahir al-Ifriqi now?" Thomas asked.

"There'll be someone else, there's bound to be." Jorge turned left in the direction Alisha had come from.

"There will be other ladies bathing, Jorge, we shouldn't be

here."

"I'm invisible to them. And you're the famous doctor Thomas Berrington. We can go wherever we wish."

"Everywhere except a lady's bathing chamber."

"I don't plan to spy on anyone, but this is where the girls work. There'll be someone else around. We can talk to those cold fish of Tahir's tomorrow."

She is there, more beautiful than anything he has ever seen, but now her beauty angers him. Or he angers himself, knowing the beauty is about to be tossed aside. Whatever the reason it doesn't matter, because anger is good. Anger is powerful.

He watches as once again a girl on each side removes Safya's gown to reveal the skin beneath, glowing with health, her swollen belly inciting further rage. He shakes his head and steps sideways and in a moment he is in the chamber, partially hidden, but no-one looks in his direction. The scent of their perfume floods through him as he steps into the alcove. He breathes hard, the time for rehearsal over at last.

Neither Safya nor her attendants hear him, and he grins, his face a rictus.

This time it will to be right!

He swings his scimitar and steps forward. At the same moment a third girl runs into the chamber. She carries a jug of some kind, skidding to a halt as she takes in his presence, then with barely a moment's hesitation she flings the jug at him. He ducks, letting it bounce from his shoulder to shatter on the floor, then he is up again, momentum carrying him forward.

The girl is brave, he gives her that. Brave but stupid. She keeps coming as though he is not armed, her hands raised as though they can stop his blade. He swings down, hard and fast. The scimitar removes her left hand at the wrist, and still she comes, as determined as those he has fought in battle. She reaches him and hammers the stump and one small fist against his chest, her blood jetting across his face. He grips her shoulder with his left hand, fingers digging deep, and turns her against him. The sword angles down, up, and the girl's writhing body goes slack. He tosses her aside. She lands hard on the edge of the bath, hangs a moment, and then slides into the water. Her blood is slick beneath his feet and he is careful as he steps forwards. The entire killing has taken no more than seconds.

Another girl screams, continues to scream as Safya turns to face him.

"What is the meaning of this? What are you doing in my private chamber?"

The tone of command in her voice is almost enough to stop him, because he is, after all, a loyal soldier. It's all he has ever known, all he has ever wanted, and obeying comes as naturally as breathing. But he controls himself. He has higher orders.

"Say goodnight, princess."

He swings the scimitar a second time, a third. Safya goes to her knees, shock on her face, but still no fear. His blows have been too quick for her to know fear. He waits a moment, judging if another strike is needed, but the gout of blood tells him it is not and he turns to the last two girls. There must be no witnesses. But already one has fled while he dealt with Safya. It cannot be helped. Even the best planned battles go awry, he knows, and he dare not pursue her. Instead he turns to the final, cowering maid.

"Shut your mouth girl and close your eyes, unless you want to see your own death coming." But before he can strike running footsteps sound, close, too close to take this last life, and he throws her to the ground and flees.

When the scream came it cut through the warm air like a blast of ice water. The terror in the voice made Jorge turn sharply and start to run. Thomas followed, leather satchel slapping against his hip on each stride.

Ahead of him Jorge skidded and careened against a wall, shouting a curse as his feet went from under him and he landed in an ungainly heap. Thomas leapt over him and kept going.

He reached a junction and hesitated, unsure which direction

to take, then another cry came, this one a sob. "Help us, please help us, she is dead!"

He turned right and ran on, looking into each of the chambers as he passed. The sight of blood brought his feet to a scrabbling halt and he grabbed at the doorway as he entered the chamber.

The scene greeting him was like some distorted battlefield. One girl knelt beside Safya on the floor while another crouched against the wall, arms wrapped around her head. A third lay face down in the bath, her blood staining the water. Safya lay on the far side, half out of the water. Something was wrong with the left side of her body.

Jorge came into the chamber and passed Thomas, reaching into the pool to drag the bleeding girl to one side. He lifted her clear with one strong movement and flipped her onto her back. He glanced at Thomas. "She's gone."

Thomas was on his feet again, moving. They reached Safya together.

Thomas knelt, feeling again as he had so recently for a sign of life at her neck. Nothing. He moved his hand. Was that something? A faint pulse? Perhaps, but surveying her wounds he doubted it.

He turned his attention to her injuries. Her left arm was almost severed at the shoulder. Blood had arced high from the initial wound, splashing the walls and floor, but now it pulsed only slowly. Her left leg was also damaged. It looked as though someone had tried to hack through that as well but failed. The wounds were clean, precise. It would have taken tremendous strength to inflict them.

Thomas sat on his heels, oblivious of his robe draping through the blood.

"Is she dead?" Jorge said.

"Dying."

"Save her."

"I can't."

"You're a surgeon. Save her!" Jorge punched Thomas's

shoulder, slapped his face.

"She's beyond saving." Thomas barely felt the blows, watching as tears filled Jorge's eyes and spilled across his cheeks. "You loved her, didn't you?"

"I love them all."

Thomas looked down, reaching once more for a pulse and stopped. The distended skin on Safya's belly moved as the child within turned, the movement fast, as though the foetus was panicked.

"My bag! Fetch my bag."

Jorge scrambled away, ran to the entrance where Thomas had dropped his satchel.

Thomas tipped the contents out, unwilling to take the time to search inside. He saw what he was looking for, a sharp blade, but any blade would do.

"I recommend you look away," he said, even as he started to cut, his mind cold now, analytical. He felt a hard blow between his shoulder blades as Jorge hit him. "I'm saving her baby! Now turn away or watch, whatever you want, but don't blame me for what you're about to see."

There was no time for subtlety—and besides, she was a patient he had no need to put together again afterwards. He cut along the base of her belly and blood pooled, not as much as there would have been if most hadn't already been emptied from her body, but enough. A roll of intestine slipped free, the metallic smell of slaughter filling the room. From somewhere in the distance came the sound of more feet on hard tile, of voices, shouting, wailing.

Thomas extended the incision, cutting upwards, pulling open a flap of skin and muscle, pushing his hand inside, searching blindly. He withdrew, judging, then slid the blade into the opened cavity and cut again, tossed the blade aside and used his hand once more. His fingers slid through blood and gore and he closed his eyes, concentrating, imagining his hand moving through the layers of the body he knew so well.

He found a tiny leg, traced it upwards.

The commotion grew louder and Thomas opened his eyes as he grasped the tiny figure within Safya's opened womb and drew it clear, glancing back over his shoulder to see Jorge standing tall between him and three guards, each with swords drawn.

"Stand aside, eunuch!"

"He is saving her."

One guard approached, his sword raised. "He has his hand inside her belly. If that's saving her then I'll save you, too. Stand aside."

"What is this? Safya, no!" The Sultan had arrived. The small bathing chamber was growing crowded.

Thomas eased the tiny figure free, knotted the umbilical cord and cut it. He slid backwards, his passage made easy by the blood slicking the floor, and dipped the child into the bath. He held the infant in the water, washing it clean of gore. It would need repeating in cleaner water but was sufficient for now.

"Thomas, what have you done?" The Sultan shook with rage. "Guards, arrest this man!"

"Malik." Thomas lifted the baby, which at that moment decided to utter its first wail, protesting at the manner of his coming into the world. "You have a new son."

EIGHT

The Sultan barely glanced at the infant.

"Take them away." He flung an arm out to encompass everyone in the room. Two guards came to stand either side of Thomas. One of the young women took the baby. A third guard went to Jorge.

"My bag," Thomas said, as he was led from the room. "Someone fetch my bag."

One of his captors stopped and looked back, an expression of distaste on his face, as though Thomas had asked for instruments of torture. *Perhaps that is how they see me*, Thomas thought, *for when I appear to men such as these, I always bring pain.*

More women arrived and one of them took the mewling infant from the girl. The tiny head turned, its mouth seeking a breast.

The men were rougher than need be as they hustled the small group through the corridors and squares of the palace. Thomas, Jorge and the two girls were deposited in a small room and the door locked behind them. A window offered a view down a sheer drop to the Hadarro hundreds of feet below.

The girls clung to each other, their thin shifts wet. They shivered, but more in fear than cold. Jorge unwound his outer robe and handed it to one. Thomas repeated the gesture for the other. The girl reached for the robe, hesitated. The grey linen was stained with blood, but finally she took it, judging her near nakedness worse.

Thomas gripped the shoulders of the older girl, although neither could have been more than sixteen. "Tell me what happened."

The girl shook her head.

It was the other who said, "A djinn appeared in the chamber and killed Safya."

Thomas turned to her. "Whoever did this, it was no djinn."

The girl shook her head. "I tell you it was a djinn. It was black, all black but on fire, his head, his body. No legs. Only a long tail he sat upon. He carried a sword, an enormous sword, and he—" She stopped abruptly, the memory overwhelming her.

Jorge reached out and drew the silent girl to him, enveloping her within his arms. "And you? Can you tell me what you saw?"

She shook her head, burying her pretty face in the folds of stained cloth.

"This is the work of no spirit," Jorge said. "It is the work of a man."

"No man can enter the harem," the girl muttered into her coverings.

"Thomas was there," Jorge said, glancing across the chamber. "And I live within its walls."

"You are not a man." There was no judgment in her voice, only a statement of fact. "And Thomas is different. He is a physician, he is allowed."

"Do you think they are going to question us, or simply behead us?" Thomas said, immediately realising his mistake as the girl shivering in Jorge's arms uttered a whimper.

"No-one's going to do anything to us," Jorge said. "We're innocent. These girls saw everything." He rose and came to stand in front of Thomas. The girl he had been comforting immediately embraced her companion.

"You saw the Sultan's face."

"What do you expect, walking into that? He'll calm down and realise Safya's death was not our doing." Jorge took Thomas's arm and drew him away to the window. "Stop talking this way. Those girls are frightened enough already."

Thomas pulled free. "Now is the time to question them, while events are clear in their minds."

"No, Thomas."

He ignored Jorge and walked across the room to where the girls were huddled together for comfort.

He crouched in front of them. "Tell me again—and think carefully, I need to know exactly what happened."

The elder girl hid her face, but the younger showed anger. "Haven't we told you enough already? It was the djinn who killed the Sultana!"

Thomas washed a hand across his face. It wasn't only the girls who were afraid. "Assuming it was a djinn then, tell me how he appeared. Where did he come from?"

The girl offered a scathing look. "Djinn's appear wherever they wish. How else could it get there? How else could it come from where it did?"

"Explain."

"It came from nowhere, from the alcove above the bath. There is no doorway, no way in. Only a djinn could have appeared as it did."

"You're sure of this?"

The girl nodded. "Of course I'm sure. Alisha came in with a pot of oil and saw it first. We had our backs turned, helping the Sultana into the water. Alisha threw the pot and it struck her first, then the Sultana. I have never—" She broke off.

"This is too soon." Jorge sat beside the girl and drew her against him, offering what comfort he could.

"Now is when they remember best."

"Now is when the scars are fresh. Tomorrow, after they have slept, they will have time to consider their memories more rationally."

Thomas rose to his feet. "Tomorrow is no good. Girl, stand, come here."

She glanced at him, at Jorge, who drew her tighter against his side.

"You're doing her no favour." Anger mixed with fear made Thomas's voice harsh.

"And neither are you. Let her be."

"She'll forget."

"Then let her forget."

Thomas shook his head and strode to the window. Couldn't Jorge see? If the man was this stubborn Thomas was starting to think it would be better to work alone.

Jorge was speaking softly to the girls, too softly for Thomas to make out his words. He tried to calm himself.

"Tell me what he looked like."

Jorge gave him a sour look, but the girl was coming out of her shock, and Thomas knew her interpretation of events was wrong. He wanted answers, but lacked the compassion needed to tease information from her. Jorge overflowed with compassion but had no sense of the urgency of their situation.

"Was he tall?" This time it was Jorge who asked the question, and Thomas wondered if he had judged him prematurely.

"He was…" Her eyes turned inward, seeking some memory. She shook her head. "I couldn't tell. He was a column of black fire. He might have been ten feet tall. I don't remember."

Impatient, Thomas took over the questioning. "When he struck Safya—how much bigger was he than her? How high did he raise his sword?" The pain his words caused was clear on the girl's face, but Thomas had no intention of easing off.

"He was taller."

"How much taller?"

The girl shook her head. It was her companion, silent until now, who supplied the answer.

"I was further away. I ran when he killed Alisha. He was… he was not much taller than the Sultana. But she is tall for a woman."

Thomas nodded. "She is. His sword—in which hand did he hold it?"

The girl frowned, closed her eyes. Thomas watched as her hands came up, moving as she replayed events.

"His right hand. He held his sword in his right hand."

"And his left—was there anything in his left hand?"

The girl thought a moment, shook her head. "Nothing."

"He knew he wouldn't need anything else, not against women," Jorge said, his features expressing his disgust.

Thomas returned and knelt before the girls once more. He reached for the hand of the eldest, who had found her courage, but she pulled away. "Did you see him enter the chamber?"

"I told you—it was a djinn, there is no entrance where he came from."

"Could he have slipped past while you were helping Safya?"

"We were facing the doorway. No-one could have entered without us seeing them. Besides, he would have been seen coming."

"And going? When he fled, in which direction did he go?" Thomas reached out and took her hand and this time she let him. It lay like a small bird, trembling within his own.

Once more she closed her eyes, and Thomas was moved by her courage. But when she opened them she shook her head. "I don't remember. I was crying, on my knees. He said... he said he was the last thing I would ever see. I didn't want to look."

"He spoke?"

"I told you."

"What were his words? His exact words?"

She pulled her hand from his, turned away. "I don't want to remember them."

He reached for her again, resisting when she tried to pull free, gripping her tight. "Tell me. Was he a Moor? His accent, what did he sound like?"

"I wasn't listening."

"Did he sound like the Sultan? Like Jorge? Like me?"

"He sounded like none of you."

"Then how did he sound? He spoke to you, you have to remember."

"I don't want to remember!" She tried to pull away once more but Thomas held her fast. He knew he must be hurting her but he didn't let go. This was too important.

"You have to." His voice was soft, but there was no comfort there. He glanced at Jorge, who stared back with an expression of disgust on his normally placid features.

The girl let her breath loose in a long exhalation and Thomas felt her fist relax within his grasp. He loosened his grip and stared into her eyes, trying to make his own sympathetic, but knew he likely only scared her more.

"He wasn't a Moor," she said. "Nor Spanish. And not at all like you." She half smiled and her gaze met Thomas's before skittering away. "I have heard how he sounded before, but—"

They all stared as the door crashed open. Thomas spun around, an instinct to protect flooding through him. Two guards stood in the entrance.

"Come with us," said one.

Thomas started forward.

"Not you. Them." He pointed at the girls, who huddled closer together.

"The Sultan will want to speak to me," Thomas said. "I should come with them."

"You haven't been asked for. You stay. The girls come." He moved forward.

Thomas blocked the way, sensed Jorge standing.

The guard stopped, a sneer on his face. "Do you want to die now? I'm happy to send you to the next world if that's what you wish." He pushed Thomas aside and reached for the girls.

Jorge moved and Thomas grabbed him, pulling him aside. "No."

The girls cried, fought, but they were small and the guards large. Thomas and Jorge watched as they were dragged from the room and the door slammed shut.

Thomas saw Jorge's shoulders slump and felt the strength leave his own body. He knew they had both been putting on a front for the girls.

"I wonder if Helena knows where I am?"

"Someone will have delighted in telling her, I'm sure."

"Those guards could have waited a little longer. I think the girl was starting to remember."

"Kitma," Jorge said. "Her name is Kitma. And her companion is Mahja. They're good girls, both of them. They should never have had to see what they did."

"But they did, and that makes them our only witnesses."

"Then we will talk to them again." Jorge went and sat against the wall, pulling his knees to his chest.

"If we are given the chance. Did you notice they stopped referring to their djinn as *it* and started saying *he*?" A nervous energy thrummed through his body. He could hardly believe they might be in danger, but he knew the Sultan made irrational decisions—had seen the evidence only the previous day. Jorge had been right to stop him talking of their fate in front of the girls. "Now they're gone perhaps we can talk about what's going to happen to us."

"That's up to Abu al-Hasan."

"He must know we were trying to help." Thomas's words sounded empty in his own ears.

"He saw you with your hands inside his wife's belly. How would you interpret such a sight?"

Thomas stared into space. "Why ask me to investigate the deaths and then accuse me of the same crime?"

"There were three men beheaded this morning, did you see?"

"And two more killed outside the city walls last night. Why were they executed?"

"Cowardice in battle. It encourages the others."

"Most don't need encouraging."

"I can see why."

"Why did you tell me? Are you trying to frighten me?"

"I told you because in this city men are executed on a whim. We both know it. All we can do is pray the Sultan comes to his senses before anger gets the better of him."

Thomas went to the door, pushed against it, pulled. He hammered his fist on the solid wood.

"Don't waste your energy," Jorge said.

Thomas abandoned the door and moved to the small

unglazed window. "It's mine to waste. How can you be so calm?"

"Because I have no choice."

Thomas's anger flared. "You think yourself safe, don't you?"

Jorge shook his head. "Why would I be a suspect? There was no blood on my hands. And the Sultan has known me since I entered the harem."

"He claims he trusts me. He says it often enough."

Jorge smiled. "Trust is a fickle commodity to stake your life on."

Thomas strode across the room and grabbed Jorge's shirt, tried to drag him to his feet. He wanted to hit someone, anyone, but there was only one person he could vent his fear against and Jorge remained where he was, a solid weight on the floor. The silk of his shirt tore and slipped through Thomas's fingers.

"Show some emotion, damn you, we might be dead by nightfall!"

"Will it do us any good? If you think so I'll gladly curse and wail along with you, but I've never found it to be of any help before."

Thomas punched the wall. He only succeeded in hurting his hand, but knew it was better than punching Jorge. He strode away, wanting to put distance between them. "We're innocent."

Jorge barked a laugh, cut it off almost at once. "The grave-yards are full of the innocent. The Sultan is angry. We can only hope his anger wanes with the daylight."

Thomas stood at the window, clutching the sill. He breathed deep, held the air in his lungs as long as he could, exhaled. He repeated the exercise. It helped, a little.

"Why kill Safya? Who has she displeased? The Sultan? The Vizier? Another wife?"

"The Sultan was excited to be getting a new son." Now an imminent attack seemed to have passed, Jorge rose to his feet.

"It could as easily have been a daughter."

Jorge strolled across the room towards Thomas. "But it wasn't. Thanks to you he has a new son. I expect he'll see the foolishness of locking us up soon enough. He knows you wouldn't kill Safya and save the son."

Thomas rubbed his nail into the lime mortar between the stone making up one side of the window. It came away, powdering onto the sill. He believed if he worked long enough he might loosen the stone and make a space large enough to crawl through. He looked down at the drop outside and stopped rubbing.

"Who would do this?" Thomas returned to the only thing worth asking, seeking to lose himself in questions. The danger they were in hovered on the edge of consciousness, but he had ignored danger before, was merely out of practice.

"Who wants to hurt the Sultan?" Jorge said.

"A thousand people."

"Exactly. Are you going to interrogate the entire city? We both know he's not a popular man. He's too harsh, and the people of Gharnatah have grown pampered and soft. The mountains protect us from Spain, but for how much longer?"

Thomas scowled at the hint of outrage in Jorge's voice. "The Spanish are your people."

"Not anymore. My life is here. I have a place in society, and women to love."

"The Moors took your manhood."

Jorge looked at Thomas. "No—you took my manhood. Part of it, anyway. Or do you forget, a busy man such as yourself?"

"I don't forget," Thomas said, uneasy at the reminder. "What I meant was the Moors took you captive, forced you into the life you have now. All I did was help you avoid pain."

Jorge pushed against Thomas's shoulder with his. "If that was avoiding pain no wonder the soldiers call you butcher."

"Would you rather someone else had performed the procedure?"

Thomas thought back sixteen years to the skinny, shivering boy who spoke no Arabic. His only crime was to be tall, pretty, and captive. The boy was the first Thomas had operated on to turn into a eunuch. He had been only twenty-five himself and newly arrived in Gharnatah. His pale skin and strange accent had, for some reason, amused the Sultan. Thomas would deliver his eldest son Muhammed, and later Yusuf, too; almost all the children in between and since. But it had been treating men in battle that had picked him out. He had been fearless, unafraid of the clashing swords and barking cannon, throwing himself into the heart of the chaos. Only a few years earlier he had been as the men around him. Worse than them, because he had fought for no cause other than greed and the rage of youth.

"What are you thinking?" Jorge said.

"Why do you ask?"

"The look on your face. You were somewhere else."

"If only that were true." He glanced at Jorge. The man had turned from pretty boy to handsome man, and Thomas considered him a friend, even closer than a friend. Although he knew the relationship might not appear so simple from the other side. "I was thinking about what you said. How you came to be who you are."

"Don't expect thanks."

"I wasn't looking for any. Can you still speak your language?" Thomas asked, uneasy at the memories their conversation evoked.

"Possibly. Can you still speak yours?"

Thomas wondered which language he could call his own anymore. His days of conversing in English were long gone, and in between he had learned and forgotten some French, Spanish, and now he spoke only Arabic like a native born to this place, as did Jorge.

"If I tried, I suspect I could, but why would I want to?"

"Don't you miss it?"

"England?"

"Is that what it's called?"

"Mercia is where I was born, on the western fringes of England."

"I was born in Qurtuba." Jorge used the Moorish pronunciation, disdaining any other he might once have known. "But I was born poor and grew poorer the longer I lived. If I hadn't been captured and turned into what I am I'd be long dead by now. I owe the Spanish nothing. Nothing at all."

Thomas heard vehemence in Jorge's voice.

"It may be worth remembering some of your old language," Thomas said. "This land won't remain in Moorish hands much longer."

"They haven't succeeded yet, and they won't. Abu al-Hasan Ali is strong, he's fierce, and the land is on our side. This is our land, not theirs. They gave it up seven centuries ago and it's the Moors who made it great. Could make it greater still."

Thomas smiled. Jorge had distracted him from the worst of his fear. He patted his friend's shoulder, who looked down as if Thomas's touch was tainted.

"I wonder what those girls really saw," Thomas said.

NINE

It was an hour before the guards returned. There were four of them this time, two to flank Thomas and Jorge as they were led through the hallways, one ahead and one behind. Thomas thought it some kind of compliment they were considered so dangerous.

But not as dangerous as he suspected. Their ultimate destination was a long chamber where three men waited, and the guards were dismissed. There was no sign of the two young women.

The Sultan sat in an ornate chair. To his right stood Tahir al-Ifriqi, the second most powerful man in al-Andalus. To the Sultan's left was Abd al-Wahid al-Mursi, the leading cleric of the city, a tall, painfully thin man with the face of an ascetic. Thomas knew him by reputation only as a man of firm beliefs. He had heard it said that Abd al-Wahid al-Mursi considered all the ills of al-Andalus could be blamed directly on its people shunning strict religious practice. It seemed he and Jorge were not the only unbelievers in the city.

Beside him Jorge moved uneasily from foot to foot, his gaze directed downwards. Thomas waited, knowing he couldn't speak first despite the thousand questions racing through his mind. Several hours had passed since the killing. The rage and grief that must have filled this room had tempered into a cold anger now displayed clearly on two of the faces.

The Sultan would want to strike out at someone for what had happened. Thomas only hoped his wrath was directed at the guilty.

"Who did this thing?"

"I don't know, Malik."

"Then who does? Those silly girls claim it was a desert spirit. What do you say?"

"They're mistaken."

"There is more to heaven and earth than you know of, physician." Abd al-Wahid's voice was as cold and emotionless as his eyes.

"Indeed there is, Imam. But it was no djinn did this."

"You don't believe in the world of the spirit?"

"I believe in what I can see and touch."

"I have heard it said you don't follow the true faith, Thomas Berrington."

The Sultan interrupted before Thomas could answer, or the argument escalate. "Faith or not, I also don't believe a djinn killed Safya. And if it was no spirit it must have been a man." He stared hard at Thomas. "You and Jorge were first there. Tell me, was this a man? Or could another woman have done it?"

Thomas shook his head. "A woman wouldn't be capable of inflicting those wounds."

"Not even with a sharp blade?" It was the first time Tahir al-Ifriqi had spoken. He was a hard man in both body and voice, his eyes cold, calculating. Thomas knew him as a tough administrator of the city, backing up the Sultan's often irrational decisions.

"There was no time for subtlety, your honour. This was done fast, and with great force."

"Could it have been more than one man?"

The Sultan waved an impatient hand. "I'm tired of discussion. Now is a time for action, not words. Thomas, I would talk with you alone."

"Sultan." Tahir al-Ifriqi reached out, almost laying a hand on the Sultan's arm before realising his error and withdrawing. "We have not yet decided if either of these men are guilty of a crime."

The Sultan laughed, a harsh sound. "Thomas is no killer."

"He has the skill."

"He is no killer," the Sultan repeated. "He saved my son on

the field of battle. He has saved many men. And he saved my newborn son. I would trust this man with my life. I would trust him above all others." The Sultan rose, looking old and tired as he turned aside.

Thomas hesitated, glancing into the faces of the Vizier and Imam. He saw no help there, no alternative offered, so he followed the Sultan outside into a shaded courtyard where water shimmered in a wide pool along the centre of the space and birds sang in the treetops.

The Sultan took a seat on a marble bench where a tree cast shade. Late afternoon sunlight caught the far side of the courtyard, cut at an angle across the water to cast dancing reflections across the tiled walls.

The Sultan patted the bench beside him. "We have lost valuable time. I should not have locked you away."

Thomas sat at a respectful distance, but the Sultan shuffled along so he was pressed almost shoulder to shoulder with him. There was a long silence while they stared at the water, the trees, the bushes. Thomas wondered if the Sultan was thinking of the loss of his wife. Did men such as him ever think that way? He had a dozen wives, two dozen concubines; surely he must feel something for each of them? But when he spoke it was as if he was more concerned for Thomas.

"Where is your robe? Shall I get you something to wear?"

"I'm fine, Malik. I gave it to one of the girls." He hesitated. The questions bubbling inside could no longer be suppressed. The Sultan was right: too much time had been wasted. "You spoke with them—where are they now?"

The Sultan shook his head. "Silly girls. I sent them back to work. Too pretty to be clever, clever enough to know not to lie. They know nothing other than what they imagined. This was no djinn."

"I agree. It was a man. This has to be connected to the task you gave me. I understand if you want to call on someone else now. Someone more suited."

"Are you refusing to help?"

"I'm saying there are people better qualified."

"But none I would trust. I want you, not some flatterer who will tell me what they think I want to know."

"You want the truth, as do I," Thomas said. "But there are other men more capable than me."

The Sultan cast him a glance. "I don't want other men, I want you. I want someone who will speak with an honest heart. You have never treated me like a master. Sometimes that has annoyed me, but right now you are exactly what I need."

"I want to examine Safya," Thomas said.

The Sultan rose abruptly and paced to the edge of the rill. He stared down into the still water. "She has already been prepared. She will be interred before sunset."

Thomas glanced at the sky. "It's important I see her, Malik. I wouldn't ask otherwise."

The Sultan turned around, his face grim. "I forbid it."

Thomas rose from the bench but didn't move closer. "Then I would pay my respects."

"Come to the internment."

"I'm not of your faith."

"Then don't come. Whatever you wish. We will talk no more of it. Find me the killer, before he chooses another of my wives to slaughter."

Thomas was unsure how hard to press, how hard he could press, but said, "Other than the girls you told me of, and now Safya, have there been other attacks?"

"A girl disappeared. Some say she ran away, some she was another victim."

"Why was nothing done sooner?" Thomas knew a commoner didn't speak to a Sultan in such a way, but he grieved, too.

"Of course we acted. Those men in there, together with myself, decided the matter was best kept within these walls. Tahir was asked to set his men to the duty. But what do scribes know of life and death? I wanted to ask Olaf Torvaldsson but was persuaded otherwise."

"He's a soldier. He knows how to deal in death, but this matter requires more subtlety."

"We wanted the matter kept private. Olaf is nothing if not loyal. But I didn't ask him. I should have come to you at the start, Thomas."

"I told you last night, I know nothing of investigating such things, Malik."

The Sultan cast a cold gaze at Thomas. "You are the cleverest man I know. And you are a survivor. You adapt. But most of all you are honest, and there are scarce few honest men in this city."

"There must be others you trust." Thomas experienced a shiver of unease at the thought he might be the only one.

"Trust—who can a Sultan trust? Muhammed wants my crown, Tahir is worried I spend too much gold on this war, and as for that prissy Imam, he considers me ungodly."

"He considers everyone ungodly."

Abu al-Hasan made a sound through his nose. "That's true. You will catch this man for me, Thomas?"

"Because I am the only man in al-Andalus you trust?"

The Sultan glanced at him. "And I'm not entirely sure I should trust you—an *ajami*." He softened his words with a brief smile.

"Then ask Olaf Torvaldsson, as you meant to. He has skills I don't possess."

"He is *ajami,* too."

"He is your man."

"And you are not?"

"You know the answer to that, Malik."

The Sultan stepped across the rill and strode to the far side of the courtyard, pulled a fig from the tree growing there and sniffed it, tossed it aside as unripe. He reached into his robe and withdrew something, holding it inside his closed fist.

"Come here." He held his hand out, whatever lay within obscured.

Thomas walked to him. He knew he could not refuse.

"Do what you must. You act under my authority. Go where you will." As Thomas held his hand out the Sultan dropped something small and heavy into it. Thomas looked at the object. A seal. "Take it," the Sultan said. "There are only three such in existence. It will grant you access wherever you wish to go. Anywhere at all. Don't let me down—whatever you do, don't let me down."

Thomas closed his fist around the seal and nodded.

The Sultan turned, leaving Thomas alone to wonder at the implied threat in the man's words.

"They told me I'm to work with you," Jorge said. "Not for you—with you." Jorge sat in the chair the Sultan had used, his long legs stretched out.

"You enjoy living dangerously, don't you. Is that really what was said?"

"It's what I chose to hear." Jorge rose as Thomas turned away.

"You don't have to help me. I may be about to make matters worse, not better. You would be wiser not associating with me."

Jorge fell into step as they entered the corridor.

"I am known for my beauty, not my wisdom."

"Where do they keep the dead before burial?"

"Safya?"

Thomas smiled, a mere thinning of his lips. And Jorge claimed he lacked wisdom? "I must examine her while I still can. There was no time before."

"You asked the Sultan?"

"He knows nothing of this."

"I don't know where she is, but Bazzu will."

"Then we go to find Bazzu."

The chamber was cold and dim, lit only by guttering candles. Thomas despatched the women still tending Safya to fetch lamps. He knew they were unhappy, but Bazzu's presence added weight to his words. The women would undoubtedly tell someone of his presence, which meant speed was vital.

Jorge stood against the wall, as if trying to press himself through it, eyes locked on the woman now wrapped in white linen sheets, her body and face obscured. The cloth was not yet tied with rope, which made Thomas's task easier. A second, slighter figure lay on another stone bench. Thomas could no longer remember the girl's name.

"You don't need to stay," he said, moving around the body. He had no intention of starting with anyone else in the room.

"She doesn't look like Safya anymore," Jorge said.

"You can't see her, of course she doesn't look like her."

"She was always so full of life, so full of fun. She would tease me all the time." Jorge's voice broke.

"Yes, she liked to tease. When Bazzu comes back I want you to return to the kitchens with her."

"I'll stay."

"No, you'll go. Seeing Safya before was bad enough. This will be worse."

"Have you no humanity?" Jorge said, and Thomas knew he was referring to what he was about to do.

"A surgeon learns to ignore what cannot be changed, to see beyond what lies in front of him. You can't cure without witnessing suffering and horror."

"This is beyond horror." Jorge started as Bazzu entered carrying two lamps. Behind her a slight figure remained outside in the corridor.

Bazzu glanced at the bodies, then placed the lamps on alcoves in the walls and retreated. Thomas stared at Jorge, waiting. Jorge returned the stare, but eventually his gaze darted aside. He took a shuddering breath, pushed himself from the wall and followed Bazzu out. Thomas closed the door before returning to Safya. He began to unwind the wrappings.

Someone had made an effort to tidy her body. Neat stitching closed the ragged wound to her belly where the baby had been delivered; more stitching drew tight the slash to her arm and leg. It took him long minutes before she lay revealed. Thomas stepped back a moment, grief rising sudden and sharp through him. Only a few brief hours before this woman had taunted him, coy and sultry in turn, more full of life than anyone he had ever known. Now she lay on a cold stone slab, all of her vibrancy eliminated. There was nothing of Safya left. He wiped an arm angrily across his face and set to work, losing himself in the routine of his profession.

It took almost an hour, and the whole time he listened for approaching footsteps, expecting to be found out, but none came. He suspected Bazzu had taken the women aside and impressed the need for secrecy on them. Whatever the reason Thomas was grateful. This woman—once so vibrant—was now nothing more than a clue in the puzzle set before him.

Finally he straightened, twisting from side to side. His body ached, weary from attending soldiers returning from battle. Thomas re-wrapped the sheets around Safya. As a mark of respect he tied the wrappings with rope. He might not share her religion, but he knew its rituals. Only when he was finished did he turn his gaze to the servant. He shook his head, still unable to recall her name. Alice kept coming to mind but he knew that wrong; this girl would have a Moorish name, not an English one. And why was he even thinking of English names? England was no more than a faint memory. Was it the thought of approaching defeat—a defeat that could no longer be denied? Thomas frowned and shook his head. He wasn't thinking of returning, not after all these years, was he? This was his home now, not some cold, distant land.

As he worked he had felt something shift inside him. Losing himself in the ritual had stilled his mind. Through the stillness had come certainty. He had agreed to help the Sultan because refusal was not an option. In this cold room, Thomas knew it was not the Sultan he would pursue the killer for, but for these two women, and the others before them. And to prevent any more suffering the same fate. He was sure if the man wasn't stopped there would be more. Would Aixa be next?

With a sigh that emptied the air from his body he turned to

the second figure and began to unwrap the coverings.

The bathing chamber had already been cleaned. Steam rose from the still water which filled the sunken bath. Water dripped from closed faucets.

"When did this happen?" Thomas said.

"They would have cleaned the room immediately," Jorge said. "It would not be seemly to leave the room tainted."

"They've destroyed any chance of us finding whatever spoor he left behind."

"It's how things are done in the palace. No-one knew."

"Someone should have known. The Sultan or Vizier. Didn't they think?"

Jorge offered a look. He had been in a subdued mood when Thomas found him in Bazzu's room, and had stayed that way the entire time since.

"A woman they loved was murdered here. They wanted no reminder."

As they walked from the kitchen to the bathing chambers, Thomas had tried to tell him of the discovery he had made, but Jorge only waved him aside and walked faster. "Too soon," Jorge had said, and the look he gave Thomas showed all the pain and anger he felt.

Now Thomas surveyed the room, moving on already. He went to the shallow steps leading into the water.

"How does this work? You belong in this place. Where would Safya be, the girls?"

Jorge had calmed a little, but his voice remained emotionless. "I may have many privileges, but witnessing a Sultana bathing is not among them."

"But you know, don't you?"

Jorge came to stand next to Thomas, pushing him aside.

"Safya would have stood here, a girl on each side helping her into the water in case she slipped. As we know, Alisha came in with a pot of oil."

Of course—not Alice but Alisha. Thomas looked around.

"From that doorway?"

Jorge nodded.

"It's the only doorway into the chamber?"

Jorge nodded again.

"And the girls—"

"Kitma and Mahja."

"I remember their names." Thomas's voice was sharp. "They said the man came at them from behind." Thomas went to the closed head of the chamber. "From here?" He turned to find Jorge staring at him, a rictus of pain across his face. "I know this is hard, but if we are to catch the killer we must put our own feelings aside."

"Easy for you to say. I don't believe you possess any."

Thomas didn't bother replying. He turned to the wall. A small alcove obscured the deepest corner of the chamber. He went to it and stood pressed against the stone.

"Can you see me from there?"

"I can see your cloak," Jorge said.

"But if you entered the chamber without expecting someone to be hiding here, would you look for them?"

"Why would you? Besides, it's not possible to be concealed there. Before Safya entered a guard would have searched the room. They always do."

"Thoroughly?" Thomas emerged into full view. "The women of the harem bathe at least once a day, sometimes more. Guards grow careless. A man could have hidden here and then stepped out to attack."

"To do that he would have to get there to begin with, to pass through the length of the palace. He would have been seen, stopped."

"Unless he was a familiar figure."

Jorge joined Thomas at the head of the chamber. "Such as?"

"Who has access to the palace? Guards and eunuchs. I can't think of anyone else."

"Sultans and princes," Jorge said. "And physicians."

"You suspect a member of the royal family?"

"I suspect no-one, I'm only stating the options. So a guard, do you think?"

"What of the other eunuchs? Could any of them have done this?"

Jorge shook his head. "Two are too old, one too young, the last too delicate."

A thought occurred to Thomas, one that raised a chill across his skin. "You said a guard would examine the chamber before Safya entered. What if that guard stayed behind, hidden in the alcove? Is there any way of finding out who that would have been?"

"There's a roster. One of Olaf's men will have it, but so will Bazzu."

"Is there anything that woman doesn't know?"

"Not much, no," Jorge said. "Are we finished here?"

"Not yet. Help me examine the walls."

"What do you expect to find? Some secret entrance?"

Thomas glanced at Jorge. "You'll make a valuable assistant if you keep thinking that way."

Jorge scowled and appeared to be about to say something, then shook his head and bent to the task. Between them they pushed and kicked at every stone in the alcove, but nothing sounded different, nothing moved.

Thomas straightened, back aching, but he felt progress had been made, a faint excitement welling within him.

"A guard then?" he said. "Perhaps even the guard meant to protect Safya. We must find Bazzu and ask her."

"She'll think I'm stalking her."

Thomas allowed himself a smile. "Will she be displeased at the idea? I don't think so."

But when they reached the kitchens Bazzu wasn't there. The girl Prea told them she had gone to attend Safya's internment.

TEN

Thomas and Jorge descended a hillside painted blood red by the lowering sun. From above came the sound of voices raised in prayer, the deep tones of the Imam rising above the others. Several times Jorge slowed and Thomas almost spoke, still wanting to raise what he had discovered during the examination. It had nothing to do with Safya. Her body, despite its injuries, offered little in the way of clues he hadn't already known. It was the servant Alisha he wanted to talk of. He didn't believe he would ever forget that name again.

When he glanced at Jorge's face it was grim, his mouth a compressed line, brows drawn down, and Thomas knew he couldn't raise the matter yet.

"She won't have suffered," he said, believing he could read the thoughts inside the man's head.

Jorge stopped and looked back up the hillside. Smoke from burning fires rose in lazy spirals, their bases grey in the palace's shadow, tops catching a new flame in the dying rays of the sun.

"I don't believe you," Jorge said. "I saw her wounds. I have suffered, too. I know what pain is."

"It would have been quick. Men take terrible injuries in battle, and only later does the pain come."

Jorge shook her head. "Safya was no soldier. Hers was a life of ease and luxury."

Thomas put his hand on Jorge shoulder. "She is beyond suffering now."

Jorge shook him off and continued his descent. As they approached the point where Helena had stopped on the climb up that morning Jorge slowed and came to a halt once more. The city lay below them. Beyond its walls cultivated land stretched to distant hills. The air had grown heavy with haze once more, the effect of the night's rainfall already defeated by the heat of the day. Out across the plain, water from irrigation canals caught the lowering sun, flickering and blinking. Dust rose from cart wheels and horses' hoofs.

"Suffered or not, she's dead." Jorge had obviously been teasing away at Thomas's response. "And for what? I should have been with her, not on some foolish quest." He paced to the edge of the drop where the land fell away beneath the trees. He kicked at a stone and it clattered away amongst the undergrowth. Birds flew up, screeching from the sound.

"It's no foolish quest, and you know it." Thomas stared at Jorge's back where tension bunched his shoulders.

Jorge reached out and wrapped a hand around the branch of a wild olive. His knuckles turned white, his arm quivering. "No, you're right, no foolish quest. When we find this man I will kill him with my own hands."

"He will be a soldier."

"Then you will help me," Jorge said, not looking at Thomas.

"Yes, I will help you. But you know one man isn't the end of this."

Jorge shook his head. "I leave the theories up to you."

Thomas scowled. "You live within the palace. The answer lies there, not with me. Why are you being so stupid?"

Jorge released his grip on the olive and finally turned to Thomas. "Because to think on why brings too much grief." He pushed against Thomas's chest, sending him staggering backwards. Jorge followed. "Because everything I love remains there." He pushed again. This time Thomas was prepared and took the blow. "Because to know who lies behind this will only bring more pain and death—most likely our own. Is that what you want?"

"I want it ended."

Jorge dropped his head. His shoulders shook. "And you think I don't? Even if it ends tonight there are too many people I love already dead." Tears flowed across his cheeks.

Thomas hesitated, then stepped forward and put his arms around Jorge. The man was four inches taller, but he leaned into Thomas like a child as sobs wracked his body. The sun had sunk behind the distant Elvira hills before Jorge recovered himself and Thomas released his hold.

For a moment they stood toe to toe, then Jorge nodded and turned away. "I'm fine. Let's go. I want to find this man before he kills any more of my women."

Helena laughed when she saw the seal.

"What foolishness is this? In which back alley did you find such a cheap trinket?"

Thomas hadn't intended to make anything of it. In fact he would have preferred she didn't even know it was in his possession—that no-one knew. But as he and Jorge entered the house he had tripped on a pile of washing left inside the doorway and his stumble sent the seal spinning from his pocket to the floor. For a moment he feared it would break, then remembered it was forged of metal. Still, even metal could shatter.

When he bent to retrieve it Helena got there first and made her comment. She glanced at the seal, giving it little attention before looking towards Jorge standing in the doorway. Thomas saw something change in her face. *Of course, she knows him.*

"Jorge and I have matters to discuss," Thomas said. "You can follow the courtyard around to my workshop."

"If you can get inside," Helena said.

Thomas hesitated a moment then reached out for the seal, waiting.

Helena examined it again, turning it over in her hands. Her eyes narrowed, and he saw the moment she recognised its authenticity.

She wrapped slim fingers around it. "This is real."

"Not according to you."

She opened her palm, staring once more at the seal. "It is real. What are you doing with this? Did you steal it?"

"The Sultan gave it me. He wants me to…" Thomas hesitated, unsure if Helena knew of the events that had occurred in the palace. "Did you hear what happened today?"

"Everyone heard." That dismissive note of scorn again, and Thomas tried to remember how long since he'd first heard it, or if it had always been there. "That still doesn't tell me why you have this in your possession." Helena's thumb stroked the rounded head of the seal, a slow, sensuous movement.

"A poisoned gift," he said. "The Sultan has asked me to investigate the killings."

"You? Why you? He has… other people for that, surely? He should have asked my father."

Thomas noted the hesitation, knew Helena had been about to say *better people*. He agreed with her.

"I don't think he trusts anyone inside the palace. Not now. If someone can find their way into a Sultana's bathing chamber nowhere is safe."

"Unless it wasn't a man who killed Safya," Helena said. "I heard it was a djinn."

Thomas started to laugh before he caught the expression on her face. She more than half believed the tale.

A flash of anger at being found out thinned her lips, drawing the scar on her face taut, distorting her features.

"It was no spirit did this. It was a man—a strong man. Someone who knows his way around the palace."

"Believe what you will." Helena tossed the seal into the air and Thomas snatched it before it could fall to the stone floor again. "Does this mean you'll be in and out at all hours? What do I tell people when they come asking for treatment?"

"Take a name and tell them I'll see them when I can. If it's urgent send them to al-Baitar."

"And if their arm is hanging off?"

"Then no doubt they'll die with or without my assistance."

Thomas knew al-Baitar was not as skilled a surgeon, but he was good enough, and better with potions and salves. Thomas used his friend's ointments in preference to his own, and in turn al-Baitar sent those he couldn't help to Thomas. Neither man was growing rich.

"Is the eunuch staying for dinner? I'm not sure we have enough food."

"Give him my share. He and I need to talk."

Helena brushed past Thomas and strode into the courtyard.

Thomas followed, stood behind her a moment, her scent enveloping him, a tension in his body brought on by the events of the day, anger at her attitude, lust for her body. After half a year he had grown accustomed to her easy availability, to the silk of her skin beneath his touch. It should have been enough.

Jorge hadn't gone to the workshop. Instead he sat on a stone bench, head resting against the wall, eyes closed. Above the wall birds swooped in pursuit of the insects of dusk, their cries filling the air.

When Helena caught sight of Jorge she came to a sudden halt and span around, only to find Thomas blocking her way. She shook her head, placed her arms on his and moved him aside. Thomas looked up to find Jorge, his eyes open now, watching them without expression. Thomas scowled and walked fast along the side of the courtyard to the workshop, not waiting to see if he followed. He pushed a heavy table to one side, pulled two chairs out and sat in one, waiting. It took Jorge only a moment to appear. He looked around with curiosity, and Thomas studied him in turn.

Jorge was a handsome man. Even in the silk and finery a eunuch was expected to wear he possessed an aura of solid masculinity. If Thomas hadn't operated on him himself he wouldn't have known Jorge was not a man in all aspects.

Jorge pulled a chair close and sat so their knees almost touched. A fragrance crossed the space between them, a residue of perfume from the harem.

"So now you live with one of the most beautiful women in all Gharnatah, eh? Some men have more luck than they deserve."

Thomas remained unsettled from his conversation with Helena. "And what would you do with such a beautiful woman?"

Jorge chose not to take offence at the sharpness in Thomas's voice. "What do you think?"

Thomas snorted a sharp laugh. "Of course, I forgot, eunuchs are all the same."

Jorge lifted a shoulder, eased back in his chair and crossed a leg. "I may lack balls, but thanks to you I still have my cock. Anyone else would have taken that as well. Don't believe everything you hear. I can get as hard as the next man…. Well, perhaps not as hard as you, I admit, but then I don't share my bed with someone as exquisite as Helena."

"You share a palace with over a hundred women. Most of them so beautiful they would make the gods hard." Jorge had recovered his usual unwavering good humour, but if anything it only served to fuel Thomas's unease.

"Ah, of course, how careless of me to forget." Jorge smiled, and Thomas knew this man—yes, he admitted, a man in all qualities but one—was used for more than fetching and carrying and preening. "What—did you think I led a celibate life? Thanks to you I have most of the equipment necessary to give a woman pleasure. In fact, also thanks to you, I have the perfect equipment for my station in life. I have this." Jorge cupped his groin, his smile flipping into a grin. "But I lack those two items that would prove dangerous to a man in my position. No surprise pregnancies. No suspicions."

Thomas's frown deepened. "If the Sultan knew you were—"

Jorge laughed. "Do you think a Sultan—especially one as old as Abu al-Hasan—can service all those young and nubile women himself? He's not a stupid man. As long as there's discretion—and I am very discrete—I am able to carry out all the duties expected of me." Jorge sighed. "I know it's a challenging role life has placed on me, but I try to rise to the occasion."

Thomas stared back, then felt a smile crease his mouth, a smile that turned into a laugh.

"How on earth is the harem going to manage without you? Perhaps I should dismiss you from service so you can return to your arduous duties."

Amusement left Jorge's face, draining like water from a broken pot. "We both know this task is the most difficult, possibly the most dangerous, of our lives."

Thomas nodded, sitting back, weariness pulling at his limbs; a weariness that would have to wait. He would never start operating on a man without knowing what outcome to expect. This task required the same skills. They needed a plan. A strategy.

Jorge leaned forward, his face expressionless. "Have you spoken with Helena about the time she was attacked?" He had obviously been sharing similar thoughts, but his mind had gone in a different direction.

Thomas shook his head. "About her injury, nothing else." He stared at Jorge's face, now serious, seeing in it the man's grief held hard in check. Jorge had loved Safya, loved her perhaps more than any other man, even her husband. This was difficult for him.

"I think a conversation would be worthwhile."

"You believe the events connected?"

Jorge reached out and rapped his knuckles on Thomas's forehead. "Come on, use that brain you're meant to have. She was attacked within the walls of the palace only six months ago. The first servant died four months later."

"Four months is a long time between attacks. And Helena lived."

"And before Helena when was the last time you heard of anyone—anyone at all—being attacked within the palace?"

Thomas nodded. "Never."

"Right. Never. I hear all the gossip, every tittle and tattle of it, and there's never been an attack on a member of the harem that I've heard of. You still believe the two events aren't connected?"

"We need to talk with her," Thomas said.

"Yes, we do. But carefully. Do you have such a thing as wine in your house?"

"Wine? Where does a eunuch get a taste for such forbidden fruit?"

"A man needs more pleasures than just those of the flesh. Do you have any?"

"Yes, I have wine."

Jorge smiled. "Even though its consumption is frowned on?"

"I'm *ajami*, remember. No-one expects me to follow the rules. Besides, I keep it for my patients."

Jorge's smile grew. Thomas rose and filled a jug from a small barrel which rested on a side bench.

The wine was palatable, just. Thomas rarely drank, but the small cask was always available. Sometimes it helped pacify a patient. Other times a great deal was needed to act as anaesthetic, although if pain was likely to be severe he preferred extract of poppy.

Jorge took a long draft, barely pulling a face.

"Where did you acquire a taste for alcohol?" Thomas asked.

"The life of a eunuch is not all scented pleasure and attending on our ladies. Sometimes we're allowed a little free time. And Gharnatah is awash with taverns."

"More so than ever," Thomas agreed. The second mouthful of wine tasted better than the first, and he was sure the third would improve yet again. He tried to remember the last time he had drunk wine and failed. It would have been before Helena came to live with him, certainly, and in the company of others. He would never have drunk alone. Jorge drained his cup and placed it on the table, casting a meaningful glance towards Thomas, who said, "Help yourself."

Jorge needed no further encouragement. Thomas placed his own cup on the table, still half full.

"Your friend the cleric wouldn't welcome seeing what you're doing," Thomas said, as Jorge drank more slowly from his refilled cup.

"My friend the cleric is friend to no man, and I doubt he'd approve of anyone enjoying themselves. He knows nothing of pleasure."

"All men know something of pleasure, otherwise what is the point of life?"

"He knows the words of Allah. They are his pleasure. Little else concerns him."

"He is a good man?" Thomas knew little of Abd al-Wahid al Mursi, other than he was the leading cleric to the Sultan.

"Abd al-Wahid is like all men who attain great power. He has lost sight of what he wanted power for and now sees only the power itself."

"He is austere."

"I'm not sure if that's a good thing or not in a cleric. Sometimes the fat, contented ones are easier to deal with. The hard men have little sympathy for those unlike themselves."

"Did he or the Vizier have any idea who might be behind the attacks?"

Jorge drained his glass but didn't refill it. Thomas sipped at his own, his head already loose from the alcohol. The taste filled his mouth, tart with an undertone of cedar.

"They made it clear to me it's our job to find the killer," Jorge said. "Did the Sultan say any more to you?"

"He sees threats everywhere and is incapable of telling what is true from false. At the bathhouse he was concerned about the nobles, but he said nothing today."

"You and I know there are men in this city who love nothing better than to plot against the Sultan. Perhaps in this instance he's right to be worried."

"Why would anyone from a wealthy family want to kill women of the harem? The Sultan, yes, even his sons. But his wives? I see no advantage in it, and too much to lose. And why the girls?"

Jorge rose and refilled his cup. "We both know it's not a fair world. The lives of servants don't carry the same value as that of a Sultan's wife. If a man is willing to kill and wants to practice his skills, what better way?" His voice was as bitter as the wine.

"And Helena?" Thomas said. "You're right, the attack on her was almost certainly the start of everything."

"But she wasn't killed."

"No. Was that because she was his first—he meant to kill her but failed?"

Jorge uttered a sharp laugh that contained no hint of humour. "I suspect whoever this man is it won't be the first time he has killed."

"A soldier, agreed. Someone familiar with the ways of death, but you said he needed to practice. The harem would be unfamiliar." Thomas watched Jorge. He was more relaxed now, the wine smoothing the lines from his face as it smoothed the pain from his heart.

"What?" Jorge said, Thomas's stare intense enough to draw his attention.

"Will you listen to me now?"

Jorge returned the stare. "Do I have to?"

"If you intend to work alongside me, yes. There are things you might not want to hear but need to hear. This is one of them."

Jorge shook his head. "I still don't understand how you could do such a thing."

"I studied them, that's all."

"Could you not allow them the dignity of death?"

"Not in these circumstances."

"You are too familiar with death—it has made you heartless."

"Perhaps so. That may be why the Sultan asked me to help—he recognises something within me." Thomas studied Jorge a moment longer before making a decision. "I learned nothing from Safya we didn't already know. The cuts were clean, deep, made by a sharp blade; but it could have been any blade. There was nothing special that I could see."

Jorge's face contorted but Thomas couldn't stop now.

"Alisha was different. Her wounds were clean, too, the same blade, but there was something else. The attacker must have gripped her shoulder." Thomas rose and moved behind Jorge. He placed his left hand on Jorge's shoulder. "Like this." He dug his fingers in for a moment, not hard, but hard enough. "And he held her tight. Much tighter than I hold you. He left a mark.

His mark."

Jorge continued to stare straight ahead. Thomas could feel the tension in the man's body. He waited, knowing it was important that Jorge ask. That to ask would bind him tighter to their task.

A minute passed. Two. Three. Thomas remained with his hand on Jorge's shoulder. Patient. He felt muscles tighten beneath his fingers.

"And?" Jorge said.

"He is missing two fingers." Thomas released his grip, returned to the seat and held his hand out, his little and ring finger folded across his palm. "These fingers."

Jorge shook his head, emptied his cup. "Half the soldiers in the Sultan's army are missing one thing or another, some of them almost half their bodies. This is meant to help us?"

"How many palace guards have those two fingers missing on their left hand?"

Jorge threw his hands up. "How am I supposed to know? Do you think I spend my time appraising the guards for missing digits?"

"It's the kind of thing you might notice," Thomas said.

"Well, I didn't. I'm sorry to disappoint you. Is there more wine?"

"You can have more wine with dinner."

"Then is it time for dinner?"

ELEVEN

They ate in the courtyard with the sky holding a pale violet line in the west. Lamps set into the wall cast a warm glow across the tiles, attracting insects which battered against the glass bowls. The moon rose behind the ramparts of al-Hamra, which appeared to loom over them.

Helena had obviously forgotten her annoyance at Jorge's presence, even bringing him a flagon of wine when he asked, then chatting about old times; meaningless conversation Thomas ignored as he examined his own thoughts, wondering how to broach the subject of the attack on her. He knew from experience how reluctant she was to relive the night her beauty had been stolen away.

Staring at her he saw how, as she always did, she ensured her hair covered one side of her face. The scar was healing well, but she would never fully recover the flawless perfection she had once possessed. Thomas wondered if she was genuinely grateful for what repairs he had managed to effect, but doubted it. All Helena saw was what had been lost, not what was recovered. No doubt she blamed him for not being a better surgeon.

Thomas fought impatience, bearing down on the pressure to do something. He knew that now, immediately after the attack on Safya, was the time to pursue the killer. Instead they sat in the warm evening air, eating a meal of goat stew, fig and apricot, while somewhere out in Gharnatah a killer was fleeing—or worse, choosing his next victim.

"Have you thought any more on what I said?" Helena asked, and Thomas frowned, trying to remember what she was talking about. She caught the expression on his face and said one word, "Lubna."

"I don't need another woman in my house." Helena had picked away at the topic for over a week, seemingly unwilling to accept his answer. Her broaching the subject on their way to the palace only that morning seemed a lifetime ago.

"Don't you want to be thought of as a great man?" Helena said.

"Why would I want that?" Thomas saw the expression of amusement on Jorge's face as he watched their conversation.

"Great men have many wives. People will believe you have your own harem if Lubna comes here. It will raise your profile. You should think of your status within the city."

"Such things are of no importance. I thought you knew me better."

"Perhaps I do—haven't you considered I might be doing this for you, not myself? You don't care enough about what people think of you. Someone has to if you won't."

Thomas tried to recall what he knew of Helena's sister. He recalled a slight girl who must now be on the pivot between youth and adulthood. Seven years shy of Helena's twenty-five, Lubna was the youngest of Olaf Torvaldsson's five daughters, the only child born of the new wife he took following the death of Helena's mother in childbirth—Helena's birth.

Olaf's seed was more adept at producing females than males, a matter he had consulted Thomas on once, but only the once, after being informed there was nothing that could be done to change or even predict the sex of a child, despite what others might say.

"I have little time to think of anything but work," Thomas said, aware both Helena and Jorge were staring at him.

"She's waiting for an answer," Helena said. "I told her you would consider my suggestion."

"You had no right to do that. I'll give the matter thought when I have time."

"She can't stay with my father forever. He won't keep her under his roof much longer, and I fear to think what will become of her then."

"When I can." A sharpness entered his voice. "There was a battle, and now this killing. How can I consider anything else at the moment?"

"She would make herself useful." Helena spoke as though Thomas had said nothing.

Thomas picked up his spoon and sawed at a piece of meat, chewed the morsel he managed to work loose, giving himself an excuse to end the conversation. He caught Jorge watching. Was that a spark of amusement in the man's eyes? A lift at the corner of his mouth? The eunuch would know Olaf, of course, and Thomas wondered what he thought of him. There could hardly be two more contrasting individuals in the entire city.

Olaf was a man from the cold, distant north, even more distant than Thomas's homeland, brought to this place along with many of his countrymen to fight for the Sultan and his predecessors. Olaf was no recent incomer but his grasp of Arabic remained poor; something he seemed determined to correct in his children.

Thomas knew Helena's elder sister continued to reside as a courtesan within the harem. The others had found places in the houses of nobles or the wealthy of Gharnatah. All except Lubna, for some reason, and what the reason might be Thomas couldn't guess. She was the youngest, certainly, and perhaps her father had run short of favours; and she wasn't as beautiful as her siblings, except for her eyes. Perhaps it was because she was half Moorish, her mother a dark skinned Berber, not exotic enough in this dry land where every other person carried Berber blood in their veins.

On the few occasions Thomas had spoken with Lubna she demonstrated a keen mind, curious about his work, often asking questions that surprised him.

"We need to talk, Thomas," Jorge said.

He looked up from his meal, aware a conversation had been going on without him.

"Later." Thomas knew he was a coward for avoiding a difficult subject.

"Jorge was asking if I had any notion who might have done such an evil thing," Helena said.

Thomas glanced at her. "And do you?" Trust Jorge to see his reluctance and offer an opening.

Helena smiled, and as always when she looked at him with compassion his heart melted and he knew, despite her sometimes difficult manner, he was grateful she had come into his life. "It might be easier to suggest who might not."

Thomas frowned. "I don't understand."

"The palace is always full of rumour, everyone trying to position themselves to advantage."

"Murder is a little more than positioning for advantage," Thomas said.

"You know the harem as well as any man other than Jorge. It's not the place of sensual ease people believe it to be. Safya was a well considered wife, but the coming of the child changed her position. It always does. If she had a boy then the balance of power shifts in her favour—"

"Except," Thomas said, "the Sultan has two older sons already. And it could have been a girl."

"But wasn't."

Thomas glanced at Jorge. He knew Helena might have discovered the sex of the child in a thousand ways, not that it mattered whether she knew or not. Soon the whole city would know of a new prince. They would also know of the killing—although the spread of that news might not be passed so keenly.

"One so far down the line of succession is little threat."

"Not just the child," Helena said. "Safya's change of status. A Sultan can sire a thousand children, but I hear it said this one is growing old, and soft in his dotage, although I don't believe that."

Thomas laughed. "Hardly his dotage. He returned from battle only yesterday. He's still strong, still respected."

"He is older than he was, and no-one lives forever. Those who want to replace him must start manoeuvring early, because if they don't there are others who will. It's how lands are ruled. You know this, Thomas. You, Jorge, know this better than Thomas, who doesn't understand the world as you do."

There it was again. The soft smile, the melting of his heart, the dismissive phrase.

"So it could be almost anyone." Thomas was disappointed. For a moment he had hoped for some useful information.

Helena pushed her chair back. "I see I am no use here. I will leave you men to discuss such weighty matters."

"I would have you stay a moment longer," Thomas said, an unfamiliar nervousness touching him. "There are questions I wish to ask."

"Questions? Of me? I know nothing of what happens on the hill these days."

"My questions are not about today. I want to ask about the night you were attacked."

Helena rose suddenly, began clashing plates together. Thomas watched her, then said, "Sit."

Something in his voice, the curtness, the certainty, stopped her. She returned the plates to the table and stared at him.

"Please," he said.

For a moment he was sure she was going to turn away. The tightness in her body where her hands pressed against the table made the hair hanging across her face shimmer. Then the tension softened, and she took her seat once more.

"What do you want to know? It was a long time ago."

"But you haven't forgotten, have you." Jorge's voice was gentle.

"Do you think I ever can?"

"Anything you recall will help," Jorge said.

Thomas leaned closer, wanting to reach for Helena's hand, but something held him back. "Did you see the man who attacked you?"

"I saw nothing that would to be of use to you. It all happened so fast, and there was great pain, and the blood. All I saw after he cut me was the blood."

"Tell us everything you can remember. Where were you

when he attacked you?"

"In the courtyard of the lions."

"Alone?"

"With Yasmina." Another concubine also no longer in the Sultan's favour.

"What time of day?" Thomas knew he should have these answers, but had never asked.

"Evening. Dark, so it must have been late."

"What were you doing in the courtyard at that hour?"

"I couldn't sleep. Yasmina was already there, listening to the water, watching the stars."

"Were there no guards?"

"Not that close to the harem. And no eunuchs either." She cast a glance at Jorge.

"What did you do when you sat with Yasmina?"

"Do?" Helena sounded defensive. "We did nothing."

"I'm not accusing you of anything. But did you talk? Walk? You must have done something."

"We talked, I suppose."

"And Yasmina was still there when you were attacked?"

Helena nodded, staring at her hands.

"Tell me everything."

"We were talking, our heads together, whispering so we wouldn't wake anyone. I think Yasmina saw him first, possibly saw more than I did. One moment we were giggling over some silly matter, the next a figure was rushing towards us. He was black, everything about him black, and he moved oddly as though... I don't..." Helena closed her eyes in an attempt to deepen the memory. "As though he hopped." Her eyes snapped open, staring at Thomas. "As though he had no legs..." Her eyes widened. "He was the djinn! I didn't realise, not then, not even today when I heard what had happened. He was the djinn, the same one!"

This time Thomas did reach across the table and took her hand between his palms, her fingers cool to his touch.

"Please," Jorge said. "Try to picture exactly what happened

that night. Everything."

"I don't want to." Helena shook her head, hair now completely obscuring her face.

"Was it you he was attacking?" Thomas said, his voice soft. "Are you sure it was you, or could it have been Yasmina?"

"Why her?"

"And why you."

"Could he have mistaken you for someone else?" Jorge said.

"Such as whom?"

"Safya, perhaps?"

"I look nothing like Safya. How could anyone mistake this hair of mine for hers?"

"In the dark?"

"The courtyard was lit with torches, as we are here. He would have been able to tell."

"Yasmina then? She is dark haired, dark skinned. Did he attack Yasmina in mistake for Safya?"

"Why? Because of the baby?"

"No-one knew of the baby, not then," Thomas said.

Helena pulled her hands free from Thomas's, scooped her hair back over her shoulders and faced him. "Not you perhaps, but in the harem women are always the first to know. Her bleeding hadn't come for two months, and the gossip was of a new son for the Sultan. A Moorish son."

"Tell me again, all you remember."

Helena breathed deeply, her shoulder tense. However gentle they tried to be it was obvious she found the questioning hard. "One moment we were alone, the next he was there, a whirling spirit cloaked in black—"

"Cloaked," Jorge said. "He wore a cloak?"

Helena shook her head. "No. Perhaps. I can't recall. I'm sorry, it was all so long ago, and the pain terrible. If I told you I saw him clearly it would be a lie."

"What would not be?" Jorge said. "Tell us what you do remember. Where did he appear from?"

"I've already told you—I didn't see!"

"What Jorge means is from which direction did he come?"

Jorge cast a glance towards Thomas as though to say *that is not what I meant,* but Thomas chose to ignore it.

Helena looked past Thomas's shoulder and he saw her eyes move as she searched her memory. "From the passageway. It was to our right as we sat, and he came from there. So fast. I remember he moved without hesitation. He..." Helena sat upright, her gaze returning to Thomas, flicking to Jorge and then back. "He didn't even glance at me. He went directly for Yasmina. Whoever he thought she was, whether he was mistaken or not, it was her he was trying to kill. Not me. Her."

"But it was you he injured," Thomas said.

"She screamed and fell backwards off the bench." Helena's eyes darted from left to right, not seeing the courtyard now but another. "His sword was raised. He brought it down but she wasn't there anymore and he caught my face as it swung around."

"Where did he flee?" Thomas said.

Before Helena could answer Jorge added, "No—*why* did he flee? He struck at you once, yes?"

"I think so. He..." Helena cast her eyes beyond Thomas's left shoulder again. "He had a sword. A scimitar—"

"You're sure of that?" Jorge interrupted.

"The blade was curved. I can see it now as he raised it, as he brought it down. He wanted to kill her. I saw it in his eyes. He—"

"You saw it in his eyes?" Jorge said, his voice sharp.

"Yes. He wanted to kill Yasmina."

"You saw his eyes?"

Helena huffed a sigh. "Did Thomas cut off your ears, too?"

"If you saw his eyes you saw his face," Thomas said. Helena reached for her wine and drained it. Jorge leaned across and refilled the cup.

Helena sipped at the fresh wine, gaze turned inward.

"He wore a deep hood. His eyes glowed like coals, but his face was in shadow."

"Afterwards," Jorge said, returning to the earlier question. "In which direction did he flee?"

Helena shook her head. "I have no idea. By then my face was split apart. I was in agony. Yasmina was screaming, and then others came, wives and concubines, eunuchs woken from dreams of whatever eunuchs dream of, and finally the guards."

"Where did the guards come from?" Jorge asked, relentless, ignoring Helena's barbs.

"I assume where they always come from. The guardhouse."

"Which is where?"

Helena cast a withering glance his way. "You live in the same palace as I did. You know where they came from. Stop asking stupid questions and go find this djinn before it kills again." She stood from the table so quickly her chair toppled backwards. "I'm going to bed. Thomas, don't stay out here all night with this..." She hesitated. "This man."

Thomas watched her go, the sway of her body, the flick of white hair, and wanted to follow. Instead he reached for the jug and poured himself more wine. The earlier cups were making his head swim. He needed to think, but had already knew he had drunk too much to stop.

Jorge held his cup out and Thomas filled it to the brim, the decision made. He had done enough thinking for one day. Oblivion offered its charms.

"Are you going back to the palace tonight, or shall I find you somewhere to sleep?"

"I can't return until this is over," Jorge said.

"Why not? Eyes and ears inside the palace would be useful."

Jorge held up a hand and started counting off on his fingers. "One: I am associated with you and this task, no longer trusted by my companions or my charges. They will tell me nothing now I'm tainted.

"Two: If this killer can enter a bathing chamber without being seen I'm not safe inside the palace walls." He held a third finger up but said nothing.

Thomas waited, watching emotions play across Jorge's normally placid features. He had known this man for over fifteen years, but never felt closer to him than at this moment.

"You loved her," Thomas said, knowing Jorge didn't want the opulence of the palace to remind him of the women who had been killed.

"Of course I loved her. I love them all."

It wasn't the first time he had said it, but Jorge's answer was beyond Thomas's understanding. He was incapable of loving the one he lived with, however hard he tried. He had emptied himself of love a long time ago.

"How can you love them all? Do you love them equally?"

Jorge glanced at Thomas, his face painted with flickering shadow from the lamps. "Sometimes yes, sometimes no."

"I don't understand."

"I know. And that's why I love you, too."

"You're doing it again."

"Doing what?"

"I'm trying to have a conversation and you belittle everything. It's as if nothing touches you."

"You're wrong." Jorge wrapped a hand around his cup. "It's because everything touches me."

"I still don't understand."

"It seems to me you understand nothing."

"You may be right, but explain to me how you can love everyone."

"Not everyone."

"Don't," Thomas said.

Jorge looked at him for a long while, finally nodded.

"All right. I'll try to explain, but on one condition."

"Which is?"

"You try to understand."

"I'll try, but I can't promise."

Jorge stood and walked to the wall. He leant back against it and stared up at al-Hamra before speaking.

"For me—and I believe for everyone, if they will let it—love is boundless. Love is the ocean. Take one thimbleful from it and an infinite amount remains. All the people in the world working together couldn't empty the ocean." Jorge turned to Thomas. "But you understand this already. You have loved, too."

Thomas turned away, the question a reminder of the pain he had wrapped tight and hidden deep within.

"You have," Jorge said, a teasing amusement in his voice.

"It was long ago, and it ended badly."

"How?"

"I don't think about it anymore."

"How did it end?"

"She…" Thomas sighed. He had never mentioned her to anyone in the years since, had no idea why he spoke of her now. "She married someone else."

"They do. Did it make you love her any less?"

"No."

"So?"

"I didn't stop loving her, but she belonged to someone else."

Jorge smiled. "Nobody belongs to anybody."

"She did."

"No," Jorge said again. "You believe she did."

"As I said, it was a long time ago."

"But it still hurts."

Thomas stared at him.

"It still hurts, doesn't it?" Jorge said.

Thomas turned away and started walking, but he muttered and answer under his breath. "Yes, it still hurts."

After Jorge had grudgingly accepted the cot in the workshop Thomas left him with the remains of the barrel of wine and returned to the courtyard. The plates from their meal remained uncleared but he left them where they were and sat on the bench beneath the balcony. Unwelcome memories flooded him, too strong to resist. He had spent more than twenty years trying to bury them deep, but had failed. One short conversation and here they were, the wounds as fresh as if they had been made that hour.

Her name had been Eleanor. He hoped it remained so, and that she continued to live—his child, too. Not a child anymore, but an adult of twenty-five. Had it been a boy or girl? He had no way of knowing. Married by now, almost certainly. Or dead. Knowing nothing of their true father.

It was for the best. Thomas had been someone different then, someone he had been running from ever since.

In his memory Eleanor possessed impossible beauty and grace, a jewel held captive inside the box of his mind, something that could never be stolen from him. Each time he opened the box she became more perfect, more angelic. Except she had been far from such a state of grace, but feral and wild as he himself had been. But her beauty—he did not exaggerate her beauty. It was the reason he had lost her, of course. The baby growing inside her belly was a surprise to both of them; no doubt even more of a surprise to the nobleman who took her from him.

Drifting aimlessly through France, lost and alone after the death of his father, he had found her by accident. His father had died on a battlefield, of course. Perhaps that was why Thomas felt the need to revisit such places, to help the wounded, to ease the pain of the dying. As he had eased that of his father when he finally accepted it was a kindness to end such suffering. It had not been the first time he'd offered such mercy. There had been others on the scorched field, but his father had been the last that day—and for a long time afterwards.

He closed his eyes and leaned against the wall, feeling a residual warmth seep into the tense muscles of his back. He tried to remember the year of the battle. He knew how long ago, knew his age at the time—but his mind no longer thought in the same measure of years they once had. In al-Andalus the year was 885. This was the one familiar to him. He knew how to perform the conversion, but his mind was tired, and wine sang in his blood. He should let it go and sleep, but for some reason it felt important to remember. It was the day he was left an orphan, cast adrift in a foreign land. Of course, that was how. He had been thirteen years old—born in the year of our Lord 1440 outside the town of Leominster, which lay in the English Marches—son of John Berrington who was squire to the Earl of Shrewsbury. He had been alone since the year 1453, abandoned by man and God close by the town of Castillon in France.

Thirteen years of age was too young to go to battle, but there had been no other choice. The sweating sickness had taken both his mother and brother—the one who was meant to go to war, who wanted to go to war—leaving behind the three of them. He hadn't thought of his sister in many long years, and it took a moment to conjure up her name. Angnes, her name had been Angnes, but however hard he tried her face refused to come, eroded by the years between. He wondered if she still lived.

Eleanor believed him dead, he knew. That was how he had been left, discarded at the side of the roadway from Ancizen to Guchen while the Count d'Arreau stole away the only woman he had ever loved. Could love truly be infinite, as Jorge claimed? It had always felt to him something to be held close in case it trickled away, like dry sand from a closed fist. What if Jorge was right? All these wasted years he had held his pain close, shunning others.

Thomas rose, the movement sudden and sharp. He shook his head, scattering pointless memories into the night. No more wine, no more conversation of love. There was work to do. Hard work. Dangerous work.

Helena was asleep when he entered their bedchamber and he stood for a moment watching her breathe. The linen sheet was cast aside and her body lay revealed in white moonlight, its perfection almost frightening. She was as beautiful as Eleanor, even more so, but standing at the foot of the bed Thomas felt nothing. Nothing at all.

TWELVE

"I don't see why I can't just stay at your house," Jorge said the next morning as they followed a narrow alley winding down into town.

"Are you sure you can't go back to the palace?"

"The women will make demands. They won't understand there are other calls on my time. But can we bring in another bed? That cot in your workroom isn't large enough to hold someone my size. And it smells strange in there."

"Herbs, that's all. You didn't touch anything, did you?"

Jorge cast him a glance.

"The inn will suit you better," Thomas said.

"I have no money."

"Money isn't a problem. You'll need different clothes, too."

So far they had seen only one other person, and that man had been too polite to stare at Jorge for long, but once in the town Thomas knew from the previous evening how it would be.

"I have other clothes. I wear them when I come to drink and enjoy male conversation."

They reached a set of steps, steep and twisting. Thomas led the way down.

"They're at the palace, I take it."

"They are."

The steps deposited them on a street running alongside the Hadarro and Thomas turned right. The day was still young and fortunately for them not many of Gharnatah's citizens were out and about. It was a different matter when they entered the square. They passed stalls piled high with almonds, fruit, vegetables, pots, local silks and imported cloth, the odours of a dozen lands drifting through the air, the sound of a score of languages babbling.

"Am I dressed so strangely?" Jorge was drawing attention even among the brightly attired stallholders.

"Not for the harem, I expect, but here? Yes. You do know you're dressed strangely, don't you? But the inn is only on the other side of the square. We'll find you a room and then get something for you to wear."

"Nothing too coarse," Jorge said, and Thomas smiled.

Khadar the innkeeper was more than happy to take Thomas's money. The room he showed them was adequate, with a small glazed window offering a view across the square. They didn't stay long, once more making their way through winding streets and then quieter, more opulent ones to the workshop of Carlos Rodriquez, set three doors down from his house.

Carlos was an acquaintance of Thomas's, one he occasionally beat at Mancala while they sipped sweet coffee or tea at Khadar's inn. He was not in the workshop when the door was opened by a wide Spanish woman, but she sent a message, and within a short time he entered from a rear door, trying to make his appearance casual.

"Thomas—have you finally come to let me dress you more appropriately?"

"I'm not here on my own behalf. I need clothes for my friend."

Distaste showed on Carlos's face, but both Thomas and Jorge chose to ignore it.

"You're sure I can't tempt you with something matching your status, Thomas?"

"He does look like some desert Bedouin, doesn't he?" Jorge said, and Thomas cast him a glance.

"I'm surprised anyone recognises him as a physician." Carlos warmed to the subject. It was an old and tired topic for Thomas, one he was determined not to be swayed over, even if Helena had now joined the chorus of those wishing to attire him like some cosseted parakeet.

"Can you do something for him, or must I look elsewhere? We want nothing fancy, for we need to pass as ordinary men."

"I may not wish—" Jorge started to speak, but Thomas cut him off with a raised hand. "I would at least prefer the materials to be less coarse than those you wear," Jorge finished.

"I believe I can promise you that," Carlos said. He approached Jorge, moving around him, measuring with his eyes. "I could have something suitable made by tomorrow evening."

"We need something now," Thomas said.

"I..." Carlos surveyed Jorge again, who was now wandering the shelves stacked with bolts of material from all over Spain, others imported from Africa, Italy and beyond. "He's tall, isn't he?"

"He is," Thomas agreed.

"And broad across the shoulder."

"And belly, a little."

"I am not fat," Jorge said, running some cloth between his fingers.

"I didn't imply you were. Well fed, I would say, no more than that."

"I may have something to fit him, but it won't be fashionable, or of fine material. If you could offer me a little more time..."

"We need to dress him now. One outfit will suffice for today, and perhaps you can make him two more for tomorrow. You did say tomorrow evening, didn't you?"

"Two outfits?"

"I like this material," Jorge said, lifting a bolt of black silk run through with fine gold thread. "This would make a wonderful pair of trousers."

"It's a special order, not for sale," Carlos said. "Besides, it's too good for trousers—and you would not wish to pay the cost if I was to use it."

"Something similar then?"

"I'll see what I can do." Carlos turned to the woman. "Teresa, will you measure him while I see if I can find something he can wear now?"

Thomas leaned against the edge of a large table where cloth was laid out ready to make up and watched as the woman expertly prodded and pushed Jorge, making him stand tall as she measured his chest, shoulders, waist and leg length, writing everything down on a scrap of paper. By the time Carlos returned Jorge was back to fingering the bolts of cloth.

"I have decided," Jorge said, "that I favour silk over cotton or linen."

"It's the silk that makes you stand out," Thomas said. "Carlos, cotton is what I want for him."

"Then I have brought the right outfit. This should fit, I believe." He laid trousers, shirt, cloak and scarf on the table. Jorge offered the garments a glance as disdainful as they deserved.

"Those are perfect," Thomas said.

"If I wear these no-one will know it's me," Jorge said.

"Exactly."

"We will leave you in privacy to change," Carlos said. "Come, Teresa, we'll use the other room to look at his measurements and decide what we can do."

"I'm not wearing them," Jorge said once they were alone.

"You can't wear what you have now."

"I told you, I have clothing at the palace."

"Which, no doubt, still makes you look like a eunuch."

"I am a eunuch!"

"But you want no-one to know you are, not for our task."

"Why not?" Jorge picked up the shirt, white, of good quality linen with a fine weave, weighed it in his hand.

"It's a good shirt," Thomas said. "At least try the clothes on and see how you feel. It may only be for a few days. Carlos will make you something better tomorrow."

"I hope so. Why couldn't I have some of that exquisite silk over there?"

"No silk. And you need to cover your head."

"But it's my second best feature."

"Only until your hair grows out. A beard would be useful,

too."

Jorge sighed, shaking his head. "What are you trying to turn me into?" He began loosening the fine silks that draped his body.

Thomas turned aside, not from guilt or shame, merely to offer some encouragement and speed him along, although he suspected an audience would be welcomed. Even if it was essential, buying clothes for Jorge was wasting time.

For a second day Thomas found himself cursing the steepness of the path from the Hadarro to the palace. It seemed irrational to him it should be separated from those it governed by a steep gorge and river. Or perhaps not. As he trudged upwards—with Jorge striding ahead hardly even drawing breath—it occurred to Thomas the separation of governor and governed was a wiser course. They frequently made poor neighbours.

"The clerks first?" Jorge asked, picking up on their initial plan, before Safya had been slain.

"I think so. And I'd like to speak with those two girls again—they may have remembered more overnight."

They drew close to the doorway where he had entered the day before, the same guard standing beside it.

"We have urgent business within the palace," Thomas commanded.

"I heard your urgent business of yesterday is dead. What else might bring you here, surgeon?" The guard drew the name of Thomas's profession out, making it clear what he thought of the practice of medicine.

Thomas delved into the pocket of his robe and drew out the Sultan's seal. "This brings me here. Now let us pass."

"Hold up, that could be anything." The guard laid his spear across the doorway, barring their way. He glanced briefly at Jorge but, with his head covered and dressed as he was, didn't appear to recognise him.

"It could be anything, certainly, but it is not." Thomas raised the seal, making the guard take a step back. "Do you want to explain to Sultan Abu al-Hasan Ali or his Vizier you turned away men on their business?"

The guard glanced at the seal, but he was no longer seeing it. The surety in Thomas's voice was enough, although face still had to be saved.

"And how do I explain letting two strangers simply walk past me while a killer is on the loose? For all I know it's one of you."

"Foolish man!" Jorge said. "Don't you know me? I belong here. And Thomas is no stranger. We've walked the palace halls longer than you've lived. Now stand aside and let us pass."

The guard was not bright, but bright enough to realise he had pushed his moment of authority as far as he could. Boredom, perhaps, had gotten the better of him. He withdrew his lance and stepped aside. Thomas passed through into the dimness of the corridor, steps rising ahead, but Jorge deliberately jostled against the guard in passing and spat quiet words in his ear.

"We need cool heads," Thomas said as Jorge caught him up. "Don't allow his stupidity to make you angry."

"I'll try to remember your words of wisdom." The sarcasm was thick in Jorge's voice. "But I never do. If I allowed stupidity to get beneath my skin I'd have been driven mad years ago. There's a surplus of it inside the walls of this place."

Thomas led the way, following the same route as the day before, except yesterday Helena had accompanied him; excited, eager to meet whoever she had been on her way to see. He had meant to ask her, but events had driven all thought of Helena's liaison from his mind.

They crossed directly through the palace and onto the narrow bridge to the Vizier's offices. They were not expected, but the seal once more gave access, and they were shown to a room where four men stood at high desks. A fifth, larger table stood in the middle of the space, scattered with scrolls, paper and books. There was a musty smell to the air. If the Sultan's chambers were the heart of the palace, the harem it's sex, then this was the head that kept track of everything that went on.

The clerk nearest the door turned to them.

"Can I help you? We don't hear petitions until later in the day."

"We're not here to petition." Thomas felt into his pocket again, searching once more for the seal. "We come on the Sultan's business, with questions."

"Ah, you're the physician. My master told me we should expect you." He looked Thomas up and down. "You don't look much like a doctor." He turned his attention to Jorge. "Nor you a eunuch."

"Needs must," Jorge said.

"Who would you question?"

"Whoever was tasked with investigating the first killings. Was that you?"

The man shook his head. "No, I wouldn't have been asked." He turned to look over the others, shaking his head slowly as though his memory was deficient. "Habib, you were involved, weren't you?"

A short man turned away from his work. The others continued, scribing information onto paper, each of them with fingers stained dark from ink.

"I was asked to record some of the conversation, but Bilal Abd al-Rahman was the one in charge."

"Can we speak with this Bilal then?" Thomas asked.

"He no longer works on the hill," the first clerk said, as Habib returned to his work, incurious.

"Then where does he work?"

"Somewhere in the city, but not here. If that's all…"

"I would speak with Habib first."

"He said he only noted some facts, nothing more."

"I would still speak with him. I take it you don't intend to refuse my request?" Thomas's fingers closed around the seal.

"Of course I won't refuse you. Habib, go into the courtyard with these men and tell them what you know."

"I have a document to finish by noon."

"We won't take long," Thomas said, not knowing if he spoke

the truth or not.

"I will explain if you're late," his master said.

Habib nodded, laid his pen on the desk and led the way through an archway into a small courtyard. The surroundings were not as opulent as those of the main palace, but there was water, trees for shade, and two stone benches in the far corner. This was no doubt a place the scribes came when they took a break from their work. It was to the benches that Habib led them. He sat in the centre of one. Thomas and Jorge settled opposite.

"What do you wish to know?" He obviously wanted the matter over with so he could return to work.

"You recorded the findings of this other man, this Bilal?"

"Some. He did much of the work himself, but at times I accompanied him to record their words when he questioned people."

"And who did he question?"

"It's been some time since those events. I'm not sure I recall their names."

"What kind of people then?"

"Oh, servants. Those who knew the girls who were attacked, those who were nearby when the attacks happened."

"And you recorded this testimony?"

"Some of it. As I said, Bilal did much for himself."

"Where are those documents now?"

"I don't know. I gave everything I worked on to Bilal. What he did with it I have no idea."

"Do you recall what was said in your presence?"

Habib shook his head. "I scribe—I don't usually take note of the words I write. Sometimes it's the safer course of action not to know."

"Weren't you curious?" Jorge asked before Thomas could pose another question.

"Curious?" It appeared to be an alien concept to Habib. "Why would I be curious?"

"Two girls were killed within the palace walls. I heard much rumour and gossip, many spoke of it."

"This is not the harem," Habib said.

"Do you remember anything at all?"

"I'm sorry." Habib shook his head. "I'm not trying to be obscure. I spend my days transcribing and recording. It would be impossible to take note of everything I write. If I could remember something I would tell you, but this happened months ago. And Bilal, as far as I know, discovered nothing."

"So why did you stop?"

"Bilal reported whatever he had discovered to the Vizier. Shortly afterwards he left his employment here."

"Left," Thomas said, "or was asked to leave?"

"All I know is he left."

"Do you know where he works now?"

"For the Jew, Hasdai ibn Shaprut. They work out of a house in the Albayzin, writing wills and contracts and land treaties."

"Was his move voluntary?" Thomas returned to the question Habib had not answered before.

The scribe looked aside. He seemed to be thinking, judging his answer, perhaps wondering if Thomas held more power than his master. "I believe he was asked to leave."

"As a result of his findings leading nowhere, do you think, or for some other reason?"

"As I already told you, I don't think anything. But in this instance there may be truth in what you say."

"Because of what he discovered?" Jorge said.

"I don't know." Habib rose from the bench. "Now, I must return to my work."

"Should you recall anything relating to this matter I would ask you to contact either myself or Jorge," Thomas said.

Habib nodded briefly. "I will contact you. But don't expect any revelations."

He returned to the room without glancing at Jorge, who said, "Do you think he doesn't like me?"

Thomas looked at him. Even in his new clothes Jorge stood out, his whole body telegraphing an instinctive sensuality. "You may be an acquired taste." '

"All good things are. Was he telling the truth?"

"What do you think? I saw you watching him."

"I believe he was. He's not an imaginative man, and his job demands he suppress any vestige of curiosity he may possess. So yes, he was truthful, if unhelpful."

"We'll have to speak with this Bilal. I know Hasdai ibn Shaprut, I've used his services on a few occasions."

"Do we go there now?" Jorge asked.

"We should finish our work on the hill first. There's little point going all the way down only to have to climb back again. And I want to ask Habib's master about the documents Bilal made, what became of them."

"They'll be gone," Jorge said.

"What makes you say so? Documents are the life-blood of people such as these. They destroy nothing."

Jorge only smiled, and when Thomas went inside it was to find there were indeed no documents.

"Why not?" Thomas said, standing too close to the senior scribe. "What has become of them?"

"They will have been passed to the Vizier and Sultan."

"So they have them?"

"No." The man looked unhappy. "All palace documents are stored here. If they existed we would have them."

"Will you look?"

"I know everything we store. They are not here."

"I still want you to look, and send a message one way or the other. If you find anything keep it safe, I wish to read what is written there."

"So who do we talk to next?"

They stood outside the clerk's offices.

"You're enjoying this, aren't you?" Thomas said.

Jorge lifted a shoulder. "Sometimes luxury and the company of beautiful women grows dull."

"I want to speak with Zoraya while we're on this side of the hill. She has rooms here, doesn't she?"

"The Sultan keeps her apart from the harem, for good reason."

"She's disliked?"

"Indeed she is."

"Because she's Greek, or are there other reasons?"

"How many do you have time to hear?" Jorge said.

THIRTEEN

Zoraya's chambers were in the north wing of the smaller palace and owed nothing to the harem which housed the Sultan's other wives. This place had been fashioned in the image of the homes of Spanish royalty. Tables and chairs were set throughout the rooms, rugs covered the tiled floor, and tapestries hid the religious messages on the walls. The hangings showed hunting scenes, court gatherings; many faces and figures, alien in any Moorish decoration, which shunned depictions of the human figure in preference to scripts celebrating the all-consuming power of Allah.

Zoraya possessed her own guards, her own clerks and minders. Thomas and Jorge were made to wait in an outer chamber while one was sent to enquire if they might be admitted. Two others remained to ensure they made no attempt to wander.

Jorge went to the nearest man. "You're aware we're on the Sultan's business?"

"Your companion showed us his seal," the guard said, unimpressed.

"So why are we kept waiting?"

"It's not his fault, Jorge," Thomas said. "We won't be here long, I'm sure."

Jorge turned, offering Thomas a look which expressed his doubt, before crossing the room to stare through a small window offering a view across the plain. From the rooms within came the sound of conversation, occasional laughter, the clattering of pans and plates, the scent of roasted meats. Thomas realised it was almost noon, but there would be no interruption for prayers here.

Minutes passed, and then some more.

Jorge left the window and sat on a chair, testing it with his weight, rocking from side to side.

"I could get used to sitting this way," he said. "I saw you have such furniture in your house."

"I'm *ajami*, remember. And the older I get the more my bones protest at sitting on the floor, however many cushions there are beneath me."

"The Sultan is almost twice your age but he keeps the tradition."

"The Sultan is a stronger man than I." Thomas lowered his voice. "Do you think she will send us away?"

"She may. Zoraya knows her own power, and believes she possesses more than she truly does. We will see. Take a seat, Thomas, rest those ancient bones of yours."

"I would prefer—" He broke off as there came the sound of footsteps from the corridor, booted feet, as befitted the style of the place. The third man had returned, shaking his head, but in confusion rather than negation.

"My lady is about to take her noon meal, but she says you are welcome to join her and the children."

Jorge raised an eyebrow in surprise and Thomas smiled at him.

"She must want to meet me," Jorge whispered as they followed the man along a wide corridor lined with more wall hangings. In rooms to right and left lay rich furnishings. "I expect she's heard of my reputation."

"She knows she can't refuse us," Thomas whispered back.

"Believe what you will. I'm not sure I like the idea of her children being with her, though."

"You concentrate on them while I speak with Zoraya. Bear in mind it appears she prefers the Spanish form of address, so use that if you still recall it."

"I don't think I ever met with much Spanish royalty, but I'll try."

Their destination was a high ceilinged chamber with many windows offering a view east to the Sholayr mountains, their peaks now almost denuded of snow, and west across the plain.

Zoraya sat at the head of a long table laid with fine plates, crystal glass and silver cutlery. She didn't rise when they entered and neither did her children, two boys and a girl, the eldest boy of an age with Muhammed, who was eighteen, the other a little younger than Yusuf, the girl somewhere between the two. All at the table were attired as though they held court in Qurtuba rather than a Moorish palace.

"I'll not ask you to sit, it would not be seemly, but welcome Thomas Berrington, you also Jorge al-Andalus." She spoke in fluent Spanish and Thomas had to make a rapid re-adjustment to understand her words.

"We thank you for seeing us, my lady. You are most gracious."

"You don't mind if we eat? Good food shouldn't be allowed to grow cold. Do you know my children?"

"By name and reputation only, my lady." Thomas had switched his mind to the alien language, knowing his words sounded coarse among such company. "They are fine children."

"And healthy. They have no need of the services of one such as you."

"I can see that. Healthy indeed. Are we free to talk in their company?" Thomas noted that Jorge had moved to stand to one side of the girl, who sat opposite her brothers. He leaned down and spoke with her, his voice too soft for Thomas to make out, but her brothers heard, leaning forward to listen.

"Talk of what, surgeon?"

Although the children were eating, they had also started to converse with Jorge as though he was an old and valued companion, and Thomas envied him his ease with people. Zoraya left her cutlery untouched, the meat on her plate cooling. Instead she lifted a crystal goblet holding what appeared to be wine and took a long drink.

"Have you heard of the task set of us, my lady?"

"We are isolated on this side of the hill, but yes, I have heard something, although the subject is unseemly to me."

"I understand." Thomas felt as though he was walking across

hot coals, the next footstep likely to lead him into disaster. "I was asked to look into the deaths that have occurred in the palace, but now matters have taken a more serious turn."

"You mean Safya?" Zoraya's voice lowered and she glanced at her children. "Perhaps it would be wise to speak of this away from the table. Your companion appears to be making a good job of amusing my little ones. Shall we leave them to it?"

Thomas nodded and waited as Zoraya rose, a slow, complex operation involving much adjusting of silk skirts. When she was finally satisfied she led the way towards the windows. Thomas had expected them to move to another chamber, but Zoraya obviously thought the short distance enough.

"What is it you want of me?" she said, a flirtatious look entering her eyes which made Thomas uncomfortable. Perhaps he and Jorge should have exchanged roles.

"A few questions, nothing more."

"Then ask, so I can return to my meal." She glanced at the table. "Although I expect it is cold by now."

"You know the mission Jorge and I are on. I must question everyone who has information that could shed light on the deaths."

"Does the Sultan know you place me under suspicion?"

"You are under no suspicion. I merely ask if you have heard any rumour that might assist us. The palace is always alive with secrets."

"I keep my place on this side of the hill, sir, and never mix with the other wives or concubines."

"I understand it was not always so, you lived within the harem for several years. You must have made friends there?"

"A few, perhaps." Zoraya stared through the window. "But now they keep to themselves. It is as difficult for them to cross the bridge as it is for me to travel in the other direction."

"It must make for a lonely life," Thomas said.

She turned from observing the view and her eyes traced the features of his face. "I have my children. And I am not a complete hermit. Friends visit me now and again."

"But none from the harem."

The fascination with his face could last only so long and she turned aside. "I thought I had already made that clear."

"In which case do you have any suspicions of your own? Any trace of an idea why someone would want to kill women of the harem? A Sultana?"

"There are always plots. Or do you not live enough in this world to know of such things? I have heard it said you are often distracted from the commonplace things in life." Zoraya's voice was cold, her gaze now locked on a distant trail of smoke rising from some field.

"I'm learning to live in the real world, my lady. You have no theories then, on why they died?"

"The girls certainly not. Safya? She was a Sultana, and women of power always have enemies. If I were you I would be concentring my questions within the harem. That is where the real intrigue lies. Ask your friend, for he must know this better than anyone. Are you finished with me?"

"Not quite." He saw the expression on her face. "One more question. Helena says Yasmina works for you now. Would you allow me to speak with her?"

"Why?"

"She was with Helena when she was attacked. I believe it was the same man."

Zoraya made a dismissive sound between her teeth. "Yasmina is no longer in my employ. She was... unsuitable."

"Do you know where she is now?"

Zoraya waved a hand. "Gone elsewhere. Malaka, I believe. Yes, I'm sure she was sent to Malaka."

Thomas decided not to press her further for now. He could always return if he needed to. Something about the woman didn't sit right, her switch from flirtatiousness to impatience was too contrived.

He watched her return to the table and sit. It was obvious she had already dismissed him from her mind. She was, he had to admit, a striking woman. Her hair was finely cut and braided, darker than Helena's, but lighter than most women in al-Andalus. It was clear from the way she moved that beneath the voluminous skirts of her robes lay a sensuous body. Her features were finely sculpted, her skin clear, but something cold lay in her eyes, marring the effect of her beauty. She reminded him of Helena.

Jorge rose from his conversation with the elder boy, and Thomas joined him as they made their way towards the doorway. He glanced back as Zoraya clapped her hands and saw a servant hustle to the table to remove her plate; cold now, as she had said. She raised her eyes and shot him a glance of such malevolence he almost stumbled. There was raw hatred there, and he wondered what had triggered such venom. Not his questions, surely, but if not them, then what?

"So," Jorge said as they left the building and started across the narrow bridge, "did she admit plotting to kill her rivals?"

Thomas had to look at him to make sure Jorge was joking.

"Did you discover anything from the children?"

"Other than they are spoiled and have ambitions to be Spanish nobility, perhaps one or two things. The girl hasn't a single thought in her head other than which Spanish prince she should marry. The younger boy enjoys hunting but not with a bird, and the elder, I believe, is also starting to weigh his marriage options. He even grew bold enough to ask me questions regarding the bed chamber."

"You, of course, told him you could hardly know of such things."

"Not quite. I dropped a few pebbles in the still pool that is his mind to stir the waters. I think he may want to talk with me again."

"There's no point questioning the children."

"Is that so? Sometimes knowledge comes from the strangest of places. You of all people should know that. So if Zoraya didn't confess to you on her knees, did you discover anything at all?"

They reached the far side of the bridge and entered the

palace.

"Only that I believe she's hiding something, but exactly what, I have no idea."

Jorge sighed. "I suppose I had better tell you of the few things I managed to uncover then. They may help explain Zoraya's attitude."

"What did you find out?" Thomas felt annoyance rising. This task was difficult enough without Jorge holding back information.

"It has nothing to do with the matter at hand."

"Tell me, anyway. You obviously believe it significant."

"I overheard you asking Zoraya if she still saw anyone from the harem."

"You could hear us from across the room? The boys, too?"

"They weren't interested."

"Whereas you were."

"You want me to be uninterested?"

Thomas shook his head. "I apologise. I'm not used to intrigue, and you were right to listen. You might have heard something I missed."

"No, I heard the same as you. She was hiding something, but it's nothing to do with our search. I believe Helena accompanied you to the palace yesterday."

Thomas stopped walking and turned to Jorge. "She did. Was that only yesterday? It feels like a month."

"Zoraya spoke the truth when she said she doesn't see anyone from the harem. What she didn't say is she's still friends with someone who used to be part of the harem."

"It was Helena who came to visit?"

"I think her eldest, Nasir, is more than a little besotted. And who can blame him? He mentioned her name twice. And then, a little later, he asked me what tips I might have to make a man a stallion in the bedchamber."

"Grow a pair of stallion balls, I hope you told him."

Jorge only smiled and started along the corridor, shaking his head. "How many times do I have to tell you, physician, a man's balls are not always as essential as most believe."

"You told Nasir that?"

"Of course not. I told him nothing. It's hardly appropriate for me to offer such advice to a young prince. I do have one other discovery that might interest you, though."

Thomas waited, refusing to ask.

Jorge maintained his silence.

"What?" Thomas said, when he could stand it no longer.

"Helena isn't the only member of her family to visit. Olaf is teaching the boys how to use a sword. It was obvious they don't like him, but he's not a man you can refuse."

"Whose idea was that, do you think?"

"All princes must know how to fight. Zoraya would have asked, or more likely the Sultan. The whole world knows he favours her and the children."

"But does it mean anything? I can't see how."

Jorge raised his shoulders. "Are we going to speak with Aixa now?"

"Do you believe we should so soon?"

"We've spoken with the Sultan's current favourite wife. It would be impolite not to speak with the previous one. After all, she may be in danger herself."

Thomas walked alongside Jorge for a while, his mind pulling at the tangled threads of information he had acquired that day, but succeeded only in tangling them further. Eventually he said, "I'm not sure I want to talk to another feted Sultana of the harem. I want to see Olaf Torvaldsson. Can you speak to Aixa for me?"

Jorge stopped, turning to face Thomas. "You think she'll speak with me?"

"She knows you well."

"As a eunuch. Not as a man who is allowed to ask her questions. We must both go, she's more likely to accept them from you. You can speak to Olaf later while I talk to the serving girls."

Fourteen

"That was a complete waste of time," Jorge said as they made their way from speaking with Aixa. Although whether interview was the right word for what had just occurred Thomas doubted. He was beginning to hate what he had been asked to do. His previous dealings with these women had been as their physician. As interrogator their attitude was completely different, their hostility clear, and he wondered if it was possible to ever return to the relationship he had once enjoyed. Even so, he thought Jorge was wrong.

"Not a total waste of time. She didn't like us questioning her, and she's obviously afraid she might be next, which tells us she has nothing to do with the deaths. She, at least, was being honest with us."

"Is there anyone you don't suspect?"

Thomas smiled. "Should there be? Other than you, me, and the Sultan?"

Jorge nodded. "Of course. And you're not sure about me, are you."

"You're going to speak with some of the girls?"

"If you can manage Olaf alone."

"I intend to ask him about Zoraya's sons. After that I need to report to the Sultan—although report what, I don't know."

They had reached the corridors which led to the bathing chambers and were about to split up when a figure stepped from a side door, blocking their way. Not a soldier. Worse than a soldier. Thomas recognised his face from the bathhouse when he had been seeking the Sultan, but not his name. The man had been with Faris al-Rashid's group, no doubt one of the hangers on to power.

"We would speak with you, surgeon." Thomas noted his use of *we* even though he was alone.

"And we are on the Sultan's business." Thomas closed his hand around the seal in his pocket but left it hidden, knowing it held little power over this man.

"Which is what we wish to speak of. Join us." The man turned into a side chamber, used to giving orders, certain they would be obeyed.

There were four men and two women in the room. The women—servants—stood to one side, invisible, eyes downcast. The men reclined on couches and cushions. The scent of strong coffee perfumed the air but so far remained unpoured.

The man who had invited them in sat, but it was another at the head of the table who spoke. "We thought we would await your arrival. Do you know everyone, or should I make introductions? You know me, of course."

The last time Thomas had seen Faris al-Rashid had been at the bathhouse. Thomas looked the small group over. Valentin al-Kamul had been at the baths, too, a long time companion of Faris, half-Spanish, half-Moor, a man whose loyalties could never be completely pinned down. The man who had confronted them in the corridor was a stranger. The fourth was a surprise to Thomas. He considered Don Domingo Alkhabaz closer to a friend than acquaintance, and his presence was puzzling.

Thomas glanced at Jorge, who stood to one side, as though once in the presence of these men he had reverted to being a servant. Except these were not men of this city, or Thomas would have known them all. He knew for certain two lived outside the walls, and he wondered what they were all doing gathered here in the palace. Wondered too what their interest in him was. He would prefer to be ignored by men such as these.

"Sit, physician." Faris's voice was thick with command. He reclined on a stack of cushions and clapped his hands. The serving girls began arranging five fine glasses encased in silver cages on the low table before pouring dark coffee.

There was no invitation offered to Jorge. Knowing his place among these men he moved away until his back was against the wall. Thomas noticed that, unlike the women, Jorge's eyes did not look down but took in each of the men in turn.

While Faris was the only member of the group of pure Moorish descent, able to trace his lineage back centuries, it was not unusual for those of Spanish extraction—if such still existed after 700 years of Moorish rule—to hold high office in al-Andalus. The Sultan and, perhaps more importantly, those who carried out his wishes, appointed the most politically advantageous person. Often money changed hands, or if not money then favours of one kind or another.

Thomas nodded to each of the men as he took a cushion then reached for his coffee. It was too hot to drink, but he allowed the aroma to rise against his face, breathing it in.

"I don't know this man," Thomas said, indicating the well-dressed individual who had invited them in, now sitting between Valentin al-Kamul and Faris.

"Don Antonio Galbretti," Faris said. "He has suffered greatly during the conflict between our nations. His lands, although extensive, span the border between our own and those of the Spanish King and Queen."

"And to which side does his loyalty lie?" Thomas was unwilling to give any quarter, aware there was meaning in every word and turn of phrase. He hoped Jorge was taking note, and not really studying the serving girls as he appeared to be doing.

"A man's loyalties lie, of course, with his master," Don Antonio said.

"At any particular time."

Don Antonio gave a slow nod. "That is taken, of course."

"Your surname, it sounds more Neapolitan or Sicilian than Spanish."

"My ancestors can be traced to most of the noble families of Europe. Naples, certainly, could be called home at one time, a century ago."

Faris interrupted, a strain in his voice hinting at impatience.

"I'm sure Don Antonio would love nothing better than to talk of his lineage all day long, but there are other matters to discuss. You know Valentin and Don Domingo, of course." Faris indicated the fourth companion, seated at the end of the table.

"You do not usually mix in such exalted circles, Don Domingo," Thomas said.

"These are troubling times. A man does what he must if he is to survive." Don Domingo's eyes avoided meeting Faris's stare, and Thomas wondered if his position at the far end of the table was deliberate, an attempt to separate himself at least a little from the others. But his mere presence in this room meant he was involved.

"Have you started your enquiries, Thomas?" Faris's question was asked in a throwaway manner, as though the answer mattered neither one way or the other.

"Barely. We are on our way now, and would have started but for your kind invitation." There was no chance he was going to mention anything he already knew.

"I want you to know we support you fully in this matter."

"And the Sultan, too, I'm sure."

"Of course. Except..." Faris hesitated, took a moment to sip his coffee. Thomas mirrored him, the dark, sweet flavour coating the inside of his mouth. "It would make little sense to trouble the Sultan with every little thing you might discover."

"Surely that is for him to decide."

"I believe you an intelligent man." The others nodded, agreeing with their master, even Don Antonio, the new member of the group. "I'm sure you will know what is relevant in this matter and what is not. Also that is why we are here, to offer you any assistance we can."

"Do you have men I can call on?"

Faris smiled. "I believe we all have men, but as you know they will be far from the city on our estates. No, I was thinking that five heads would be better than one at deciphering this riddle. I have no plans to return to my fields for some time. I'm not sure if I can speak for my companions, but believe me when

I say I am at your disposal."

"You do me much honour offering me the gift of your time." Thomas glanced around. "All of you. But—"

"I would suggest we meet here at the end of each day, just after evening prayers, so you can update us on your progress."

"That won't be possible," Thomas said. "There are times when I'll be away from the city, and a regular meeting, coming all the way to the palace every day, would be inconvenient." He made no mention of the Sultan asking him to do exactly that.

"Then somewhere else. In the town, if you wish. Don Antonio has a fine house on the banks of the Hadarro. I'm sure he would make it available to us."

"Of course," Don Antonio said.

"I thank you," Thomas said, "but regret I find myself unable to accept your offer. Who knows what may happen, or where I may be? And my time is better spent on investigation, not discussion."

"I wish to be appraised of any findings," Faris said, steel entering his voice even as he made an effort to appear relaxed.

"After I have informed the Sultan, perhaps, and with his permission."

"If that is your wish," Faris said. "But the Sultan has no need to worry himself over our arrangements. He has matters of greater importance to consider."

"I will not go behind his back," Thomas said.

"Nor I." Jorge spoke for the first time.

Faris raised his eyes, distaste on his features. "We were not speaking to you."

"I've been set this task alongside Thomas," Jorge said. "I take those orders seriously. I would never offend the Sultan."

"No-one said anything—" Valentin al-Kamul spoke for the first time, his outburst cut dead as Faris raised a hand, master in this small domain.

"I see you have set your minds on the matter. Both of you. Very well—but remember my offer—help is at hand. All you need to do is ask. There are no secrets here, only honest men offering honest advice and assistance."

"I won't forget your words," Thomas said, starting to rise.

"We are likely to remain in this chamber until prayer is called," Faris said. "Should you wish to return you will be made most welcome." His eyes didn't take in Jorge.

"Physician." Don Antonio spoke, stopping Thomas in the act of turning away. "Don't think you can act independently in this matter. Faris has made you a generous offer, but we make just as good enemies as we do friends."

Thomas turned back, reaching out his hand to stop Jorge moving forward. "There is no reason for us to be enemies. All we do is follow the Sultan's wishes."

"An old man," Don Antonio said. "Who knows how many years he has left? You should consider looking to the next generation."

"The Sultan returned from a great victory only yester—"

"A great skirmish," Faris interrupted. "You forget I was alongside him."

"I saw little sign of blood on your clothing," Thomas said.

Jorge continued pulling against Thomas's hand, which remained gripping his shoulder.

Faris smiled. "Some of us fight more elegantly."

"And further from the chaos." Jorge couldn't hold his anger in check any longer. Faris didn't even glance in his direction.

"Don't get confused over where true power lies in this land, physician. Abu al-Hasan Ali is a figurehead, no more. It's gold that counts here, just as it does throughout the civilized world."

"Not for everyone," Thomas said.

"I've heard it said you are not like others. If that's true then you're an even bigger fool than you've already led me to believe."

"Enjoy what little power you have, while it lasts," Thomas said, "for the Spanish are coming just as sure as winter snow on the Sholayr."

Faris smiled. "The Spanish are the same as everyone else. They love gold as much as the next man."

"Don't expect to see either of us again," Thomas said, turning once more from these men he despised.

Don Antonio rose to his feet, moving fast. His hand fell to a dagger tucked into his belt, but he didn't draw it.

"Expect to see me again, Thomas Berrington. Expect to see me when—" He stopped abruptly as the door opened to admit a giant of a man.

Olaf Torvaldsson, the Sultan's general, glanced at Thomas and Jorge, then to the others, a frown touching his brow. He was someone else Thomas hadn't seen since the day the soldiers returned—but was glad to do so now.

"Thomas, I have been searching for you everywhere. The Sultan waits. You are to come with me now."

Thomas saw Don Antonio's hand fall from the hilt of the dagger.

"We were about to leave." He made a bow, as though these men meant something to him. "It has been a pleasure I look forward to not repeating any time soon. Good day, gentlemen."

Fifteen

The Sultan waited in the throne room, an austere place designed to impress. Unusually for Moorish accommodation there was a physical throne, an ornate object carved of dark wood from Africa. It was positioned in an alcove where light entered behind so that whoever sat there would be bathed in illumination, their face obscured. At the moment the throne was empty. Instead the Sultan lounged on cushions against one wall, a jug of sweet tea scenting the air. He looked at ease, as though he had no worries, and Thomas wondered at the man's powers of recovery. The Sultan was closer to his sixtieth year than fiftieth, his eyesight failing, but he appeared to have shrugged off the events of the past week—a battle, murder, plots—as though such things happened every day. Perhaps for someone such as him they did.

"What have you found out?" he asked, his voice curt. It was his way. The man made a score of decisions each day and had no time for the niceties of conversation.

Thomas stood at a respectful distance. "We have made a little progress, Malik. I have spoken with Aixa, some servants and Zoraya. Tomorrow we—"

"You spoke to Zoraya?"

"Yes, Malik."

"Why? Who gave you permission to do so?"

"I told you I would need to speak with everyone, Malik, and you said I could do so. I didn't know I had to provide a list for approval. I can't judge who possesses information until I've spoken to as many as possible."

The Sultan made a noise. "I expect she wasn't pleased."

Thomas tried not to smile, trying to gauge the Sultan's

mood. "You are correct, Malik."

"Will you be visiting her again?"

"I don't know." It wasn't a complete lie. Thomas didn't want to air his suspicions of Zoraya, not to the man it was claimed loved her above all his other wives. Later, if need be, but not yet. "We have a new line of enquiry."

"Tell me." The Sultan clicked his fingers and the girl standing against one wall padded across and poured tea into a silvered glass before resuming her position. None was offered to Thomas.

"In the morning we go to speak with the clerk who carried out the first investigation."

The Sultan made a noise again and Thomas recognised the dismissive nature of it, wondering if this was how the man conducted all his business, through hints and subtle body signals. This was a new side to the man and Thomas realised he had stepped across an invisible boundary. Before, he had been the respected physician, the man who had saved his son, who birthed his children. Now he was just one more instrument, to be directed and used.

"I remember the investigation. He discovered nothing. I had him stop and return to more fruitful work."

"I still believe speaking with him may prove useful, if only to rule out certain lines of enquiry."

Abu al-Hasan Ali nodded, sipped at his tea. "Return tomorrow, after evening prayers. If I am not here then speak to no-one else."

"Are you expecting not to be here, Malik?"

The Sultan waved a hand. "There are reports the Spanish gather on our northern borders. It seems my victory at Tajar has stirred up a hornet's nest. I may have to leave without warning. If I do you are to continue your work, understand? And report only to me."

Thomas decided to keep his meeting with Faris al-Rashid to himself for the moment.

"What about your son, Malik?"

"Which one? I have a surfeit of sons at the moment, yet one more thanks to you."

"I meant Muhammed," Thomas said. "Should I not speak with him in your absence?"

"No. Particularly not that son. I'll likely be here tomorrow anyway and you can report to me directly. But if not then tell no-one, understand?"

Thomas nodded. "As you ask, Malik."

The Sultan's curt signal was a dismissal and Thomas backed from the room, head bowed. Before he would have turned and strode out, but something had changed in their relationship and he felt his old position slipping away from him.

Olaf and Jorge stood outside the throne room where Thomas had left them. "We need to talk to those two girls and see if they've remembered anything else."

"It's Bazzu again, then," Jorge said.

"Olaf, I would speak with you later," Thomas said.

"You know where you can find me." The tall northman turned aside in the direction of the barracks.

"Is he under suspicion?" Jorge asked as he led the way through the courtyard of lions.

"At the moment everyone and no-one is under suspicion. But yes, after what Zoraya's children told you, he is. And don't forget Olaf sold his services to the Sultan many years ago. A man who is willing to do so might sell himself again to a higher bidder. And he sees the way this war is going. Who would blame him for protecting himself?"

"Then be careful when you see him. Olaf thinks nothing of killing men, even you."

They turned right. The smell of spices and cooking came as they moved deeper into the working rooms surrounding the palace. Eventually they entered a large, busy kitchen. As they passed through Jorge stole fresh bread from a girl who swatted him and laughed when he swatted back. This was his world, Thomas knew, one Jorge felt comfortable in. Unlike himself, who could work in the palace, but was glad to live on the other side of the river.

In Bazzu's room the same wide table lay scattered with scrolls and vellum, which looked identical to those of the day before.

"Kitma and Mahja," Thomas said, raising the subject of the two servants who had witnessed Safya's murder, too impatient to respect the niceties. "I want to speak with them." The girls had been little use the day before, but perhaps by now, with some distance from their fear, they would remember more.

Bazzu looked up from the document she was reading. "Did Alisha suffer? Her wounds were fearful when I helped prepare her." She had obviously been giving thought to the attack on the girl.

"She wouldn't have known she'd been struck before her heart stopped. It was swift."

"That is good, I suppose. But I have bad news for you. The other two are no longer here."

"We were with them yesterday," Jorge said.

"I know you were. And I spoke with them afterwards and they had only kind words for the pair of you. But they have been sent from the city."

"Where? By whom?"

"Tahir sent them early this morning, before dawn. A caravan was traveling south to Malaka carrying silks and salted meat. It seems a message came a few days ago requesting additional servants to be sent south. Tahir came and asked me himself if he could send those two."

Malaka again, Thomas thought. How convenient. "Why both of them?"

"I don't usually question the commands of the Vizier, but this time I did. It seemed strange after what had happened. He said he was worried about them, that staying within the harem would remind them of what happened, and if the killer returned they would be in danger. It made sense so I agreed. Did they really see who it was?"

"You've heard the rumours," Jorge said.

Bazzu snorted. "A djinn? Of course it was a djinn. A far more serious suspect than any man, I'm sure."

"Did you believe the Vizier?" Thomas said.

"What reason would I have to doubt him? He appeared concerned for their welfare. I'm sorry—had I known you wanted to question them again I would have held them back. I suppose you could always catch them up. A caravan moves slowly, and two men on fast horses would reach them before morning."

"I'm no horseman," Thomas said, his days of fast riding long in the past.

"Nor I," Jorge said. "Besides, I doubt they'd be any more help than they were yesterday."

"If they've gone, so be it," Thomas said. "We also wanted to speak with Yasmina, but it seems she's in Malaka too."

"Yasmina?"

"She was with Helena—Hulyah—when she was attacked." Thomas remembered the name Helena had been known by those within the harem, doubting Bazzu would know who he was speaking of otherwise. "Nothing was made of it at the time, but I believe the two events are linked."

"You suspect it's the same man? After all this time?"

"That's what I wanted to find out. It's some time ago now, but Yasmina might have recalled something that she missed in the shock of what happened."

"I understood she was still in the employ of Zoraya."

"No longer, "Thomas said. "We have spoken with Zoraya, and I doubt we would be welcome again soon."

Bazzu rose, the interview at an end. She came around the table and hugged Jorge, released him and turned to Thomas. She hugged him too. Her succulent body pressed against his in a way that made him uneasy, and when she finally released him it was with a sultry laugh. "Ah, my two beautiful men. Such memories, such bliss. Look after yourselves, and each other. Catch this killer and perhaps I will reward you in ways you have never been rewarded before."

"I look forward to the moment," Jorge said, kissing her once more.

They had reached the doorway when Bazzu called after them.

"Thomas—how is Hulyah now? I was sad to see her leave the palace. She was such an asset to the harem. Such an enthusiast." Thomas turned and Bazzu stared into his eyes, knowledge within her own.

"She is well. I'll tell her you were asking after her."

"She's an agreeable companion for you?"

Thomas tried to interpret the smile on Bazzu's lips as anything other than knowing, and failed.

"I'm not sure whether she's happy, but I don't believe her unhappy."

"I am curious—do you enjoy living with her? She's a skilled woman in many ways. I hope she's making those ways known to you."

Thomas felt his face warm. "I prefer to keep that side of my life private. I'm sorry if I offend you."

"Offend me?" Bazzu glanced at Jorge as she laughed. "Tell him, my beautiful man, is it possible to offend me?"

"She cannot be offended, Thomas. God knows, I've tried often enough."

Sixteen

"We are blocked at every turn," Jorge said as they re-entered the kitchen. Only a few workers remained, and Thomas realised it was close to Asr, the time of afternoon prayer.

"If I was a suspicious man I'd be questioning what's happening here."

"You are a suspicious man."

"I didn't used to be, but I'm learning."

"Do you wonder about the manoeuvring behind these events?"

"Or just coincidence?"

"Certainly one should never underestimate the subtlety of coincidence. Still, it would have been good to talk to the girls again. They'll have slept since the murder and perhaps recalled something new."

"Yasmina might have know something too, if we'd been allowed to talk to her."

"If," Jorge said as they reached a junction. "But the attack on her and Helena was half a year ago. She would have forgotten much."

Coming from the kitchens they could have turned right back towards the palace, or left and make their way out through the Alkazaba. The small township to the east of Al Hamra housed workers and businesses servicing the palace with goods, furniture, fruit and vegetables, as well as livestock. It was a whole town above a town, one raised both physically and, if one were to believe the inhabitants, socially and spiritually as well. It was where the Sultan had asked Thomas to live.

"I believe we have no-one else to question today," Jorge said.

"Perhaps we should return to the city."

"I have more questions."

"Of whom?"

"I want to speak with Olaf Torvaldsson. If he's been training Zoraya's children he might have seen or heard something."

"Do you really believe she's behind these deaths?" Jorge slowed, stopped.

"I don't know what I believe. I need more information, and Olaf might provide it. For all I know it's he who is behind everything, or the pair of them together. Zoraya's a beautiful woman—enough to tempt any man."

"Even if they were lovers why would he want to kill Safya? Or anyone else within the palace?"

Jorge turned left, the barracks lying beyond the township, and Thomas fell into step beside him, thoughts tumbling together in his head, each one demanding attention. "Because he was asked?" he said.

"By Zoraya?"

"Men have done worse than kill for a woman. Olaf's a soldier—killing means less to him than other men."

"Killing a Sultana?" Jorge said.

"I believe Olaf regards his adopted land as home now." Thomas worked through ideas as his feet carried him down the slope, thoughts coming to him in a rush he barely filtered. "The war goes badly. What if he believes he can change its course?"

"Make himself Sultan?"

Thomas shook his head. "Not Sultan, he wouldn't be accepted as such, but king?"

"King Olaf?" Jorge barely suppressed a laugh.

"He knows the Sultan is making mistakes. He sees it every time there's a battle. Abu al-Hasan isn't the man he once was. Everyone sees it, not just Olaf. Zoraya wants to protect her children, to give them a future in a unified Spain. A long war puts that outcome in danger."

"You just said Olaf believes he can win the war."

"He's cleverer than that. It's not the war that needs to be

won, but the peace. Peace with honour."

"Abu al-Hasan doesn't believe we can make any kind of peace, honourable or not."

"Exactly."

They stepped to one side as a cart pulled by two mules came trundling down the dirt roadway. Empty barrels bounced and knocked against each other on the back, the sound a rattling cacophony, dust rising from its wheels.

Jorge squinted against the sun and rubbed at his head where stubble was starting to show. "Did you know Olaf's first wife?" It seemed he was as weary of the intrigue as Thomas, seeking a little gossip to lighten their mood.

"Hardly. I was fifteen years old when she died, and a long way from Garnatah. I had enough troubles of my own to deal with."

They reached the edge of the township and stopped. A roadway led down through trees to where the barracks stood, housing almost a thousand soldiers.

"Could you have saved her if you'd been there?" Jorge said.

"Not at fifteen, no. I don't even know what was wrong."

"But if it was now. You've saved others."

"And had others die."

"It's said if a birth is difficult, Thomas Berrington is the man to call on."

"Don't believe everything you hear. I'm human, the same as every other physician."

"But better than most."

Thomas preferred his work to be appreciated rather than acknowledged. "It's ancient history. We should be talking about Zoraya—she has light hair and fine features—"

"A fine body, too," Jorge interrupted.

"You would notice that more than me."

Jorge only smiled.

"She resembles the northern women," Thomas said, "and we know Olaf still misses his first wife. I'll keep a watch on him, but I want to talk to his men, too. One of them might have seen something, heard something, suspected something. You go back and talk with any servants you can find. Soldiers and servants, those are the eyes of the palace, even if they don't speak of what they see. Meet me at the eastern entrance when they call *Maghrib*."

"You know, I considered my choice for this task as some kind of cruel joke," Jorge said. "What can I bring, I wondered? And then, as I lay unable to sleep last night, I made a decision. Perhaps choosing me is deliberate, and is meant to cause us to fail. But if so they have underestimated this eunuch. I'm more of a man than all of them put together. I will catch this killer, with your aid, and when we do I may just strangle him with my bare hands."

Thomas nodded and slapped Jorge on the shoulder. He left his hand there a moment, feeling the play of muscle beneath his palm. Before this was finished they might have need of that strength.

Thomas found Olaf in his rooms adjoining the barracks and practice yard. The accommodation was spartan, with no decoration or finery. From beyond Olaf's workroom came the sound of female voices, but too low to make out what was being said.

Olaf rose and embraced Thomas, almost squeezing the breath from him. Thomas had known the general a long time—stood beside him in battle, witnessed the ferocity of the man—but this was the first time he had ever felt uneasy in his presence.

Olaf appeared not to notice Thomas's discomfort.

"So, what do you want with me—am I a suspect, too?"

Thomas gave the big man a glance, but Olaf's face was unreadable.

"Why weren't you asked to look into this matter after the first killings?"

"I understand the reasons. I'm not a subtle man. Give me a sword and a battle to fight and I'm content, but don't expect me to think."

"You miss little, though. What have you seen or heard? Where should I be looking?" Perhaps a direct question would provide some answers.

Olaf took a seat, a straight-backed chair which he dwarfed; it seemed he too preferred wood over cushions. "Have you eaten today?"

"I had something at the inn with Jorge this morning."

Olaf nodded at the mention of the name. "He might have made a good soldier had they not made him soft. Have the two of you made any progress?"

"We're asking a lot of questions."

Thomas was concentrating so hard on Olaf's body language he almost jumped out of his chair when the man raised his voice and called out. A moment later a slim figure entered the room. She caught sight of Thomas and hurriedly drew her scarf across her face.

"Bring us water, and some of the lamb left over from midday. A little of that bread you made, too."

"I don't—" Thomas started, but Olaf raised a hand.

"Eat. You've met Lubna, haven't you?" Olaf nodded at the disappearing figure. "Helena tells me you are going to offer her a place in your household."

"She tells me the same, but I'm undecided." Thomas wanted to get the conversation back on track, but Olaf had seized its direction for now.

"I would consider it a personal favour if you took her in," Olaf said. "She cooks better than Helena, and she's a willing worker. Not a beauty like my other daughters, but not displeasing to look at either."

Thomas wondered exactly what was being offered. A blunt man, with few social graces, Olaf no doubt considered his offer generous.

"No, she's not displeasing to look at." Thomas knew it was the wrong thing to say but didn't want to risk antagonising the man just yet.

"Think on it, my friend. But perhaps we should discuss the

matter later," Olaf said as Lubna returned with plates and cups. She laid them on a side table and withdrew, but not before her eyes met Thomas's, and he read a hope there that troubled him.

Olaf took bread and meat and chewed. After a moment Thomas did the same, only recognising his hunger as he put the food to his mouth.

"Did your wife make this?" he asked.

"She and Lubna. The girl bakes well, don't you think? And she has other skills, too."

"I will give it consideration," Thomas said. Were the entire family this persistent? "Why has she no place already?"

"She did have. But Lubna is a girl of strong principle and wouldn't comply with all the duties expected of her by her master."

"I see."

Olaf only nodded. "So what do you need of me, in return for this favour you intend to do my family?"

Thomas pulled more meat from the chunk on his plate and wrapped it inside the still warm bread. And Olaf claimed he lacked subtlety?

"I want permission to talk to your men. I need to discover if someone could steal into a Sultana's bathing chamber and take a life and escape without anyone seeing them. The man who did this must have been covered in blood." Thomas stared at Olaf's face, seeking any clue to what was going on in the man's mind.

"The same with the other killings, too. These attacks were not subtle."

"You saw the first bodies?"

"I am the Sultan's General. He called for me, just not for the clever stuff."

"Were they the same?"

"Swift and clean. Fine executions." Olaf stopped as he saw the look on Thomas's face. "Forgive me, but I am what I am. Death is what I deal in, and these deaths were done with much grace and strength."

"A soldier?" Olaf was either the cleverest man in Gharnatah

or Thomas's suspicions, vague as they were, had been wrong.

"Only a trained soldier could have done it so well."

Thomas leaned forward. "But why wasn't he seen? I don't understand. A man covered in blood, fleeing through the palace, someone must have seen him."

Olaf nodded. "However skilled the man it would be impossible to get close enough to kill in the way he did and not get caught in the spray, not when a blade cuts that deep. But he wasn't, and I don't know why not. There are people throughout the palace who should have seen him and didn't."

Thomas chewed his food a moment, watching Olaf keenly as he started looking for the answers he really sought. "We visited Zoraya this morning."

Olaf nodded. "A strange woman." No reaction.

"I believe you're teaching her sons to use a sword."

Olaf laughed. "Teaching them badly. Or they are poor students. I only hope they never need to use my lessons in anger, for both are poor swordsmen. I wager even you could beat them in a fight."

Thomas smiled. "Was it the Sultan who asked you to train them? I would have thought a man as important as you would not bother with such lessons."

"Zoraya came to me," Olaf said. "I tried to persuade her to use one of my armsmen, but she insisted she wanted me."

"You have a reputation," Thomas said. He licked his fingers clean and stood. "Can I talk with your men, ask if they have heard anything?"

"You will need to be careful, but ask. There may be some rumour that hasn't reached my ears yet, although your friend Jorge is better fitted to that kind of work. The girls of the harem will have been closer than my guards, who are not allowed in all places."

"We will speak with them, too, but I want to talk with your men first."

"As you will. Say it is with my permission." Olaf rose. He had agreed readily enough to the questioning of his men—but if he had carried out the attacks himself then he knew Thomas would discover nothing. And it seemed there was a price to pay for his agreement. "I'll tell Lubna to come to your house this evening then, shall I?"

SEVENTEEN

It was dark by the time Thomas and Jorge made their way down the lesser slope from the Alkazaba. Maghrib had been called as they met at the gate, the faithful within the palace moving away to say prayers. It formed a natural punctuation to their questions. By the time they reached the inn on al-Hattabin square the devout were returning to the streets to find and eat their evening meal.

Thomas slowed, looking for a spare table. He saw Carlos Rodriguez deep in conversation, and hoped the man hadn't seen him in turn, but Jorge had caught sight of the merchant, too.

"Do you think my new clothes are ready?"

"The ones you're wearing will last a day or two yet. I'm too tired for conversation, and if he sees us he'll want to play Mancala. The way I feel, he might even win."

"I can't wear the same clothes again tomorrow," Jorge said, a look of horror on his face.

"You're no longer in the harem. I haven't changed my robes since the day before yesterday."

"And it shows, my friend, it shows."

Thomas turned away. "Let's find a quiet corner and get something to eat, then I might feel more in the mood to pander to your sense of fashion."

Thomas saw a table set back against the wall and started towards it. He supposed he should be grateful to Rodriguez for providing Jorge's clothing, but the day had already been long and his mind seethed with possibilities, the constant worrying details sapping his energy.

Jorge remained on the edge of the tables and Thomas

noticed he didn't stand out as he had the evening before, although he continued to draw attention, but now it was because of his height and beauty. If anything he was more handsome without the clothes of the harem.

All around him people ate, talked and drank. Some, like Thomas, dressed in plain robes and headdress, although few with the full tagelmust. Others were attired more ornately in an attempt to advertise their wealth. And then there was the detritus to be found in any city. The waifs and strays in rags, boys and girls in equal number, but cleaner than in many places thanks to the washing fountains and basins scattered throughout the streets and squares. There were fewer women, but more than might be expected. Some covered themselves completely, but these were the minority. Most wore a simple headdress to cloak their hair, others going bare-headed. The city was a melting pot for the cultures of the south and west, drawing in the peoples of Africa, Arabia, Turkey, Italy, France, and Spain beyond the borders of al-Andalus. In spite of over three centuries of warfare, trade continued to thrive, both inward and out. The fertile plains around the city provided much needed food for the rest of Hispania. Almond and olive groves climbed the foothills of the Sholayr, together with mulberry, fig, olives, pomegranates, lemon, lime and orange. Al-Andalus was still the larder of Spain. In return other goods made their way inwards. Wine, of course, in spite of it being against the word of Islam. And other, darker trades: weapons, armour, raw metal. War was war, but trade was trade, and Thomas knew that in the end trade always won.

"Thomas!" Khadar al-Abidah came weaving through the tables, still lithe despite his age and size. "You want something to drink, to eat? Where is your friend?" There was only the slightest of hesitations, but after a day listening with suspicion to a hundred answers, Thomas's ears were finely tuned to such subtleties.

"Yes to everything. And my friend is over there trying to decide whether fashion or hunger is more important to him."

Thomas saw Jorge turn towards him and waved.

"Does he like the room? I have others now if he wishes to change."

"You were full this morning," Thomas said, "claiming extra payment, as I recall, for the room you did manage to find. What happened in between?"

Khadar moved aside to allow Jorge to seat himself. "They fear the djinn! It's the talk of the city—a demon stalks our streets hungry for blood."

"There is no djinn," Thomas said, but Khadar wasn't listening as he called to a serving girl, who snaked between tables clearing them of bowls.

Unfortunately Jorge's passage had not gone unnoticed.

"Do you have time for a game tonight, Thomas?" Carlos Rodriguez asked, approaching the table as Khadar moved away to organise their food.

"Not tonight, I'm sorry."

"Are my new clothes ready?" Jorge asked.

"You may call for them in the morning."

"Tonight would be better," Jorge said.

"My storerooms are closed for the night."

"But you have a key," Thomas said.

"You ask a lot of a simple merchant."

Thomas smiled. "If you were a simple merchant then perhaps I would be, but everyone knows you are not that. And no, don't pretend false modesty. I would be grateful if you would help Jorge out tonight."

"Perhaps the promise of a game of Mancala will loosen my resolve, before we have to leave at this ungodly hour to do *trade*." He spat the final word as though tainted.

"Fetch the board in a while then, but after we have eaten."

A serving girl arrived, tiny, dark haired, sullen faced, her expression changing when she laid eyes on Jorge. She stopped dead in her tracks, eyes wide, the tray containing two bowls of stew and a jug of wine starting to tip forward. Thomas reached out and retrieved the tray before their supper landed on the floor.

"Boo!" Jorge said, his voice quiet so as to attract no further attention, loud enough to make the girl jump. She stepped back, staggered across a tilted paving stone, turned and ran.

"I thought I was meant to be passing unnoticed," Jorge said, looking down at his clothing.

"It's because your head's shaved," Thomas said. "And there's a softness about you she recognises. I thought women were meant to like you."

"Some do. Some don't. I've ceased worrying about the latter, as there is always a surfeit of the former." Jorge helped himself to the larger bowl of stew and drained half his flagon in one draft. "What am I to do? I can't woo them all, however much I might wish it. And she was a little young and skinny for my taste. Pretty though, if she would only stop scowling."

"Khadar only employs the pretty ones, boys and girls both. He says it's good for trade."

"I suspect he's right. This stew's good."

"Better than that made by my... by Helena?" Recently Thomas had to stop himself calling her his wife. He had no idea how the notion of marriage kept popping into his head. It wasn't one he welcomed. Even so he knew most men would be jealous of his position. A courtesan, even one with a damaged face, would be highly prized. Thomas wondered if it was Helena's beauty he was afraid of—a reminder of what he had lost, the pain carried across the years in memories he kept hidden even from himself.

"I thought you must have a maid," Jorge said.

"No, Helena cooked the stew."

"I would offer her congratulations, if I wasn't sure she would be upset I knew she cooked."

Jorge fell silent as he filled his belly, tearing off hunks of dark bread and dipping it into the fragrant stew. Either mutton or goat, no matter what it tasted good. Thomas spooned the mixture into his mouth, hungry again. When he was finished he wiped his bowl with the last of his bread while Jorge looked on with an expression of mild disgust. He must have known hunger, Thomas thought, but perhaps not for some time. He knew from his own experience it wasn't something you forgot.

"What did you find out from Olaf today?" Jorge asked. "Anything to help us?"

"In a moment. I want to hear what you discovered first." Thomas had important news, but a lassitude filled him almost too deep to ignore. He lifted his cup of wine and sipped, determined to make it last.

"Nothing. I spoke with everyone I could within the harem, the courtesans, wives, servants, the other eunuchs. Nobody admits to knowing a single piece of useful information."

"You pressed them?"

"As hard as I dared. I have to return there when this task is finished."

"If it ever is."

"And you? Did you talk with Olaf? Is he under suspicion or not?"

"I'm undecided. He's not the kind of man you accuse to his face, not if you want to walk away alive. He appears innocent enough, although if I had pushed him harder... I don't know."

"It might come to that. How would we handle the situation if it did?"

"We'd need men of our own."

Jorge learned forward. "That noble who threatened us—he did threaten us, didn't he?"

Thomas nodded. "I believe so. What of him?"

"I don't like him. Don't trust him. Another one for our list?"

"Another one for the list," Thomas agreed. "Together with Zoraya, her sons, and Olaf. And..." Thomas recalled the Sultan's order to report only to himself. "Muhammed, too, perhaps." He watched Jorge closely, interested in his reaction.

Jorge was unsurprised, which told Thomas much. "Muhammed has eighteen years now. He's a man full grown and believes he can run this city better than his father."

"Except Abu al-Hasan isn't ready to step aside yet," Thomas

said.

"And in truth I believe Muhammed a weak man compared to his father. You know him well enough, what do you think?"

"He's strong in body, certainly, but he lacks the inner confidence needed to rule, to get men to follow him without question."

"Olaf wouldn't take his orders," Jorge said.

"Could they be in this together?"

"All three of them?" Jorge sat back and looked around. "Against his own father?"

"Maybe not all three. I don't know. Muhammed and Olaf?"

Jorge shook his head. "I can't see it. Nor Muhammed and Zoraya, either. No—we're wrong, Muhammed might be weak but he wouldn't plot to kill his father's wife."

"There are other sons." Thomas saw his words bring a smile to Jorge's mouth. "You spoke with them. They're close in age to Muhammed. Are they ambitious, too?"

"Ambitious enough to plot murder?" Jorge said. "Perhaps. And they will no doubt be afraid of what happens to them if Abu al-Hasan is deposed."

"Retaliate before you're attacked. A good strategy," Thomas said, and something in his tone made Jorge frown. "Zoraya is raising them as Spanish nobility. You know why, don't you?"

"Of course. She sees the way the war goes. While the Spanish fought amongst themselves we were left alone. Since Ferdinand married Isabelle they have a common purpose, and powerful allies. I don't know how long until we are defeated, a year, ten years, twenty, but defeat is our ultimate destination. What better way to maintain power than to become Spanish yourself?"

"And what better way to gain power than to kill your rivals."

"Muhammed is their rival, not Safya or Aixa."

"They are powerful in their own right. The mothers of princes always are. And they would want to make the Sultan and his sons appear weak. If he can't even protect the women in his own harem how can he protect a city and a land?"

"How do we prove any of this?" Jorge said. "Prove it well enough to make an accusation against the woman the Sultan loves more than any other? Even if we had her confession he might choose to ignore it."

Thomas felt the little energy their conversation had sparked drain from him. Jorge was right. They were dealing with far more than a simple crime here. This was politics, and he hated politics.

"We have to ignore that possibility and continue as if we can make a difference. That or give up."

"We can't give up. We wouldn't be allowed to, and I wouldn't want to." Jorge dragged his thumb and forefinger across his cheeks, tiredness there, too. "So tell me, if you didn't confront Olaf—and I don't blame you—what did you find out?"

Thomas knew Jorge was right. They had to go on. He took a breath, trying to summon his energy. "I talked to the guards. I went to the barracks and spoke with those on duty yesterday. It took me longer than it should because I found myself checking their hands."

Jorge smiled. "And did you find our three-fingered culprit?"

Thomas shook his head. "I found a score of them. Have you any idea how many soldiers are missing those two fingers? A hazard of their profession, it seems."

"Even so the killer does have those fingers missing. It's one of our few clues."

"I don't dismiss it," Thomas said. "But as with you, everyone claims to have seen nothing, nothing at all. The consensus is it truly was a djinn that carried out the attack. The guards all claim it would be impossible for someone to find their way into the harem without being seen. Particularly a man dressed head to toe in black as our killer is."

"So we're no further forward." Jorge drained his cup and re-filled it. He held the jug out to Thomas, who nodded.

I am a weak man, he thought, *I allow myself to be seduced by Helena, and now I'm getting drunk again for the second night running. What next?*

"Not quite," he said. "As I was returning I stopped to speak with a guard I hadn't seen before. I had to show the seal to gain re-entrance to the palace. I almost neglected to ask him, thinking only of finding you and getting away. But something made me turn back. This one seemed more intelligent, more obliging that the others. He claims it is possible for someone to find their way into the harem unseen, if they have the right knowledge and a little assistance."

"Assistance? So are we looking for more than one man?"

"Or a man and a woman. The assistance required would not demand strength. The guard's name was Galib ibn-Ubaid. Do you know him?"

Jorge shook his head, smiling. "Guards don't talk to me. I think they believe I might contaminate them. In truth I make them uneasy. So no, I might recognise the man if you pointed him out, but the name means nothing. Is he a Moor?"

"Arab, I think. Tall. Strong."

"Sounds interesting."

Thomas gave Jorge an irritated glance, never sure how much the man meant when he spoke this way. "He told me there are ways a man can pass through the palace undiscovered, secret ways to move from place to place unseen. They are there for a purpose. For a concubine to find her way to a room for a secret assignation. For a man to gain access to the harem when he shouldn't."

"I have heard tales, but as far as I know such places don't exist."

"Oh, they exist all right. Galib says he will show me tomorrow how it can be done."

"Not today?"

"There wasn't time. He had duties to return to, and he said he wanted time to consult with others and to work out how a man could find his way to where Safya was killed. I plan to return first thing in the morning and have him show me. Our killer may have left some sign of his passing."

"This Galib ibn-Ubaid, can he be trusted?"

"I don't know the man, but he appears loyal and honest. I'll talk with him more tomorrow. Perhaps Olaf can assign him to assist us."

"Stranger things have happened on the hill. By the way, that merchant has been staring at you for the past five minutes. If we're to get me more suitable clothing, I think you owe him his game. Are you going to let him win?"

"I never have yet."

"But tonight you will?"

"Why would I do that?"

"Because you are a kind and generous soul who wouldn't wish to see me garbed in rags."

Thomas sighed. "You realise my reputation will be lost."

Jorge shrugged. "You expect me to care?"

EIGHTEEN

In the darkness of the night Helena shook Thomas's shoulder. He came awake slowly, exhaustion clouding his mind. He saw nothing, sensing only a shape as she sat up and leaned towards him.

"I'm tired," he groaned.

"My face hurts. The scar—it burns."

He sat, the last trace of sleep departing. There had been a dream of being chased through corridors, but it faded at once as he turned to Helena, feeling out for her in the dark. She wasn't where he expected and his hand grasped at air. He moved it left, bumped into something soft and curved, her right breast, and jerked away. When he returned he found her shoulder and traced her neck to the jawline. Delicately he touched her cheek. The scar felt warm beneath his fingertips and Helena gasped.

"I need light." He turned and found his way by touch to the door. Outside in the hallway an oil lamp burned low, always lit in the event he was called out during the night. When he returned Helena was sitting up in bed, the covers pooled at her waist. Thomas tried not to stare, but concern overrode any sense of shame and he moved the lamp close to her face.

"Is it bad?" she said.

"A little inflamed, no more. I'll make up a fresh cream to soothe the ache."

"Some poppy would make me feel better." Helena reclined now his examination was finished, making no effort to cover herself.

Thomas sighed. "It's not wise to overuse some medicines."

"But it aches. It aches deep inside my face." In the lamplight her eyes glittered and Thomas knew he could refuse her nothing.

"Perhaps a little, then."

"Thank you." She smiled, relaxing against the pillows. "The Sultan showed great kindness in sending me to you."

Thomas drew a robe around himself and descended the stairs, the lamp held high. Outside the courtyard was starlit, pale cloud streaking the sky. On the hillside, lights burned in the al-Hamra's many windows. The night was not quite silent, it never was, but at this hour it was as quiet as the city ever became. Occasionally a dog barked, a man shouted. Here in the Albayzin life was good and bad in equal measure. The people, too.

Thomas pushed open the workshop door and went inside, lighting more lamps. The poppy first, he thought, a weak mixture, just enough to take the edge from Helena's pain. He turned to his workbench, almost dropping the lamp in shock as a slim figure moved beneath a blanket on the narrow cot where he had slept himself on so many nights.

"Thomas, is that you? What are you doing here?" Lubna tried to sit up. Unlike her sister she held the blanket against her body, covering herself to the neck.

"I could ask the same of you."

"I..." Lubna wiped a hand across her face, more asleep than awake. "My sister came for me. You told my father I could come, didn't you?"

Thomas tried to remember one conversation among the many he had had over the past two days, and suspected she was right as he recalled the way Olaf had tricked him. Not a stupid man, despite his protests. Thomas knew it would be difficult if his suspicions proved correct—how would he deal with accusing a man whose daughter shared his bed? And now a second one in his house.

"So you came. Why are you sleeping in the workshop?"

"Helena told me this is my place. Is there somewhere else I should be?"

Thomas shook his head. "No. Not at the moment. Do you

plan on staying?"

"I have nowhere else to go." Lubna cast her eyes down. When she raised them they contained a question. "Didn't you mean what you said to my father?"

"I'm a man of my word," Thomas said, uncomfortable.

"Then I will stay."

"I'll find you somewhere better to sleep."

"This cot suits me fine. I'm small, and I like the smell in here. What brings you downstairs in the middle of the night?"

"Helena's scar pains her. I need to make up some cream for her, and mix a little poppy." As Lubna swung her legs to the flagstone floor he turned away, conscious for a moment of the delicacy of her feet.

He listened to the sounds she made as she rose, a rustle of clothing.

"You can turn around now." There was a murmur of amusement beneath the words. "Can I watch you work, or will I disturb you?"

"You won't disturb me. I'm only mixing herbs and oils. Heating some poppy heads to extract a tincture. It's not exciting."

"I'm interested. I was looking around earlier, you have so many different things here. I recognised a few, but most are a mystery."

"Did you touch anything? Some of these bottles contain poisons." For a moment he scanned the shelves, searching for anything out of place. So many bottles, pots and phials, each labelled in his own hand, so many of them lethal if used in the wrong way; sensel, meterre, gemoro, burbira. He stopped looking, afraid.

Lubna smiled. "I touched nothing. But I am interested."

"Truly?" Thomas turned away, reaching for a bundle of poppy heads that hung from a hook. He pulled three loose and examined them for signs of white putty being exuded. He found none so reached for more. If he couldn't find any it would take an hour to steep the seeds in water. He knew he should make time to prepare a supply of the liquor—both for Helena and his other patients. But time was a commodity he had in short supply.

"What are you looking for?" Lubna came to stand close beside him, her slight body leaning inward as far is she could without brushing against him.

"The heads of the poppy, if they are mature enough, exude a white milk. This is the opium that eases pain. I am looking for signs."

Lubna reached for some more poppy heads hanging from a hook to the left, barely able to reach. Her fingertips knocked them loose and she caught the tied bunch before it landed on the bench. She bent close, examining each in turn, and Thomas smiled at her concentration.

"You really are interested in all of this, aren't you."

"Shh…" Lubna said, focusing on her task.

Thomas's bunch of heads yielded nothing and he pulled three more free and broke them up, allowing the small dark seeds to drop into a mortar. He turned and retrieved dry straw and twigs and started making a small fire in a depression set into the stone wall. He let the fire catch and returned to the bench, began adding water to the seeds.

"Is this what you are looking for?" Lubna held two heads out to him. Each exhibited a sticky substance oozing from cracks in their sides.

"It is." Thomas took the poppies from her.

"Can I watch how it's done?"

"If you want." He used a small knife to open the sides of the poppy head and scraped the milk, now partially dried, into a small bowl. By the time he had removed the sticky milk from the outside the head was oozing more and he teased this out and added it to the first.

"Get me that bottle over there, it's raw alcohol."

Thomas watched, making sure she retrieved the right one, pleased when she showed only a little hesitation. She turned and held the bottle up to him, a question on her face, and he nodded. He poured a little of the alcohol into the bowl and swirled it around. Lubna, now back at his side, was fascinated.

Thomas glanced down, amused at how she leaned forwards, eyes keen. He recalled someone else, even younger than her, doing the same beside an old man in a stone hut high in the mountain range that separated France from Spain, and how that fascination had sparked an interest that ended up bringing the boy to where he now stood.

"Do you think you can do this?"

"Me?"

"Swirl the alcohol around in the bowl, let it dissolve all the milk until only liquid remains." He demonstrated.

When Thomas placed the bowl on the bench Lubna reached for it, hesitant.

"You can do no harm."

Her slim brown fingers closed around the bowl and she lifted it. Her first attempt almost sent liquid spilling from the rim, but she quickly adjusted, soon her movements mirroring Thomas's almost exactly.

"Good," he said, pleased to see the smile that fleetingly touched her lips before she suppressed it. He turned away, picking out the herbs and mixtures for the salve. He had a little still in a jar, but it was always more effective when freshly mixed.

Thomas set a small brass scales on the bench and weighed the ingredients, adding some to one stone bowl, the remainder to a second. He caught Lubna trying to watch him at the same time as mixing the opium tincture.

"How's that coming along?" he asked, and her eyes darted back to the bowl. She came across to show him. He nodded. "Ready. Pour a little over half into a cup then add wine from the barrel over there. Mix it well and take it to Helena."

"Me?"

"Yes, you."

Lubna tipped the contents out. Thomas watched to ensure she didn't add too much, pleased to see she took her time, pouring only a little more than required. She took the cup to the barrel and opened the tap gently, allowing dark wine to dribble in.

"Enough?" she asked, her back turned but knowing he was watching.

"A little more… yes, good."

Lubna straightened and left the workshop without looking back, and Thomas returned to the salve. It was already half finished when she returned several minutes later.

"She drank it?"

Lubna nodded.

"All of it?"

She nodded again, something taut in her face, as though she held some emotion in check.

"She can be rude when she's in pain," Thomas said. "I've learned to ignore her."

Lubna made a soft snorting noise. "Then she's been in pain much of her life." She came and stood beside him again, her left arm touching his side. Thomas was conscious of her closeness, the pressure of their contact rising and falling as he mixed first one bowl then the other.

"I can help with one of those."

"I expect you could. But this is no job for a woman."

Lubna let her breath loose. "Are there no women doctors?"

"There are. What I meant was…" Thomas hesitated, his hands still working, and then he pushed the bowl along the bench. "It needs to be done hard. Everything must be ground to a soft paste."

The tendons in Lubna's arms stood out as she put effort into the mixing, and slowly her breath came harder. Thomas returned to the other bowl, a mix of seeds and berries, and started to grind them to a fine powder. When it was done he took down two jars, one containing a white cream extracted from the grease which coated a sheep's wool, the other a pale golden oil. He put a little of each into a third bowl, poured in the fine powder from his own then went to see how Lubna was getting on.

She glanced at him, her mouth compressed from the effort, then asked, "Is it finished yet?"

"Stop a moment." Thomas dipped the tip of his finger into the mixture, ran it along the side of the bowl, feeling for any residual coarseness, before nodding. "It's done," he said. He took the bowl and scraped the contents into the one he had already completed, used a wooden spill to stir the mixture.

Lubna came to stand beside him, once more close enough to press into his side, her eyes locked on his work.

"How do you know all these things?" she said.

"Books, good teachers, a lot of practice. I was given a note of introduction to the school in Malaka. I spent three years watching and learning, and then they allowed me to practice a little, and then to practice some more. But you never stop learning."

"Not all doctors are as you," Lubna said.

"No, not all. Some have lost their way. When we ruled this entire land we knew more than we do now."

A smiled touched Lubna's lips. "We, Thomas? Are you a Moor now?"

He smiled and patted his chest with his palm. "In here I am. And you? You're not like your sister." Even as he spoke Thomas knew his words might be interpreted the wrong way, but Lubna seemed to accept what he said.

"After Helena's mother died my father lived alone for some years before he took a Berber wife. I think he believed she might bear him sons, but she doesn't. I'm the only child they have, and I'm sure when I was born he lost heart and gave up the pleasures of the flesh for fear of bringing even more women into the world."

"You're not bitter?"

"Why would I be bitter?"

He shook his head. "I don't know. It sounds a sad tale, somehow."

"Not sad. My father is incapable of being sad. Pain and loss and anger, all those emotions he has in plenty. But sadness he doesn't recognise. I think he simply moved on."

"And your mother?"

"She lives in his house still. Cooks his meals when he's home, which is rarely. He lives to fight, revels in battle."

"I like your father," Thomas said, because it was the truth—he had liked Olaf a great deal, and found himself conflicted now the man had come under suspicion.

"So do I. I love him. But I know him for what he is. A hard man."

Thomas shook his head. "You do him a disservice."

"Then perhaps you know him better than me." Lubna turned away. "Have you finished your salve? I'm tired now, I'd like to go back to bed."

"I'm finished." Thomas took the bowl and carried it to the doorway. He stopped, meaning to apologise, but Lubna had her back to him, already drawing her robe over her head, and he turned away quickly.

As he started to close the door she said, "You and the eunuch are the talk of the hill with this fruitless task you've been set."

Thomas hesitated. Lubna sat on the cot, the rough blanket pulled to her chin.

"Why pointless?"

"No-one expects you to succeed. How can you when you seek a spirit?"

"You believe in the djinn?"

Lubna shook her head. "No. But most do."

"You think we're wasting our time."

"You have better things to do."

He hesitated, wanting to tell her she was wrong, but all that came was, "I made a promise to the Sultan."

Lubna released an arm from beneath the blanket and waved it at the shelves, the books, the instruments. "You know all of this. I've heard it said you're the best surgeon in al-Andalus, most likely the best in the whole of Spain. You're wasting your talents on this stupid investigation."

"I made a promise," Thomas said again. "And people have died."

"And if someone dies because you're not doing your job?"

It was the same accusation Helena had made, but from this slip of a woman it cut deeper. Thomas wondered why he felt such an obligation to complete the task, to find the killer and whoever guided him, and all he could come up with was duty. That sense of duty made him a good surgeon. That same sense of duty wouldn't let him turn away from the quest, however ill-equipped he might be. And he believed they had made some progress. There were threads to untangle and trace, one more to follow when dawn came, which was not far away. He turned from the room without giving Lubna an answer.

The sky was lightening in the courtyard as he passed alongside the wall. From the mosque beneath the hill the muezzin began calling the faithful to prayer.

When he entered the bedchamber Helena was asleep, the opium bringing her relief. She sprawled on the bed, and Thomas stared for a moment, awed as ever at her beauty, but feeling no other emotion. Her effect on him was purely physical, and it was no longer enough. Perhaps it never had been.

He knelt on the bed and applied the salve to the red line across her face. She stirred in her sleep but didn't wake, and when he was done Thomas dressed and went into town.

NINETEEN

Jorge was snoring softly as Thomas entered the room. Instead of waking the sleeping eunuch he turned to the small table and took a seat. Let the man enjoy his dreams a while longer. It was too early for the palace to be awake, and Thomas was tired as well. He had barely slept three hours before Helena had woken him.

As Thomas stared at the sleeping man a smile softened his normally stern expression. Even in repose Jorge was distinct from other men. He lay half turned on his side, chest uncovered, one arm beneath his head, the other draped over the side of the bed. A leg had crept clear of the rough blanket and Thomas watched the foot twitch. Thomas turned his attention to Jorge's face and saw his eyes roll beneath closed lids. He had observed the same in other men, women, and some animals. Dogs dreamed this way, their legs running as they chased imaginary hares. He wondered what Jorge might be dreaming of. The women of the harem, or something darker? His face looked at ease, so perhaps it was the women.

Jorge's skin was soft, smooth—partly a result, Thomas knew, of the mutilation done against him. Lying revealed as he was, the changes were even more dramatic. Dressed in the rough clothing Carlos Rodriguez had supplied Jorge might pass for an ordinary man, but even then people noticed him. Thomas had seen them stare, men and women alike, seen them look and turn away, unsure what it was about the man that attracted them; perhaps feeling guilt at the attraction. Thomas knew Jorge was aware of it too, but he never seemed concerned. He wondered if it was that way within the harem, and whether Jorge resented being a pretty plaything to the women there.

It was all conjecture, fantasy, and Thomas laid his head on the table and closed his eyes; for a moment only, he promised himself.

He jerked so hard he kicked out and sent the other chair tumbling. He had slept, unaware of the moment when he slipped from consciousness into slumber. A noise sounded from below, barrels rolling into a cellar. It must have been this that had roused him.

He stood, unsteady a moment, then took four paces and shook Jorge's shoulder, the skin smooth beneath his hand. Jorge rolled over, burrowing beneath the covers.

"No sleep for either of us until this is over," Thomas said.

"I have an urge to kill someone," Jorge muttered into the bedclothes.

"Then make use of those urges and get up. Khadar has put out bread, cheese and olives for us." Thomas returned to the small table. "We have much to do today."

"Turn your back on me at your peril." Jorge grunted, swinging his legs from the bed.

"I hear that said often in regard to eunuchs, but I dismiss such rumour."

Jorge dressed in the clothes they had bought from Carlos Rodriguez the night before, the merchant holding out for a high price even after winning his first ever game of Mancala against Thomas. Dressed, Jorge looked less conspicuous than on the day he'd arrived, but still there was an other-worldly aura around him that made him stand out. There was nothing that could be done; it was part of the man himself. He started to wrap a length of dyed cloth around his head.

"Wait," Thomas said, rising.

"What, you want to study my head now?"

Thomas reached out and ran a hand over Jorge's skull, feeling the roughness of stubble. He ran the back of a finger along Jorge's cheek.

"And I love you, too, my friend, but later," Jorge said.

"You hair is growing out quickly."

"Of course it is. I've had little enough time to remove it. I've been busy, or have you failed to notice?"

"Let it grow. On your cheeks, too. It will be a good disguise. No-one believes a eunuch can grow hair."

Jorge rolled his eyes. "Show me this poor excuse for a meal, surgeon, and let's get this day begun the sooner it will be finished."

They went first to the garrison quarters beside the palace, a large stone building with a red-tiled roof. Thomas wanted to find the guard he had spoken with the day before, eager to discover more of the secret ways he claimed ran through the palace.

They asked for the duty officer of the day and were directed to a small office at the rear of a long building. Thomas expected to have to introduce himself and their purpose, but as they entered a stocky man looked up and said, "So you're the two, are you? I'm told I must do whatever you ask, by order of the Sultan and Vizier both." His face showed what he thought of such orders. "So what is it you want?"

Thomas made no effort at drawing the meeting out. "I spoke with one of your guards yesterday, Galib ibn-Ubaid. I want to speak with him again."

The officer uttered a short bark that could be interpreted as laughter. "So you speak with the dead, do you, surgeon?"

"I spoke with the man yesterday."

"As well you might. But today he's dead, and the one who slew him has fled the city."

Thomas looked around, pulled a stool from beside the wall and sat. "Explain."

For a moment he thought the officer was about to refuse, and he reached inside his robe and closed his hand around the Sultan's seal. Something in his eyes must have shown his resolve, because the officer lost all bluster and breathed out, sitting back in his chair.

"It was a falling out over, of all things, a game of dice. Galib threw three sixes in a row. Darras accused him. Galib grew angry. Darras angrier still. Knives were drawn. Someone tried to stop them and was cut. Darras stabbed Galib through the heart. He died at once." The brusque repeating of the facts appalled Thomas, but he knew death was a constant presence among these men; something they believed lay around the next corner for any of them. The less attention they gave it the less power death held over them.

"This Darras, is he being searched for?"

"He'll be long gone. He stole a horse, and in the confusion nobody saw in which direction he rode. He could be thirty miles away by now."

"Was this truly a stupid argument, or did something else lie behind it? Had there been friction between the men before?"

The officer lifted his hands in a gesture of hopelessness. "As I said, one is dead, the other gone, that's all I know."

Thomas sighed. "And nobody here knows anything, I suppose?"

The officer smiled. "They told me you were a clever man."

Thomas stood, his blood quickening with anger. "Who gives you your orders?" he said, voice louder than he intended. "Who are you really working for?"

The officer also rose to his feet, facing up to Thomas. "Working for? I work for the Sultan, and below him the Vizier, and below him—"

"You know what I mean!"

"Thomas, leave it." Jorge pulled at his robe. "Anger won't help us. Let's seek answers elsewhere while the day's still young."

"This man knows something." Thomas raised his hand, pointing. "And he's keeping it from us."

"Am I? Is it treachery you accuse me of?" The officer started around his desk, a hand dropping to the hilt of his sword.

Jorge tugged harder at Thomas's robe. "Come away. There are other means. Come away now, while you still can."

"I won't forget this," Thomas said, allowing himself to be led out through the barracks.

Once outside he turned to Jorge, still angry. "That man is part of this. There's something more behind this than a simple killing, can't you see that?"

"Of course I can," Jorge said, surprising Thomas. "Do you think me stupid? But antagonising men like that won't help your cause. He's a cog in a pulley, nothing more. Someone else pulls the strings. Let's go, you already know who can help us."

The barracks might have been full of men so soon after dawn, but when they reached the kitchens only a few bleary-eyed girls were preparing pots and carrying in boxes of oranges, limes and pomegranates. Thomas more than half expected Bazzu to still be in her bed, but she was in the same place they had left her the day before, as though she had not moved since. She looked rested, eyes bright, skin clear, and he studied her a moment with a professional eye and knew she was in robust health.

"Jorge! I knew you couldn't resist my charms for long. Come in, send this *ajami* away, and give an old woman something to remember."

"You forget I am *ajami,* too," Jorge said.

"You are a good Spaniard. As I am a good servant of Allah. This physician is from far off." She cast an amused glance at Thomas. "Unless he wants to make himself useful and join us. Ah, those were good days, weren't they?"

Thomas glanced at Jorge and raised an eyebrow. Jorge lifted a shoulder.

"I'm afraid we seek your help once more," Jorge said.

Bazzu sighed deeply. "Not even a quick coupling before we break the palace's fast? You know I'm more than enough woman for both of you. The surgeon's a little skinny for my taste, but he may be hiding a treasure beneath his robe."

"We must disappoint you for now, sweet dumpling. We are on the Sultan's business."

"I never forget a debt, you know that," Bazzu said. "And your debt is increasing day by day."

"I will repay it three-fold, I swear."

"What is it you want of me now?" There was more amusement in her voice than anything else, and Thomas wondered how much reality lay behind her teasing.

"Thomas spoke with a guard yesterday and was told of a means for someone to find their way secretly through the palace. You may not know of such ways, but—"

"I know of what you speak."

"Good. We went to find the guard this morning, but it appears he's been remiss overnight and gotten himself killed."

Bazzu's face showed concern. "How? Were you involved?"

"A game of dice turned bad, nothing more."

"Such things happen. Usually no more than fists and a broken nose, but sometimes... these men are trained to kill, they find it hard to hold back when anger takes them."

"So I believe. But we would know more of these secret ways. If anyone can help us I know it's you."

"As I said, at one time I would have happily taken you along any secret passage you wished to explore, but regrettably these hips no longer allow me to assist you."

"But there will be someone you know who can, I'm sure."

Bazzu sat back, staring up at the low ceiling. From beyond the ever open doorway the sound of work rose in the kitchen as others started to arrive. Clashing pots, running water, a myriad of scents and sounds drifted in. Thomas and Jorge waited, patience forced on them.

Bazzu leaned forward. "Prea!" Her voice, so soft, so sultry, became commanding. "Prea—come in here girl, now!"

There was the sound of a pot banging down then bare feet running. A waif of barely fourteen years darted into the room and bowed her head.

"Yes, Bazzu, how can I serve?"

"I have a task for you, girl, one that's highly important. You will help these men, do whatever they ask. Understood?"

Prea looked up, dark eyes taking in Thomas and, apparently

finding nothing to fear, she checked Jorge and looked less sure. A frown touched her brow.

"You already know Jorge. This other is Thomas Berrington, surgeon to the Sultan and the harem."

"Welcome, sirs." Prea's voice caught, unused to serving such dignitaries. Although, Thomas thought, looking at her with sympathy, they were not such dignitaries as Bazzu was trying to make out, but he saw the point. This girl would better serve those she feared.

Bazzu signalled the girl close and whispered in her ear. She grinned, her eyes flashing as they took the two of them in. Bazzu is a marvel, Thomas thought, one brief whisper and the girl had gone from uncertainty to excitement in a heartbeat.

"Go with them," Bazzu said. "Do as they ask."

The girl bowed and accompanied Jorge from the room. Thomas was about to turn away when Bazzu's voice stopped him.

"Thomas, take care of Jorge. He is very dear to me. And take care of yourself, too, even though I know little of you other than by reputation. Jorge seems to like you, so I have decided to like you, too. And when you know something, I want you to come back and tell me." She steepled her short, plump fingers and gazed at him. "Know this—I can be of assistance to you in whatever manner you desire. I served as a concubine for many years, and I have served the Sultan's household faithfully ever since. I know everyone and every place in this palace. These killing have disturbed our peace, and I would have it returned for whatever small time we may have before the infidel Spanish rape our fertile land."

Thomas felt a tightness in his throat. This still beautiful woman held within her a love of this kingdom as deep as his own. "Of course we will return."

"But most of all keep him safe. I place on you that responsibility, and will hold you to it."

Thomas nodded and rushed after Jorge and the girl. He found them in the corridor beyond the kitchen. Jorge had gone onto one knee so his face was level with the girl's. He glanced up as Thomas approached.

"I've explained our purpose, and Prea says she knows these secret ways well. One of her jobs is to take small favours to those inside the harem and elsewhere without others knowing. She also tells me she has, on occasion, been asked to spy on certain individuals and report their actions to Bazzu."

Thomas smiled. "And I wonder what she does with such information?"

"Only what is best for the palace. Now, where would you have this waif lead us?"

Thomas turned to the girl. Despite her thinness, her short-clipped hair shone and her skin was clear and smooth, eyes bright. She might be a servant at the bottom of a long pecking order within the palace, but she was well cared for.

"How much do you know of the harem, Prea?" Thomas deliberately used her name, wanting her at ease.

"I know all of the palace, sir."

"You heard of what happened two days past? To Safya, and the others?"

Prea lowered her eyes, her face losing some colour. "I heard, sir. It was terrible."

"You know where the killings occurred?"

She nodded.

"Are there ways a man might find his way through the palace unobserved? Can you show them to me?"

She nodded again, but her dark skin grew paler still.

"Show me how someone could get close to that place without being seen."

"There are many ways, sir, but they are narrow and twisting." She looked Thomas up and down, appraising him. "I think you might pass, but this one?" She cast a glance at Jorge, her face making her meaning clear.

"I'm not built for tight spaces," Jorge said. "But I have some ideas of my own. Go with the girl. I'll go into town and make enquiries there. We'll meet at the inn this evening."

For a moment neither men knew how to part, then Jorge stepped forward and hugged Thomas, a strange gesture in the palace corridor.

When Jorge was gone Thomas found Prea staring at him and his face flushed for some reason he couldn't fathom.

"Show me. I want to see all of these ways, and hear everything you know of them."

"A day may not be long enough, sir," Prea said, leading the way.

"Then show me what is important. And you don't need to call me sir."

"How am I to know what is important, sir? I'm a serving girl. I do what I'm told, nothing more."

"You're more than a serving girl, I see it in your eyes. You have intelligence and wit. And call me Thomas."

"Of course, sir, this way, there's an entrance nearby."

TWENTY

Prea turned into a narrow corridor before stopping opposite an arched window which presented a view across the Alkazaba. Thomas expected her to lead him to some side corridor, but instead she turned away from the sunlight. Her nimble fingers searched the wall below the writing which ran throughout the palace, almost all of it stating the same, stark message: There is no victor but Allah.

Her fingers found a depression. There was a click and a small section of wall opened. Prea pushed her arm in almost to the shoulder, straining. Her face showed satisfaction when a louder clunk caused the panel to hinge outwards. Thomas looked at the opening with growing wonder and not a little uncertainty. He had been expecting quiet corridors, hidden alcoves, not this.

Prea turned to him, a grin flashing small white teeth against a dark face.

"You have done well," Thomas said, hesitation colouring his voice.

She nodded as though praise was her due and turned to slip into the darkness. Thomas stepped to the opening and breathed in, angled himself sideways and pushed, his robe catching on stone. He realised he'd done the wrong thing and released the air from his lungs. As his chest deflated it gave him enough room to squeeze into the passage. He was glad to discover the tunnel itself was wider than the opening, but not by much. Prea pressed against his side as she reached behind him. The panel closed, shutting them into darkness.

"How do we find our way through this?" Thomas blinked, the darkness remaining as dense as before.

"Wait here, and don't move." Prea moved away and Thomas

was left on his own, trapped inside the walls of the palace. The air was damp, cold against his skin. He rubbed his sandal across the floor and found it covered in a fine grit. He touched the wall to one side, then the other, a hand on each, his arms barely parted. He tried to turn so he was facing directly along the passage but couldn't. The only way to make progress was by shuffling sideways. Panic tightened his chest and he found it difficult to breathe, as if the walls were already crushing him. Then Thomas realised he could make out movement, a shape ahead of him that resolved into Prea. Light filtered in from somewhere, brighter ahead than where he stood.

Prea spoke quietly, her voice barely a whisper. "See? There are channels and spy holes cut throughout these passages. They admit some light, enough to find your way if you know where you're going." Prea stood directly across the tunnel, slim enough to make it appear roomy. Thomas couldn't make out her features, but a sudden flash revealed her teeth as she grinned. "Is it a little snug for you, Thomas?" She used his name now, an equal here in her domain.

Thomas tried to match Prea's tone, aware of peopled rooms just beyond the walls. He wondered what would happen if they were discovered spying on the occupants. "How close are we to the bath chamber where the attack took place?"

"A little way. We need to pass beneath the courtyard of lions and then climb to the level of the harem. Come, I'll show you. And keep up. If you lose me you'll never find your way out on your own."

"I won't lose you," Thomas said, starting after the slight figure.

Progress was hard, and Thomas knew Prea had to keep stopping for him. She would dart ahead, almost disappearing from sight, and panic would start up, then she would wait for him to catch up, his heart slowing, only for her to rush off again.

At intervals the light grew brighter, and then they would pass a small niche, a shelf, some marker, and there would be a narrow aperture in the wall. At first Thomas stopped at each to peer through. Most rooms he gazed on were empty, but in one he glimpsed a woman dressed in a long silk robe.

"How many people know of these passages?"

"Only a few. Those like me who are asked to deliver contraband, sometimes…" She hesitated, her voice trailing to silence. She shuffled onward, her bare feet almost silent on the coarse floor. Thomas followed, his own movements loud in his ears.

"Sometimes what?" he said, raising his voice now there was no aperture.

Prea halted and he bumped into her slight figure. The passage was almost pitch black, the last illumination lying beyond the last turn. Nothing showed ahead but velvet darkness.

"Sometimes I'm asked to escort a concubine for the pleasure of the royal household. Sometimes a woman from outside, if they are especially beautiful or skilled."

"And men? Do you lead men through these tunnels?"

"Most men don't fit. You are thinner than most men I have known."

"You've known many men, have you?" Thomas smiled, amused at her precociousness, knowing full well female servants, even those as young or younger than Prea, were often the thoughtless playthings of high-ranking nobles and officials.

"I work in the palace, sir. I perform the duties demanded of me."

Thomas felt sad for this slip of a girl, then thought of Bazzu, the mother hen at the centre of everything. Did she look out for the innocent and protect them? Thomas believed she did.

"Is it far now?"

"Not far. Soon we climb some steps and then we're almost there."

"It's dark here. Will it grow lighter ahead?"

"Not for a while. Would you like some light?"

"You can do that?"

"Of course." In the dimness Prea put her feet against each wall, extended her hands and climbed upward as though she had been doing so all her life, which perhaps she had. She wedged herself and reached sideways, tugged at something and a shaft of light flooded in, the sudden brightness blinding Thomas for a moment.

"There are vantage points everywhere," she said, her voice once more barely audible. "Many are closed off, those that show the more delicate vistas are only revealed to those who know. Would you like to see, Thomas?" She used his name again, amusement colouring her voice.

"See what?"

"Climb up and you'll discover for yourself." Prea shuffled along, still maintaining her position, making room for him. He tried to emulate her but his sandals kept slipping on the rough stone and he kicked them off, managing to gain traction with his bare feet. His ascent was halting, and at one point he slipped all the way down and had to start again, but eventually his head came level with Prea's. She had left enough room for him to stare through a narrow vertical slit. Thomas found himself gazing at Aixa in her chamber. She was starting to rise from sleep, her face soft, reminding him the day was still young, and that Sultan's wives had no need to rise at dawn with the rest of the populace. Thomas had treated Aixa in the past and knew her body well, but seeing her now was different, a voyeuristic thrill running through him as she turned aside, revealing breast and belly and sex. Thomas's feet lost their grip and he tumbled to the ground, landing awkwardly, wedging himself in so tightly he feared he was trapped, his knees locked solid against the stone.

Prea closed the slit with a block of wood and slid down to squat beside him.

"You are too loud, Thomas." She leaned close, spice on her breath. "The passages amplify any sound you make. You must be silent as a mouse, even quieter if you can. I don't think the Sultana heard you, but you must take more care. She is beautiful, isn't she?" Once more her teeth gleamed in the dark.

"I've treated her often in my role as a surgeon," Thomas said, his whisper robbing the words of any note of authority he sought.

"But watching her now is different, no?"

"Do you spy on people often?"

"You call it spying, I call it doing my duty."

"Always duty?"

Thomas sensed movement in the dark. It was Prea shrugging. "Duty-duty-duty. Sometimes a person grows tired of duty all the time. I like to gaze on beautiful things."

"And what else do you see?"

"You can use your imagination, can't you? Come, we're almost there." Prea moved away.

"Prea," Thomas called after her and she stopped, turned back. "I don't think I can move."

She giggled, covering her mouth with her hand to mask the sound. "Perhaps I ought to leave you where you lie."

"Help me. Please."

She put her hands on her hips and stared at him, finally nodding. "All right, although I'm tempted to leave you, except you'll start to stink the tunnels up and I wouldn't want that." Prea knelt and cocked her head to one side, judging Thomas's position. She reached in and grabbed an ankle, tugged hard.

"Ow!"

"Be quiet. This is all your own fault."

Thomas grimaced as she tried the other leg. His knee scraped along the wall, and then was free. He twisted, aware of how inelegant he looked, but Prea had already turned away and was moving along the passage. Thomas used his hands to pull himself upright, sore, blood seeping from one knee, and followed.

A set of steps led upwards, turning on themselves, turning again, so that by the time they reached a higher level Thomas had no idea in which direction they were facing. There was more light, frequent gaps in the walls casting patterns against the rough hewn stone, and he realised they were passing between two carved arches above a doorway.

They descended stone steps then Prea stopped at a particularly light section.

"We are here." She raised her hand and Thomas turned to gaze through several small holes bored through the wall.

The bath chamber was occupied. Two concubines who Thomas knew by sight but not name lay in the water, steam rising around them, while two servant girls washed their bodies. A third entered the room carrying a jug of oil and a blade. She slipped into the hot water and each concubine in turn raised their arms, allowing the girl to remove all trace of hair beneath. Thomas stood, stunned, growing aroused and guilty, forgetting about the slip of a girl standing beside him until a movement distracted him. He glanced sideways. Prea, too, was staring into the chamber, her eyes bright in the light catching them. She also watched as in a trance, unaware of Thomas in turn observing her.

"This is the same chamber?" Thomas asked, and Prea jerked, startled. She might have flushed, but her face was too dark to show if she did.

"The same chamber," she said. "I heard no-one wishes to use it now, but these two are minor concubines and have no choice. They remove every trace of hair from their bodies, other than on their head. Did you know that?"

"I live with a concubine. An ex-concubine."

"You do?"

"It's a long story."

"I like stories."

"It's not for now. Would there be an entrance into the bathing chamber?"

"I don't know of one, but I can look." Prea moved away along the passage.

"Wait. Let them finish. No-one must know of what we do."

Prea padded back, a grin on her face. "A secret, Thomas? Is this our secret?"

"Not a secret. A surety. I believe someone stood where we stand now. That they entered the chamber and killed Safya, spilling her blood into the water. I seek this man, whoever he is—"

"He will be as skinny as you, then. How could someone like that be strong enough to wield a sword?"

"I have wielded a sword," Thomas said.

"In anger?" Prea resumed her observation of the chamber, the bright rays of light splashing against her skin painting it with cold fire.

"I have fought in battle when I had to, when there was no other choice. But my calling is to save lives, not take them."

Prea nodded, Thomas unable to tell whether she believed him or not. More likely, as everyone else did, she considered him a coward.

"They're removing the hair from their sex now. You should watch. It's very arousing."

Thomas sat against the wall, hunching his knees tight to his chest. "I would prefer not."

"They use the blade and wax. It looks as though it should hurt, but the women appear to show no pain. Does someone grow used to such a thing?"

"Their skin is soft from the water. And the hair grows more slowly after a time, and less dense. It becomes easier the longer they perform the act."

"Perhaps one day, when I'm no longer a servant, I will do the same. It's an interesting idea."

"You have ambition?" Thomas asked, curious.

"I've been told I'm not unattractive. I might snare a man, a rich man, and have him take me as one of his wives. It would be a better life than the one I have here."

"Are you mistreated?"

"They don't beat me, but to those within the palace I barely exist. I just am. I fetch, I carry, I take. I believe they don't even see me. I am as the air, essential but invisible."

"Were you born in Gharnatah?"

"In the desert beyond the sea. I was captured and carried across the narrow water."

"I'm sorry."

Prea glanced at him a moment, quickly returning her

attention to the ablutions being performed in the bath. "Don't be. I recall nothing of my life from before, other than a memory of hunger and fighting. My tribe was always at war with some other. There was little food. Here I'm not mistreated and they fill my belly all I want, they let me wash and keep myself clean. All I lack is freedom, and freedom is overrated."

"What will you do when the Spanish come?"

"The Spanish? Why would the Spanish come?"

Thomas realised the girl knew nothing of the world beyond the palace walls.

"They're finishing now, they'll be leaving soon." Prea crouched against the wall, mirroring Thomas's position, except she didn't look as though she'd been wedged in place. "When they've gone I'll look for a doorway."

"How will you find it?"

"There are signs. You can watch and learn."

"I want to thank you for helping me."

"It's what I was asked to do, and I do as I'm told."

"But you didn't have to show such willingness. I'm truly grateful."

"Will you pay me then?" Her teeth gleamed.

"If you would like me to, yes." Thomas searched inside his robe for his purse.

"Not now. Afterwards. When the day is done."

"What will you do with money?"

"I don't know. I might go into town and buy myself something pretty. I've never had money, so it will be an adventure. Do you need a servant, Thomas?"

The question caught him by surprise.

"My needs are simple. And the life of a servant in my house would lack the luxury of the palace."

"It would? I thought you were an important man."

"But not rich."

"In that case you don't need to pay me much." Prea stood and gazed through the spy-hole. "They're gone. Come on, let's search for an entrance."

Twenty-One

When Thomas found him the Sultan Abu al-Hasan Ali was preparing to leave the city. He strode the barracks' yard issuing orders while soldiers ran to obey. Horses clattered, carts creaked, swords and armour clashed as men armed themselves for battle. The air stank of horse dung and sweat. Thomas stood to one side, waiting his chance, uneasy because Olaf stood beside him.

"When does he go?" Thomas said. "Tomorrow?"

"Today."

"It's gone noon. How far will they get before dark?"

"There's a full moon. The men will ride until midnight. Word is the Spanish are a small force, but have come as far south as Aznalloz."

"That's barely a day from the city."

Olaf nodded at the bustling soldiers. "Hence the urgency."

Thomas glanced at the general. "You seem calm enough. Is someone preparing your horse?"

"Apparently I'm not needed on this expedition. The Sultan said I would prove more useful here, in case of insurrection."

"Insurrection? The city is peaceful, surely?"

"There are rumours," Olaf said.

"I have heard none."

"My daughter tells me you don't have an ear for rumour."

Which daughter, Thomas wondered, knowing there was only one answer. "I do at the moment."

"Of course." Olaf nodded. "He's free now if you want to talk to him."

Thomas offered a final glance at Olaf, whose face showed he would rather be preparing for a skirmish than left to babysit a city.

Abu al-Hasan Ali caught sight of Thomas as he crossed the yard and finished giving hurried instructions to two men. One of them lacked two fingers on his left hand, but Thomas had seen the same disfigurement too many times now to be suspicious. He had discovered those fingers were often damaged while holding a shield.

"I have little time, Thomas, so tell me what you know." Another soldier approached and the Sultan waved him away. "Give me a moment, I won't be long, and then we leave. Quickly, Thomas."

He hesitated a moment, trying to work out where to start, how much to say. "We have made some progress, Malik. I've discovered how the man gained access to the bathing chambers." Thomas took the opportunity of urgency to neglect telling of the tunnels. For some reason he didn't yet wish the Sultan to know he had almost certainly been watched on his visits to the harem. "I've also identified the man who conducted the first investigation, and plan on talking with him in the morning."

"You have done well." The Sultan clapped Thomas on the shoulder. "I may be away several days, it depends on whether this band of Spaniards are alone or have company." He stared around at the men milling across the yard. "In my absence I want you to report to Olaf. He asked if he could remain behind, and I agreed. It's a good idea not to leave the city undefended. This move may be a feint to draw us away. Have you a suspect yet?"

"Not yet, Malik. Perhaps by the time you return." He considered it unwise to mention his suspects were the woman the Sultan loved and his trusted general.

"It would be good if you did. Time is passing. And..." He hesitated.

"Is there more, Malik?"

"The nobles. Faris al-Rashid, those who swarm to him. I hear they have been visiting the palace, and I would like to know why. Have you investigated any of these men?"

"I have spoken with some," Thomas said, "but not questioned them. Do you think they know something?"

The Sultan looked around at the organised chaos. "They are close to my son." He didn't need to mention which one. "It might be worth your time looking into their affairs. Or I may only be seeing plots where none exist."

"I will do as you ask, Malik."

"I want this matter settled before I return."

"It may not be—"

"Settled, Thomas. The others took too long—I expect better from you. Do what you have to and find me the killer." His voice was cold, and Thomas wondered what might happen if he failed in the task.

The Sultan turned away, leaving Thomas standing alone while around him soldiers hustled to make good their preparations. As they drew together, men mounting horses, the Sultan raised his arm and led them through the gate, turning east towards the rising foothills of the Sholayr.

A movement caused Thomas to turn his head, to find Olaf walking to join him.

"The Sultan thinks this may be a trap to draw him away from the city."

"If he thinks that he should have stayed and sent me instead. I can deal with a band of Spaniards as well as he."

Likely better, Thomas thought, puzzling over the discrepancy in their stories. "He said I'm to report to you, not the Vizier or Muhammed."

Olaf turned to stare at him. "To me? Why?"

"I think..." Thomas shook his head. "No, I don't know what I think."

"Unless you have something positive to tell don't bother finding me. I would rather you direct your energies towards finding this culprit than talking to me. Are you making any progress at all?"

The question sounded innocent, but Thomas only told Olaf the same as he had the Sultan, once more missing out the revelation of the tunnels.

"Is Jorge proving any use to you? Helena has no time for him, but…" He left the sentence unfinished.

"He's better with people than I am. They like him, and I trust his judgement."

"He's no man of action."

Thomas smiled. "Neither am I."

"Perhaps it's not men of action we need. Don't listen to me, Thomas, all I know is how to fight. I'm sorry, I have to go. The young princes need my attentions." He started away towards his quarters.

"Zoraya's sons?" Thomas called after him.

Olaf stopped, his face was puzzled as he turned back. "Yes, the young princes. I am teaching them swordplay, although they are enthusiastic more than they are skilled, as I told you before, and boys need to know how to wield a sword. I only hope they never have to use one in anger."

"Can I join you?" Thomas asked.

"Haven't you more important matters to attend to?"

"Will Zoraya be there?"

Olaf's frown deepened. "She comes to watch sometimes, but not always. Why?"

"I talked to her yesterday, and would like to talk with her again. She might be more relaxed if I'm not alone with her."

"If you think it will do any good. Come if you want, but if it was me I'd be following the Sultan's orders and looking for the killer."

Yes, Thomas thought, *I am.*

He sat on a stone bench set in the shade, his back to a wall. The small courtyard was uncluttered, the middle cleared of all planting and furniture. He saw Olaf had been right about the princes' skills. The two boys stood stripped to the waist, sweat streaking their chests while they followed the general's instructions, but enthusiasm only went so far. Thomas's professional eye studied them. Slim but not muscled, clear-skinned, fit enough. He compared them with his memory of himself at their age. He had arrived in France young but strong, years of work on his father's farm building muscle. He had also been fast, and naturally gifted, as the local boys in Leominster discovered. Later, as he wandered alone through the French hinterland it was those skills that kept him alive. He had honed them in the field until he believed himself invulnerable. That had been a long time ago, and he no longer possessed such certainty.

Nasir and Said took a break, both breathing hard. They drank water from a jug a servant brought to them. Thomas was waiting for Zoraya to appear, but already he had been there half an hour and she had not shown herself. He rose and walked to the small group gathered in the sun, meaning to make his excuses and leave. Olaf was trying to explain a move to the boys. They listened attentively, but it was obvious they didn't understand what he was trying to teach them.

"Thomas, come here and show them what I mean."

"Me?"

"You have been on the battlefield. Don't pretend you are innocent in the ways of war. They need to be more aware of what is happening behind them."

"How can we do that?" It was Nasir, the eldest, who spoke. No doubt he considered himself the leader. "We don't have eyes in the back of our heads."

"But you have other senses," Olaf said. "Your ears most of all. And your bodies, your noses—these all tell you what is happening around you. You must learn to use them if you are to survive."

"Do you think we will ever need to fight?" Said asked. He was a little younger than Yusuf, the Sultan's youngest son by Aixa, and slimmer. He had the face of a scholar, not a warrior.

"The Spanish are coming."

"Mother believes the Spanish will save us," Nasir said.

"People respect strength," Olaf said. "If you *can* fight you don't *need* to fight. If you can't fight you will be taken advantage of." Olaf reached out fast and took the sword from Nasir's hand, snatching it away before the boy could react. He swung it through the air and tossed it towards Thomas.

Without thinking, the blade turning as it came at him, he raised his right hand and snatched it from the air.

"See?" Olaf said. "Thomas has seen battle. He was prepared. Take a seat, lads, and see how men fight."

"I don't want to fight with you," Thomas said.

Olaf grinned. "Then you will demonstrate how the weak are slaughtered. That is a valuable lesson they also need to learn. Take off your robe."

Thomas shook his head.

Olaf paced forward, his own sword descending quickly. Thomas raised his arm and blocked the move, instinct taking over.

"Take off your robe. I will turn my back on you. Come at me as if you mean it." Olaf stepped close and lowered his voice. "I know you can do this. Helena told me she has seen your scars. A man doesn't get scars like those working as a surgeon."

Thomas paced backwards. He had told Helena nothing of what he had once been. But it was true she had traced the scars on his body with her fingertips, and he had seen the curiosity in her eyes. No doubt she had made up stories for her father, inventing some heroic past that might put her in a better light—concubine to a hero rather than a physician. Her father would have instilled in her respect for those with strength rather than the knowledge.

Thomas loosened his robe and tagelmust and tossed them away, feeling the boy's eyes on him. Unbound, his brown hair fell free to curl against his shoulders. The sun warmed his skin and he stepped softly as Olaf turned his back on him, his own badges of honour criss-crossing his skin.

The swords were deliberately blunted, but they still carried weight and could inflict damage in the right hands—and Olaf's were the right hands. Thomas moved fast and swung at his broad shoulders.

Olaf twisted, quicker than seemed possible, and their blades clashed. The general was grinning, a fierce light in his eyes. This is what he lived for, even if his opponent was a poor excuse for a challenger.

"See," he said, "I heard Thomas approach. Feet on sand. I saw his shadow from the side of my eye."

"A battlefield is a noisy place," Nasir said. "You would not hear him with the sound of battle all around you."

"Then come make some noise," Olaf ordered. "Nasir, fetch another weapon and fight me, see if Thomas can get to me then."

Nasir smiled, enjoying the game; this was far more interesting than practice. He retrieved another sword and he and Said ran at Olaf, shouting at the top of their voices. Olaf deflected their blows easily, used to far better opposition. Thomas watched carefully, picking his moment, then attacked, sure Olaf was distracted, but the man swung his blade behind him, not even bothering to turn, and Thomas's own was jarred and knocked aside. The boys, believing they had an advantage, came at Olaf harder, but he only yelled and forced them back until Said stumbled and fell over. Then he spun and came at Thomas, his face cold.

Thomas raised his blade, deflecting a rush of blows. When they stopped he was breathing hard, his own chest sweat-streaked. He caught movement from the edge of his vision. Zoraya had come out and stopped, observing the scene. She called to her sons, who ran across the courtyard. Words were exchanged, too faint to carry.

"Shall we show them how men truly fight, Thomas?" Olaf said.

"It would be a poor show."

"Would it?" Olaf's gaze took in the scars on Thomas's chest, shoulders and belly. No match for his, but they were not the scars a scholar should possess. "I'm curious about the tales my daughter tells. Are you really the warrior she claims?"

What had Helena told the man? "She knows nothing of me," Thomas said.

"My daughter knows men," Olaf reminded him. "She is skilled, or so I have been told. Come then, surgeon, show this family what you are made of." Without hesitation Olaf came at him again, his blade flashing in the sun, his blows a constant barrage against Thomas's sword.

Thomas fell back, deflecting strike after strike. They came faster and he darted aside and counter-attacked, almost landing what, with sharpened swords, would have proved a fatal blow, but Olaf's sword parried just in time.

"Good, this is what they need to see. Two grown men fighting for their lives." Olaf's gaze moved to one side, for a moment taking in Zoraya, and Thomas thought he saw something in the other's eyes for a moment and attacked fast.

Olaf had expected the move and parried. Thomas came again, twisting, turning, his blade sparking shards of reflected sunlight across the shadowed wall.

"Yes, Thomas—come at me, show them what real men do!" Olaf attacked again. Thomas parried. Olaf increased his blows and Thomas stumbled. The general grinned, raising his sword for what could be a killing blow. A strike to the head or neck would prove fatal, blunt blade or not.

Thomas allowed himself to fall as Olaf's blade swept through the spot where his head had been a second before. He hit the ground and rolled, coming instantly to his feet to launch into a fresh attack. Olaf parried, fell back. Now it was Thomas's turn to increase the pressure, strike after strike landing as blades clashed. Thomas felt his rational mind fade, replaced by a heat he had not experienced since he came to this city. He allowed it to fill him as he fought even harder. It was as though the world stilled, awareness drawing in until there were only the two of them, moving fast in the sun.

Olaf counter-attacked and Thomas deflected the blows easily, buried muscle-memory returning to him as though it had never gone away. He had no notion of how long they fought, but gradually he knew he was gaining the ascendancy. He was younger than Olaf, and, he realised, a more instinctive fighter.

Thomas put together a rapid series of blows, a deliberate diversion. He saw it laid out, the moves, the execution, exactly as he saw the moves to the end of a game of Mancala.

Thomas's blade came down hard against Olaf's exposed neck.

Thomas almost carried through with the blow, but at the last moment he held back, laying the blunted blade against Olaf's skin. A sharp blade, fully executed, would have removed his head. Even with this one it would have been a killing blow had he put enough power behind it. That was when Thomas felt a pressure against his ribs and looked down to see the point of Olaf's sword pressing against his chest.

"I think we can call that a draw," Olaf said, grinning. He lowered his blade and slapped Thomas on the shoulder, drawing him against him, his sweat-slicked skin slippery. "I always thought Helena was exaggerating your past, but I think she might have underestimated you. Where did you learn to fight that way?"

Thomas stepped away, shaking his head, offering no answer. That was when Nasir and Said, sensing their chance, came at him from behind.

Thomas swung around, his body still pulsating with a remembered skill. Said's blade flew off in one direction, Nasir's in the other.

"Stop! Stop this now!" Zoraya strode out to stand between Thomas and her sons. She was breathing hard, her face flushed, and Thomas realised watching him and Olaf fight had excited her. He shook his head and tossed his own blade to the ground, disgusted with himself.

"I'm sorry, my lady, we were lost in the moment. I meant no harm to your children."

"And you, Olaf, what were you thinking?"

"We were teaching your sons a valuable lesson."

"You were showing off, that's what you were doing."

Thomas studied the interaction between them. Olaf was at ease—although Olaf was at ease in almost all situations, certain of his status and power—but Zoraya exhibited some masked emotion. Could they be lovers? Was that the hold she had over Olaf? Was that why he was involved in the plot? Thomas knew he couldn't simply throw an accusation at her, particularly not here. He wasn't even sure he could let the Sultan know of his suspicions, because the man loved this woman. He walked away and retrieved his robe.

"How did you learn to fight that way?" Nasir came to stand close by, but not too close.

"I have tried to forget," Thomas said.

"If I could fight like that I would never want to forget."

Thomas ruffled the boy's hair, even as he made the gesture recognising how inappropriate it was, but it seemed his demonstration had given him permission. "When you are older and have seen more of the world you will understand."

"I am old enough now," Nasir said. "And I have seen much of the world. I have travelled. And..." He hesitated, his eyes tracking Thomas's face, and a sly smile came to his mouth. "And I have known women. I am a man. Mother says I am a man, and that a man must know all there is to know."

"And books?" Thomas said, tired of this strutting cock of a prince. "Have you acquired the knowledge that comes from books?"

Nasir scowled. "Princes have others to do that for them."

"Of course." Thomas felt an urge to argue, to try to convince him there was more to life than position and prestige, but knew it was a hopeless task. Nasir was right, anyway—princes only had to surround themselves with clever men, they didn't need to be clever themselves.

"Boys, come inside and bathe, you stink like commoners." Zoraya clapped her hands and her sons ran to obey.

"I would speak with you again," Thomas said.

"On what matter?"

"The same one."

"I told you all I know the last time. I have nothing more."

"I would still speak with you. The Sultan commands me to

talk with everyone."

"He does not mean me, surely you know that?"

Thomas watched Olaf dressing, gathering together the blunted weapons. The man seemed uninterested in their conversation, but it could be a pretence.

"I take his instructions seriously, my lady, and so should you. One Sultana has been killed already. Where one is attacked so might another. Have you considered you might be in danger?" He watched her carefully for a reaction, but her face remained as cold as it had the entire conversation. If she was behind the plotting then she would know she was safe. "I will talk with you, out here or in your quarters, but we will talk. And this time you will answer me truthfully."

TWENTY-TWO

"And she let you question her?" Jorge's face showed disbelief and amusement in equal measure.

"For what little good it did." Thomas kicked Jorge's legs aside and dropped onto the bed. His body ached from the fight with Olaf, his mind from the verbal battle with Zoraya. The latter had been harder than the former. Zoraya was stubborn, convinced of her own invulnerability. Thomas had refused to back down, even when she resorted to tears. It made for an interesting meeting.

"Tell me what she told you."

"Later. I need food and wine. What did you find out?"

Jorge smiled. "I can play coy as well as you. And I'm also hungry and thirsty. When we first went to your house you told me you didn't drink wine."

"I lied. Are we going downstairs? If that merchant is down there again I refuse to give him a game of Mancala. Losing once was bad enough."

"But he gave me such beautiful clothes,"Jorge said, holding his arms out and grimacing. "Nobody looks at me in these."

"I believe that's the point." Thomas pushed off the bed. "Come on, let's go downstairs, and I'll tell you what I know."

The stew was indistinguishable from the previous night's, and no doubt would be tomorrow and tomorrow's tomorrow. The same girl brought them bowls and a jug of wine, today her scowl washed clean. Her pretty face reminded Thomas of Prea. The city was full of girls and boys like her, making their way the best they could. He pressed a coin into the hand of this one, hoping she didn't misinterpret his generosity.

"Tell me," Jorge said, reaching for his cup of wine.

"You first. Did you find anything out?"

"Other than the entire city believes the foolish tale a djinn did the killing, I know no more than I did this morning. And you—have you had more luck?"

Where to start, Thomas thought, and told Jorge of his meeting with Zoraya, because for him it felt the most significant event of his day, even above the tunnels.

Jorge listened without comment, sipping at his wine, staring out over the crowd.

"Did you ask her outright about Olaf?" he asked when Thomas had finished.

"I didn't want to show my suspicions openly, but she knew the implication was there, and I saw in her eyes she understood what I meant."

"They are lovers?"

"I don't think so. Although…"

Jorge waited a moment. "Although what?"

"Olaf and I fought."

Jorge laughed. He leaned across the table and gripped Thomas's chin, turned his head to one side, the other. "No, it's still attached. For a moment there I thought you said you fought with Olaf."

"Afterwards Zoraya was excited."

"As in sexually excited?" Jorge grinned.

"I believe so."

"If only I'd been there I would have known for sure. So she's aroused by men fighting. But does that mean she takes the general into her bed?"

"I wish I could say yes. It would make our job simpler. I pressed her, came at her from different directions, and although I discovered a little more she remains stubborn. But her stubbornness only makes me more suspicious. Why not answer me openly unless she has something to hide?"

"You have made an enemy of her."

"She was already that, I believe, but yes, even more so now."

"Will she strike out?"

"At me?"

"Or someone else. Someone close to you. Helena, perhaps? If she does it would be proof of a kind."

"I would rather Helena remain alive and have less proof."

"Tell her to be careful. Zoraya will know of others close to you as well."

"We can't protect everyone."

"We won't have to. Most will be safe. People like Yusuf are always surrounded by guards and servants. But she may try to attack us directly, so we need to bear that in mind, too."

Thomas took a mouthful of wine and swallowed. "When did you become so filled with suspicion?"

Jorge smiled. "Oh, there is enough plotting and intrigue in a harem to outshine even the cleverest generals. So—do we accuse them? Tell the Sultan?"

"Abu al-Hasan Ali's not in Gharnatah. He's off fighting more Spanish. He left Olaf in charge."

"This gets better and better. Not only have you upset Zoraya, our prime suspect is now running the city. My life was so much simpler a few days ago."

Thomas looked around, thankful he couldn't see the merchant Carlos Rodriguez anywhere among the busy tables. He caught the eye of the girl who had served them earlier and pointed at the almost empty jug of wine, and she nodded.

"I was thinking it through as I came down the hill, and I'm not so sure Zoraya and Olaf are behind it after all. Both of them have too much to lose, and what do they gain? Olaf is already the Sultan's general—he has no ambition other than that. And if Zoraya is uncovered the least she can expect is banishment, the worst execution."

"Abu al-Hasan Ali loves her. The entire palace knows it. They might believe themselves invincible."

"Olaf already believes he is invincible." Thomas drained his cup and reached for the jug, but it was empty. "When we fought today I think he tried to kill me."

Jorge leaned forward. "What?"

"He was training Zoraya's sons with blunted swords, claimed he wanted to demonstrate some technique. I was a fool."

"He tried to kill you?" Jorge looked into his own cup. "Where's that little serving girl? Thomas, if Olaf tried to kill you, you would be dead. No question. I was joking before, but I'm not now."

Thomas shook his head, not in disagreement, more in wonder. "I'm sure he did."

"So why are you still here?"

Thomas didn't want to explain himself, not in this. "Luck. Ah, here's our wine."

The girl replaced the old jug with the new.

"I think you have an admirer," Thomas teased.

Jorge smiled. "Is wine medicinal? You're the man to ask."

"I believe there are differing opinions on the matter."

"And yours is?"

"Moderation is the key. I've seen men with distended bellies from swollen livers, their skin the colour and texture of parchment, who have drunk too well and too often over many years. And I've seen others who live beyond any expectation, who partake of a little wine on occasion."

"I believe I'll follow the practice of the latter."

"How did you acquire the taste, Jorge? Alcohol isn't allowed within the palace, is it?"

"You'd be surprised what's allowed within those walls. But tell me, I've waited long enough, how did you get on with that ruffian of a girl today? Was she useful, or did she lead you down another false path?"

"She was useful."

"So are there secret corridors in the palace?"

"More than that. The place is a warren of tunnels. Prea showed me only a few, but she says there are others."

Jorge looked off into space for a moment. "Have I been spied on?"

Thomas smiled. "Almost certainly. There was much to see, and many surprises..." Thomas hesitated, remembering his unease at spying on the women of the harem. There would be men willing to pay a great deal to be awarded such a privilege.

"So Bazzu has been of use again. I didn't recognise the girl, but there are many such as her, too many to take note of them all."

"Prea's different. She's sharp and observant. And she was more than helpful. There's a way a man might make his way through those hidden passages from a score of secret entrances. We found our way to the bathing chamber where the attack took place. It was in use, but once the ladies left Prea discovered a secret doorway and we were able to enter. The opening is hidden behind the balustrade. It would be possible for someone who knew those tunnels to enter the chamber unobserved."

"Is that what happened?"

"I know it is, but we had to be quick, fearing discovery. I want no-one to know what I'm seeking yet. I believe Galib ibn-Ubaid was killed because of the little knowledge he imparted to me. He didn't know he was in danger, but I'm convinced the argument over a game of dice was manufactured, and his killer instructed to remove him. I wouldn't want Prea to be placed in the same danger." Thomas smiled. "She asked if I could find a position for her."

Jorge laughed. "She's too skinny for any position I can think of."

"As a servant," Thomas said, but his smile remained. He had been enchanted with the girl's intelligence, the way she quickly grasped what he wanted. "She pretended to bathe while I used the secret entrance and crept up on her. It wasn't completely realistic, because she knew what was happening, but between us we concluded it was possible for someone to approach the bath without being seen until the very last moment."

"Someone dressed in black from head to foot," Jorge said. He had finished his stew and pushed the bowl away, filled his flagon with more wine.

"And who might easily be mistaken for some supernatural being with their miraculous appearance and disappearance.

Once we fathomed how the deed could be done I examined the passageway and door. I found several signs of his presence." Thomas reached inside his robe, drew out a canvas sack and shook out a few scraps of material.

Jorge leaned over. "Can I touch them?"

"Help yourself."

Jorge lifted a strip of cloth, one edge ragged where it had caught on something and been torn. The strip was small and seemed to have been trampled on, the material stained so badly it was impossible to tell its true colour.

"There's little we can discover from this," he said, "other than the man wore black, which we already know."

"There were more signs I couldn't bring. Marks on the stone inside the tunnel, as might be made by a sword catching against it. And the ground was disturbed more than the passage of Prea and I would account for. Jorge, those tunnels honeycomb the palace. With enough knowledge a man might travel anywhere he wishes, perform any act he wishes, and disappear as though into thin air."

"A djinn." Jorge stared through the small window. "He might truly appear as some djinn, might he not? But it would be a huge risk. How often are these passages used? What if someone discovered him?"

"I wondered that, too, so I asked Prea. She said they may be used only once a month, at other times more often. She recalls one time she was sent through them four times in a single day, but more usually it's less often."

"Still, how could he know when someone might discover him?"

"She showed me how it's possible to avoid discovery as well. As I said, she's a sharp little thing. She bid me move around a corner and give her a few moments, then to return swiftly and find her. I did as I was told. I tell you, I was hidden from her less than a minute, but when I returned she was nowhere to be found."

"Another passageway?"

Thomas laughed. "Not at all. But it would require someone with strength and agility to do as she did. As I stood there puzzling, I felt something rap against the top of my head, and when I looked up she was wedged against the ceiling like a spider. Had she not dropped a pebble onto me I would never have seen her."

"Whoever did this would need to know the passages well. And of how they are used, their frequency, the escape routes. They would need to know many things."

"Indeed they would."

"Someone who knows the palace well."

Thomas nodded. "As do you."

"You suspect me now?"

"Of course not. For one thing you wouldn't fit inside the tunnels. I became wedged myself at one point and Prea had to free me." Thomas experienced an inner shiver at the memory of being trapped inside the walls.

"Who then? Not Olaf, for sure, if you said you had difficulties."

"Olaf has a thousand men under his command, any one of whom would do his bidding without question." Thomas drained his cup, refilled it. "And Zoraya's sons are slim. Either would be comfortable in the tunnels."

"But?" Thomas knew Jorge had caught the hesitancy in his voice.

"The wounds I saw on Safya's body were made by a strong man who knows how to wield a sword." Thomas didn't like the reminder of how the life had been stolen from the Sultan's wife.

"And?"

"The boys are poor warriors. Even you could defeat them."

"Don't overestimate me," Jorge said. "Perhaps they were hiding their skills in front of you. Are they suspicious?"

"The boys? No. Zoraya, yes, but not her boys."

"You discovered something else, didn't you," Jorge said.

"Perhaps. Zoraya spoke of much, to distract me I think. She never answered a question with a direct answer, but there were answers hidden in what she said, even more in what she didn't. She let slip the Sultan visits her often, and I now know Helena goes there regularly." Thomas's expression wasn't lost on Jorge.

"You already knew that."

"Not that she visits most days. Why have I not noticed before now? What have I been doing? Or not doing?"

"Who does she visit?" Jorge asked. "Zoraya, or..." He didn't need to finish.

Thomas reached for his cup and drained it. He didn't want to think what Helena had been going to Zoraya's rooms for. There was more than friendship going on.

"Can it work to our advantage?"

"What—ask Helena to spy for us?"

"She's a gift to you, Thomas, she has to do whatever you demand of her."

Thomas rubbed a hand across his mouth. "It's too late for that, not after the way I've treated her."

"It's never too late with one such as her."

Thomas looked at Jorge, surprised at the coldness in his voice. "You never liked her, did you?"

Jorge shrugged and refilled their cups. "I love many, but not all."

Thomas didn't need to ask Jorge why. He had lived with Helena long enough to know that—despite her obvious charms—she lacked something of humanity.

"I see why she and Zoraya are friends."

"And the boys...?" Jorge said, not needing to say more.

"Yes, the boys. And then she—" Thomas couldn't go on, the sense of betrayal too painful. The thought of Helena's perfect body lying next to one, or both, of those spoiled brats was more than he could bear. He didn't want the woman under his roof a moment longer, but saw no easy way to evict her. She was a gift of the Sultan, not someone to be easily tossed aside. It seemed to him all the Sultan's gifts were tainted in some way.

Jorge leaned forward. "So did you discover anything we can use against her?"

Thomas saw what his friend was doing and was grateful. "Yes and no. Zoraya told me little that was new, but it was her attitude I found more interesting. She believes herself above the law. I pressed her hard, far harder than on our first visit. I let her know I suspect her involvement. She was angry, defensive, even aggressive, but not once did I sense fear."

"The Sultan favours her. The children, too."

"It was more than that. She has a certainty about her, a sense of invulnerability. I believe she has connections with Spain. She plays Moor off against Spaniard, Spaniard against Moor. Whichever side wins she knows she is secure."

"Why kill Safya? That I don't understand. What gain does it bring?"

"It clears the ground for her ascendancy. Without the other wives the Sultan is free to make her sons his heirs. She rises with them. Most mothers work for their children, not themselves. I think Zoraya does both. I have never met a colder, more calculating being."

"You said other wives, Thomas. Do you believe Aixa the next victim?"

"If I'm right, then yes, there will be more killings."

"And it's Olaf who does her bidding? You said the boys are not skilled enough, but that man has access to the best warriors in the kingdom. We have to unmask the pair of them." Jorge banged his fist on the table, setting the jug rattling. "I will have no more deaths in my harem. None."

"We need proof. Solid proof. Tomorrow we visit this Bilal, who was first given the investigation. Someone stopped him before he could find out who was behind it. Knowing who did that would tell us who carries some of the guilt."

"Then call for me early," Jorge said. "for you scare me with this kind of talk."

It was late before Thomas arrived home. Despite the ache in his limbs he was energised. At last progress was being made. He was tired, but knew sleep would elude him. The fight with

Olaf had sparked old feelings. A coldness still filled him, and if Helena was at home he knew he might not be able to stop himself taking her by force. He didn't want such an act on his conscience.

The house was quiet as he entered, and he went into the kitchen to get a cup of water. Lubna was sitting at the table, a book open in front of her. She glanced up as Thomas entered, started to stand.

"Are you hungry? Shall I make you something to eat?"

"Sit. I ate with Jorge. Go on with what you were doing." His thoughts of Helena had turned to instant guilt.

Lubna continued standing, and Thomas hesitated as he passed the table, glancing at the book. She had placed a knife to mark her place and the cover had closed itself.

"Is that one of my books?" Thomas leaned closer to examine the title.

"I only borrowed it, I'll return it if you wish."

Thomas picked it up, allowing the knife to fall free but retaining her place with his thumb. "This is al-Sahwari, isn't it?" He glanced towards Lubna, who stood with hands clasped in front of her, eyes downcast. "Look at me, girl, I'm not angry. Do you read well enough to understand any of this?"

"I read as well as anyone," Lubna said, but she didn't raise her eyes. "And I understand the words well enough."

Thomas turned the book in his hands. He reached for the knife and used it to mark Lubna's place once more, replaced the book on the table.

"You are curious?"

Lubna nodded, and he felt an enormous gratitude. Her interest had distracted him from memories of his past, reminding him of the man he had become.

"About the art of medicine, or the world in general?"

"Both."

"Does your father encourage you in this curiosity?"

"My father has many great traits, but admiration of a woman's curiosity is not among them. He doesn't discourage me, he merely fails to understand."

"You wish to know more?"

Once more Lubna nodded. Perhaps the lack of any edge to Thomas's voice offered encouragement and she raised her gaze to meet his. "I could help you with your work if I gained a little knowledge."

"Do you think I need an assistant?"

"Would it help to have one? Was it water you wanted, or wine?" Lubna turned away.

"Water. I've had enough wine to last me the rest of the year. What would your sister say to you helping me?"

Lubna poured cold water from a jug and brought it back, handed the cup to Thomas.

"She would consider it a waste of time. Not suitable work for a woman. But I can do the work she asks of me and help you as well."

"What work is she asking you to do? I understood you were a guest in this house."

"A guest who must pay her keep. I've washed her clothes, and yours, too. I cooked a meal and tidied the rooms. I would have tidied in your workshop, but I wasn't sure what I could touch and what I couldn't."

"You've only been here a day," Thomas said. "And what has Helena been doing with all this free time you've gifted her?"

"She visits friends."

"Friends on the hill." Once more a sense of betrayal washed through him.

"I don't know. She didn't tell me where."

Thomas sat and reached for the book, seeking distraction. "If you truly want to learn I'll find you something better to start on than this. And you can assist me if you wish, or offer your services to some other physician, I wouldn't mind if—"

"I wouldn't want to work for anyone else."

"And I wouldn't make you do so." Thomas stood. "Come into the workshop, I'll put out some texts more suitable for you to start on. Do you have any area you are particularly interested in? Herbs? Medicines?" He smiled. "Surgery?"

"I would know everything there is to know," Lubna answered.

"You are indeed a strange one," Thomas said as he moved towards the door. Lubna, following close behind, so different to her sister, reminded him of himself, a long time ago.

TWENTY-THREE

If what the Vizier's clerk told them three days before was true, the man who had conducted the first investigation now worked for Hasdai ibn Shaprut. He maintained offices on the edge of the Jewish quarter in the south of the city, knowing his clients wouldn't wish to venture to his household. Jorge rapped on the sturdy door and a few moments later it was opened by a boy little more than a child.

"We have business with your master," Thomas said, and the boy ducked his head and led them inside. Within was a single room ten paces deep by five across. To either side, men worked at tables, fingers stained by ink, heads bent over papers.

Hasdai ibn Shaprut resided over this industry from his own larger table set at the far end of the room. Thomas saw him raise his eyes from his work and watch them approach.

He rose, nodding to Thomas, surveying Jorge with curiosity. "You have business with me, Thomas Berrington? I haven't seen you in more than a year. Do you have some new contract you wish me to draw up? Some payment you need chasing?"

"You know I don't chase for payment," Thomas said. "I'm here on the Sultan's business."

"The Sultan has his own scribes, does he not?"

"This is business of a different kind."

"I heard a rumour you were set a task," Hasdai said. "So it's true?"

"That depends on what the rumour is," Jorge said.

Hasdai afforded him a brief glance. "We are intelligent men, Thomas, there's no need to play games. I don't believe I'm likely to be involved in anything to help you."

"We seek someone who works for you. His name is Bilal

Abd al-Rahman."

Hasdai's eyes flicked away from Thomas to find something beyond his right shoulder. "Yes, he came to me four months ago. A good worker." He raised his voice. "Bilal, these men want to speak to you."

Thomas turned to see a slim man seated half way back along the room start to rise. There was little space and he had to come from behind the table, moving faster than necessary. A second clerk blocked his way, preventing Bilal from reaching the central walkway, and all at once he pushed against the table, tipping it over. Papers scattered, an inkwell and oil lamp broke against the tile, and then Bilal was running towards the door.

Thomas remained where he was, rooted to the spot in surprise. It was Jorge who reacted first, launching himself after the man, moving fast. He would have caught Bilal, but one of the other clerks came from behind his own desk and Jorge careened into him, both of them falling to the floor. The tumbled clerk cried out in pain. Jorge skidded beneath a desk, scrabbling to recover.

Bilal crashed through the door and was gone.

The room erupted into chaos. Two clerks stamped at papers set alight by the shattered lamp. Another picked up those not being trod into the tile, while yet another attempted to right the overturned desk. Clerks milled along the central aisle.

"Back to your desks!" Hasdai shouted. "Back to your desks now! Ibraham—stop destroying those documents, the fire is out." Hasdai clapped his hands, walking through the centre of the chaos as men ducked behind their desks and made some pretence at a return to work.

Jorge climbed to his feet, rubbing at his side.

"Are you hurt?" Thomas asked.

"Nothing that needs your skills, my friend. I would have caught him if that fool hadn't tripped me."

Thomas turned to the other man, only now sitting up. He had a cut on his forehead which bled profusely. Thomas pinched it with his fingers, satisfied it needed no stitching or bandage.

Instead he reached into his satchel and held some linen against the wound and told the man to press hard.

"What just happened here?" Hasdai asked.

"You told me he was a good worker."

"He was skilled, needing no instruction for any task he was set."

"Did you know he worked for the Vizier?"

"He didn't say, but it was obvious he knew what he was doing. I had no doubts about his work, none at all. Nor, until this moment, about the man himself. I liked him."

"Where does he live?"

"In the Albayzin, of course. Where does anyone who does the real work of this city live? But exactly where I couldn't say."

"Would anyone else know?"

Hasdai lifted his shoulders, looked around. "Is anyone here a friend to Bilal?"

The men kept working, their heads down.

"Tell them you don't blame them," Jorge said quietly. "They worry you will taint them with his deeds. Better still, is there somewhere you can go for a moment while we ask our questions? They'll answer more honestly if you're not here."

Hasdai looked as if he was about to object, then nodded and walked to the end of the long room. A small door set into the wall admitted him to another chamber. He closed the door behind him.

"It's important we speak with Bilal," Thomas said, raising his voice so all could hear. They had stopped working now their master had left the room, the excitement of the moment still fresh. "We're here on the Sultan's business."

"Is he wanted?" the man three places down from where Bilal worked asked.

"He's wanted to ask questions of, nothing more. He's not under suspicion of anything." Although Thomas knew that was no longer the case. Why would an innocent man flee?

"I wouldn't call him a friend, but we've walked together once or twice after work, on our way home. He lives close to me, a little further up the hill."

"You know his lodgings?" Jorge asked, and Thomas stepped backwards, allowing the eunuch to continue the questioning.

"Not his doorway, no. He continues on when I pass through my own. But he's nearby, for he said so one evening when we said goodnight."

"Will you show us?" Jorge said.

The man's gaze flickered to the end of the room. "I have work to finish."

"We will ask your master," Jorge said. "If need be we'll pay for your time. How far is your room?"

"Half a mile, no more."

"How far up the slope of the Albayzin?"

"Near the top, beyond the city wall."

Jorge nodded as though that was the answer he expected. "Thomas, go speak with Hasdai, offer him coin if you have to. I'll speak with some of these others and see if there's anything else they know."

Hasdai had been happy to accept fair payment in exchange for the man's time, and Thomas was content to pay, knowing there was no uplift in the expected fee. Jorge chatted with the man as they climbed the slopes of the hill across from the palace. The higher they climbed the narrower the alleyways became, doors letting out directly onto the street. The steepness of the hillside meant the houses lacked any courtyard or gardens. The buildings were barely deep enough to accommodate a family, let alone the luxury of outside space.

Thomas picked up a little information about the man as they climbed, enough to know he lived alone and shared rooms with other workers, but mostly he tried to puzzle through why Bilal had fled. It made little sense, unless he was guilty of something. Or feared something. It had been a long time since Thomas had been feared, and he believed that the life he once led was left far behind when he came to this land.

"What did you and Bilal speak of on your journey home?"

The clerk turned his head as he strode forward, walking fast, used to the climb. "What do single men talk of when they're alone? You know how it is."

Thomas caught Jorge smiling.

"He didn't speak of his life before he came to work for Hasdai?"

"I never asked and he never offered. We walked together once or twice a week and always spoke of insignificant matters. I don't know why he ran."

"He'll likely be caught by now," Jorge said.

Thomas slowed. "Caught? How?"

"One of the clerks near the door went outside after Bilal. He said he was gone already, and that two soldiers were in pursuit."

"When were you going to tell me this?"

"I'm telling you now, so you needn't wear yourself out on the climb. I expect we'll see him coming back down any moment. Under arrest."

"Perhaps the soldiers weren't chasing Bilal," Thomas said.

"And perhaps I'm a full man."

They reached the city wall and passed through an unguarded gate into an area beyond its protection. The ground finally levelled off, rough-built houses pressing close on either side, some using the city wall as their own. The clerk stopped in front of a doorway.

"My rooms lie within. When we part Bilal continues to the end of the alley and turns right."

"That's all you know?"

"It's all I know. May I return to my work now?"

Thomas pressed a small coin into the man's hand and watched as he trotted back down the slope.

"He's keen to return to his labours," Jorge said.

"Some men are made that way."

"You realise we're no closer to Bilal than we were in the workshop."

"Of course we are. The man said he lives nearby, that he turns right at the end of the alley."

"We'll go and see then, shall we?"

Thomas shook his head at Jorge's intransigence and led the way. At the end of the alley they turned right along one even narrower, lined on one side with accommodation no different to that they had already passed, but on the other the buildings were more scattered and rough scrub rose along the hillside.

"We've left civilisation behind," Jorge said.

"You think civilisation ends at the palace walls."

"I'm here, aren't I?"

Thomas wondered if Jorge was finding his change of circumstance difficult to adjust to. The first few days had provided a distraction from his usual life, but now his interest might be waning.

"Leave if you want," Thomas said, his tone sharper than he intended. Bilal could be a genuine lead to something, but he was aware he was ignoring the only other lead they had in pursuit of a man who didn't wish to be found.

"I didn't mean I wanted to go," Jorge said. "But how do you plan to find this man? He could be in any one of these rooms. Or even beyond." Jorge waved a hand towards an alley which dipped away from them, barely wide enough to accommodate a man's shoulders. It wasn't the first one they'd passed. "Do we knock on every door?"

"If we have to."

Jorge looked around. "This isn't the kind of place that welcomes strangers."

"Whether they like it or not we've little choice." Thomas approached the nearest door and hammered against it.

There was no response.

"These are the homes of working men," Jorge said. "Their inhabitants won't return until evening."

"I lived in a place like this when I first came to the city," Thomas said, moving the few paces required to knock at the next door.

"Then I feel sorry for you."

"It was an improvement on my life up until then. I thought

I'd discovered the most wonderful place on earth."

Jorge laughed and patted Thomas on the shoulder. "And what do you think of life now? Living with two beautiful sisters in a large house, friend to the most powerful man in the land?"

Thomas scowled. "Sometimes I miss the simplicity of those days." He hammered on another door. "Is there no-one home anywhere?"

"As I said—" Jorge stopped as there came a commotion from the end of the alley. A woman ran shouting from a doorway, waving her arms. Her words were Spanish, spoken too rapidly for Thomas to make out more than one or two, but he only needed to understand one, derived from Arabic. *Asesinato*—Murder.

The woman was distressed, and Jorge took her to one side, his voice calm, one hand on her shoulder, the other holding her hand. Thomas watched, impressed and jealous of the man's ability to put people at ease. While Jorge extracted her tale Thomas entered the doorway she had rushed from.

Within was a narrow hallway with more doors leading off to left and right, at the end a small window lacking glass looked out across the city, the minarets of the many mosques rising above the ochre roof tiles. In any other house it would have been a view to appreciate, here it was no more than a means of admitting a little light.

A doorway three rooms down stood ajar, and Thomas went there to discover what had frightened the woman. He knew from the smell what he would find even before he saw Bilal's body tumbled across a narrow cot. Papers lay strewn over the floor, some torn, others stained with the blood that pooled on the bedclothes and tiles. Bilal lay on his side, a slash across his neck so deep his head lolled at an unnatural angle. Even so, Thomas knelt, careful to avoid the blood, and felt for a pulse, unsurprised when he find none. The body was still as warm as that of a living man, but all life had fled.

Thomas stood and surveyed the space.

The room was tiny, a narrow cot taking up half the floor, with a small desk jammed hard against the opposite wall. There was no chair, and Thomas imagined the man sitting on the bed to work, writing contracts in his own time. It was one explanation for the papers scattered about. Thomas knelt and retrieved a few, turning them over. Most were written in Arabic, but here and there he found a few in Latin, Greek, Spanish, too. Bilal had been a learned clerk. One who took private work outside that given him by Hasdai. Had the old Jew discovered this, Bilal would have been dismissed immediately.

Thomas turned as Jorge came into the room.

"She collects laundry from these rooms and others along the alleyway. She says she doesn't enter the rooms themselves. Each man leaves a sack outside the door. Bilal's is still there. She said the door was open when she came to it and glanced inside, saw him as he is now." Jorge studied the body a moment with a cool gaze and shook his head. "We're seeing too much death lately."

"Did she see anyone else?"

"Not a soul when she arrived. She tells me this building is empty during the day. Filled with single men at night." Jorge glanced around. "It's a depressing life."

"I never found it so," Thomas said.

Jorge smiled. "Why doesn't that surprise me? You're unlike other men, that's for sure. Anyway, she said she saw no-one here, but on her approach two men almost knocked her over they were running so fast."

"In which direction?"

"She came from the far end of the alley, the opposite direction to us or we'd have seen them as well."

"Could she describe them?"

"It happened too quickly, but she said she thought they were soldiers of some kind."

"In what colours?"

Jorge shook his head. "That she couldn't say. I pressed her a little on the matter, as hard as I dared without putting a scare into her. She's had enough scares already today, but she knew no more, I'm sure."

"You said a clerk saw two soldiers running after Bilal when he fled the workshop."

"It's too much of a coincidence that someone else came to kill the man at the same time, don't you think?"

"Too great a coincidence they were there at exactly the same time as us," Thomas said, shaking his head. He knelt and began to collect together the scattered papers. "Help me gather these. Is the woman still outside?"

"I sent her to find a guard. Someone will need to know of the death."

"I'd prefer we weren't here when they arrive," Thomas said. "Is his laundry sack still outside?"

"It was when I came in."

"Fetch it, I need something to put these papers in."

Jorge straightened. "You've no need to tidy the room, he's too dead to care."

"I think the papers are important. They could be the reason he was killed."

"Wouldn't they have taken anything of importance already?"

"Soldiers? How many soldiers do you know can read? They may have taken something, but they wouldn't know what was important or not. Go fetch the sack."

Jorge sighed and ducked through the doorway, returned with a small linen sack. He emptied the contents on the floor and held the neck wide while Thomas stuffed documents inside.

He hesitated, taking a last look around the room, searching for a place Bilal might have hidden anything else. These papers had been in plain view, but if the man possessed something secret it would be elsewhere. Thomas lifted the bed. Nothing beneath. He pulled the small desk away from the wall and up-ended it, examined it for a hidden compartment. Again, nothing. He started tapping on the walls.

"Are you looking for more tunnels?" Jorge asked.

Thomas gave up. The room was too small, the walls too thin for a hiding place. He nodded and pushed Jorge towards the door.

"We're done, there's nothing here for us anymore."

Outside in the alleyway it was as quiet as when they arrived. This high on the Albayzin was deserted during daylight, the hubbub of the city far below. Thomas led the way he considered the fastest route to his house, although he didn't know the area at all and found their passage blocked on several occasions. Eventually he came to a place he recognised and their progress grew faster.

"That woman will tell the guards we were there," Jorge said.

"It doesn't matter. I have the Sultan's seal, and it seems the entire city knows of our quest. I'm more worried about the soldiers that chased Bilal. I don't believe they were waiting for him."

"Do you think they were following *us?*" Jorge said, and once more Thomas knew he had underestimated the man.

"I was hard on Zoraya yesterday. I wouldn't be surprised if she told Olaf about it and he sent someone to follow us. It means we're getting closer."

"It means we're in more danger," Jorge said. "What if they were following us until we came to a quiet spot, and then attacked?"

"If that was the plan they wouldn't have gone after Bilal. Whoever is behind this is a step ahead of us. They know where the threats are, and are shutting them down one by one. The soldiers followed Bilal and killed him because they knew he was a danger to whoever gave them orders. And who better to give soldiers an order than the Sultan's general?"

"It's a dangerous game they play," Jorge said. "If word gets back to Abu al-Hasan, Olaf will find himself without a head. His daughters will be in danger, too. Plotting against a Sultan is no slight matter. You have seen how he treats those who displease him."

"What about Faris al-Rashid? He accosted us in the palace itself, as good as threatened us, and he knows his way around. Is he Olaf's master? I wonder, when Olaf found us in that chamber with him, did he already know we were there?"

"He would know Zoraya, too. I didn't take to the Neapolitan, but he's just the kind of man who would appeal to Zoraya. Naples and Greece are close in spirit as well as geography. Would Faris order a man killed?"

Thomas didn't bother replying to the question, the answer self-evident. "Faris is fond of his head, though, and even more aware of the dangers than Olaf."

"He is used to plot and intrigue, and a far more credible suspect than Olaf, now I think on it. He is also more useful to the Sultan. His money, and that of his friends, prop up the Sultan's rule. And he has men of his own. Strangers to the city, which would be an advantage."

"We have too many suspects," Thomas said as they turned into the alley leading to his house. "Why did Faris invite us to join him? There's more going on here than we know. Have there been rumours of insurrection?"

Jorge laughed as they entered Thomas's house. "Rumours of insurrection? You overestimate me. I'm a mere eunuch who doesn't trouble himself with such things."

"Your entire life is plot and intrigue."

"Ah, but of a different kind, and all in the pursuit of love, not death. As for Faris wanting us to join him, don't they say you should keep your enemies close?" Jorge stopped as Lubna came from the workshop.

"You're early," she said. "My sister's not at home, and I haven't started the evening meal yet. But if you're hungry I can find something. And someone called for you, Thomas."

"We don't want to eat. Who was the caller? A patient?"

"They didn't say."

"Did they leave a name?"

Lubna shook her head. "I never thought to ask. I'm sorry, Thomas."

"Did they look ill?"

"Not at all. They gave me a message for you. It's in your workshop."

"When did they call?"

"You have missed them by minutes."

"Did he look like a soldier?"

Lubna looked at him. "Who said it was a man?"

"A woman?"

She nodded, and Thomas sighed, tension leaving his body.

"I need your help. Jorge isn't staying."

"I'm not?"

Thomas lifted the sack of papers. It rustled. "Do you read Arabic? Latin? Spanish even?"

"You know I read nothing."

"Then I have more useful work for you. Go to the barracks, find Olaf and tell him of Bilal's death. See if you can slip something into the conversation and ask him if he sent anyone to follow us. You can say for our protection if it sounds better."

"And of course he will tell me all of this."

"Thank him for the lesson he gave me yesterday. His answer, one way or the other, will prove enlightening."

Jorge nodded, accepting his task. Once he was gone Thomas took the sack into the courtyard and emptied its contents onto the table where he, Jorge and Helena had eaten.

Lubna came to stand at his side.

"I want you to help me read these, as fast as we can."

"Some of the pages have blood on them," Lubna said.

Thomas glanced at her, but saw no sign of revulsion; she was merely stating the obvious.

"I'll take those," he said. "Do you read Latin or Greek?"

"Arabic only."

"Then start on those, I'll read the rest."

"What are we looking for?"

Thomas drew a seat to the table and reached for a document, glancing at it before passing it to Lubna. "I don't know until we find it, or even if there's anything to find. But the man who possessed these documents is dead, and the reason why will be hidden somewhere here. If you find anything significant tell me at once."

Lubna gave him a look that contained an entire conversation, then chose to sit on the stone slabs before starting to read.

TWENTY-FOUR

Thomas finished with the last of the documents written in Spanish and broke off, twisting to ease the pain in his back. He rose stiffly while Lubna turned from those she held in her hand and looked up at him. For a moment he caught some fleeting emotion in her eyes, something he couldn't decipher, and wondered how the world might change if he threw Helena out.

A breeze had started up, plucking at the loose papers. Thomas went to the edge of the courtyard and retrieved four round stones used as decoration, carried them back and laid them on the pages.

"I need to walk around for a moment. You should take a break, too."

Lubna put down the paper she was holding immediately and rose as though she hadn't been sitting on the tiles for over an hour.

"Do you want water?"

"I can get it," Thomas said.

Lubna glanced at the sky, studied the shadows in the courtyard before turning away.

"What time did Helena leave?" Thomas asked, following her into the kitchen.

"Early, for Helena at least. She didn't say where she was going."

"Friends on the hill."

"She misses her old life."

"Hmm."

Lubna poured cold water for them both and drained half her cup in three fast gulps. "The life she led wasn't real, was it? What you do is real. What my father does, even what the Sultan does, is real." She stopped with an expression on her face as though she may have said too much.

Thomas detected no hint of jealousy in her voice, only a note of disapproval. He ignored whatever might be there. "Have you found anything?"

Lubna drank again and when she had drained the glass shook her head. Water had spilled from her chin and marked her shift. "Nothing that makes any sense to kill a man over. Bills of sale, contracts for land, a request to fund an expedition of exploration. Any of it might mean something, but without more to go on I can't tell."

"Is there anything with the name of Faris al-Rashid on? Or Valentin al-Kamul, Antonio Galbretti, Domingo Alkhabaz?" Thomas reeled off the names of the men who had been in the palace chamber two days earlier. He no longer suspected them of direct involvement, but their interest still puzzled him.

Lubna held a hand up, shaking her head. "Stop, stop, too many names. Say them again more slowly."

Thomas repeated the list. When he was done Lubna shook her head again. "Perhaps, I don't know. I wasn't looking for any name in particular. You should have told me this before we started. Now I have to go through all those papers again."

"You're right, I was too impatient. You continue with the others and I'll check the pages you've already read."

"No—keep working on those I can't read, it won't take me long to skim them for names." She glanced beyond him to the courtyard. "I should prepare a meal. Helena will want to eat on her return."

"Don't bother on my account," Thomas said, "I'll eat with Jorge later."

"And drink, no doubt." A smile tugged at her lips.

"You're right, he's not a good Muslim, but neither am I."

"I meant no criticism." Lubna cast her gaze from his, busying herself refilling their cups. "I only meant I found him amusing in his enthusiasm for wine."

"Yes, I believe women find him amusing. We'd better get back to work if time's short." Thomas took the cup from her and turned away.

It was Lubna who found the first document, signed and sealed by Valentin al-Kamul, his name printed neatly, which was fortunate because the signature was made with such a flourish it was indecipherable. Like the man himself, Thomas thought.

He leaned towards Lubna as they both read the document.

She placed a finger on the paper. "Why would he buy a share in a mine?"

"Why would any man? For profit, I suspect. I doubt very much he even knows where it is."

Lubna turned the sheet over and Thomas tried not to show his annoyance.

"Qasada," she said. "The mine is outside Qasada." She frowned. "Where's that?"

"A day's ride east. It's a small town in the foothills of the Sholayr."

"A day east? Is it our territory or Spanish?"

"The last I heard it was ours, just. It passes between us time and again, but at the moment it's Moorish."

"A dangerous spot to go into business," Lubna said.

"Commerce is commerce, and this man is no more a Moor than I am. He'll be able to deal with whoever claims title to the territory. How large is his share in this mine?" Thomas tried to take the paper from Lubna but she kept hold, bending close to study the words.

"A quarter share, it says here." She glanced up. "He paid a great deal of money for it."

"How much?"

When she told him Thomas shook his head. "Valentin is a rich man, that isn't a large sum for someone like him."

"I could live my whole life in luxury on such an amount."

"He already lives in luxury, and his investment will only

bring him more. Do we know who the other shareholders are? Does the document say?" Once more he reached for the paper. Once more Lubna retained her hold.

Thomas waited—half amused, half annoyed.

Lubna shook her head. "It doesn't. There's another signature, but I can't make it out, and the corner of the paper where the name is printed is stained with blood and the seal indistinct."

"Put it aside, we can return to it later, but it may be significant. You did well."

Lubna found three more documents containing names she was searching for, Thomas only one. He started on the balance of Arabic documents and came across something that intrigued him even though it wasn't connected to the task in hand. A bill of trade for a roll of cloth made out in the name of the Sultan's son Muhammed. He would have missed it altogether except the trader's name was Carlos Rodriguez.

Thomas read the bill of goods then tossed the paper into the stack already read. Interesting but irrelevant.

The shadow cast by the courtyard wall touched them. The breeze picked up, snatching at the papers, which would have scattered had they not been trapped beneath stones. Lubna looked up, stretching.

"I ought to prepare that meal for my sister's return."

"You weren't brought here to be a servant."

"Say that to Helena, not me. I don't mind. I'm not like her, I need to be kept busy." Lubna stood, as lithe as before, and padded into the house on bare feet.

Thomas watched her go, continuing to stare at the empty doorway long after she had disappeared.

Eventually he returned to the small pile of documents they had set aside, picked them up and went into his workshop. He spread the five documents across the table and leaned in to study each in turn, searching for something he was unsure he would recognise even if he found it. From the corner of his eye he saw another piece of paper and reached for it, but it was only the note his visitor had left and he tossed it aside unread. He had no time for the pleas of patients.

* * *

"Olaf swore he sent none of his men to follow us," Jorge said in response to Thomas's question. They were back in the room above the inn, day turning to night outside the window.

"Did you believe him? Those men were soldiers."

"Not all soldiers belong to Olaf. When I talked to him I got a different impression than you. I no longer believe he's involved."

"The soldiers in this city are under his command. Whoever they were knew to follow us, and they knew who Bilal was. Or do you think Bilal was their quarry all along? And why did Olaf try to kill me?"

Jorge laughed. "Olaf doesn't know his own strength or speed. You surprised him, you were a little more skilled than expected, he said. I think he just reacted, nothing more."

Thomas shook his head, reluctant to let go of Olaf as a suspect yet. "Whoever is behind it, why wait until now to kill Bilal?"

"Because he wasn't a threat until we came looking. Safer to leave him be and not raise suspicion. Bilal was a clerk to Tahir—secrecy and confidentiality will be seared into his bones. I doubt he would have told us anything."

"I'm not so sure." Thomas paced the room while Jorge sat on the bed. Lamps burned across the square, and the sound and scent of eating drifted in through the open window. "Imagine how he must feel, dismissed from his position, forced to work in a back street sweatshop. You saw how many clerks were crammed into that space. How would you feel if they tossed you out of the harem and you had to exist as some front of house in a brothel?"

"A man makes what he can of life, the highs and lows both. But you're right, perhaps he would have spoken to us."

Thomas picked up the small pile of documents he and Lubna had identified as of interest. "I don't understand why we didn't find anything else."

"Such as?"

"You know what. Bilal undertook the first investigation. I don't believe he would have destroyed his findings. If he has these papers, he would have kept the notes he made as well. But they're missing."

"Is that what they were after?" Jorge said. "Soldiers who can read after all."

"And these?" Thomas waved the papers in his hand. "Does someone else know of their existence? Surely these are a threat, too."

"Perhaps, perhaps not. But if they're all we have tell me what they contain, and see if I see the same pattern as you."

Thomas pulled out a chair and sat at the small table, spreading the papers across its surface. "That's my point, there is no pattern that I can see. The only thing linking them are the names of the men we saw with Faris."

"Is Faris himself named on any of them?" Jorge made no attempt to rise and come across.

"Not directly. But look, here's Valentin al-Kamul on this one, and this." Thomas pushed two pages to one side. "Galbretti on these three. All of them linked."

"But in what?" Jorge said. "Tell me the matters listed there."

Thomas shook his head. "It makes no sense to me. Here Valentin has bought a quarter share in a mine—iron ore, it seems. The other with his name on is for farmland. Poor farmland, at that. It makes no sense."

"Is the land close to the mine?"

Thomas examined the papers again, although he knew the answer, had pored over the pages long after they'd stopped making any sense. "Perhaps half a day's ride apart. Both in the foothills of the Sholayr."

"Could it be there's more iron beneath the farmland?"

"It would make sense, but there's no mention here."

"Which there wouldn't be, otherwise the price paid would be considerably higher. Valentin may know more than is shown on these pages. Is there benefit in playing along with them so we get a chance to question them without drawing suspicion on ourselves?"

"These others." Thomas said, ignoring the question as he pushed the papers around randomly. "Another tract of farm-land, this one a day from the mine in the other direction, along-side al-wādi al-kabīr. That land might be in Spanish hands by now. And here, Galbretti has *sold* estates in Sicily and is having the proceeds sent here."

"And Don Domingo?"

"Title to a house in Qurtuba—what link lies there? Nothing that I can see."

"Don Domingo is no fool, despite mixing with those men. He sees the way the war is going, and his blood is Spanish, not Moor. When this war ends—and it can end only one way—he will have his place secured." Jorge leaned forward, his face in shadow but eyes bright. "Are you thinking the same thing as me, Thomas?"

"I don't know. What are you thinking?"

Jorge sat back, smiling. "There are two possibilities here." He held up a closed fist before raising a finger. "First—these papers mean nothing. They are the random dealings of wealthy men and we should dismiss them as no more than that." He allowed a second finger to pop loose. "Second, these men are planning something and, I believe, are connected with the killings. Whether they're behind them directly or not I haven't made up my mind about yet, but they're plotting some mischief, I'm sure, and are involved in some way."

Thomas stared at Jorge a long time before nodding. "And Zoraya? Is she involved or not?"

"What's to say they're not all in it together?"

"We need to know more about these land acquisitions. Is there anything here we don't see yet? They are all border land. It will be the first to go when the war finally comes. But if they are involved together why was Bilal killed?"

"For something he knew that was *not* written down? He was a man of letters, as aware as you of the power of words. He would never commit something so important to ink and paper."

Thomas looked away through the window. "So whatever knowledge he might have possessed is gone." He turned back towards Jorge. "You think he had worked it out? The answer we seek?"

"He was a learned man, and no fool. Yes, I think he knew who was behind this. Likely not the killer himself, but the man is merely the sacrificial pawn. It's his master we seek, the one guiding the assassin's rage."

Thomas said nothing, his mind as exhausted as his body. This task was as hard as anything he had ever experienced. Too many suspects, not enough evidence.

"But you're no fool, either, Thomas," Jorge said. "If Bilal was able to discover who lay behind the killings then so can you."

Thomas shook his head. "Your faith in my abilities are sadly misjudged. I think I have less idea now than when we started."

Jorge smiled. "If we assume for the moment Olaf and Zoraya are *not* behind the plot—and we can always come back to them— then who? You must have had suspicions when we started."

Thomas returned the smile. "I thought Faris behind it, of course. And you?"

"Too simple, too obvious," Jorge said.

"As I quickly realised. So who did you think?"

"What about Muhammed?"

Thomas nodded. "I considered him, too. Because we're looking for those who have something to gain. Not from the deaths, but from who will be damaged by them."

"That would be the Sultan," Jorge said. "Muhammed wants his father's position."

Thomas nodded again. "It's the only conclusion I'm able to come to. Not who gains but who loses. But it's not Muhammed, either. He would suffer as much as the Sultan."

"Explain the loss to me," Jorge said, leaning forward.

"I don't need to, you understand it better than me. You live among these people, know their ways more intimately than anyone. The only thing keeping the Sultan in power is strength, real or imagined. He's regarded as a strong leader, a warrior, and this land needs a warrior at the moment more than it needs a ruler. If he goes his son is tainted the same way as him and will never gain power."

"If the Sultan can't stop people dying within the walls of his own palace he's no longer seen as strong, but weak. The wolves start creeping closer, sensing that weakness."

"Are we back to Faris then?" Thomas said.

"Faris wouldn't be accepted by the people."

"Then Faris plotting on someone's behalf?"

"Which brings us once more to who gains most from the Sultan's removal."

"His sons."

"Which sons—Aixa's or Zoraya's?"

Thomas groaned and put his head in his hands. "I can't think on this anymore tonight. My thoughts are as shattered as broken glass. I need sleep, I need to forget plotting until the morning."

Jorge rose from the bed. "Then let's go and eat, then walk the streets for a while. Even visit the bathhouse and find some relaxation." He came across the room and put a hand on Thomas's shoulders, lifted his chin so he could look into his eyes. It was an uncomfortably intimate gesture. "Sometimes these matters are best left to mature in darkness. Turn off your mind and think of good food, good wine and, if you wish, a good woman."

"I have a woman."

"Then eat and drink and go home and make love to her. But turn this off." He rapped the top of Thomas's skull with his knuckles.

Thomas made for the door. "I'll try, but it's not easy. All I want is some idea of where to look. Who'd have thought we would end up with too many suspects?"

"Forget it," Jorge said. "By morning the idea may come fully formed to you."

"By morning we might both be dead."

"In that case let's enjoy living for as long as we can."

TWENTY-FIVE

As he ascended the dark alleys of the Albayzin, Thomas realised he wasn't thinking of Helena but her sister. The image of Lubna at the start of the day, bright eyed, fascinated as she mixed herbs and powders and oils, filled his mind. Each time he made an effort to expel it a moment later there it was again, a longing for something he couldn't express. Thomas considered himself weak-willed for allowing the jumble of images to cloud his mind, but at least the wine had loosened his thoughts and allowed something else to briefly occupy them. Jorge had been right about that.

Narrow steps brought him to a level roadway paved with smooth stones. Thomas stopped to catch his breath, looking back at the palace which dominated the entire city. As it was meant to.

He was missing something and had finally worked out what it was. The documents recovered from Bilal's room were noise, nothing more. There had to be others.

Something sounded below, down among the twisting steps he had just ascended. A foot kicking a stone. In the still of the night it clattered away. Thomas walked back to the head of the steps and looked down. Only darkness. A hundred men could be hidden there. He waited, alert, but nothing more came. Some creature—a dog, a cat, a rat? It could have been anything. He hurried on, the night not finished yet.

The house was quiet, and he moved carefully, not wanting to wake Helena, knowing he would disturb Lubna, unless she had found somewhere else to sleep.

She was curled on the cot, a weak candle guttering on the floor beside her. Thomas moved carefully across the dim room, knowing his way precisely. He touched the wooden bench and pulled on a drawer, easing it open. His hand searched inside, found what it sought.

"Thomas?"

"Go back to sleep. I'm going out again."

She sat up, clutching at the sheet as it threatened to reveal her. "It's the middle of the night."

"Not yet. Go to sleep." He stepped away from the bench, slipping the object he had retrieved beneath his robe.

"What are you hiding?"

"Nothing."

Lubna gave a laugh that contained no humour. "I can see you hiding something, and it's not nothing. Or do you lust for my body now too, as well as my sister's?"

Thomas glanced down.

"I felt the need of some protection," he said, drawing out the knife he had taken.

Lubna swung her legs to the flagstones and rose. "What are you planning?"

Thomas sighed. He admired Lubna's sharp mind, but for once would have preferred her not to ask so many questions.

"Those documents we read aren't the ones I seek. Bilal must have others I didn't find."

"You said the soldiers took them."

"I don't think so, not anymore. I believe they're still in his room. We searched, but not hard or long enough. I'm going there now, and not coming away until I find them."

"If they exist."

"If they exist I will find them."

Lubna shook her head. "Wait then, I'll come with you."

"Stay here."

Lubna frowned at the roughness in his voice.

Thomas closed the space between them and put his hands on her shoulders, only realising he still held the knife after he had done so, but Lubna didn't flinch.

"Why do you think I came back for the blade?" he said.

"I can keep watch while you search."

"If I'd wanted help I'd have asked Jorge." Lubna was not to know the idea had only just occurred to him. "There's no-one about at this time of night. Go back to sleep, I'll see you in the morning." He turned and strode away fast before she could say anything.

Far up the hillside the Albayzin looked different in the dark, and Thomas found himself lost more than once. At one point he feared he would never find Bilal's room again, then he stumbled onto the city wall and followed it, knowing the accommodation lay just outside its gate.

When at last he found the place he discovered it had taken no time to let the room again. The outer door was open, and he counted down five doors. He expected his push to open it, but instead found it locked. He knocked, then again, louder. There was no response from within but voices came from behind other doors. Thomas knocked again, eventually rewarded by the throwing of a bolt.

A short man peered out, his eyes barely open. "I have done nothing wrong."

"I need to search your room."

"I am a stonemason, sir, I possess nothing of value."

Thomas reached into his robe, withdrew a gold Maravedi and pressed it into the man's hand. "You do now." The coin was more than the man could earn in three months. "I need an hour alone in your room."

The man shook his head and peered out, looking for the woman.

"I only moved in this evening, I don't understand what—"

"Do you want the coin or not?"

The man looked down at his hand, nodded.

"Find somewhere else, then. Go sit on the hillside and enjoy the stars."

The man backed into the room and started to dress in rough clothing. Thomas stepped in after him, already looking around.

The small window let in some moonlight, but not enough for his task. On a stone shelf lay an oil lamp and flint, and Thomas lit it. After climbing the hill through the night the little light it gave out was dazzling.

"An hour?" the man asked, standing in the doorway.

"No more. I will call you when I finish." For a moment Thomas thought a second coin would be needed, but the man nodded and disappeared.

Thomas held the lamp high and looked around. A stain still marked the floor where Bilal had died. Only the bedclothes had been changed, everything else remained the same. Next week it would be this new occupant placing his soiled clothing in a linen sack outside the door. Life goes on. For a moment Thomas wondered if the man had thrown out anything of Bilal's, but he doubted it. Whatever remained behind would be considered good fortune rather than bad luck: new clothes, perhaps even some money.

He had already searched the small desk, but did so again, placing the lamp as high as he could so its glow filled the room. Already its brilliance was fading as his eyes grew accustomed to the light.

There were three drawers in the desk, shallow but deep. Thomas pulled them all the way out and laid them on the bed. They contained unmarked paper, some quills, and a small bottle of ink, as well as the makings for more. A few small coins lay scattered in the bottom of one. Thomas tipped the contents onto the bed and turned each drawer over, but they were nothing more than what they were. He turned his attention to the desk itself, upending it and going on his knees, feeling underneath, tugging at the joints. Nothing there, either.

He stood and surveyed the room. The only other piece of furniture was the bed.

Thomas replaced the items in the drawers and slid them back into the desk, then pulled the thin mattress from the bed and leaned it against the wall. He overturned the bed as he had the desk and worked his way along every inch of it, with the same result. He tried the mattress, probing its paltry comfort with his fingers, even taking his knife, easing loose the stitching and feeling inside. He kicked the bed in frustration. Only the walls remained, and he thought of the tunnels running through the palace. Perhaps.

He began next to the door. The room wasn't high, and Thomas could reach the ceiling without stretching. He pushed against each stone, used the knife between courses, but everything remained firm. He cursed the builders, because the structure was sound, not a single loose stone that might be used to conceal secret documents. Thomas pulled the bed into the room and searched the wall by the window. He took special care around the narrow opening, but once more the masons had done a good job.

He muttered under his breath and stepped back, defeated.

Something moved under his heel and he almost lost his balance.

He stepped to one side and went to his knees. His fingers splayed across a rough slab and he pushed, rocking it slightly. Thomas took the knife and forced it into a crack. The mortar joint was loose and he levered, the slab lifting a little. He pushed his fingertips beneath one edge, used the knife again and the slab came clear. Thomas laid it to one side. A small chamber had been hollowed out beneath. It must have taken Bilal a week to make this hiding place; unless it was already here and he had only discovered it as Thomas had. Within lay something wrapped in oiled cloth.

Thomas lifted the parcel out and unwrapped it enough to see what lay within. Documents. He laid them to one side and worked the stone slab back into place, dragged the bed back and re-made it. He looked around one last time. There was nothing else here for him. He had uncovered the secret he came looking for.

Another hundred paces and he would be at his door. Helena would be asleep in their bed, but it was not one he wanted to share. He shook his head. What other man would turn their back on such a woman, even if she had betrayed them? Helena had been raised to be used. Other men would use—and abuse—her, but Thomas knew he was not one of that kind. His head spun with fatigue but he knew he couldn't sleep until he had examined the documents tucked beneath his robe.

He shook his head to clear it and turned aside, stopping at a sound from behind, up along the steps he had recently descended. Thomas stood silent, listening for the second time that night. For a time nothing, and then, on the edge of hearing a scrape, a second following close behind. Someone was coming down the steps in near silence. Thomas walked on a dozen paces before slipping into a narrow doorway, just deep enough to hide him from the street. He drew his dark cloak around himself, loosened his headscarf and covered his face, waiting.

He was beginning to think he had been overly cautious when a figure moved across the doorway's entrance, robe flowing behind, feet running. Thomas listened as the steps moved away... slowed... stopped. There was a scuffling sound and then they started to return, slower now.

Thomas felt beneath his robe, his hand seeking and closing around the handle of the knife. He drew the blade, readying himself, fearing he was a poor soldier in comparison to whoever came after him. Then his body chilled as voices sounded. There were two of them.

One must have been waiting further along, close to his house, in case the follower lost him. Two men. Two men pursuing him. As two men had pursued Bilal. There was no other reason for them to be here, to be acting in this way. Thomas pressed himself hard into the small protection of the doorway, trying to calculate if he was safer there or in the open where he would have more freedom of movement. As the footsteps came closer the whispered voices grew louder. He tried to make out what they were saying, but nothing made sense, and Thomas realised they were speaking a language he didn't understand. The odd word caught in his memory and he tried to place them.

A chill ran through him.

They were speaking the language Helena used with her father, Olaf still uncomfortable with that of his adopted homeland, grateful for anyone who could ease his mind with words he readily understood.

Two northmen.

Was there significance in that? There had to be. Coincidence could stretch only so far. But if there was significance, what was its nature?

Then they were on him, Thomas still trapped in indecision. He closed his eyes, not wishing to see his own death coming. The voices grew louder, peaked and faded. They had walked right past his hiding place. Thomas let out the breath he had been holding, opened his eyes and peered around the edge of the doorway, not believing they could have walked by without seeing him.

The men moved along the alleyway, approaching the foot of the steps Thomas had descended only a few moments before. They were dressed in black robes, black leggings, but their heads were bare. The hair of one looked dark in the starlight, the other's almost white. Thomas considered slipping from his hiding place and making a dash for home. The door would be unlocked, and once inside he could bar it from within. There was a second entrance at the side which opened directly into his workshop, but that was always kept locked.

The men stopped and spoke. One turned and Thomas ducked into the shelter of the doorway, but he was too late. A muffled shout sounded, followed by running feet, and he dashed into the alleyway, running as fast as he could for home, not even knowing for sure if these men meant him harm, but convinced in his heart they did.

He knew they had caught him ten paces short of safety when something tugged at his billowing robe, the loss of momentum sending his sandaled feet skidding. He stumbled, caught his footing and turned, the knife held in front of him.

The men stopped, grins lighting their faces in the gloom.

"What are you running from, surgeon?"

"Why are you following me?"

"We are two soldiers on our way home from the brothel. Why would we want to follow you? Or do you have women we could share? Perhaps a beautiful concubine with skin white as milk and hair like snow?"

"Who sent you—was it Olaf?"

"Olaf?" The dark-haired man laughed. "He's the Sultan's man." The soldier's accent was broad, his companion yet to speak, but Thomas knew from past battles always to watch the silent ones. As the man spoke both moved slowly apart, giving themselves space for an attack. Thomas's stupid knife felt tiny in his hand. Even tinier as the blonde man drew a scimitar.

Thomas heard the whisper of steel from the other but didn't turn his head, eyes locked onto those of the silent attacker.

"Come on then, kill me if you can." Thomas feinted forward, pleased and surprised to see the man take a step back. That had been the time to attack in turn, to move swift and sure, to finish him. Thomas had seen it often enough in battle. Some men blustered, putting on a good show, but when it came to the job of killing they were reluctant. He had also seen those who walked away alive, and they were the ones who showed no hesitation. They were not evil men, but he had seen something turn off in their eyes a moment before they flung themselves into battle. The same thing he felt drain from himself as he followed their example, keeping his momentum going, slashing at the blonde man, his blade flashing in the starlight, the world dark and cloaked in confusion.

Thomas sensed rather than saw the second man moving in, too slowly, too cautious, and Thomas, filled with a rage of exultation, of blood lust, struck out. He spun, knife darting, and felt it catch on something as the dark-haired man staggered back, swearing in his own language, calling out to his companion.

The man made too much noise. The other, at least, had sense.

"Help!" Thomas yelled at the top of his voice. "Murder! Help me!"

He turned again, dismissing the loud attacker, lunging fast against the silent one. The man had recovered his wits and didn't fall back this time. He jerked to one side, narrowly avoiding Thomas's blade, then slashed back, his sword coming in from the side. Thomas darted away and the blade hissed through the air, its passing catching a fold of his scarf and slicing clean through. Thomas didn't flinch but stepped forward again, inside the attack, and the second blow held far less force than the first. He lifted his left arm and took the blade against his robe, the thick folds cushioning the strike. He thrust his knife forward, satisfied when it met resistance. He twisted and the blade caught, tugged from his hand. The man gasped, fell back, his sword sliding along the fold of Thomas's robe, the movement of razor-sharp steel doing what a blow had failed to, slicing through linen, slicing through flesh until it met bone. Hot agony flared in Thomas's arm and he stumbled away, the sword catching for a moment before slipping free. He staggered, clutching at his arm, already blood pulsing from the wound, knowing he was finished.

TWENTY-SIX

"Thomas!" It was a female voice. Not Helena but her sister. A wave of nausea and dizziness swept through him, the world swimming away.

Something jarred against his side. *So this is how it ends, after all this time, all the miles I have travelled, all the things I have seen and done, it ends here in an alley in the dark.*

He looked up, wanting to see the stars one last time, waiting for the thrust that would end his life. But his attackers were falling back. One of them clutched his chest on the left side. The other held a hand to his waist. They moved faster as windows were thrown open, doorways flung wide. All at once there were people around him, hands assisting, and Thomas found Lubna at his side, her tiny frame trying to take his weight and half succeeding before other hands came to her aid, leading Thomas inside the house.

"Take him through the courtyard to the workshop. I will bring a light."

Men half carried him to the cluttered space he loved more than any other in the world. *A fitting place to die,* he thought, the world tilting once more as he looked at his arm, blood pulsing from the wound, a dark stain spreading across his robe.

Something caught the back of his knees and he sat hard, finding himself on the narrow cot, its mattress still warm from Lubna's slumber. Three men stood around him, dressed in a ragged mix of shirts and robes, one with a rough hank of cloth wrapped at his waist.

"Thank you, gentleman."

"Thank your servant. It was she who saved you."

He knew each of these men, considered them friends to one

degree or another.

"Where did she go?"

"She's fetching a lamp." The speaker looked at Thomas's arm, turning away quickly.

"Get me a blade. They're on the bench. Quickly."

For a moment none of them moved, then the slap of footsteps approached, a wavering light, and as Lubna entered the room holding a lantern high a man moved to search, returning with a sharp knife. Thomas took it and slit the remains of his robe on one side, letting it fall away to reveal a deep gash along the outer edge of his arm, half way between his elbow and wrist. Thomas let his breath go, relieved. The cut lay on the outer side, and bone had stopped the blade. Blood continued to flow, but Thomas knew it wouldn't kill him unless it went untreated, and who better to treat it than the best surgeon in Gharnatah.

"I'll look after him now, sirs. You have my thanks for your help." Lubna started to herd them out. The confusion of the attack and swift flight indoors was leaving Thomas now, a deeper nausea replacing it as he recognised how close he had come to death.

Lubna returned a moment later and knelt in front of the cot, staring at the hand covering the wound on his arm. No fear or revulsion showed on her face. Even through his pain Thomas noticed she wore only a thin cotton shift that revealed the shape of her body beneath.

"Tell me what I have to do."

"Silk and a needle. You'll find both in the middle drawer of the bench. And there's an instrument. It looks like scissors but has blunt edges. Fetch that, too."

Lubna ran across the room. She rummaged inside the drawer, returned with the items in her hand.

"Are these what you want?"

"Thread the silk, then fetch a candle and light it. Hold the needle with the instrument and thrust the head into the flame until it glows. Then pass it to me."

Lubna brought a candle, lit it from the lamp and did as he asked. Thomas saw her mouth draw into a tight line as the tip of the needle glowed red and then, briefly, white. She grasped the silk and released the needle so it hung loose. Thomas took it, burning his fingers. He gritted his teeth and thrust the needle into his flesh, eyes watering, the pain exquisite, but he worked on, pushing the needle through and out the other side.

"I'm sorry, I can't do the next part with one hand. Pull the silk through until there are two inches either side the wound. Then cut it off and tie it tight to draw the edges of the wound together.

Lubna nodded, drew on the thread, its passage through his flesh a tiny agony. She cut it, looked around for somewhere to lay the needle.

"Don't put it down. Here, give it to me."

She handed the needle to Thomas, returned to his arm and tightened the thread, drawing on it. The flesh pulled together and she raised her eyes to his.

"Tighter. As tight as it will go, but careful it doesn't tear the skin."

She complied, twisting as though she too felt his pain. "Enough?"

"Good."

"Give me the needle," she said, "I'll finish the rest."

"You don't know how." His head started to swim again. Shock, he knew, more than loss of blood, but there had been some of that, too.

"I'm a good seamstress. It seems to me far simpler than stitching a buttonhole in a lady's dress." She took the needle from his limp fingers and Thomas slumped against the cot, barely feeling anything as Lubna pushed the needle into his arm and out the other side of the wound.

"If I pass out, pour raw alcohol into the wound when you're done. And clean it with a cloth soaked in the same. There are fresh bandages in one of the drawers in... I'm not sure, but in one of them. Bind my arm tight. Then make a draught of poppy, I may need it when I wake, for the pain."

Thomas closed his eyes and drifted. He felt the tug on his flesh as Lubna added more stitches, but the pain was distant, no more than someone pinching his skin.

When he next opened his eyes she was standing across the room unrolling bandage, and Thomas wondered how much time had passed.

"Where's Helena?"

Lubna gave a short laugh. "She's sleeping."

"I expect she knew she could be of no assistance."

"She didn't even wake." Lubna turned and came to the cot, the bandage in her hand. "She asked me for poppy again."

"You shouldn't have given her any. She's developing too much of a liking."

"I didn't, I refused her."

"You did?" Thomas lifted his arm, looking down at Lubna's handiwork. The stitching was exceedingly fine and he smiled, wondering if it would be possible to fit a button through the raw gaps between, and doubting it. She had tied at least three times more stitches than he would have, and it would be painful removing them all, but the scar would be smaller, he had to admit.

"I'm aware of what opium does to people," she said. "I've seen it in the houses I worked in. I wouldn't do that to my sister, but she went out, and when she came back she had acquired a little from someone else."

"One of my so-called friends."

Lubna glanced at Thomas. "My sister has always been able to twist men to her will."

"I won't need the poppy after all. You did a good job on my arm. I'll be able to sleep unaided." He started to sit up and Lubna placed a hand against his chest and pushed him down.

"I'll make some for you anyway. I know you're not the kind of man to grow dependent. You're going nowhere. Stay here. Sleep. I'll watch over you."

Thomas let her push him back onto the cot, lay half-awake,

only the throbbing in his arm preventing sleep from taking him. He watched as Lubna took poppy heads and drew the sticky milk from them. Dark hair tumbled over her shoulders, but viewed from the side she could be mistaken for a boy: slim-hipped, slight, steady on her feet. Thomas couldn't ignore the reaction she was starting to trigger in him. She wasn't beautiful in the way of her sister, but her elfin grace, her infectious smile, hinted at something genuine which Helena lacked. Even as he recognised his infatuation Thomas suppressed it, acknowledging some kind of loyalty to the woman sleeping upstairs, even if she had shown little to him. Whatever he felt towards Lubna he swore, even as watching her, he would never act on it.

Lubna returned and knelt as his side while the poppy steeped in a little wine. She stared at him a long time, a frown creasing her brow.

"There's something I don't understand," she said.

Thomas smiled. "There are many things I don't understand."

"Why are you still alive?"

"Because you came to my aid."

Lubna shook her head. "No. The two attacking you were soldiers. You're a doctor, Thomas. They should have killed you in an instant. Instead you fought back, you wounded them. I did nothing, neither did your neighbours. It was you who fought them off." Her frown deepened. "Where did you learn to fight like that?"

"I was lucky, or they were careless."

"No." She shook her head harder, making her hair fly. "I saw you. You fought like..." She sat back on her heels and let her breath out. "You fought like someone who has done so before."

"That poppy will be ready now."

"I heard them as they ran," Lubna said. "They spoke the language of the north. The language of my father."

"I know. I didn't understand the words, but I recognised the sounds. They were northmen."

Lubna continued to stare at him. "My father wouldn't send men after you."

Thomas closed his eyes, waiting for her to grow tired of questioning him.

"I heard a name," Lubna said. "Sven."

Thomas sat up. "Which one was it?"

"I don't know. All I heard was the name, and what they were saying to each other."

Lubna brought the poppy and helped him sit up.

Thomas patted his robe, searching for the document that had caused all of this. Panic flashed through him when he couldn't find it. Lubna tried to make him drink and he pushed the cup away.

"I had something in my robe. An oilskin package."

"It's yours? No-one was sure. It was lying outside on the roadway. One of your neighbours picked it up. It's on your bench, over there."

Thomas sank back, saw Lubna's muscles tense along her arm as she tried to hold him upright.

"Keep it safe. I must read it, but not tonight. Don't let me sleep late."

The draft of poppy eased the pain in his arm, sleep engulfing him like a sudden thunderstorm, dark and heavy and loud with dreams, and he tossed his head and muttered unintelligible words.

Twenty-Seven

"Well—I'd better move my things down here and let you two share the marital bed!"

Thomas woke to bright sunshine filling one corner of the workshop. Helena stood in the doorway, the light beyond casting her perfect body into clear profile. Lubna's head lay on his chest, her legs tucked beneath her. As she dozed her arm had snaked across his belly. The sound of her sister's harsh voice stirred her and she sat up, rubbing at her eyes.

"When do you want me to move out?" Helena said.

"This isn't what it seems." He tried to sit, his head still spinning, but he gripped the edge of the cot and breathed deep until the world steadied.

"There's little room for mistake, short of me catching you in the act." Then Helena's eyes caught sight of the bandage on Thomas's arm and she put her hand out to steady herself against the side of the door.

Thomas glanced down. Blood had seeped through the linen, staining it dark. It needed changing, and the wound would have to be cleaned again. He tried to sense the level of pain emanating from his arm but was unable to judge if it was better or worse than during the night.

"What happened here?" And this time Helena wasn't referring to Lubna and himself.

"I was attacked on my way home. Your sister and our neighbours came to my help."

"Are you hurt? Do you need a surgeon?" Helena was unaware of what she had said.

"Lubna sealed the wound for me. Helena, there's nothing untoward going on here, I promise. She's a fine seamstress."

Thomas smiled, directing his gaze at Lubna, who stood to one side, arms clasped around her slim body. "I couldn't climb the stairs. I was barely able to sit. Lubna dressed my wound and watched over me. You should be thanking her."

Helena's eyes darted across the room. She offered a brief nod. "Thank you, sister." She looked back to Thomas. "You are well?"

"I ache, but I'll survive."

"Good. Now, I'm hungry. Lubna, prepare some food." Helena turned away without waiting for an answer.

"She needs to dress my wound first."

Helena stopped, turned back, her body flaring in the sunlight and Thomas felt himself tugged in directions he didn't wish to consider. His life had been easier before women came into it, his needs more easily slaked by the girls of the bathhouse.

"Of course. Forgive me, I wasn't thinking. I'll dress and go into town to break my fast." She turned once more, feet delicate against the warm tile of the courtyard, and Thomas sighed, wondering where she might really be going. Two days ago he had been sure she was sharing the bed of Zoraya's son. Now the whole idea seemed preposterous.

Lubna approached, tentative.

"You've done nothing wrong," Thomas said, grateful for a distraction from his thoughts. "The opposite, in fact. Were it not for you those men would have killed me last night."

"You were doing well enough on your own."

"What brought you out?"

"Your shouting. I came immediately." The dusky skin of her cheeks showed darker as she flushed. "I should have taken time to dress properly, but you scared me. You were obviously in danger. Shall I look at your arm?"

"Once you're dressed."

Lubna glanced down at herself, the linen slip falling only half way down her thighs. "It's a little late for that, don't you think? Besides, you are master in this house, it is allowed for you to look on me. Allowed for you to use me for your pleasure if you wish. I am nothing and you are everything."

Thomas turned his head away. "Get dressed, Lubna. This house is different to others you might have been in. You're no slave here, not even a servant. After last night you're an equal." He waited, listening to movement, the rustle of clothing, and wished he felt less uncomfortable. "I hardly know anything about you. We met on only a handful of occasions before you came here. You've lived beneath this roof only a few days, but in that time I have seen something in you."

"What have you seen?" She was smiling as he turned back.

"You show interest in my work, or am I wrong?"

Lubna returned to the side of the cot, clothed more appropriately in a cotton robe that fell to her ankles, but her head remained uncovered. It was the attire of a servant, and Thomas disliked seeing her dressed that way. He realised it was probably all she possessed, and felt determined to do something about it. He saw the need for another conversation with Carlos Rodriguez once events settled. Lubna went to the bench and picked up a bottle of raw alcohol, some cloth, and a roll of linen bandage.

"What you do fascinates me," she said.

"Since you came here, or before?"

"Since I was a little girl. Helena joined the harem when she was very young, her beauty recognised early, but I was dragged around after my father, cleaning his armour, preparing his food. I saw the work of surgeons on the battlefield. I met you first when I was twelve years old, but you won't remember."

"I think I do. It was at al-Munekhar? The Spanish were attacking from the east. Your father killed a score of men that day. You were a tiny thing, all wiry strength and attitude, as I recall. We met in his tent at sunset."

Lubna appeared pleased at his recollection. "Father likes nothing better than to kill Spaniards."

"Even though he's no Moor?" Thomas thought back to the two northmen who attacked him. Would Olaf Torvaldsson know who they were? Or was Olaf the one who had sent them?

"He's loyal to the Sultan. More loyal than any man in al-Andalus." Her words, even if true, did little to resolve the questions in his head. "Do I cut the old bandage loose?"

"On the bench you will find a small instrument. It looks like a very small knife with a sharp blade. Use it to cut the outer layer and then unwind the rest. And bring me that package."

Lubna brought the blade but left the oilskin wrapped papers where they were. She started work on the bandage, pulling the sticky, blood-soaked linen away. When she came close to the skin it stuck, and as she pulled, it ripped the hairs along his arm free and Thomas winced. "That hurts almost more than the wound itself. I want to read those papers of Bilal's. Get them for me."

Lubna laughed. "You wouldn't last a second in the harem." She eased the last of the stained bandage away and gazed at the wound, her head to one side. "And you can read the papers when I've finished. I tried but they're in that old writing I can't read."

"Fetch them."

"Later. You are more important."

Thomas saw she wasn't to be deflected and leaned back against the table, forcing himself to be a good patient. It was a role unfamiliar to him. "Tell me how you see the wound this morning."

She glanced at him. "Are you training me, Thomas?"

"If you wish to learn, and show ability, I will help you."

"I'm not clever enough to be a surgeon, and besides I'm a woman. But I can nurse for you, give assistance, if you will let me."

Thomas wanted to berate her but knew it would be the wrong thing. Too many women, too many demands. Her presence beside him carried a strong pull of attraction, not just because she was pretty, but for the assistance she could bring.

"There are female surgeons," Thomas said. "Our civilisation doesn't put shackles on women as others do. There has been enlightenment here for seven centuries."

"Then I am not clever enough. But I can be of help."

"We'll see how far you progress. But yes, if you wish, I will train you in all you can learn. It would be a boon to have someone who can make up medicines and salves, to apply bandages and treat wounds. Speaking of which, you have not yet made your diagnosis."

Lubna returned her attention to his arm. She leaned close. Her fingertips touched his skin, close to the angry wound but not too near. Her touch was soft, soothing. She leaned closer still and sniffed, and Thomas was pleased.

"Well?"

"There's no infection, but it will need cleaning again. I have better light now and more time. But I fear I will cause you pain."

"Pain is soon forgotten. Use the cloth and water to begin with. Then the alcohol, for I believe it cleans a wound better than water alone."

Lubna rose and filled a bowl with water. She stroked a wet cloth across his arm, teasing loose the flakes of dried blood, working harder against the clots that had formed. Thomas bit down hard and tried not to cry out, watching the back of her head as she bent in concentration, not wanting her to know how much she was hurting him.

Finally she was finished and Thomas inspected the wound.

"It's good work. You have a talent."

Lubna smiled.

"Now the alcohol. Pour it liberally into the wound, into any open sections, then apply more on a cloth and rebind the arm."

"You friend will be wondering where you are," Lubna said as she poured clear alcohol into the wound, taking care to treat every part.

"He'll still be asleep," Thomas said, and the strain in his voice stilled Lubna's hand and she sat on her heels and looked at him.

"This is hurting you."

"It's doing me good. The pain will pass. Finish the work. If you really mean to do this you have to learn there are times to ignore your patient's pain. We are still too ignorant of a reliable means to stop it. It must be possible, because opium dulls a pain. There will be other medicines too if we search long enough. Finish it. Work fast and hard, and ignore me."

Lubna did as he told her. "Is this the reason you are called by that name?"

"What name is that?" Although he knew the one she meant.

"Butcher," she said. "*Qassab.*"

"Ignorance."

"So there's no truth in it? I have heard my father call you it."

"Ignorance," he said again. "There are physicians in this city who would have their patients love them. I would rather my patients live."

"Many don't," Lubna said. There was no trace of accusation in her voice. She continued working, rebinding his arm.

"You know what I am," Thomas said. "You said yourself we first met on a battlefield. There's no time for softness when lives are at stake."

"Why do you do it?" She checked the tightness of the bandage, stood and returned the instruments to the bench, standing with her back to him.

"It's my job."

"There are those who refuse."

"All the more reason for me to do it. This land is at war. To pretend otherwise is foolish. Turning away doesn't make the danger less. And without me many soldiers would have died. We need all the soldiers we can get."

"*Ajami* soldiers," Lubna said, "like my father."

Thomas was about to say 'He's a good man', then recalled his suspicions of Olaf. Instead he said, "It's how things work here."

"The Moors should fight for themselves."

"Some do."

"Not many."

"The Sultan does, his sons, too."

"Few others. I despair at my countrymen. Don't they realise what is being lost?" Her shoulders hunched as she washed the instruments. "This is our land. We have as much right to it as the Spanish."

Thomas said nothing, knowing what she said was true, but he was a stranger here, too.

He left Lubna tidying the workshop while he ascended to his bedchamber. He tossed the bundle of papers onto the unmade covers and stepped out of his torn and stained robes. The room was thick with the scent of Helena's body and perfume and he felt his manhood thicken, despising his own reaction even as it sent a thrill through his belly. He wished he could be as other men, those who never experienced guilt over their lusts, wished he didn't have to debate with himself about such things as much as he did.

He washed as best he could and dressed in fresh clothes. Then he sat on the bed and opened the papers. There were only eight sheets, written on both sides in a small, neat hand; the unmistakeable hand of a scribe. Bilal had tried to hide their content by using Greek, and Thomas's was rusty. He sat and started to read. When he was finished he went back to the first page and read the words again.

"I cleaned your instruments," Lubna said over her shoulder. "I placed them in boiling water and wiped them with alcohol. Is that sufficient?"

Thomas tossed the bundle of papers onto the bench. "You said you didn't read these?"

Lubna glanced at them. "Couldn't, not didn't."

"He accuses the Sultan's son."

"Which one, and by which mother?"

"Muhammed. Yusuf would never betray his father."

"Was this Bilal a clever man?"

"I think so, yes."

"As clever as you?"

Thomas shrugged. He didn't believe in false modesty. Why pretend to the lack of something when it was self-evident? "Not as clever as me perhaps, but clever enough. I'm not sure what you're saying. Do you believe his claim or not?"

"He worked in the palace, didn't he?"

"For the Vizier. I know where you're going with this. And yes, Bilal would have possessed a political sensitivity greater than mine."

"Take them to Jorge, ask what he thinks."

"Jorge can't read Arabic, let alone Greek."

"But he can listen, can't he?"

"Are you going to tell me what you think?"

Lubna shook her head. "Not yet. Now—did I do right cleaning your instruments?"

Thomas swept his fingers back through his hair. Why did he only gather awkward women around him? "When did you learn to do that?"

"I've been watching you, and reading the books you gave me." Her vibrant, mismatched eyes sparked. "You have so many books."

Thomas looked at the shelves lining one wall of the workshop. He had grown so used to the pages they held he had forgotten how they might look to someone else.

"They contain the knowledge of centuries. Some can be traced to the time of the Greeks, others are Arabian, some from further East and from this land too, many from this land." He walked to the shelves, studying the parchments and bindings, their scent as always reminding him of his calling. He reached out. "This one is good when you finish the others. It's old, but we've forgotten a great deal since it was written and discovered little that's new. Study this, but make up your own mind. Don't close yourself to new experiences or learning and I will turn you into a surgeon yet."

"I will clean the house as well. And there is washing to be done. You might want to impart knowledge to me, but my sister regards me as her servant."

"Don't let her bully you."

"She isn't you, Thomas. She doesn't consider me other than what I can do for her. And truly, I don't mind. There are many hours between dawn and dusk, and I don't sleep away the afternoons like many others."

"I need to find Jorge and then return to the palace. I want to speak with your father if I can. The men who attacked me—"

"They were northmen, I know. I saw the hair of one, heard their speech, and one of their names."

"I know, you told me, but did you hear anything else? Did you hear what was said?"

"All I heard was as they ran, and most of it concerned your lack of parentage. They hadn't expected you to fight like you did. Certainly hadn't expected you to be as skilled."

"Exactly how much did you witness?"

"Enough. As they made their escape I overhead one say 'He will be displeased we have failed', and the other replied, 'He is only a surgeon, no threat to anyone. The eunuch is the danger'. And then they were gone, still talking, but I could make out no more."

"That was enough. Thank you. But you should have told me this last night."

"You needed rest."

Thomas felt an upwelling of gratitude, an urge to pull her slim body inside his arms and hug her. He bore down hard on his emotions and turned away. "You've been of assistance in more ways than you can know. I hope to return before dark, but who knows?"

As he left the house the alleyway outside showed no sign of the disturbance of the night. Thomas felt a momentum building. His attackers had fled, but he had the name of one of them, and their nationality. Olaf might know more, and if he didn't, if he showed reluctance... well, that would be progress, too. The documents he clutched in his hand appeared to prove Lubna's father innocent. Thomas wanted Jorge's opinion, but hoped he agreed with the findings—Olaf would make a far better friend than enemy.

Thomas increased his pace, eager to talk with Jorge, concerned about Lubna's comments, which meant his friend might now be in danger.

TWENTY-EIGHT

"**M**uhammed?" Jorge said. He had lain on the bed while Thomas sat at the small table and read the document to him. He only needed to hear it the once. "I can understand him wanting to oust his father, but why kill Safya? What benefit does that bring?"

"Safya is new information that Bilal didn't have. He couldn't know what was going to happen in the future, only what had happened in the past. Remember he undertook his investigation months ago. The logic was sound at the time. He identified the attack on Helena and Yasmina as a mistaken attempt on Zoraya. Helena said it was Yasmina who was being attacked, but memory is a fragile thing, and in the darkness who knows what the killer saw? But we know why Muhammed would want Zoraya dead."

"And the girls? Why kill the servants?"

"Practice," Thomas said.

"You can be cold sometimes," Jorge said. "They were my girls. They are all my girls."

"So you keep saying. Then revenge them."

Jorge raised his head and stared at Thomas. "Are you convinced by those papers?"

"I believe I am."

"Hm." Jorge sat up, swung his legs to the floor. "I'm not."

"Did Bilal make a mistake?"

"Not at the time. But events have moved on. I can't believe Muhammed is behind an attack on Safya. She was not his mother, but she was part of the inner circle in the harem, and close to his real mother. He wouldn't attack anyone there."

"I'm not the only cold one," Thomas said. "Once Muhammed

gets rid of Zoraya he'll have to dispose of her children, too. They're the real threat to his inheritance."

"What inheritance? If the Sultan found out his son had killed Zoraya, Muhammed would be executed, prince or not. You might be cold, but a Sultan's heart is made of ice."

"Which is why Safya was killed. Zoraya will be next. Even his own mother might be in danger. You can't kill one Sultana without killing them all. Muhammed wants his father's position. Abu al-Hasan Ali would have to die, possibly even before his wives. For all we know he's already dead. It would be a simple matter to sneak an assassin into his company."

"No," Jorge said. He stood and paced the room, clearly upset. "You might be right, but I need proof before I believe it."

"Then we will get proof."

"From where?"

"Olaf," Thomas said. "Those men who attacked me were sent by someone—most likely Muhammed himself. Olaf will know who they are. I have a name. And they're both injured."

"As are you," Jorge said. "You should take a few days to recover."

"There's nothing wrong with me. Besides, we can't stop now." Thomas rose and grabbed Jorge by the shoulders, stopping his pacing.

"I should have been with you," Jorge said. "Those men wouldn't have attacked two together."

"How skilled are you in swordplay? Does a eunuch of the harem get much practice in arms?"

"You got lucky, didn't you? Besides, don't underestimate this eunuch. Sometimes more is expected of us than simply pandering to the wishes of our ladies. I decided long ago looking beautiful wasn't enough and learned how to use a sword. I considered it wise in case my charges are attacked. But at the moment I was needed, when Safya was in danger, where was I?"

"The palace is meant to be safe, and you can't be everywhere at once."

"I wish it had been otherwise."

"I meant no criticism. Had you been there you would likely be dead as well."

"And Safya alive. I would gladly make that sacrifice."

"Wish all you want, we have to accept what the fates send us. But now there is something to go after." Thomas had told Jorge everything he knew, including what Lubna had translated, and the still mysterious knowledge that put him in danger.

"Why am I a threat?"

"You know something, or at least they believe you know something."

Jorge shook his head. "I know nothing. Nothing at all."

"I will tease it from you when we have time." Thomas released Jorge and led the way from the room, walking fast.

"Is Olaf Torvaldsson to be trusted?" Thomas had told Jorge he intended to find the soldier first. "These men are from his land. What if they're in it together? You escaped last night, Thomas, but Torvaldsson is another matter entirely. That man kills for pleasure, and he's good at it."

"I've seen the light in his eyes when he looks at his children, when he looks at his wife. Savage he may be, but only when he needs, and there's a gentleness in his heart for those he loves."

"And he loves you, does he? Only yesterday you were convinced of his guilt."

"He loves his daughter who is in my care. Two daughters now."

"There are many would be jealous. Two sisters living under your roof. There'll be gossip circulating already."

They walked out into the square, which was starting to grow busy. People and animals and goods moved to and fro, the air loud with conversation, barks and brays, thick with the scent of fruit and spices. It was later than Thomas had hoped and he wished Lubna had not let him sleep so long.

"Talk. Nothing more than talk. Lubna did well stitching my arm—I'm thinking of training her. She would make a fine nurse." Thomas didn't mention the confusion of emotions she raised within him, although he knew Jorge was just the man to talk of them with, and was tempted to open himself up.

"If there's talk you'd be a fool not to give it substance. I would."

"I'm sure you would."

"Supposing the old northman is willing to help us, supposing he knows who these men are, or recognises a name. What do we do then? Do you believe one of them is our killer?"

"No. The killer is a better warrior than either of those two. If it had been him I would be dead. But they may know who he is. They will certainly know who their orders came from."

"They won't have come from Muhammed directly, not if he's really behind the plot."

"Agreed. But there will be a trail leading to him."

"Are you going to tell Olaf you suspect Muhammed?"

Thomas cast a glance at Jorge. "I'm not that stupid."

Olaf Torvaldsson laughed. "Sven? Is that all you've got to go on?"

"At least it's something. One of them was dark haired, the other light, like you."

"Do you know how many northmen there are in Gharnatah?"

"Not exactly, no."

"Well I do. It's my job to know. I know to the last man. There are seven hundred and forty-three. Not all within the city walls at one time, but that is the count I can call on when required. And do you know how many of those men are called Sven?"

Thomas shook his head, feeling like a child being scolded.

"At least an eighth, possibly more. I will get a roster of Sven's drawn up if you wish, but are you going to speak to all of them? And some will be on patrol, some on loan to other cities. It would be like trying to pin down a hundred cats. As fast as you finish with one everything will have changed."

"They won't all have blonde hair," Thomas said.

"But you don't know that man was Sven. It was dark. You saw one light and one dark haired man. That covers about every Sven I have. You need to bring me more than a name."

"I don't have more."

Olaf shook his head. The three of them stood in what passed for his offices, although the room lacked even a desk. Olaf wasn't a man to sit when he could stand, not a man to stand when he could walk. He paced now, to the window, to the door, across to the wall where shelves held papers—likely the list of Sven's—back to the window. It looked across a dirt square where soldiers drilled and practiced.

He stopped, his back to the window, and crossed his arms.

"Tell me more of the attack. Were you hurt?"

"A scratch, nothing more," Thomas said, making light of his injuries.

"Show me," Olaf said.

"Why?"

Olaf lowered his brow, obviously not used to being questioned. "Because I ask it. Show me this scratch."

Thomas pulled back the sleeve of his robe and extended his arm. "It's bound up. Your daughter did this for me."

"Helena? Helena bandaged your arm?" The incredulity was thick in Olaf's voice.

"Lubna."

"Of course. She always did show interest in things it wasn't her place to know."

"She could be a fine help to me."

Olaf shook his head. "She serves you now, do as you wish. No doubt you are her best employer yet, so I have no fears in that direction. I cannot see your so called wound with all this stuff around it."

"I would prefer not to untie it."

"Eunuch, help him. I need to see the wound if I am to help."

Thomas knew he either had to untie the bandage or withdraw, and he was not ready to give in. He had no idea why Olaf needed to see his arm, but Olaf obviously had a reason.

Thomas raised his arm and tugged at the knotted linen with his teeth.

"Let me do it," Jorge said, stepping to his side.

"You don't look so much like a eunuch today," Olaf said.

"I'm glad to hear it. You still look like a soldier."

"I'm glad to hear that, too." Olaf directed his attention back to Thomas, watching as Jorge unwound the linen. The bandage was cleaner than the one Lubna had removed that morning, barely stained with blood, but as the arm revealed itself the wound was red and bruised, the stitches weeping. Thomas took the opportunity to study himself dispassionately. He decided there was nothing to worry about. A dull ache filled his arm to the shoulder, but he knew that would pass in time.

Olaf leaned close, not touching, his face hovering to take in the spectacle presented him.

"It was a sharp blade," he said.

"A scimitar."

"Scimitar? Northmen don't fight with scimitars. Are you sure you have this right, Thomas?"

"They both carried scimitars."

"And you had what, a sword of your own?"

"A knife."

"A knife? A big knife?"

"A small knife. Middle sized at best."

Olaf straightened. "You're telling me you were attacked by two northmen, in the dark, and you saw them off with a middle sized knife, receiving only this scratch in return?"

"It's hardly a scratch," Thomas said.

"Hm."

"And I injured them, one badly I think. My knife went into his side, about here." Thomas patted his own chest on the left, low down where the ribs ended. "Wrong side for his liver, but he'll be damaged, I swear to it."

"My God, you are a mystery to me, Thomas Berrington. I have great respect for you, for your profession, and you seem to treat my daughter well—damn it, both my daughters now. Are you trying to create your own harem? Ignore that. What I'm saying is, if these were my men you are either the best fighter I have seen in a long time, or they were not my men. If I had sent men to kill you, you would be dead by now."

Thomas was unsure how to take the outburst. Had Olaf forgotten their fight in front of Zoraya's children already?

"Are there other northmen?"

"A few, I'm sure. The Vizier employs his own troops, there could be some in his offices. And no doubt there are others who came down because they hear of the riches of al-Andalus, its luxury, its gold, its abundance of food..." Olaf smiled. "And even after they discover the lie they don't return home. So what I'm saying is searching among *my* northmen is a waste of time. Look elsewhere."

"Help me," Thomas said, but he was addressing Jorge, who proceeded to re-bandage his arm. "Then how do I proceed? We are two against who knows how many. Where do I start?"

Olaf shook his head. "Ask, but I have no answer. I'm not a clever man. I obey orders, go where I am told, kill who I'm asked to, but I don't think beyond that. You're the one with a brain in his head instead of straw. I leave this work to you."

Thomas knew Olaf underestimated himself, knew equally well he was impossible to argue with. It was as if the man regarded stubbornness as a positive trait.

"Then we will seek. One of them is injured, I know that—"

"As injured as you believe?"

Thomas heard the incredulity that remained in Olaf's voice, but he was sure of what his senses told him. "I felt the knife go in. I twisted. The blade caught on something, a rib almost certainly, and was pulled from my grasp. So we are looking for a man who would have bled greatly, in possession of a middle sized knife that is not his own."

"I'll ask around. It's possible my men may know something. They have friends, and we of the north stick close together. Even you, Thomas Berrington, might have northern blood running through your veins. Try to keep it there and spill no more, for the sake of my daughters."

"Send a message if you discover something, however small."

"I will come myself."

"And stay for dinner," Thomas said.

Olaf frowned. "Who will cook, Helena or Lubna?"

"Helena seems to have lost any small love of cooking she might once have had since her sister arrived."

"Then I may stay and eat. Now return to your quest, and I will pass word quietly to a few of my most trusted men. News of this attack shouldn't spread for fear the culprits flee, or return to silence you as they meant."

Twenty-Nine

"So, what now?" Jorge asked as they walked from the barracks through hot morning sunshine. The scent of flowering bushes filled the air, the sound of running water carried on the breeze, but the glittering beauty of the palace felt distant, separated behind an invisible barrier.

"According to Olaf, the Vizier employs northmen, too. We need to speak with him."

"Without an appointment?"

"I have the Sultan's seal." Despite the attack it remained safe in the pocket of his robe, transferred that morning to a fresh one.

"As does he. He's a cold fish—do you trust him?"

"He's odd, certainly, but he's the Sultan's man. Whoever's behind this has a deeper motive than simple murder. But I want to see someone else before we go to his offices."

"Who might that be?"

"Your friend." Thomas smiled. "Bazzu, and Prea."

Jorge laughed. "*Your* little friend. What else did you get up to in those tunnels? Did spying on the women get your blood boiling so hot you had to take her there and then?"

"Don't judge all men by your own standards," Thomas said. "Besides, I have seen practically every woman of the harem naked."

"Ah, but that was work, wasn't it? It must be different when you're hidden, spying on them from a secret vantage point. Very different indeed."

He was about to press Jorge on how he knew about such things, but they were approaching the palace and almost at the kitchens, serving girls and boys running to and fro, and

Thomas realised it was close to noon. Soon the faithful would be called to prayer, and on their return would want to eat. He increased his pace, wanting to find Bazzu before she was called away.

As they approached the kitchens, Thomas saw a familiar slim figure ahead and called out, "Prea! Stop a moment." He trotted up as the girl slowed, but when she turned it wasn't whom he thought.

"Can I help you, sir?"

"I'm sorry, I thought you were someone else." Even close to, there was a remarkable similarity. Her height, her colouring, her hair, even her eyes and features.

"Are you looking for Prea?" the girl said.

"You know her?"

His question was greeted with a laugh, momentarily covered by a hand. "We share a room, of course I know her. You're Thomas the surgeon, aren't you. She has told me all about you." A smile.

He was unsure what to make of the news, or the smile, which was too knowing. "Do you know where she is?"

"Working. Our duties keep us apart during the day."

"Bazzu will know," Jorge said, having come to join them, and the girl, sensing their interest in her had reached an end, darted off on whatever errand Thomas had interrupted.

They found Bazzu in her usual lair, the kitchen beyond a hive of activity. She embraced Thomas, even pecked his cheek, and when he asked to speak with Prea she called a maid and sent her to find the girl.

"She was of help to you?" she asked, slipping behind her desk, papers neatly arranged before her, lists of special requirements, recipes, notes on expected visitors and their preferences. Thomas read a few scraps upside down, noticed one that stated: *Spanish Priest—bread and water*, and wondered if it was the man's wish, or some punishment for being an infidel.

"A great help. I trust you didn't spread word of our undertaking?"

"Not about what you told me you were doing." No wonder Jorge got along so well with this woman, they were cut of the same cloth.

"It wouldn't do for anyone—and I mean anyone other than us here—to know of what she showed me. The man who first told me of these passages is dead. Another man was killed only yesterday. I wouldn't have the same fate befall you or Prea."

"We are no threat to anyone, but you are right. No-one will know your secret." Her eyes glittered and he gave in.

Prea arrived silently on bare feet and Thomas left Jorge and Bazzu to talk together as he led her aside. Once alone she took his hand and tugged him.

"You got my message then? I have something to show you, Thomas. Something important."

"What message?"

"I came to your house yesterday and left it with your woman. Bazzu helped me write it. I have some words, but not enough."

"That was you? You should have left your name."

"My name was on the note."

"Whatever it was will have to wait. You haven't told anyone else about what you showed me, have you?"

"Only Bazzu. You asked me to keep my silence and I have."

"And the money I gave you?"

Prea's face turned hard. "If it was too much, sir, I have not spent a single coin. I will return it all."

"I don't want it back. If anything I didn't pay you enough-"

"I have never seen so much money in my life. I thank you with all my heart, Thomas."

"But you can't spend any of it. Not for now, at least. Can you be patient?"

"I can wait. It's many times more than I ever possessed before. The spending will prove all the sweeter for waiting, if that is what you ask."

"I will try and come back as soon as I can."

"I'm at your call, day or night, you need only ask."

Thomas wondered as he walked back to Bazzu's office

whether he had not indeed paid her too much, and whether she had misinterpreted his generosity. It wasn't unknown for wealthy men to buy the services of girls as young as Prea for their pleasure. He wouldn't have her entertain he held such ideas, but had no simple way of telling her short of blurting it out, and knew she would simply deny any such suspicion were he to do so.

Jorge sat on the corner of Bazzu's desk and Thomas was sure, in the moment before he approached, her hand rested on his thigh, both of them drawing apart as he entered the room.

"There was a man here asking for us," Jorge said, standing and coming around to his side of the desk.

"On what business?"

"You said you wanted to see the Vizier—well it seems the Vizier wants to see us. This instant."

"That saves us the trouble of making an appointment. I thank you once more, Bazzu, and remember what I said."

She waved a hand. "You doubt my memory, surgeon? Help yourself to some sweetmeats as you pass through the kitchen. You look as though you need feeding up."

Thomas and Jorge nibbled at morsels of fruit wrapped inside strips of lamb and pigeon. They returned the way they had come, before turning to follow the opposite ridge of the hill to the Vizier's palace. Less grand than al-Hamra, it was still an imposing structure, and was where the real power of Gharnatah lay. The Sultan was a figurehead and general. It was the Vizier who made the city run, collected taxes, paid mercenaries, bribed enemies to stay their hand. Tahir al-Ifriqi was a teak-dark Berber who had crossed the narrow sea as a boy and risen through the ranks. He owed nothing of his position to patronage, and was perhaps sterner as a result. He ran his own parallel seat of power, employing troops loyal only to him. As they made their way to his chambers Thomas tried to decide how much he could reveal.

They were expected, a guard despatched to the gate to escort them inside. As they entered the Vizier's public room Thomas was surprised to find company, and strange company at that.

The cleric Abd al-Wahid al-Mursi might have been half expected, dressed as always in black, but the other man was an anomaly and should never have been in the same room as the first. He too was dressed in black, but instead of a turban covering his hair he wore a wide-brimmed hat, and hanging against his chest was a large silver cross. A Catholic priest, here in the grounds of al-Hamra.

Thomas and Jorge bowed to Tahir.

"I hear you were injured, Thomas Berrington," Abd al-Wahid said. "I trust your wounds are not serious."

"A scratch, no more," Thomas replied, sure these three would not want him to remove the bandage to check his honesty. "We are making progress, your honour." He addressed himself to the Vizier. "I have some questions, but don't wish to bother you with trifling matters. If you permit me I would speak with your chief guard about the men who attacked me."

"Should there be time, perhaps, but there are more pressing matters."

"More pressing than murder?" Jorge said, and Thomas sent a sharp glance his way. They should not antagonise the Vizier.

"Politics is always more pressing that murder, eunuch." The contempt the Vizier held for Jorge was clear in his voice, which softened as he shifted to address Thomas. "You know Qurtuba, I believe?"

"I have visited there. The library, when I was young, but most of the books had been destroyed by then."

"Heresy has no place in a godly city." The priest spoke in stilted Arabic, his soft voice belying the harshness of his words. Thomas glanced his way, but no-one else appeared to even hear what was said, so he bit back a reply, wanting to ask what heresy there was in knowledge.

"I want you to go there on a mission for the Sultan, and also to assist this gentleman and his superiors."

"We are in the middle of a pursuit, your honour. I am, of

course, at your command, but do I need to remind you this task was given me by the Sultan himself?"

"I have spoken with him on the matter, and he agrees with me that this takes precedence. You can be of great service to your country. You too, eunuch."

"Thank you, sir," Jorge said, but if the Vizier recognised sarcasm he chose to let it pass.

"Let me at least speak with your general, Vizier, if only to ask him to do something while we are away." Thomas knew refusal was impossible. He had no idea why they were being sent away now, or on what pretext, only that he felt a momentum building that couldn't be wasted.

"There is no time. Tell me what it is you want and I will pass a message on. Time is of the essence here, and you leave before the day ends."

"I must return to my house and make arrangements. I have patients to care for. A household to organise. And I must send a report to the Sultan before sunset."

"Once more, a message will be sent."

"I need clothes for travelling, your honour, or—"

"Enough! I will stand no dissension." The Vizier stood, trembling. For a moment Thomas feared he would strike him. Then the man breathed deeply and calmed himself. "Walk with me, Thomas, I would speak with you in private. This man will instruct you further, eunuch."

Jorge turned to face the Catholic priest, who was stony faced.

"I take no orders from an infidel priest!"

"He will give you no order," the Vizier said, his voice cold, "only information. Thomas will carry the message I wish to pass to the powers in Qurtuba."

"Their graces the King and Queen of Spain, their highnesses Ferdinand of Aragon and Isab—"

"Yes, yes, we know who they are. Thomas, come. Eunuch, remain here and try not to kill our friend before I return."

Thomas glanced at a scowling Jorge and followed the Vizier

into the garden.

"Why are we being sent away?" Thomas said. "I have proof of who is behind the killings." Thomas had not intended to show his hand, but he needed some way to prevent the Vizier sending them away.

"Is your proof the same as that the scribe brought me?"

"His name was Bilal abd al-Rhaman."

The Vizier waved a dismissive hand. "Yes, something like that. He came and made foolish allegations. False, of course. He couldn't remain in the palace after making up such lies."

"I believe he was an honourable man."

The Vizier stopped next to an orange tree and reached out, plucking a white flower and holding it to his nose. The scent of the flowers filled the small courtyard, rich and cloying.

"He was a dangerous man. As you will be if you continue with false accusations. Do you understand what I am saying?"

Thomas felt the heat rise through him. "Yes, I understand. But I'm a surgeon, not a diplomat."

"Which is why several weeks away from the city will be good for your health."

"I'm not going," Thomas said.

"Of course you are. The priest comes with a request from the Spanish royal palace, one which cannot have been made lightly."

Thomas shook his head. "Why choose me, when we are close to—"

Once more the dismissive wave. "We have been asked to send our best surgeon to Qurtuba, where a young prince lies injured."

"The Spanish have doctors of their own."

The Vizier made a sound through his nose. "We both know the quality of Spanish doctors. There is more of superstition and hope in their treatment than science. They may not like it, but their majesties are not stupid."

"If this prince is injured, he's likely dead by now. How far is it to Qurtuba? A week? At least a week since they sent their priest, another for us to return. He will be dead before we even set out."

"Do you take me for a fool? I have asked all of these questions. It is a matter of bones, it seems, something broken that will not set. Their own physicians have tried and failed, and so they seek our help. Privately, of course. No-one can know this."

"The Sultan—"

"Do you believe the Sultan does not know? It was his idea to send you. I have to admit I had someone else in mind, but he said you are the best surgeon in the whole of Spain. He was insistent."

Thomas wondered how the Vizier had access to the Sultan while he did not. It felt as though their investigation—the closer it came to success—was being baulked.

"Why would the Sultan help the Spanish? And what of this other duty he has given me?"

"He said you were making little progress. He should not have chosen you in the first place, should not have put you in danger. He knows you are a man of peace, not war. This new duty is more suited to your skills, is it not?"

"But we *are* making progress." Thomas's head spun with too many conflicting suspicions.

"The same progress the scribe claimed he had made? I have already told you his suspicions had no foundation in truth. Don't make the same mistake he did. Go to Qurtuba. When you return my men will have found the true culprit and you can return to your peaceful life."

They had reached the far end of the courtyard and the Vizier stopped, turned and waited.

"I refuse," Thomas said.

"You spurn me, spurn your Sultan?"

Thomas looked back along the courtyard. He could see Jorge standing beside the dark-robed priest, both men looking away from each other. Could he make the decision for Jorge, too? Was there any choice? He took a deep breath, filling his lungs with the sweet air.

"Yes. I refuse the task. I already have one that is more important. Send the man you preferred and let me finish what I have started."

"You cannot refuse." The Vizier's voice was soft. Thomas would have preferred anger.

"But I do."

"Are you aware of the consequences?"

"No, but I still refuse."

The Vizier's face reflected an inner pain. "Then you are cast out." He lowered his gaze, shook his head. "Go. Take that creature with you and leave the palace, both of you, and never return."

Thirty

There was nowhere to go but home, but first they had to follow the convoluted corridors of the palace to reach the outside world.

"Did you have to make the decision on my behalf?" Jorge said.

"They didn't want you, only me, but they saw us working together, that is all."

"And still you included me?" Jorge's voice was tight with anger.

Anger at me, Thomas thought, and wondered if he could have done things differently. He was no diplomat. Jorge should have been with him, he might have made a better decision.

"I didn't include you, they did. You're tainted by association, and for that I'm truly sorry. But you know we can't go to Qurtuba, don't you? Spend at least two weeks away, likely more? How many others would be dead on our return?"

"Maybe none. This might be the end of it. Did you tell him about your suspicions of Muhammed?"

"He already knew. He called them foolish."

"So you have banished us for nothing!" Jorge's voice rose. "You have banished *me*! This place is my home. I know or want no other, and now I'm never to return?" He shook his head, sharp tears in his eyes. "What have you done? Can you even begin to comprehend what it is you have done?"

"They will forget," Thomas said. "A week. A month. They will forget and forgive. Likely not me, but you they will forgive. They know this is my doing, not yours."

"We will end up like Bilal. Power protects itself. What have you done, Thomas? I am disgraced by you."

"We are no scribes. I am a supposed friend to the Sultan, you an honoured eunuch. Can you see your women allowing you to be banished?"

Jorge snorted. "Sometimes I wonder how you have managed to live so long. Well—that state of affairs could change soon."

"If we left now we would be traitors. My loyalty lies with the Sultan, not his Vizier."

"The Vizier *is* the Sultan. Why else was he sent a message?" Jorge walked faster, trying to distance himself.

Thomas grabbed at him before he could move away. Jorge turned, pushing Thomas hard, his arms strong and Thomas still weak.

"All right, go ahead." Thomas steeled himself for blows. "Hit me if it makes you feel better, then go show my bruised face to the Vizier and say you'll go to Qurtuba with his other physician. Save yourself, Jorge."

"It's not me they want. Why would they send a eunuch unless I was with you? We are bound together and I wish you had never come to me!"

Thomas lowered his face and waited to be struck. Instead Jorge stepped close and drew him against his chest, drew him into a tight embrace as he began to weep.

"You are a mad man, Thomas Berrington. But I love you like a brother. I will not abandon you now."

"Nor our task?" Thomas's words emerged muffled against the taller man's chest. It was curiously comforting to be held this way, even by another man. Especially by this man.

Jorge's chest hitched. "Our task is ended. We are cast into the wind. We have no access, no assistance from any quarter. The killer will go free, his master undiscovered, and we must make what we can of our lives."

Thomas waited, allowing Jorge to release his pain. When he finally loosened his hold Thomas held his arms and looked into his friend's face.

"No—I think if you go back you will be forgiven. They know this is all down to me."

"Don't disrespect me, Thomas. Have I had no part to play in any of this? It's not who I am, it's what I know that banishes me." Jorge shook his head. "They never wanted the truth, only a cover-up." He made a noise, half laugh, half sob. "What useless creatures are they to pick first the scribe and then us, expecting both to fail?"

"They wanted us to fail, didn't they? What are you going to do?"

"What can I do? I am a eunuch. All I know is how to please my ladies, how to care for them."

"There are other harems. You could go to Malaka. To al-Muneckhar."

"My place is in this palace. I will find somewhere to hide and wait for the disgrace to pass, if it ever does. I'm strong enough, and I can be subtle when needs require. And you have friends. Perhaps one of them has a place for the likes of me in their household. I will do what I have to and hope, one day, I am able to return."

"I had friends," Thomas said. "Once word spreads they will fade like the morning mist over the Hadarro."

Jorge looked along the corridor. "I think it wise we leave by a less subtle exit than the main entrance."

"You know of somewhere?"

Jorge smiled and wiped the back of his hand across his eyes. "Of course I know of somewhere."

"What are you doing home?" Helena's face showed a coldness it frequently exhibited when Thomas annoyed her.

"I live here. This is my house." They stood in the main room, a wide doorway looking onto the courtyard where Lubna had finished hanging the washing and now pushed a brush around, picking up fallen leaves, feathers and dust.

"You were sent for by the Vizier."

"I was, and now I'm back."

"But—but—"

"I'll go and say hello to Lubna," Jorge said, stepping around

Thomas.

"What is he doing here?" Helena asked.

"You know full well why he's here. We're working together on Safya's murder. What is wrong with you, Helena? I thought you'd be glad to see me."

"You're not meant to be here!"

"In my own house? Why not? And…" Something in what she had said rose to the surface. "How did you know the Vizier sent for me?"

"It's all over town." Helena waved her hand as though Thomas was an idiot. "I heard he was sending you away. Something to do with the Spanish king and queen, although why we would be helping them, I don't know. When is it you leave, Thomas? Soon?"

"You want me gone so badly?"

Something changed in Helena's face, some realisation she might have pushed too hard. A sly look settled in her eyes, one Thomas had noticed more of recently. He believed she thought the look seductive, but he had grown to associate it purely with her needs, not his.

"I want you in my bed, Thomas, of course I do. But a summons from the Vizier can't be ignored. He's an important man. Think what this will do for your career."

"I don't have a career. I have a calling. And I doubt I have either any longer."

"We could be living on the hill again. Not in the palace, perhaps, but the Alkazaba is a hundred times better than… than *this*!"

"I like this."

"And I don't. I'm used to refinement and luxury and servants. I can't live this way any longer."

He stared at her. How long had she felt this way? All the time she had lived under his roof?

"Then leave!" Thomas snapped. "If I make you so unhappy, go—make your own way in the world."

Her face changed again, collapsing in on itself, tears flooding her eyes in an instant. "I'm sorry. I have overstepped my place, and I apologise."

"I'm not staying."

Helena stepped towards him, her face tilting to the side so hair fell across her scar. "Oh, Thomas, I have angered you without need. Of course I will miss you. Both here, and here." She touched a hand between her breasts, over her heart, and then again on her belly, low down. "So you will go to Qurtuba? For me? When do you leave? Have we time to go upstairs one last time?"

One last time? Did she really mean to say that?

"Jorge is waiting. And I'm not going to Qurtuba. We're close on the trail of our killer. I can almost taste him on my tongue. Now's not the time to abandon the chase. But I won't return here until I have him. Don't overwork Lubna. I hope this matter will be concluded within days, a week at most." He leaned in to kiss her cheek but she drew away.

From beyond the courtyard the sound of the muezzin calling afternoon prayer floated through the air. Helena turned her head at the sound.

"I must pray," she said, moving quickly towards the door, drawing her scarf across her head and face, leaving only sharp blue eyes exposed.

"Pray?"

"Yes, the muezzin is calling the faithful. I will see you on your return. Try not to get yourself hurt any more than you already are."

With that she was gone. Thomas stood in the centre of the room, puzzling through the encounter. He tried to remember the last time Helena had shown the slightest interest in prayer. She must have done so with the others in the harem, but he hadn't seen any sign since.

He ascended the stairs. He had enough concerns without adding Helena's sudden conversion to the list. He threw clothes into a bag, returned to the courtyard to find Jorge and Lubna in conversation, sitting side by side on the bench beneath the balcony. Thomas felt a momentary pang of jealousy and dismissed it. He had nothing to be jealous about; nothing at all.

"Be ready to leave," Thomas said, and Jorge nodded. Thomas went to his workshop and took down a leather satchel, began to pack herbs and potions inside, as well as a sample of instruments, not sure what might be needed, unwilling to abandon his home without at least something.

There was a textbook open on the bench and he moved it aside, sensed a presence and turned to find Lubna beside him.

"I started reading that one," she said, reaching to take the book. She marked her place with a feather and closed it, then pressed against his side as she reached across, remained pressed against him even after she had returned the book.

"Did you know Helena prayed at the mosque?" Thomas asked, her sudden departure still puzzling him.

"Helena? Pray? You mean my sister Helena? Or surely some other I'm not familiar with. It is *Asar* already? I didn't hear the call."

"It's a little after. You were talking to Jorge."

"Excuse me, I will be in the courtyard. If I'm finished before you leave remember to say goodbye."

Jorge had come in and sat on the cot, watching the conversation without expression. Thomas scowled, making Jorge laugh.

"What," Thomas said. "You're going to tell me you want to pray as well?"

"I have done so at times, certainly," Jorge said, "but only because my masters expected it of me. You know I follow no gods other than the god of sensuality."

"Ah, that one." Thomas continued filling his satchel, looking around, trying to decide what else might be needed. He saw a bottle containing extract of poppy and added it, together with a sticky cube of hemp resin. He could think of nothing else, so went to sit on the cot beside Jorge.

"Are we leaving?" Jorge asked.

"In a moment. I want to say goodbye first."

"She said only if she had finished."

"We'll wait."

Thomas returned to the bench and opened a wide drawer. He stood for a long time looking at what lay inside as the soothing music of Lubna's prayers drifted in from the courtyard. Finally he reached in and withdrew the sword he hadn't worn since arriving in the city many years before. It was a little short, for he had been younger then, but it was better than a medium sized dagger. He tied the belt around his waist and covered the weapon with his robe.

When he turned Jorge was watching. "Do you believe we have need of weapons?"

Thomas gave a curt nod. "We would be foolish not to go prepared."

"I have nothing," Jorge said.

"I considered that might be the safest option, but you're right." Thomas turned and drew a second sword from the drawer, took it across to Jorge. Both possessed long, straight blades, unlike those carried by the Moors.

Jorge made no move to take the weapon.

"Do you want it or not?"

"What are you doing with two swords, Thomas? Or even one? These weapons are not new. But you have kept them honed and clean."

"You're right, they're not new. It would take too long to tell you why I possess them, but they are mine, both of them."

"And have seen fighting?"

Thomas nodded. "And have seen fighting, yes."

Finally Jorge took the offered sword and laid it across his knees.

Thomas sat beside him once more, the cot creaking as his weight settled. The two were silent, listening to the soft cadence of Lubna reciting the words of the prophet. She was just visible in the courtyard, sunk to her knees, legs splayed to one side, head covered as she faced east. Thomas watched the sway of her head, her shoulders. She had come to his house not a week since, but already her presence felt more a part of it than her sister who had lived there half a year.

Allāhu akbar

Allāhu akbar

Lā ilāha illallā

Lubna remained a moment longer, head bowed, then she rose in a single lithe movement and turned, her face lighting up to find the two of them still sitting inside the workshop.

"I thought you were gone. I expected you to be gone."

"We're going now. Jorge wanted to say goodbye before we went."

"I—" Jorge started to object, stopped. "I did. Of course I did." He rose and went to the tiny figure of Helena's sister and enclosed her in his arms, lifting her from her feet and swinging her around until she squealed with joy. Jorge deposited her on the tiled floor and kissed the top of her head. "Take care, little one."

"You too, big one." Lubna smiled and glanced shyly towards Thomas. He knew what he wanted to do, what she expected, but instead he only stood and nodded, the satchel already around his shoulder.

"We will return soon. Take care of your sister for me."

"I will, Thomas. Perhaps she will pray alongside me this evening."

"Perhaps she will."

He had reached the door to the alley when Lubna ran after him, stopping abruptly.

"You take care, too. No more fighting. And keep a watch out for this one," she said nodding at Jorge. "He might look dangerous, but I sense he is not."

Thomas smiled. "Oh, I know he is not. Goodbye, Lubna."

She came onto the street and waved as they made their way to the steps which would lead them into town. When Thomas turned back just before Lubna was lost from sight she was still waving.

THIRTY-ONE

The hottest part of the day was still to come and the city of Gharnatah slumbered the afternoon away, even the city's cats and dogs seeking shade. Jorge lay on the bed in his room while Thomas sat at the table, staring out through the open window onto the square. An occasional figure passed across it, but they moved slowly through waves of heat that shimmered from the flagstones.

"Why the haste?" Thomas said. "Why do they want us gone from the city so badly?"

"That thought crossed my mind, and there's only one reason I can think of. They want everything hushed up."

"They can't hide Muhammed's guilt and pretend nothing's happened."

"He's a prince. He might be Sultan one day, even sooner than we think. Powerful men work to different rules than you or I. Muhammed will have been taken aside, told he has been found out, but if he stops now all will be forgiven." Jorge's face reflected his pain, and Thomas knew this was hard on him, for he had lost people he loved.

"I can't just walk away," Thomas said.

Jorge stared at him. "You've fought before, haven't you?"

Thomas said nothing.

"You've fought against odds such as these. I see it in your eyes. See it in your lack of fear. You're not like me. I do this despite my fear. You?" Jorge shook his head. "You have none."

"I have plenty of fear," Thomas said.

"But only for others. Tell me, Thomas. I need to understand—why do you think we can win? What makes you believe we can possibly win now?"

"I haven't always won." Thomas smiled. "No, perhaps that's a lie. I thought I had lost, but that loss was what brought me here, through a long, circuitous route, so perhaps it was a victory as well, even if it didn't feel so at the time."

"Who was she?" Jorge said. "The woman you loved?"

"How long have you been thinking on that?"

"What was her name?"

"Eleanor," Thomas said, wondering why he was talking about her at all. Perhaps some of the poppy still clung to him, eroding his resistance. "And she wasn't a woman. She was a girl on the point of becoming a woman."

"How old were you?"

"Sixteen. We were both sixteen years old, but it felt like more."

"And you loved her." There was no hint of a question.

Thomas nodded, not meeting Jorge's eyes, but he knew they were on him. "Yes, I loved her."

"And you've never loved since."

Thomas shook his head. He felt emotions well inside him and pressed them down hard.

"Let your barriers down," Jorge said, as though he could see directly into Thomas's heart. "You have nothing to lose but the pain you carry. Allow someone else in. Not Helena, not that bitch. But Lubna. I can see how you feel about her. She feels the same about you. It would be funny if it wasn't so tragic."

"She's a—"

"Yes, yes, I know, you keep saying. She's a help to you. Does that stop you wanting her? What happened to her?"

Thomas knew Jorge had slipped into the past; they were back with Eleanor.

"I don't know. She was promised to someone else but she chose me. We were going to have…" No, he wouldn't go there. "We were ambushed. So many men against just the two of us. I fought. She did, too." He smiled and knew there were tears on his face. "She was a wild creature. You would have liked her."

"Are you sure? Go on."

"Too many men," Thomas said. "I was injured, then injured again. They took her, kicking and screaming and scratching. I lay on the ground bleeding my life away and watched them bundle her into the back of a cart and take her away to the man she was promised to. A count. Older than her by twenty years."

"But you didn't die. And I can't see you abandoning her, either."

"I didn't mean to. I woke a day later, still on the side of the road. People must have passed. It wasn't a quiet road, but no-one had stopped to help. No doubt they thought me dead. I lay there another night before I could move. A fox came sniffing at me and I scared it off. Then something larger, but I still had my sword. I dragged myself into the undergrowth and waited to die. Except I didn't. It was a week before I could move. Two before I could walk. She was gone. The count had fled with her, whereas I was never discovered." Thomas raised his gaze to meet Jorge's. "I looked for her. I spent half a year looking. Then his men came for me. I must have made myself known—all the questions, all the anger. This time they made sure. They threw me off a cliff."

Jorge sat silent. Thomas saw there were tears on his cheeks, too. Then Jorge smiled.

"Is it even possible to kill you?"

"I expect so."

"Why didn't you die?"

"I hit a tree growing from the cliff face. Hit it hard enough to break my arm and thigh. It should have been enough, stuck half way down a cliff wedged into a birch tree, but somehow I managed to climb down, although god knows how. This time I knew I wasn't going to make it so I crawled away, seeking high ground, and an old man discovered me and took me in." Thomas stood and walked across the room. "Make space. I'm tired of talking and want to sleep."

Jorge shifted his legs and Thomas fell across the bed. The moment he closed his eyes the world faded. He expected dreams but none came.

* * *

When he opened his eyes the room was still bathed with light, but he felt refreshed. Jorge was shaking him by the shoulder.

"I've remembered," he said.

"Good." Thomas draped an arm across his eyes. "What is it you've remembered?"

"Why I'm considered a danger."

Thomas sat up. "Go on."

"I know who the killer is, or I can identify him, at least."

"You—" Thomas banged his head against the wall. "You'll recognise the killer? Why didn't you wake me at once?"

"Because it won't do us any good until we find him."

"How do you know him?"

"Ever since you told me, I've been trying to work out what it is that marks me out, and failing. I don't lead an exciting life, not in that way. And then I thought back, wondering if this knowledge wasn't recent, and it came to me."

Thomas waited, saying nothing. Eventually Jorge went on, staring down at his hands, speaking softly.

"It was a month, perhaps two, before Helena was attacked. There were new guards, two or three of them, I think. They change the guards often, not wanting the same men close to the harem for too long. The temptation, you know." Jorge smiled. "There was this one man, a Berber, good looking, slim, friend-ly. Too friendly."

Thomas watched Jorge. "Too friendly? Do you mean he-"

Jorge waved a hand. "No, nothing like that. He asked ques-tions, as some men do. About life within the harem. Except... when I think about it, his questions were about specific mat-ters, too. How often the ladies bathed. Where they relaxed and conversed. He asked about the hierarchy, who had position, who didn't."

"You said many men ask questions, it's understandable. What was different about this one?"

"I'm a fool not to have seen it sooner." Jorge looked up, met Thomas's eyes. "The day after Helena was attacked I saw him.

He was shaken, upset. And I said, 'Don't worry, they won't blame you'. He almost jumped out of his skin, asking me what I meant. For a moment I thought he was going to strike me. It was the last time I saw him. The following day he was gone."

"Punished for his mistake?" Thomas said. "If that's the case then he's already dead."

"Perhaps. But secrets are hard to keep—his kind of killer even harder to find. Perhaps he was only pulled out for a time, given more information, told who his targets were, and then sent back."

"If you're right, and he is the murderer, it still brings us no closer to the person behind it."

"He was a guard. The guards are chosen from the ranks of the Sultan's troops. Do you think Olaf will allow us to interview each man? I would recognise him again, I'm sure." Jorge held up his left hand. "And he had two fingers missing." He closed the little and ring finger against his palm. "These two. Exactly as you described the marks on Alisha's body."

"We can't go to Olaf, not now. And how many troops are there in the city? A thousand?"

"Less within the walls."

"Which means less chance he's still here. But you're right, we have to try. When the light fades we'll try to find Olaf and see if he's willing to help."

Thomas pushed off the bed and went to the small window looking for some fresh air. The square remained almost deserted, still an hour before people left their houses. On the far side five soldiers appeared from the roadway leading to al-Hamra. Thomas watched the certainty of their movement, their single-mindedness. They wavered neither left nor right, coming directly towards the inn.

"Off the bed now—we're leaving."

"It's too soon. We should wait an hour at least, preferably two."

"Wait if you want, but there are men coming to arrest us."

Jorge rolled from the bed and came to the window. The

soldiers were half way across the square.

Thomas grabbed his satchel and ran for the door, descending the stairs with Jorge close behind. They passed Khadar al-Abidah as they ran through the kitchen where the fat innkeeper was preparing lamb and goat for his evening clients.

"There are soldiers coming," Thomas said. "When they ask tell them we haven't been here. We have never been here."

"Everyone knows you come to my inn, it would be foolish to pretend otherwise."

"Then tell them nothing of Jorge, only that I come in the evening to play mancala and drink tea."

Without waiting for a reply they rushed on, appearing in the shaded alley behind the inn. Thomas looked left and right, undecided. Left would take them to the wider streets leading from the square, from there to the Albayzin, but they would know where his house was and were no doubt searching there as well.

"You're sure they're after us?"

"No. But do you want to wait and ask?" Thomas went left, turning right when he came to Babole then running fast along the wider avenue. The stalls and shops were still closed for the afternoon, their shutters drawn, panting dogs the only life to be seen.

From behind came a yell and the sound of running feet.

"They have us, Thomas. Run!" Jorge shouted, and Thomas skidded right, climbing steeply through a narrow alley, cutting left, right, right again. They came to a dead end, a single oak door marking the entrance to a bathhouse. Thomas tried the door but it was locked. He hammered, knowing the gesture was useless.

"Do you hear anything?" He stood still, trying to listen above the pounding of blood in his ears. There were distant sounds, shouts masked by the maze of alleys they had run through.

"They're searching for us." Jorge looked around, trying to find some means of concealment.

"I'm lost. Perhaps they are too and won't find us." But

Thomas gave the lie to his words as he drew his sword. The air in the alley was like an oven, close and fetid, and sweat trickled down his face. He felt it running across the skin beneath his robes.

"Are we going to fight?" Jorge said.

"If we have to."

"Soldiers?"

Thomas nodded, said again, "If we have to."

Jorge laughed. "I've probably lived long enough anyway. It's all downhill from now on, especially after what we've done today." He drew his own sword and the two faced the alley, waiting. The sounds of their pursuers grew, faded, grew again, and Jorge said, "They're not giving up, are they?"

"They have their orders, as do we."

"Except they're obeying theirs."

"Do you want to go to Qurtuba? To the court of the Spanish king and queen? I hear they pride themselves on not washing and haven't bathed in two years. They have destroyed all the baths in the city, claiming that bathing is the work of the devil and un-Christian."

"I always knew my people were stupid," Jorge said. "I'm grateful I was brought here so you could remove my balls."

There was a commotion at the end of the alley and two soldiers appeared. At first Thomas thought they were going to walk past without looking in their direction. One of the men moved beyond his sight, but the other stopped at the end of the alley and turned his head. His shout was instantaneous, his companion running back. Thomas expected them to attack at once, but they only stood there. Then one spoke to the other, who sprinted off in the direction from which they had come. It was a mistake.

Thomas grinned and ran at the remaining man, screaming. The soldier stepped back, shock on his face, then defended himself as Thomas fell on him. Swords clashed, the man crashing against the far wall from the force of Thomas's sudden attack.

"Take his legs!" Thomas shouted to Jorge, defending himself

as the man countered his blows. From the corner of his eye he saw Jorge step close and swing his blade, trying for the back of the man's knees, but leather leggings resisted Jorge's slashes. Seeing the danger the soldier swung sideways at Jorge who stumbled, falling in his haste to retreat. The soldier followed through on his advantage, turning from Thomas, dismissing him as little threat, raising his sword to swing down upon Jorge.

Thomas judged his spot and slid his sword forward. As the man lunged Jorge raised his arms uselessly, stumbling backwards, Thomas sliced cleanly through the back of the attacker's right knee and his leg buckled. He screamed, trying to drag himself to his feet, but the leg was hobbled. He turned to Thomas, swinging wildly, unable to reach.

"Run," Thomas said, tempted to aim a kick at the man's face and resisting. Instead he pushed Jorge, who was simply standing there staring.

"You didn't kill him."

Thomas pushed at Jorge again, eventually getting him to move, urging him faster. Blood pounded through his veins and exultation filled him. He no longer saw the alleys twisting and turning around them. His mind had returned to a time he hoped had been put behind him, but there it still was, only waiting patiently for him to call it into life. The blood lust. The fire in his veins. The elation of battle.

"You should have killed him," Jorge said, his face a mask of shock.

"There was a time I would have without a second thought. But we're men, Jorge, not animals, we have control over ourselves."

"He would have killed you."

"Then I'm not like him."

Thomas grabbed Jorge's robe and dragged him along, running as hard as he could. There had been shouts behind when they fled the alleyway, but they had lost their pursuers. Perhaps the men were nervous, their prey more dangerous than they had been told.

There were now only four men pursuing them, and Thomas ran, Jorge close behind, skidding and tripping on the cobbles as the city began to wake slowly from its afternoon slumber.

THIRTY-TWO

There were no names to the alleys they ran through. Anyone coming to this place did so for a reason and already knew their destination. Thomas's house stood on the eastern slope of the Albayzin where the residences were larger and looked across to the palace. Here on the western slope the buildings were crumbling, the alleys lacked cobbles, only bare sand and soil beneath their feet. Naked children played in the dust, laughing at the strange men who ran through their midst, some of them running alongside as though this was a fine game.

At the crest of the hillside, in the shadow behind the great mosque, they crouched to recover their breath.

"We have lost them, surely," Jorge said. He had kept pace beside Thomas the whole time, fitter than he looked.

"They won't stop looking. They mean us dead."

"Or captured?" Jorge said, a note of hope in his voice.

"Those men didn't come on a whim. They are following orders. Someone sent them."

"Muhammed?"

"If he is the guilty one. I need to study those documents again before I make up my mind. He wasn't even under suspicion until now. I'd rather draw my own conclusions than accept another man's judgement blindly."

"I can't believe he would harm us. You saved his brother's life. His father trusts you. As for me, I mean nothing to him."

"There are bigger stakes at risk here than you or I. And Muhammed bears me no friendship, none at all."

"Does he have men of his own?" Jorge asked. "Is that who he has sent after us?"

"He has access to men, but none of his own. He has to be

working with someone."

"Who?"

"I don't know. Olaf? Faris? I don't like that snake but it doesn't mean he's involved."

Shouts sounded from somewhere behind and below and Thomas turned quickly. The alley curved down and away, but there was no sign of pursuit.

"We have to leave the city," Jorge said. "We're not safe as long as we remain within its walls."

"And go where? To Qurtuba as we've been asked?"

"I suspect it's too late for that. To one of the villages in the hills. Somewhere we won't be looked for."

"We can't run and hide, not now we're this close who's behind the deaths. When you're under greatest threat, that is the time to attack."

"Or a route to a slow and painful death," Jorge said. "I would prefer my death to be slow, and at the end of a long life, and I would wish to avoid any hint of pain."

"Go if you wish," Thomas said. "I intend to finish this thing before any more die."

"How?"

"I'll confront Muhammed. Accuse him."

Jorge barked a laugh, falling into step beside Thomas as he started along the alley. "And how are you going to do that with a sword in your guts? He'll kill you. You've shown courage and skill today, but Muhammed is a warrior like his father, and he's never alone."

"He won't kill me, not if the Vizier and Olaf are present. I have a plan to draw him out, to confront him in the presence of them both, to lay his treachery bare."

"Then he will kill you all."

"No, he will kill no-one, not with Olaf there."

"I had better stay then, in case you need my protection, too. Where are we going now?"

Thomas glanced at Jorge and smiled. "Back to my house."

"There will be guards."

"Not now. They believe we are in hiding, on the run, the house will be empty. I need a change of clothes and another satchel of tools. Then we implement my plan."

"I can't wait to discover more. But if you don't mind I'll stay outside, in case someone wants to try and kill me."

The house was quiet, for which Thomas was grateful. There had been nobody outside waiting for them, nobody within. For a moment he stood in the entrance hallway looking into the courtyard beyond, listening.

Silence. Complete silence.

It was as the house had been half a year earlier, when he lived alone. Except now the silence was different, echoing a lack of something, of someone. The house had grown used to the sound of voices, the scent of a woman. The lack of one left a resonance that whispered of a need to be filled. Thomas realised how sterile his life had been before the coming of Helena. How tainted it was now by her betrayal.

So much change over so short a time. Could he ever hope to restore the routine of a few days earlier? It seemed so much had happened that his old life was a shadowed dream never to be re-captured. He returned to the street and called Jorge inside.

"Shall I fetch your clothes from upstairs?" Jorge asked.

"I've changed my mind. We need to travel light, and I can buy clothes if I need them. Carlos will be glad of more trade." Thomas went into the courtyard, left towards his workshop.

"If he doesn't turn us in. There'll be a price on our heads by now. The entire city will know we're outlaws."

"Carlos is a friend."

"Sometimes I really do wonder how you've managed to live this long." Jorge looked around, sat on the narrow cot that was becoming Lubna's.

Thomas started gathering more instruments, no longer his best, those now lost at the inn, irretrievable until this affair was done. Instead he selected the best of those he had owned the longest, no longer modern but adequate should he need them.

His supply of herbs and potions was low and he took what he could. He went in search of something to store them in. He had used his one good leather satchel, so went to his knees and pulled out boxes, sacs containing something he must have once considered important but had lain beneath the bench for years. Far in the back he found what he was looking for. A second satchel, this one also leather, stained almost black with age. It was not Thomas's but a gift—from the old man in the Piranneus who had saved his life when he was sixteen and set him on the path that brought him to this point in time.

"Thomas!"

He banged his head on the bench, backed out, aware of the undignified sight he must make. Lubna stood in the doorway, looking between him and Jorge.

"I thought you were out."

"I was upstairs making your bed, hanging clean clothes." She stood barefoot, a homespun shift falling to her knees, head uncovered because she was indoors and alone, leaving herself uncovered now because she considered herself Thomas's servant and Jorge's friend.

"Has Helena returned?"

"She was downstairs earlier while I was working. Is she no longer here?" Something showed in Lubna's eyes, a flicker of disappointment, but it passed as swiftly as it had come.

"We're not staying," Thomas said, ignoring what he had seen.

"Again."

"What?"

"It's all you do these days. Come and go. Come and go."

"We're close. We have to act now, before they can stop us."

Her expression changed. "Who, Muhammed?"

Thomas had pondered on who could be helping the Sultan's son as they had made their way through the back streets and alleyways. There was only one man with sufficient resources to have sent men so quickly. But he couldn't make the accusation, fearing it would wound this waif of a woman further.

"Muhammed and others, I can't say who. But you will know soon enough."

"You don't trust me."

"I trust you. But I would not have this knowledge place you in danger. Jorge and I are fugitives. If anyone comes here looking for us tell them you know nothing."

"That won't be difficult."

"You're in no danger, but if you need to, you must betray us."

Lubna shook her head. "I can never do that."

"You might have to. If it comes to it, do it, don't even think, just do it."

"I'm not my sister, Thomas. I will not betray you."

He stared at her. The intense eyes, her shadowed skin lustrous in the afternoon light.

"No, you're not. I know you're not." He saw his words pain her as she interpreted them differently than he meant, and said, "You're far more than she could ever be." But it was too late. He saw she didn't believe him.

"I must finish my chores. Helena will want a meal ready when she returns. She's as bad as you at the moment, never home."

Thomas watched her go, wanting to run after her, knowing he couldn't.

"You're a fool, Thomas Berrington." Jorge had sat on the cot the whole time, a silent observer.

"A fool if we stay here. Come on, we have plans to put into action."

Jorge rolled his eyes. "Whatever they might be. I wait with anticipation to hear what my clever friend has conjured up. Come then, at least the streets are cooler now. Where are we going?"

"To the baths."

"Of course, how foolish of me. I haven't bathed today, and my sweat must offend your sensitive nose."

"They won't look for us there, you fool."

They passed into the courtyard and stopped.

Three armed men stood in the shaded area. One of them held Lubna tight, making no effort to be gentle, an arm gripping her across one breast, another around her waist. She tried to break free but only succeeded in tightening his grip.

Helena stood to one side, as though distancing herself from what was happening.

"You brought them," Thomas said, addressing her, satisfied to see her eyes shift away in guilt.

"You are under arrest, you and that creature both. Take them," the soldier in the centre ordered.

The man grasping Lubna let her drop, drew his scimitar and came forward.

Thomas leaned across to Jorge. "The back door," he whispered, drawing his sword and making as though to confront the approaching man. He feinted as he sensed Jorge backing away. Thomas intended to give him a moment, inflict a flesh wound on the man to the right and then follow. The thought never once entered his head he was in real danger.

He heard Jorge run, the throw of bolts, and then the door crashed open. Thomas feinted left, twisted, brought his sword around onto the arm of the man to his right, exactly as he had seen it in his mind, except the blow caught on a leather armpiece. Thomas turned to run, only to see more men spilling through the door Jorge had so conveniently opened for them. Thomas lowered his sword, recognising the hopelessness of the situation. When he turned back to the men in the courtyard they made no attempt to approach, content to wait.

Beyond them Lubna darted to one side and pushed against the captain of guards, throwing him off balance. She snatched a knife from his belt and leapt on the back of the man who had held her, brought the knife around in a sweeping arc.

"No!" Thomas shouted, but Lubna's eyes had lost all rationality.

Another soldier threw himself against her, tapping her skull with the hilt of his sword. The knife had enough momentum to strike the man her legs were wrapped around, to scratch his flesh, but it lacked force and fell free to clatter against the tiles.

"Bitch." The soldier twisted, grabbing Lubna as she slid from his back. He lifted her at the waist, rushed forward and slammed her into the wall. Lubna's head cracked against stone and she went limp. The man glanced over his shoulder at his captain, requesting permission.

The officer looked, raised a shoulder: do as you wish.

Thomas yelled, but other hands came from behind, taking his sword, pinning him to the spot.

"What about the whore?" the other soldier said.

The captain looked at Helena, still standing apart from the group. Her earlier expression of spite and triumph had faded and she looked afraid.

"We have orders, she's not to be harmed." The captain's face showed disdain. "Bring these two, and the whore. And Ahmed, be quick."

"He always is," someone said, the words greeted with laughter.

Thomas struggled, trying to break free, but the men holding him were strong, and for all his writhing they only gripped him more firmly.

The man grasping Lubna pawed at her shift, his intentions clear. Thomas yelled again and the other soldiers laughed, watching their companion with amusement.

"She's too skinny for you, Ahmad, she looks like a boy. Might as well turn her round and pretend she is one."

"I heard he likes it that way," someone else said.

Thomas lurched, one arm pulling clear only to be instantly caught. He could see Jorge equally trying to break free, tears on the big man's face. Jorge's strength was greater and he pulled his right arm loose, swung it hard and smashed his fist into the side of one captor's head. He almost broke loose, but a man came behind and hit him on the back of the skull with the pommel of his sword and Jorge's knees went slack.

Thomas kicked backwards, his heel striking a shin, but the

blow was only greeted with laughter.

"The surgeon thinks himself a fighter."

"Let me loose and I'll show you who the fighter is, you coward."

Thomas felt the hands gripping him loosen, not believing these men were so stupid as to rise to such a challenge. Hope flared for a moment before the captain said, "Keep your hold. You can fight him when he's safe inside the palace if you must, but not here."

The man turned and strode to the doorway from the courtyard. Thomas was dragged after. Lubna, who lay slack in Ahmad's grasp, came alive, twisting and screaming. She reached down and grasped the knife from his waist and this time her blow was true. Instead of lifting her arm she turned the knife, bringing it up into the man's stomach, grunting with effort as she buried the blade deep.

Ahmad started to keen, his right leg jerking up and down as though he had trodden on a hornet. Lubna fell away, her stomach and thighs slicked with the man's blood.

"Oh shit," the captain said, his voice tired. "Now we have to take the girl with us, too. She has a lesson to learn." He strode across to grip Lubna's chin hard, staring into her face, took the knife from her grasp and tossed it aside. "You don't kill one of my men and survive. Tonight you will learn what it's like to be impaled on the cocks of a regiment."

"Safer to kill her here," someone said.

The captain drew his sword, staring at it a moment. Thomas tried once more to pull free but his captors' arms might as well have been iron shackles.

The captain sheathed his sword. "No, bring her. But she's mine first. Afterwards you can do as you will, but I go first. And bring the whore, we are to deliver her safe."

"Thomas, stop them!" Helena shouted as rough hands grabbed at her, grasping her breasts, her belly, her sex. She twisted and turned, but the movement only made the men laugh more as her silk clothing tore. "Thomas!" she cried again, but his heart had gone cold. The woman who had shared his life for half a year had betrayed them all.

"She is not to be harmed," the captain reminded his men, but his eyes took in the exquisite flesh revealed by torn silk.

The men gripping Thomas bundled him forward. His foot caught on a terracotta pot and he stumbled. The hands holding him loosened and he jerked free. He sprinted across the courtyard, hitting the captain with his shoulder, reaching for the man's sword. He spun, crouching, ready to die, but instead something hit the side of his head and the day turned dark.

THIRTY-THREE

Thomas woke to intense pain, a pounding in his temples, a throbbing in his arm, and fled back into unconsciousness. The second time he came round, the pain was still there but he ignored it, teasing out a strand of thought like a tangled thread, searching for its source. It had come to him in an instant on waking. Whether he had worked it out in a fevered dream, or his mind remained active while his body lay comatose, the truth emerged crystal clear, fully formed. Bilal had been wrong.

He groaned. Small hands pulled at his arm. On the other side someone stronger drew him upright to sit against a hard wall, but he immediately slumped sideways.

Thomas forced his eyes open and looked around. They were in a cell, the only illumination a flickering glow from the corridor outside, coming through a small barred opening in the solid door. To his left Lubna knelt, her torn shift drawn around herself. To the right Jorge sat with his legs stretched out, blood on his face and ear.

"I was starting to wonder if they'd killed you," Jorge said, "but then I thought, no, it was only his head."

"How long…"

"Some hours. Evening prayers have been called. It's likely dark outside but we have no window to tell."

"Where?"

"Somewhere in the palace. Not a place I've seen before."

Thomas tried to sit upright, his head spinning, and again Lubna came to his assistance. Recollection came slowly as he looked at her, not seeing the woman but remembering her sister. Misinterpreting his stare she drew the torn cloth across her breasts.

"I had something to repair that in my bag," Thomas said.

"They took nothing," Jorge said. "Your bag is over there. Do you want it?"

"Fetch it for me if you would. My thanks." Thomas tried not to think why they had left him his bag. It wasn't a good sign. More than likely it meant they had no intention of releasing them.

"My, they did hit you hard, didn't they."

Thomas accepted the battered satchel and opened the clasp, searched inside until he found the items he was looking for. He pulled out a needle and silk and handed both to Lubna. Then he shook some dry bark into his hand and popped it into his mouth, chewing the bitter willow, hoping it would ease the pounding in his head.

Lubna stood and walked to the door on the far side of the dungeon, where enough light filtered in for her to see more clearly. She turned her back on Thomas and Jorge and began to pull together the separated parts of her clothing.

"How is she?" Thomas whispered, putting his head against Jorge's, calmed by the touch against his own. He wanted to close his eyes and sleep, fought against it.

"Subdued. She wonders why she's here, why the soldiers didn't keep their promise."

"There's only one answer. You know it and so does she. They were Olaf's men. He wants us dead, but he won't harm his daughters. You heard what they said to Helena."

"I tried to tell her," Jorge said, "but I don't think she listened. She's too calm." Jorge's voice was as soft as Thomas's, neither of them wanting Lubna to overhear.

"And Helena? What became of her?"

Jorge shook his head. "They separated us as soon as we reached the palace. She'll be with him now."

"So why is Lubna here? Why not take her as well?"

"She killed one of them. Even Olaf has to be seen to punish murder. But she'll be spirited out of the city to somewhere safe."

"Not murder," Thomas said. "Self defence."

"That won't be how they see it."

"Zoraya and Olaf together, after all," Thomas whispered. "What a pairing."

Jorge nodded, his gaze flicking across to Lubna, but she remained with her back to them. "You've worked it out as well, then. I couldn't understand why Muhammed wanted Safya killed. She was too close to his mother, as good as a mother to him. It didn't make sense. None at all. But Zoraya wanting her dead—that makes a lot of sense."

"For what good the knowledge will do us now." Thomas leaned closer, lowering his voice further. "Don't tell Lubna. She must know nothing of the truth if she's to remain safe."

"Her father will protect her."

"He will try, no doubt, but Zoraya is a cold operator. Olaf will need to watch his back once her son takes the throne."

"We made a good team, didn't we? Your brains and my subtlety?" Jorge's smiled, and Thomas battled between love and frustration for the man.

"And we found those behind the killings, even if we can't do anything about it."

"Whisper all you want, I can hear you perfectly well," Lubna said. "I will never believe my father guilty of what you accuse him of."

Thomas said nothing. It was Jorge who felt a need to fill the silence. "You, like Thomas, have a sharp mind. You'll see the truth when you think it through. It's plain who's behind this. And your sister was feeding him information all the time. No wonder it felt like we were fighting our way into a sandstorm."

"Helena betrayed you, yes," Lubna spat. "You, who took her in when no-one else would, who treated her like the princess she believed herself to be, instead of the lying, vicious bitch she is. But my father would never do the same. It must be someone else who aids Zoraya."

"Who, if not your father?" Thomas said, his voice gentle. It hurt to see Lubna in such pain, but he had never denied the truth, and wasn't going to start now.

"How am I supposed to know? You're the man with all the answers. Tell me why we're locked in here instead of dead? I don't understand why we weren't simply disposed of."

"You know why you're alive," Thomas said.

"They can't kill us," Jorge said. "You're the Sultan's physician."

"We'd never be found."

"But we would be missed. Half the city knows what you have been doing. Your disappearance will raise questions."

"Which might last a day and then pass. There is always some new gossip in Gharnatah."

"Then the Sultan won't forget. It was he who entrusted you with this task at the outset. He wouldn't let your disappearance go unnoticed."

"Unless it's him behind our capture," Lubna said. Thomas glanced at her, wondering if she was going to blame the entire population before accepting her father's involvement.

"Why would he want us captured? Why send me to find the killer and then lock us away?"

"Because he didn't expect you to succeed. He couldn't allow you to succeed. He killed the last men he set to do the task."

Thomas sighed, his headache starting up again. "But it's not him we are accusing."

"Not now, no. But when your accusations against my father prove false you will look elsewhere, and he knows the trail leads to him."

"So now you accuse the Sultan? Why not Jorge and me, too? It's the Sultan who banished your sister to my house, why would she plot with him?"

"Because you've done too good a job. She is beautiful again, and she was a favourite in the harem. You know her skills as well as any man. She can't be resisted once she sets her mind to a thing."

Thomas didn't like the reminder of his own weakness. "Why did she betray me? Haven't I been good to her?"

"Because she hates you. She scatters hurt like a farmer scatters wheat. It's her stock in trade."

"Lubna speaks the truth," Jorge said. "You know she does."

"You tell me this now?" Thomas raised his voice. "What kind of friend are you not to warn me when she came to my house?"

"The kind of friend who was pleased for you. Yes, she has her problems, but she's also beautiful and highly skilled. I thought you might enjoy the education."

Thomas shook his head. "I ache, and what brains I possess are bruised too badly to function. I can think no longer."

"You have to. It's what you're good at. Don't look to me for intelligence, my skills are of a different kind."

Thomas almost smiled. The willow was finally starting to work on his head, the throbbing in his arm lessening. He wanted to remove the bandage and check the stitches, convinced they had torn loose with the strain put on them.

Lubna padded across the cell and sat beside him, her left leg touching his right. She handed back the needle and silk. She had roughly drawn the front of her shift together, but it would never be high fashion.

"Tell me what you believe, Thomas. Jorge told me some story while you slept, but he made no sense."

"Thank you," Jorge said.

"My pleasure. This can't be the work of my father. I refuse to believe he's capable of such a thing."

"As was I," Thomas said. "But the more I look the more I see no other explanation. I saw with my own eyes how he was with Zoraya. Olaf is one of the few who could have us arrested and thrown in here."

"Why would he want Safya dead?"

"Not *he*. Zoraya. He knows her well, will have acted as guard to her on many occasions. He admitted to me he visits her rooms. I have seen him train her sons with my own eyes. And she is beautiful, as Helena's mother was."

"My mother is beautiful, too."

"Of course she is." Thomas lowered his gaze, then lifted it quickly for fear Lubna would think his eyes sought her body. "Your mother is a fine woman, but these ladies of the harem are... are something different." He felt a moment's grief arc through him like a bolt of lightning. In an instant a thousand and one memories flooded his mind. Of the night Helena came to his bed for the first time, her skin pale gold, her hands delicate and knowing as she loosened his clothing. The sounds she uttered as they made love. The skills she demonstrated, acts of sensuality Thomas had never dreamed of.

"I still won't believe it of my father. Olaf Torvaldsson is pure and loyal. He has fought beside the Sultan for thirty years. He couldn't do such a thing."

Thomas saw a brightness in her eyes, heard a quiver in her voice, and knew she was trying to convince herself, doubts already settling in her mind, gnawing away at certainty.

"No doubt he believes what he does is best for Gharnatah."

"What—to have the Sultan's wives murdered?" Lubna turned her face away.

"It would not be all the wives. Without Safya or Aixa, Muhammed's claim to the title is weak, Yusuf's weaker still. The city would pass to Nasir."

"I understand all this. I'm not stupid, but I will never believe my father is part of such treachery. Never."

"What you or I believe is of little use tonight." Thomas lifted his arm. Lubna hesitated a moment, then lay against his side, and he drew her closer, both comforting and comforted. He stared into the gloom, only the flickering glow of the torch beyond the door casting a weak illumination on them. "I assume someone has checked the door is locked," he said.

Jorge snorted a laugh. "Oh, of course, they would throw us into an unlocked dungeon."

Lubna slipped from beneath his arm and went to the door. She rattled the lock, pushed and pulled, but it was as solid as the wall surrounding it. She came back, a wry grin on her face. "Suppose it had been? Wouldn't we look fools?" She slid down beside Thomas, snugged tight against him once more, and he moved his head a little and breathed in her scent. None of them smelled too sweet after this day, but still her smell soothed him.

He closed his eyes. For a moment only, he promised.

He woke to a scuttling sound, at first part of his dream, then solidifying.

"Rats," Jorge said. "This far below ground they'll be everywhere."

"It's not rats," Lubna said.

"What's not rats?" Thomas said.

"You're awake at last." She moved away from him and his side felt cold where she had lain against him.

"I wasn't sleeping, only resting."

"You snore loudly when you rest," Jorge said.

"What rats," Thomas said.

There came a sound from the passage, a scraping.

"Those rats," Jorge said.

Thomas rose stiffly and went to the door. He tried to lift up far enough to see through the bars, but they were too high. He pressed his ear against the wood, sprung back when something banged against the far side.

"They're coming for us!" His stomach filled with ice, his heart beating hard in his chest.

The sound of scuttling resolved into a heavy key turning in the lock. The door swung inward.

"Hello, Thomas."

"Prea!"

"You will have to pay me even more now, won't you?" Her face showed a manic glee.

"Where are the guards?"

The girl laughed. "Sleeping the sleep of angels. Or devils. We heard about your capture and Bazzu sent me down with a special meal for them, a thank you for capturing the wicked palace killers."

"Is that what we're blamed of now?"

"Everyone within these walls believes it. Well, almost everyone." She smiled.

"And who first raised this news?"

Prea shook her head. "How am I to know? By the time we heard of it in the kitchen it was rumour built on rumour. Are we going to stand here all night, or do you want to escape?"

"Yes, we want to escape." Thomas wanted to hug her, but knew she might misinterpret such a show of affection. Not to mention Lubna.

"Follow me, then."

Prea darted out into the passageway. Jorge pushed past Thomas, but Lubna waited beside him until he finally took a step, and then she stayed close as they made their way out. Torches lit the passage at intervals. Other cells led off on one side, the other solid stone, likely the wall part of the foundations of the palace.

When they turned a corner three guards sat slumped around a glowing brazier. Thomas stopped, but Prea laughed and ran forward to slap one across the face. The guard's head rocked, but his eyes remained closed.

"Bazzu made a fine meal for the likes of these. They will sleep till morning."

"Where are you taking us?" Thomas whispered, still afraid the guards might wake.

"To the kitchens. They are the closest place of safety. Bazzu knows I have come looking for you. She will hide you until the small hours and then we will sneak you out."

"When did you know we were prisoners?"

"I told you, it's the talk of the palace. They say you are the killers, that you fooled the Sultan into asking you to investigate when it was the two of you behind everything. You, Thomas, were driven mad by Helena's whisperings in your ear, and Jorge was the, ah, the man on the inside. They say you planned it all between you."

"I assume you didn't believe what was said?"

Prea laughed, darting ahead, the passage wider, the scent of clean air coming to them.

"Bazzu refused to believe such a thing of Jorge. She has such softness in her heart for that one."

"I am right here," Jorge said.

"And I knew you were no traitor, Thomas. You spent an entire day with me in the passages. You could have killed me any time you wanted, to hide your secret, but you didn't. So we knew the rumours were false, spread by whoever is truly behind this."

"And who would that be?" Jorge asked. "Who started the rumours?"

"Who starts any rumour?" Prea said. "They appear as if by magic, from out of thin air. I truly believe they have no source, but simply are. However, Bazzu believes this one likely started in the barracks."

"Olaf Torvaldsson," Thomas muttered.

Lubna, walking beside him, her head down, made no comment, but Thomas saw her shoulders tense, and wished the truth was otherwise.

Thomas manoeuvred to put Lubna into the lead, with Jorge between himself and Prea. He dropped back, touching the girl's shoulder to let her know to fall behind, and once a space had opened up he whispered to her, "You know Lubna's sister?"

"The courtesan? Your wife?"

"Not my wife, but she is the one. She was taken at the same time we were, but to the barracks I think. Have you heard anything of her fate?"

Prea gave a sigh that was half muffled laughter. "That one has no fate. Bazzu told me all about her. She is like the cockroaches—she can survive anything. I heard she is with Zoraya."

They reached ground level and Prea led them on through dark courtyards, only the occasional lamp flickering a weak illumination here and there.

"I sent you another message, but you didn't come."

"I received no second message." Thomas realised he hadn't even read the first one. He looked ahead to where Lubna and Jorge walked. He was too far away to hear their conversation.

"My friend brought it. She said you mistook her for me the other day. She left my message at your house, with your wife."

Thomas nodded, understanding coming slowly.

"What did this second message say?"

"The same as my first, that I have discovered something important. I have found his clothes."

"The killer's clothes?"

Prea favoured him with a look. "He has them hidden away on a high shelf close to an entrance. I think it's where he enters that world. I have been waiting and watching, but he hasn't come yet."

Thomas stopped, grabbing the girl's arm. "You mustn't do that, Prea. This man's a killer. He'll strike you down without a second's hesitation."

"I'm not stupid, Thomas Berrington. He will never discover me. I have a safe place to hide. You know how well I can hide."

"Don't go back there."

"Will you let me show you?"

"It's too dangerous, we are wanted, all three of us. You can't be seen associating with me."

Prea laughed and started along the corridor. They were close to the kitchens, and even now in the small hours the scent of fresh bread, fruit and meat reached them.

"Now is the time, when everyone is asleep. Just you and me, Thomas. We can pass like ghosts and no-one will see us."

Bazzu was awake when they arrived at her room, sitting behind her desk, as alert as if the hour was noon. She rose when they entered and went directly to Jorge, drawing him into her arms. Thomas looked away, allowing them a moment. His gaze fell on Lubna, who was watching him in turn, her face expressionless.

Prea tugged at his hand and he saw Lubna's eyes shift to the girl, back to his.

"We must go now," Prea said. "Bazzu will look after these two, and we need to sneak you out before dawn." She tugged him again.

"What does she want with you?" Lubna said, her voice as cold as her face.

"She wants to show me something."

"I expect she does. You had better go then." Lubna turned away, leaned against a wall and slid down, her head dropping.

Thomas wanted nothing more than to go to her, but Prea was still pulling at his hand, and he knew whatever she had found might be important. He allowed himself to be led away.

Once they had left the kitchen behind Prea said, "Is she your girl, too?"

"Who, Lubna? No, of course not. You know who I live with."

"The woman with the white hair. Do you look at her the same way you look at this girl?"

Thomas slowed and glanced at Prea. How many years did she have? More than fourteen, less than sixteen. So much wisdom in such a small package.

"I know where my duty lies. Now show me this place so I can get out of here."

Prea walked away, muttering, thinking Thomas couldn't hear, but his ears had always been sharp.

"I would like it if someone looked at me the way you look at her, but never mind about me."

THIRTY-FOUR

The entrance Prea led them to wasn't one Thomas had seen before. It lay close to the outer wall of the palace, near the barracks. For a soldier it made a perfect place from which to gain access—a little used corridor which would be deserted most of the time.

Prea reached into the wall, her face a rictus of concentration. A moment later she grinned and Thomas helped her swing a wooden panel open.

"How do we see inside?" The palace slumbered around them, only small lamps or candles burning, not enough to illuminate inside the tunnels.

"There is a lamp already here. He must come at night, and the man is well prepared." Prea disappeared into the darkness. A moment later Thomas heard the strike of flint and a faint illumination showed him the way. He drew the panel closed behind him but didn't let it latch shut.

"Are they here?" He surveyed the space. This spot appeared no different to any other. Grey stone enclosed a narrow passage leading into darkness, grit scraped beneath his feet; claustrophobic.

"It's not far." Prea went ahead and Thomas felt a chill of fear as he imagined being alone in these tunnels, lost in the dark. What else used these passages other than men and women?

But Prea made good her promise. After less than two minutes she stopped and indicated a shelf cut into the wall.

"It will be easier if you reach up. I had to climb."

Thomas stretched, going on tiptoe, and still could only just reach. His searching hand found something soft and he jerked it away before realising it was what he sought. He tugged and a garment fell, fine silk billowing. Prea stepped back to avoid it touching the guttering lamp.

"Is there anything else?"

"Look," Prea said.

Thomas reached again, his fingers walking across cold stone. They found nothing, and he withdrew.

Prea sighed. "Here, hold this." She thrust the lamp at him and clambered up the walls, legs spread, until she perched on the edge of the shelf. She reached in and the light caught on something bright. Then she was handing him a curved sword.

"Careful," she said, "it's sharp."

Thomas wrapped the blade inside the silk, placed the lamp on the ground and took the hilt. Prea slid down and landed beside him.

"When did you find this?"

"Two days ago. I sent you the first message immediately."

"And you have been watching for him?"

"When I could. I have duties, but I also have friends who help cover for me. There's another shelf a little way along—large enough for me to lie concealed on. I have been waiting there, but he hasn't come."

Thomas shook his head. "He would have killed you. It was a foolish thing to do."

"You would rather I didn't do it? Rather I not tell you of this?"

"I would rather you showed me this before."

"I sent a message and you didn't come! What was I supposed to do, ignore it? How would you feel if he struck again and I had done nothing?"

"What were you planning to do? Confront him?"

"I was going to follow him and find out who he was," Prea said.

Thomas knew her discovery was important. He would have come at once if he had read her messages. He wondered whether Helena had not passed the second message on deliberately. He cursed himself for not reading the first when Lubna mentioned it, but he had been too engrossed with Bilal's documents.

"Will you put it back?" Prea said.

"No, I want to examine the items in better light."

"If he returns he will know he has been discovered."

"Good. Then he might abandon his future plans and run. Or we will flush him out."

Prea looked at him, the wavering light of the lamp catching in her eyes. "I don't think he's the kind to run."

"No, you're probably right. Still, losing these will give him pause. Let's find Bazzu, dawn can't be far away."

In the kitchen Thomas laid the garment across Bazzu's table and he, Bazzu and Jorge leaned over it. Prea had disappeared, and Lubna slept, or pretended to.

"This is unusually fine," Bazzu said, rubbing the silk between finger and thumb. "And the colour is like nothing I have ever seen. Almost black, but this gold thread running through gives it a shimmer. This must look wonderful when worn."

"It's the killer's disguise, if you can consider something so beautiful a disguise."

Jorge picked up the material, draping it across his arm, a frown troubling his face. "This material is familiar. I've seen it somewhere before."

"In the palace?" Thomas said. "Have you seen someone wearing it?"

"Not the palace, somewhere else, but I can't remember where." Jorge lifted the garment and let it hang loose. It moved in the lightest draft, the colour shifting as it did so. "Can I wear it?"

"Now? Will it fit you?"

"Of course it will. We could both fit inside it. Aren't you curious to see how it looks?"

"If you must." Thomas saw Bazzu smile. Without waiting Jorge disrobed until he stood naked, unashamed. Bazzu openly admired him. Even Thomas was impressed. Jorge's chest was broad, muscle clearly delineated beneath smooth skin, his legs long and shapely. Not to mention that element of his manhood Thomas had not removed.

He slipped the robe over his nakedness and closed it with delicate ties, before drawing the deep hood over his head, almost completely obscuring his face.

"Move around," Thomas said, and Jorge walked to the door. The robe followed his every move, accentuating the figure beneath.

Jorge returned and took the sword which lay on the table. He returned to the door, went out into the corridor. Thomas saw Bazzu frown.

Jorge rushed into the room, turning, twisting, the sword raised high. He slashed down, turned again, struck once more. Something about the sound, his movement, roused Lubna, and she screamed as she took in the whirling figure.

Thomas went to her and laid his hand on her shoulder, but Lubna's gaze was locked on Jorge.

"The djinn," Bazzu said, a note of awe in her voice.

"Indeed, the djinn," Thomas said, then softer to Lubna, "It's not real."

As Jorge moved, the robe—so light, so responsive—wrapped itself around him. His legs fused into one, his shoulders flared. The minute gold threads shimmered, offering a hint of fire. "It's easy to see how the women were deceived. This is clever. It masks the man within and makes it impossible to judge his shape or size. Someone planned this with great precision."

"And money," Bazzu said. "I have never seen a cloth so fine."

Jorge stopped showing off and returned the sword to the table.

"I want to wear it forever," he said. "It kisses the body like a thousand lips." He bent and briefly kissed Bazzu. "But where have I seen this cloth before? It has to be the same, and the same purchaser. There can none like it anywhere else in Spain."

"You might want to wear it but you can't," Thomas said, and Jorge nodded.

"If I must, but I will miss the kisses."

Thomas turned his back while Jorge disrobed and dressed once more in his own clothes.

"What do we do with it now?"

"Hide it," Thomas said. "Bazzu, do you have somewhere safe?"

"I have a place."

Thomas nodded. "Good. I want to make use of it again when we confront the killer. The sword, too. Tell Prea she did well."

"You should reward her," Bazzu said.

Thomas gave her a quizzical glance. "I will give her more coins, of course, she—"

"That isn't what I meant."

"Then make yourself clear." He was in no mood for subtlety.

"She talked with me about you—it seems you have an admirer."

Thomas sighed. "She is young and impressionable, and—"

This time is was Bazzu's laugh interrupting him, and he scowled.

"She doesn't want to share your bed, although no doubt she would if asked. She is bright, and can do better for herself than work in the palace kitchens."

Thomas returned Bazzu's stare and waited, half an idea where she was going.

"She told me you needed a servant. An important man such as yourself without at least one servant is in danger of looking foolish."

"I don't need—"

Bazzu held up a hand and Thomas wondered if she was ever going to allow him to finish a sentence.

"You know she is sharp, and eager to do whatever is asked. Do you truly not have a place for her?"

"There is no room," Thomas said.

"Then make room. She deserves more than just payment for what she has done, don't you agree?"

"She has been a great help."

"Shall I tell her you will consider my request?"

"Your request, or hers?"

Bazzu studied his face, smiled. "It comes from me, so my request. Would you turn me down, too?"

Thomas wiped fingertips across his forehead. His head ached, his body hurt, his thoughts swooped and curled like swallows in flight, but with far less precision.

"I will consider it. Although whether I'm ever going to be able return home is in question. But yes, if I'm allowed to return to my work I will consider your request."

Bazzu smiled and he knew she had won, wondering how he would accommodate yet another female in his household. Of course, there was every likelihood Helena would not be returning, in which case.... No, he shook his head, too many thoughts, too many questions.

"In a few days you will be back in your house, surrounded by women." Bazzu stared at him, something in her gaze sparking discomfort inside him. "I have known you only a little time, Thomas Berrington, but even I can see you are incapable of what you are accused of."

"Events aren't always so simple. There are politics involved here too."

"Then Jorge will take care of those." Her eyes narrowed. "You know he can deal with such matters, don't you?"

Thomas glanced at his friend. "I know he hides his abilities well in order to play the fool. I need another favour from you and Prea, if you will ask her." He turned his head to check on Lubna, who seemed to have slumped back into a doze, before lowering his voice. "I know who is behind these killings and plan to set a trap. I want both of you to play a part, if you're willing."

Bazzu nodded. She had won her small battle and could afford to be magnanimous now.

Thomas drew up a chair and told her what he wanted.

THIRTY-FIVE

The day was just starting as they slipped from the back of a cart returning from carrying flour to the palace. Stallholders were erecting tables and setting out wares, the markets and side streets busy with focused activity, assailed by noise and smells. Dressed in the clothes Bazzu had found for them all three looked like poor merchants, each with a tagelmust obscuring their features.

"Where do you plan to hide us today?" Jorge asked. "We're starting to run out of places that will have us."

"We won't have to hide long. This will end soon, one way or another."

They negotiated their way through the back alleys of Gharnatah and came to the edge of al-Hattabin square. Thomas called a halt. He stood a moment looking around but saw nothing to raise suspicion. With luck they had not been missed yet. Thomas wondered how long they would have been left in the dungeon had Prea not come. Forever? Locked in the dark and left to starve? More likely someone would come looking for them today, if not already, planning their disappearance.

Thomas Jorge and Lubna moved along the edge of the square, unwilling to risk its open expanse, crossed over the Hadarro at the head of the square and took the roadway along its banks until they came to Aamir's bathhouse. Here the street was busier, people coming down from the Albayzin for work, others to cleanse at the start of the day.

They avoided the busy main entrance and instead took a narrow alley, cool from never seeing the sun. Thomas rapped on a small door set deep into the wall. Steam venting from grills set in the stone rose into the air. There was no reply so Thomas rapped a second time, harder, and eventually heard the sound of bolts being drawn. A young boy peered out, suspicious.

"You must use the front door. This one isn't allowed."

"I'm a friend of Aamir's, he will let me use this way."

The boy looked unconvinced. "I will need to ask." He started to push the door shut, but Jorge leaned his weight against it and the lad had no option but to give way.

"Aamir will be displeased if he hears my friend and I have been turned away. Thomas is a distinguished surgeon, and this woman is the daughter of Olaf Torvaldsson."

"You are Thomas Berrington?" The boy's eyes widened, and Thomas nodded. The boy's resistance gave way and they entered the baths, the scent of oil and soap heavy in the steamy air.

The boy darted ahead, stopped. "I'll tell my master you're here. Don't move, he'll want to see you."

Thomas slumped, the release of tension sapping what little reserves remained to him. Jorge placed his palm flat on the wall and lowered his head, breathing as though they had run all the way. Lubna looked around, an expression on her face Thomas hadn't seen before.

"I don't like this place," she said.

"The baths? Why not?"

"It's a place of sin."

Jorge chuckled, and Thomas smiled. "It can be. But it's also a place I visit often, but not for sin." He chose not to mention all the times in the past when he had come here for exactly that purpose. "How then do you bathe?"

"I wash with a cloth and bowl of water, as the prophet demands."

"Hot or cold?"

"Usually cold. I can't always get hot water."

Thomas laughed. "I'll ask Aamir to provide you with your very own chamber so you can discover the ultimate pleasure of a hot bath. A massage too if you wish."

"I need neither."

Thomas leaned over and sniffed. "Are you so sure?"

Lubna turned aside, rewarding him with a moment's shame at his teasing. The past day had seen the cornerstones of her life crumble. First Helena's betrayal, and now her father's guilt. He put his hands on her shoulders and turned her to face him.

"I miss her, too," Thomas said. "I worry what may become of her."

"Helena?" Lubna shook her head. "She'll find a new man, as she always has. You know it isn't Helena I'm thinking of."

"Much as I might wish to, I can't protect you from the truth."

Lubna looked as though she might strike him. Thomas wouldn't blame her if she did, happy to accept her blows if they helped.

"The things you believe are not true," she said. "You may think so, but I know, in here, you are wrong." She punched herself in the centre of her chest. Once. Twice. "I know my father can be cruel, but he isn't underhand. He would never betray the Sultan."

"Everything I know points to it being so," Thomas said.

"Then everything you know is wrong!" Lubna turned away once more. She hunched her shoulders and took several paces along the corridor. "I hate this place."

Thomas followed, laid his hands on her narrow shoulders again, but she shrugged him off. "Don't touch me. I'm no longer your servant."

"You were never my servant."

"Not in your head, but everyone else saw what I was."

"I thought you wanted to learn. I can help, if you allow me."

"I could never stay in your house with this between us. You see one truth and I another. I have nowhere left. And now I am on the run for murder! I won't go to my father and tell him of your suspicions, I owe you that much. There has been enough betrayal already."

Thomas placed his hands on her shoulders a third time, and although Lubna tensed, this time she didn't pull away.

"Go to my house. Your house. You will be safe there, and

it's close to the mosque. Get something to eat. Sleep. Wash. Wear some of Helena's clothing as a disguise. Stay as long as you wish. For ever, if you want."

"And you?"

"I will return, if I can."

"If you can?"

"The path I choose isn't without danger. If I survive I will return to you."

Lubna's shoulders trembled beneath his hands and he saw a quiver in the fall of her robe. He was unsure if this waif could manage her pain alone, but asking her to stay would only make the pain worse. Thomas pushed at her and released his grip.

"Go. This place isn't for you."

Lubna walked away without looking back, wrapping a scarf around her head.

"She needs time," Jorge said. "The news of her father has come as a shock, but she will learn to accept the truth. She has a brain and knows how to use it."

"I don't know if I care anymore. I've had enough of women and their ways."

Jorge smiled and patted Thomas on the shoulder. "You, too, will change your mind."

"I heard there were three of you." Aamir came bustling towards them. "Is your companion nearby?" He ignored Jorge, stopping in front of Thomas. "I prepared a private chamber if you wish to make use of it."

"She's not that kind of companion. And besides, she's no longer here."

Aamir shrugged. "Then you will have to make do with the eunuch."

"I need you to find me some items once I have bathed. I will pay well."

"You know I will take no coin from you, Thomas."

"It will make me feel better to pay."

Once more Aamir raised his shoulders, and as he led them to the promised bathing chamber Thomas gave him his list of requirements.

They stopped a moment outside the chamber as Thomas finished talking with Aamir. By the time he entered Jorge had already stripped out of his soiled clothing and was pouring hot water over himself, a contented smile on his face.

Thomas discarded his own robes and stepped beneath the water gushing from a spout set in the wall, it's weight beating against his head and shoulders. It was an hour before they emerged. Aamir had provided a small room with two cots, a meal, wine, and the supplies Thomas had asked for. There were no chairs or table in the room, so Thomas sat cross-legged on the floor, dipped a quill into dark ink and started to write.

"Love letters?" Jorge asked, already starting on the food.

"Of a kind. It's an invitation, anyway. Leave me some of that food."

"Don't take long, then."

But Thomas took his time. The document had to look authentic.

He scattered fine sand on the paper and shook it, tipped the sand onto the floor, then lit the candle Aamir's boy had brought. He felt inside his robe, for a moment experiencing panic he had lost the seal, but it was there, caught in the side of a pocket.

He melted dark wax and let it run onto the folded paper, pressed the seal, holding it there while the wax solidified. After he had eased it clear he checked carefully. The document looked authentic. No—the document *was* authentic; it possessed the seal of the Sultan of Gharnatah. It would be unquestioned.

Thomas laid it aside and took another sheet of paper, started to write a second note. This one—less formal—required no seal.

Lubna didn't wash, nor did she visit the mosque, even though midday prayer had been called. Instead she cleaned the blood from the courtyard tiles, forced herself to eat some fruit and nuts, then gathered up the papers she and Thomas had studied and laid them on the table in his workshop. Those written in symbols she didn't understand were reluctantly laid aside.

Those in Arabic she set apart. When there were two piles—those she could read containing three times the quantity of those she couldn't—she sat and began to work through them again.

She didn't believe her father guilty of the crimes Thomas accused him of. These documents were the only means she had of proving his innocence, and if proof lay somewhere within these pages she meant to find it.

Lubna barely noticed the chatter of the swallows as they swooped above the courtyard, or the movement of the shadows on the walls as the afternoon passed. The city of Gharnatah slumbered in the heat as she continued to read, over and over again, the minutiae of commercial life within the city.

THIRTY-SIX

The market was a tumult of sound and scent and texture, men and women shouting, great brass pots cooking food from a dozen countries, chickens, geese, goats and sheep milling about underfoot, boys and girls in rags running through it all on errands and mischief. The noise was overwhelming.

Thomas sat deep in the alcove of a merchant's house, hidden behind a stall selling lamps from across the narrow sea, rolls of cloth from Egypt, lengths of dark wood from the forests of Africa, and sticky balls of resin extracted from poppy, together with a score of other items, none related other than by the fact each might turn a profit.

He was watching the crowd that surged and ebbed like the tides of the ocean, and waiting. Thomas knew all he wanted of the ocean, of its ebbing and flowing, its waves and storms. He had seen more than enough and wanted never to see or cross it again. Thomas searched the crowd for a sign. It had not come yet, but he was patient.

Jorge spent the time either standing nearby looking furtive, or wandering the stalls while he also studied the milling throng.

It was late morning before Thomas saw what he was waiting for.

Two merchants talking together were startled as a slim figure darted between them. One of the men turned and shouted, believing the girl a pickpocket, but Prea had already disappeared into the crowd. Thomas lost sight of her for a moment, then she was standing not twenty paces away, looking around. She was searching for him, but his alcove was shaded and the square bright.

Thomas scanned the crowd both near and far, then took

two paces forward so sunlight fell on him. Prea's face showed excitement, cheeks flushed, this intrigue beyond her usual experience. She ran to him.

"He's on the way?" Thomas asked, grasping her shoulders to prevent her hugging him.

"He'll be here any moment." Prea turned, lifting on tiptoes as she surveyed the crowd. "I see Bazzu, I have to go. Come and find me later if you can. And thank you for saying you will take me in." This time he couldn't prevent the hug. Thomas knew he needed to be firmer. First Olaf had tricked him into taking Lubna, now Bazzu was making promises to this girl on his behalf, but he couldn't be displeased. He only hoped he lived beyond tomorrow so there was a place for her to come to.

When she eventually released him he retained his grip, preventing her from moving away. "You haven't been back to the tunnels, have you?"

"You asked me not to," Prea said. She tugged away again, this time breaking free.

"Don't—" But she was gone.

"I think you have another admirer." Jorge appeared at his side like the djinn they were chasing.

"Just what I need. A fourteen year old girl. Did you know Bazzu is sending her to me as a servant? How long have you been there?"

"Long enough." Jorge looked Thomas up and down. "How do you attract all these women to you?" Jorge shook his head. "It's not even as if you're good looking. And we both know fourteen year old girls marry and have children." Jorge shrugged. "Or maybe not even bother with the marrying part."

"So now I'm *marrying* her?" Thomas caught sight of Bazzu moving through the far side of the crowd. For a large women she was light on her feet, her body twisting through gaps that appeared too narrow for her size. Behind her trailed a line of boys, none much older than Prea, and as Bazzu chose their goods the merchants loaded the baskets they carried. Despite the lateness of the morning Bazzu was a familiar figure most days, and the stallholders always held back some of their best produce for the palace, where price was no object.

The last boy in line was dressed the same as the others except for a tagelmust which obscured most of his face. His dark eyes darted as Prea's had, searching. Thomas saw Prea approach the boy and lean in to speak. They drifted from the end of the line, the boy still carrying his empty basket. Bazzu, who expected the move, continued shopping as though nothing had happened.

"Time to hide you even further," Jorge said, and Thomas rose and moved without haste to the rear of a stall selling silk and linen owned by Carlos Rodriguez. The Spanish merchant no longer dirtied his own hands in the markets, but he had briefed his stallholder, and informed Thomas the man could be trusted.

As he approached, the grey cotton cloth which covered the table top and fell to the ground on all sides was lifted to offer him a place of concealment. Thomas ducked beneath into warm dimness. A moment later the side cloth was raised again and the small figure of the Sultan's son, Yusuf, crawled in. His face glowed in the filtered light.

"Thomas—this intrigue is far more exciting than battle." Yusuf clapped Thomas on the shoulder, what would be a familiar gesture from an older man incongruous in one so young, but Yusuf had been raised as a prince and didn't act as any normal child. His enthusiasm, however, was still that of a fourteen year old boy.

"You received my message then."

"That girl—what's her name?"

"Prea?"

"She's pretty."

"She is."

"Do you think if I spoke with her she would spend some time with me?"

"It depends what you have in mind."

Yusuf's olive skin flushed, but he said, "I tire of princesses and the ladies of the harem. They are all so proper and perfect. I want to run and play with someone my own age."

"Then ask her. Although be aware if you do she will say yes to anything you ask."

"Tell her she can do as she wants, but if she wants to play then she can do that, too. Will you tell her, Thomas?"

He smiled. Yusuf was such a sweet child, unlike his brother. Unfortunately it was his brother Thomas had to deal with.

"I will tell her." He laid a hand on Yusuf's shoulder, feeling the tremble there. "Now, I need you to take a message for me, and it must go to one person and one person only—"

"My father is away from the city."

"This message is for your brother. I must speak with Muhammed, and speak with him tonight."

"You will come to the palace?"

"Muhammed will come to Aamir's bathhouse."

"He likes to visit there."

"I have heard he does. But tonight there will be no women, not until he has spoken with me. I have something important to discuss."

"Can I come, too?"

"No. Our conversation might be... difficult." Thomas had been about to say dangerous, but feared the word would only attract Yusuf the more. "Do you have any notion of the task been set of me and Jorge?"

"I heard you are searching for the man who killed Safya. Do you have him, Thomas? Is that what you want to speak to Muhammed about? They say in the palace you and the eunuch are the killers, but I don't believe it. I'm not sure about my brother. He repeats the charges against you as though they are true."

Thomas knew he had no time to argue his case. "We know who is behind the plot. But I can't tell you who, only your brother, and hope he recognises the truth when he hears it. Will you do this for me, Yusuf? It's a dangerous task I ask of you. There will be those in the palace who wish to seek out and destroy me for what I know. Tell no-one, no-one at all, other than Muhammed."

"I promise, Thomas." The thrum through Yusuf's body grew, his small frame barely able to contain his excitement. "This is real intrigue, isn't it? Bazzu and Prea are in the plot, too, aren't they?"

"You can't mention either of them, or they will be in danger also. Return to your place and then to the palace. Find Muhammed. He is in the palace, isn't he?"

"He was when I left. But you know Muhammed, he likes to hawk and hunt. But he prefers to go out late in the afternoon when the day has cooled. He goes into the hills behind al-Hamra and chases down rabbits and pigeons."

"Then tell him tonight he can't hunt but must come to me."

"Shall I tell him why?"

"This letter will tell him why." Thomas pressed the second letter he had written into Yusuf's warm hand. "You must tell him it's important I see him today. Now go."

Yusuf crept away, stopped and scuttled back. He half climbed onto Thomas's lap and hugged him, a small hard body pressed against his. Thomas knew he should discourage the boy from such shows of affection, but couldn't bring himself to do so. There was still an innocence within Yusuf he wished to see last as long as possible. As the younger son he had been spoiled, allowed to hold on to his childhood longer than his brother. Soon enough he would have to act as a prince and learn the cunning needed to survive in the world on the hill. Thomas pushed him away and this time Yusuf didn't turn back.

Thomas backed out from his hiding place, face streaked with sweat, and strolled back to the shaded alcove. Jorge had remained, keeping watch in case any guards had followed the kitchen party.

They watched Yusuf retrieve his basket. Bazzu placed a few token objects into it before turning and weaving back through the crowd to return to the palace.

* * *

They reached the bathhouse before noon prayers, while the streets were still busy. As Jorge lay on a cot, Thomas used his teeth to untie the knot on the bandage covering his arm. The wound beneath itched, and he needed to know if the itch was from healing or something more sinister.

With the stained bandage removed Thomas held his arm close and sniffed deeply. He detected no hint of infection.

"You should wash that," Jorge said.

Thomas smiled. "Are you the doctor now?"

"I've spent enough time around one to know you should wash it."

"I was planning on that next."

"How is the arm?"

"Healing," Thomas said.

"Do you want me to re-bandage it afterwards? I know I'm not as skilled as Lubna, but I will try if you ask."

Thomas studied the arm. "I think I'll leave it open to the air. The stitches have knitted now and the wound is no longer weeping."

"So you'll live," Jorge said.

"Allah willing."

"The girl is rubbing off on you."

"It's a saying," Thomas said. "Nothing more."

"She's a pretty thing. And bright."

Thomas gave Jorge a look and the eunuch shrugged. "I'm only saying what I see, in case you happened to miss it."

THIRTY-SEVEN

Muhammed came after sunset. Smoke from the many lamps spiralled upwards to be captured by the vaulted ceiling. Thomas watched from the vantage point of the balcony which ran around the large bath in the centre of the building. He hadn't expected the prince to come alone—no member of the royal palace went anywhere alone, unless like Yusuf they sneaked away—but Muhammed entered accompanied by only two guards. He swaggered. He always swaggered, the affectation becoming more pronounced the older he grew.

"You'll have to separate him from his guards." Jorge stood beside Thomas, his head and cheeks rough with stubble, his clothing creased. Thomas knew he looked equally as unkempt. It was almost a week since his last shave, in this same bathhouse. He would ask Aamir for a barber when their business was done. If his head still remained on his shoulders.

"Separating him won't be easy."

"Why not just ask him to send them away?"

"Ask him?"

"That's right. Tell him you must speak with him alone and to send them away."

Thomas laughed, raising his hand to mask the sound. "And he will agree, of course."

"He will once you're both undressed and he sees you can do him no harm. He's a vain man and wouldn't believe it possible for you to attack him on your own."

"In that he's right. Muhammed, for all his arrogance, is a skilled warrior."

"I have heard him say so on many occasions."

"It's true. I've seen him, he's a dervish."

"You haven't done so badly yourself," Jorge pointed out. "You surprised me when you attacked those soldiers."

"I did? How?" Thomas was only half listening, watching Muhammed speak with Aamir, the old man making a suggestion the prince seemed not too keen on.

"You're still alive. I didn't expect that."

Thomas turned away and moved along the balcony, heading for a set of stairs at the end. Jorge fell into step beside him and he stopped.

"Go back to the room. He won't see me if you're there."

"He fears me?"

Thomas didn't bother with any reply other than a smile.

As he made his way along the corridor Thomas wondered if he was making a mistake. What if Bilal had been right after all and Muhammed *was* the guilty party behind everything? But it was too late, the die had been cast, and all he could do now was see how it fell.

The prince waited in a small bath chamber set deep in the rear of the building. It was close to the one Thomas and Jorge had shared the evening before. The same damp rock formed one wall, the same girls and boys moved about, carrying soaps and scented oils, each dressed at most in a strip of cloth.

Muhammed turned when Thomas entered, a grin breaking across his face.

"I have you now, Thomas Berrington. Guards, arrest this man. He is wanted for murder."

Thomas held his hands up. "Murder now, is it?"

"And treason. You will lack a head come morning, and not before time."

"Your brother gave you my message?"

Muhammed glanced away. "He did. Some foolishness about the killer and a plot against my father. As if anyone would plot against Sultan Abu al-Hasan Ali."

"Indeed. But he told you the truth, at least as much as I passed on to him. I would speak with you if I may. I deserve to be heard after what I have done for your family."

"What you have done? You have done nothing. My father has already been far too indulgent. I would not have been so soft."

"I know you wouldn't, but I have never asked a single thing of him. What he gave me were gifts of his own choice, not ones sought. Dismiss your guards and let us talk, and then, if you still want you may take me to the palace and throw me into a dungeon again."

"Again? Why would I send my men away—so you can kill me like you did Safya?"

So Muhammed didn't know of our arrest?

"I killed no-one." Thomas pulled at his robe, loosening it, allowing it to drop to the floor. "You can see I'm no threat, and I'm wounded." He raised his arm, showing the livid scar that ran from elbow to wrist. "You are twice as strong as me, and ten times the fighter. You don't need these men to indulge in a moment's conversation."

Muhammed glanced at the guards, back to Thomas.

Thomas watched the thought processes flow through him.

"Leave us," Muhammed said. "This *ajami* is no threat. Wait outside. But come at once if I call. Now talk."

"I would prefer if they were out of earshot."

"They will be, so long as you don't shout. Now, what more would you have me do, *qassab*?"

"Nothing, my prince, and I thank you." Thomas stepped beneath the flow of hot water falling from the sluice set into the wall. Beneath lay a stone bench and he sat, stretching his legs out, resting his arms along the ledge on either side. The water felt good, warmth seeping into his tired limbs.

When the guards had departed Muhammed sat on the side bench, his eyes searching. Thomas knew he was tracing the scars on his chest, and tried to act as though he wasn't aware of his study.

"You're not joining me, prince?"

Muhammed laughed. "You're an insolent man, aren't you?"

"It was only a question."

"That will never happen. Unless you wish to turn around and let me bugger you. Now *that* would be interesting."

"I'm sorry to disappoint you, prince, but my arse isn't on offer."

"I wouldn't want it if it was." Muhammed was amused, a state of affairs Thomas preferred to continue. Despite his protest the prince began to remove his clothing: fine silk and linen, freshly washed and pressed that morning, perhaps even a new outfit to venture out in this evening. He folded nothing, letting it lie where it dropped. Naked, he stood before Thomas, displaying himself.

The man—for despite having only eighteen years he was definitely a man—possessed broad shoulders and a flat stomach, the owner of his own set of scars which traced across his chest and arms, three on one leg, two on the other. Prizes of battle proudly displayed. Thomas took in the whole of the prince and nodded as if impressed. Only then did Muhammed step beneath his own fall of water.

He stared at Thomas, an expression of open contempt on his face.

"What is it you want of me, *ajami?* Much as I enjoy your company, Aamir was telling me of two new girls he has. They are fresh from Africa and he says their skin is like burnished charcoal, and they have skills no Moorish woman possesses. So tell me quickly, before I grow tired of this game."

Thomas told him.

When Thomas returned to the room Jorge was stretched out on one of the beds, staring at the ceiling.

"So, did he dismiss you without listening?"

"It was confusing. When I told him I suspected Olaf of being behind the killings he didn't appear in the least surprised. He asked why was I telling him this, so I said I needed his help. He laughed."

"Laughed? I know there are times you are extremely

amusing, particularly when you don't know you're being so, but murder is a serious business."

"I think he enjoyed watching me beg. He hates me, I know he does, and loves it when I'm beholden to him."

"You told him what you wanted?"

"I did. I expected resistance, disbelief, but he agreed with all I said. He told me it made a great deal of sense, that Olaf Torvaldsson possesses too much power, and if anyone in this city might plot to overthrow his father it would be him. With the palace guard behind him who could stop the man?"

"You don't think we're making a mistake?" Jorge said, reflecting Thomas's own doubts. "If Muhammed agrees this easily, does it mean he's hiding something?"

"I think not. The more I spoke the more I gained the impression nothing I said was new to him, that my suspicions matched his own. Was Bilal's document a deliberate misdirection, do you think? He was part of the palace. The entire investigation could have been a show, a distraction from the truth, nothing more."

"Why protect Olaf? The Sultan wouldn't hesitate to execute him."

"Are his men loyal to the Sultan or loyal to Olaf?"

Jorge nodded. "I suppose we'll find out. Did Muhammed agree to help?"

"I'm not sure help is the word I would use. He will do what is best for Muhammed. In this case what's best for him is best for us. He agreed to have my letter delivered, and to provide soldiers when we confront Olaf. We'll see what happens then."

"Did you say it would be better if the Sultan was present? If it comes to a confrontation between Muhammed and Olaf I'm not sure where the loyalties of the soldiers will lie."

"I tried to say so without demeaning his authority. But he says his father is away from the city, and nobody knows exactly where."

"So we go ahead anyway?"

"I would prefer the Sultan there, but failing that I believe

Muhammed has the authority. Perhaps it won't come to asking anyone to decide. Once Olaf knows his plotting is uncovered he may submit."

"And if he doesn't?"

"Then I'm a dead man."

"We are both dead men," Jorge said.

Thomas shook his head. "You stay here. If I don't return by nightfall find Lubna and flee the city, take her to safety. You must leave al-Andalus, you won't be safe within its boundaries. Qurtuba is three days ride on a fast horse. Go there first. You're a Spaniard, you'll be fine."

"But Lubna is not."

"Who is Spanish these days? The Moors have lived here so long no-one possesses pure blood anymore. I wager even King Ferdinand and his queen have a little Moorish blood flowing through their veins."

"I'll remember not to mention that fact should I ever be unlucky enough to meet them."

"Take care of her, Jorge. I have grown fond of her in a short time."

"And her sister?"

"Is nothing to me now."

"You take care, too, Thomas. The path you follow is a dangerous one."

"Which is why I remind you, if I fail to return you must leave. By nightfall tomorrow either we'll be together again or you'll be fleeing through the western gate. There's money at my house, hidden beneath the bed. There's more in the workshop. Take it and run."

"You state a hypothetical case. By this time tomorrow we will be back in your house drinking that awful wine of yours and laughing at our fears."

"I pray it is so."

"If you prayed."

"Then Lubna will pray for us."

"I'm sure she will," Jorge said. "Whether we deserve it or not."

THIRTY-EIGHT

Thomas climbed the hill with Jorge close behind. There was no room to walk side by side. The track was barely passable through dense bushes, the soft soil to their left falling away sheer to the Hadarro.

"I don't like this path," Jorge said.

"I told you to stay behind."

"And let you walk into danger alone?"

"Lubna needs you."

"No, Lubna needs *you*. She likes me, but she needs you. And I still don't like this path."

"Would you rather we knock on the main gate? I expect there's still a dungeon waiting for us."

"Why couldn't we go directly to Muhammed?"

"Because I need the robe Prea found, the sword too. They are our only physical evidence, and I have a plan for them."

"You and your plans. I wish I'd turned you down when you asked to me for help. You should have told me there would be danger."

"You were keen enough at the time." Thomas knew Jorge wasn't serious—he wouldn't be here if he was.

The path narrowed and he turned sideways. The sheer wall of the palace to his back felt like it was trying to push him into the ravine.

"You're sure there's a doorway?" Jorge said, following Thomas's example. "I know of no entrance on this side of the walls."

"Prea told me of it. The door is small and used to smuggle people and goods in and out."

"I can imagine the kind of people. The kind of goods, too."

"And you such a paragon of virtue."

The path opened out a little and came to an end. Thomas turned to face the wall.

"There's no doorway," Jorge said. "You've been sent on a fool's errand. That girl should be punished."

"The door is here," Thomas snapped. "If it was easy to find it wouldn't be secret, would it."

Thomas edged along the stained rock forming the base of the palace wall, which soared high above, appearing to lean outward, everything conspiring to push the unwary out into the void. He ran his hands over the stone. At one point he stopped and pushed his hand into a crevice, but it was only where mortar had fallen loose.

"I still say we should continue to the meeting place."

"The door is—ah, I have it." Thomas reached into another crevice, his arm disappearing to the shoulder this time. "Prea tells me the door is used often, so the mechanism should work easily." Something made a metallic noise, muffled by stone. "See?"

Thomas withdrew his arm and pulled at where a section of rock had created a gap. "Come and help me."

Jorge looked at the narrowness of their perch, at the chasm to their back, and stayed where he was.

"I'll remember how helpful you were," Thomas said, leaning out over the drop. The door swung to his touch and he retained his hold, pulling himself back upright and ducking inside. The air was cold and damp, the only light coming from behind.

"I don't—"

"Yes, I know, you don't like it. Then stay behind if you wish, or meet me at the place we agreed on, but I'm going inside. I want to see Bazzu and Prea before we go on." Thomas moved forward, bent almost double in the low passage.

"How far does it go on like this?" Jorge had come to stand in the entrance.

"Prea didn't say, but it can't be forever. I see more light ahead. Are you coming or staying?"

"Coming, I suppose."

"Pull the door closed behind you then. We don't want someone stumbling in on us."

"As if anyone else is going to take that pathway," Jorge said, but he did as requested before following Thomas along the dark passage.

Soon steps rose steeply upward, turning on themselves again and again, rising through layers of rock, dungeon, chamber, until they came to a solid wall.

"Do your magic," Jorge muttered.

Thomas searched, found the niche he knew would be there, and a wooden panel opened to his command.

"You're getting good at this," Jorge said. "When I return to the harem I'm going to have to be more careful in my assignations."

"Don't worry, I have no wish to enter these tunnels ever again."

They found Bazzu in her usual lair, but there was no sign of Prea.

"You got my message?" Thomas asked.

"I did. And that boy was asking about Prea as well."

"He's a prince."

"Prince or not, he's still a boy. Perhaps he found her, for I haven't seen her since yesterday. There is work to do and she decides to go missing."

"You have the robe and sword?" Thomas said.

"Of course, exactly as you asked." She nodded to where a rolled blanket sat on a shelf. "Disguised, as you also asked."

Thomas knew Bazzu's shortness was caused by fear—her fear for Jorge, mostly. Having a plan didn't mean it was going to succeed, and there were a hundred ways it could go wrong.

Thomas unrolled the blanket and checked the contents.

"It's all there," Bazzu said. She reached a hand out to Jorge, who was perched on the corner of her deep table, and he took it.

"Can we go?" Jorge said. "I never thought I would say this, but I'm nervous inside the palace now."

"I want to speak with Prea before we leave. Are you sure you have no idea where she is, Bazzu?"

"She returned with me from the city. The prince took your message to his brother, and she..." Bazzu frowned, trying to call up a memory. "She said she had one more task to do for you, but didn't say what."

"I gave her no task," Thomas said.

Bazzu's frown remained. "I'm sure that's what she said. 'One more task for Thomas'."

His blood chilled. There was only one place she might have gone. The place he'd asked her not to go. The girl thought she was too clever for the killer. Thomas bundled up the blanket once more and thrust it at Jorge.

"I have to check something before we go. Wait here."

"How long are you going to be?"

"Not long. Not long at all. But if I don't return within an hour follow the plan without me."

Jorge scowled. "What plan, Thomas? Without you there is no plan."

"Then I will return."

It should have been a matter of moments to reach the entrance to the tunnels from the kitchen, but Thomas was forced to hide in doorways and alcoves each time he heard someone coming. It was mid-morning, and the palace was busy with guards, officials and servants, but eventually he reached the quiet side chamber and thrust his arm into the opening he had seen Prea use.

A panel jerked open an inch and he drew it wider, clambered through and immediately stopped, one leg inside, one still in the sunlit chamber. There was an odour in the air, one he recognised. The stink of the battlefield. The smell of freshly spilled blood. He ran to where Prea had shown him the cache of robe and sword, ignoring the pain in his shoulders as they scraped and banged against the walls.

She sprawled awkwardly in a lake of blood, and Thomas saw how it had happened. Prea had lain in hiding on the ledge she had shown him, so pleased with her own cleverness. But something had gone wrong. Perhaps she had moved, dislodged a pebble, or the man sensed her, smelled her. The how was irrelevant, because the what lay tumbled on the floor of the tunnel. Thomas went to his knees and moved her gently, re-arranging her tangled limbs.

Prea's face was calm, at peace, and he hoped the attack had come too fast to cause her much pain. She had been dead some time, a day at least. The rigour had come and gone and her limbs lay slack beneath his hands. Her once vibrant eyes were now dull, staring at nothing, and he reached down and closed them, fatigue flooding through him as he closed his own eyes, breathing deeply, trying not to think of what he had brought to this girl who had barely started to live. He stayed that way for minutes before shaking himself. Weakness now would only make her death more futile.

He knelt and searched her slight frame, finding wound after wound. One had pierced her heart and he prayed that had been the first blow. Others ran through her belly and thighs, another to her neck. Any of the blows would have proved fatal, and Thomas recognised most as redundant. These were strikes made in anger. The killer had returned for his robe, his sword, perhaps to continue his work, to take another victim, most likely Aixa, and Prea had been in the way. This wasn't over yet. Unless he was stopped, Safya wouldn't be the last.

Thomas lifted Prea's slight figure and carried her along the tunnel. He kicked the panel out, no longer caring who knew what lay beyond, and walked with her in his arms through the corridors, making no effort to conceal himself. Around him people stared. There were cries of fear. Some ran. Others came towards him only to be stopped by the look of feral rage in his eyes.

Bazzu screamed and fell to her knees wailing as he laid Prea on the floor. Jorge stood to one side, his face pale.

"Who remains in the palace?" Thomas said.

"No-one. They are all at the hillside, as you planned."

"She must be washed and prepared."

"I will care for her." Bazzu reached a trembling hand towards Prea, hesitated.

"Was she religious?"

"A little, yes."

"Then prepare her in the way of Islam and have her interred. Spare no expense, I will pay."

Bazzu looked at him, anger replacing the grief in her eyes. "Don't you *dare* try to buy your way out of this guilt! This is your doing, Thomas Berrington. Didn't you see the girl worshiped you? She would have done anything for you, anything at all—"

"I specifically forbade her to do this."

"Do you honestly think that would make any difference? She did it for you!"

Thomas looked down at the body. "Then I will bear the guilt. I deserve it. But another struck the blow, and I will kill him. Jorge, are you still with me?"

Jorge didn't appear to hear. Thomas went to stand in front of him.

"Are you with me or not?"

"I... I..."

Thomas nodded. "Of course, I understand. Stay and help Bazzu." He went to the table and lifted the blanket holding the robe and sword. He was halfway to the door when Jorge's hand swung him around. For a moment Thomas thought he was going to strike him, but instead Jorge pulled him into a hard embrace.

"I am with you, Thomas."

He glanced at Bazzu in the moments before Jorge released him. Her eyes continued to burn with a hatred he knew would never fade. So be it. He deserved her hatred, welcomed it, drew it into himself, feeling it turn his heart to ice. All emotion drained from him. Fear. Pain. Grief. He pushed Jorge away and left the room, discarding his humanity as he walked through the corridors of the palace. No-one challenged him. No-one dared.

Thirty-Nine

The sun shone from a sky dotted with bright clouds. It was one of those days when a light breeze carried down from the mountains, cooling the heat of the day. An occasional updraft swirled across the ground, lifting blades of dry grass into the air, raising dust, and the trees rattled and shook before stillness returned. One of the miniature storms hit as Thomas and Jorge lay side by side on a rise in the ground, looking down on Muhammed's hawking group in the shallow valley below. A tent had been erected on the flat ground, horses tied behind.

Thirty or so men were arranged in two groups. Muhammed and three others stood apart from the rest, their guards close by. Muhammed held one arm extended, a hawk sitting at his hand.

A cry came, one of the men pointing, and Muhammed launched the bird upward. It soared into the air with rapid wing beats, hovered. A further group of men appeared from the far tree line, driving everything ahead of them. Birds flew in all directions, caught sight of the men and swooped aside. The hawk continued to hover, then its stance changed, the quiver of its wings growing taut, an arrow ready to be loosed. The hawk fell, its prey unaware of danger until talons struck. There was a burst of feathers without sound. The hawk dropped to the ground, its curved beak tearing at meat.

The sound of laughter drifted up the hillside.

"I can see Olaf," Jorge said.

"So do I. In that group set apart, and he has men with him."

"Not as many as Muhammed."

"Three to one. Is that enough? Olaf's men are the best there are."

"They will do nothing. Their loyalty is to the Sultan, and after him the Sultan's sons. As is Olaf's."

"As was Olaf's," Thomas said.

The wind came again, died.

"Are we going to lie here all day?" Jorge said.

Thomas said nothing, studying the men, their positions, trying to work out the tensions between them. Muhammed was at ease. Olaf watched the young prince with what appeared to be disdain. Muhammed ignored everything other than his hawks.

"You're sure he's expecting us?" Jorge said.

"Have you ever been hunting with him?"

"Me? I'm a creature of the harem. Muhammed hates my kind. He recognises the need but wishes it wasn't so."

"I have been with them, at the Sultan's request."

"He likes you."

"I wish that weren't so."

"It's better than the alternative."

"Being ignored would suit me."

"I think that wish is about to end." Jorge nodded down the slope. A man was observing the hawk, concerned at its behaviour. Thomas looked up. The bird hovered directly above them, hanging unmoving in a rising breeze lifting off the ridge. When he looked back, men were pointing. One swung onto a horse and started up the slope.

"Hold him up a minute if you can," Thomas said, rising and moving back to a cluster of olives.

"Hold him up? Me?"

Thomas ignored Jorge as he stripped out of his clothes. He bent and retrieved the opulent silk robes from within the blanket, slipped them on, ignoring the sensuality against his skin as he ignored the raging of his emotions. He had to be cold now. He sought deep for the memory of how he had once been. He pulled the hood over his head, allowing it to drape until it hid most of his face. Then he knelt and drew the sword. He swung it through the air as he stood, ready, memory flooding him with cold fire.

The rider reached the ridge and reined in, sat watching as Thomas walked towards him. Unease touched his face.

"Stay here," Thomas said as he reached Jorge. "Hide. Watch. And remember, if anything happens to me, take Lubna to safety."

"I would rather be at your side."

"And I would rather you stay safe. Too many have died already. Can't you for once just do as I ask?"

He started forward without waiting for a reply. The rider tried to block him with his horse.

"Who are you? What are you doing here?"

"I am death," Thomas said, pushing the horse aside, knowing the beast would respond to his touch.

The rider tried to get in front of him again. "You're the surgeon. The *qassab*."

"I am he," Thomas said.

"The prince expects you." The man glanced back to the ridge. Jorge was no longer visible.

The horse knocked against Thomas again, and he fought the urge to strike out at the man. Cold. He needed to be as cold as the snow that tipped the Sholayr.

"Walk on then," the rider said. "We have been waiting on you, and the prince waits for no man."

Thomas took his time descending the shallow slope, knowing all eyes were on him, exactly as he wanted. From within the shadow of his hood he observed Olaf, waiting for recognition to show.

The closer he came the more Thomas's doubt grew. The old soldier's cohort was closest to him, and so far nothing showed on the man's face.

Thomas stopped as Olaf started towards him. So this was the moment. Would Olaf strike first, or try disguising the truth? Thomas wondered if he could kill the man. He had killed men bigger and stronger, men who considered themselves great fighters—but Olaf?

"What are you doing here? They told me you were the killer.

This is a dangerous place for you." There was no hint of deception in the general's eyes, and his concern appeared genuine. Olaf looked him up and down. "And why are you dressed like this? Do you know we wait for the Sultan?"

So Muhammed had delivered the message. Thomas smiled. "The Sultan isn't coming. Do you not recognise these robes?"

Olaf shook his head. "Should I?" He took a step closer and Thomas tightened the grip on his sword. "The cloth is extremely fine, but they are cut as a fighting man's robes, not those of a surgeon."

"Today I am a fighting man."

Olaf laughed. "You?"

"Have you forgotten our lesson? I was barely trying that day."

Thomas studied the general's face. His eyes were clear and without guile; but he was a trained fighter, well versed in concealing his thoughts. Except... in all the time Thomas had known Olaf, he had considered the man incapable of hiding even the slightest of feelings. Thomas had seen him cry openly in response to Helena's injuries, weep at the memory of his first wife.

Thomas looked beyond Olaf, searching for some indication of the truth. It had to be here somewhere. This gathering involved everyone other than the Sultan, and it had been he who put Thomas on the trail in the first place. The killer would be here. Thomas had worried he might be with Abu al-Hasan, but Prea's murder had shown him the man was close.

Muhammed was to their left, in front of the tent, his heavily leathered arm now at his side. Faris al-Rashid stood close by, as he always did, a whisperer in the ears of men who possessed power, a supplier of coin where coin was needed, always willing to buy favour.

The other men from Thomas's earlier encounter in the palace were scattered through the group. Men of influence. Men of ambition.

Olaf's troops were watching their general, tension in their

stance.

"What is my daughter doing here?" Olaf said, looking beyond Thomas.

For a moment Thomas thought he meant Helena, but then he saw the direction of his gaze and turned. Jorge and Lubna were coming down the hillside. Lubna ran ahead, something fluttering in her hand. She had closed half the distance when she stopped abruptly, her feet scrabbling in the dust.

Thomas turned again at a commotion, a murmur amongst the troops, a shifting of attention away from him to a group of men coming down the far slope. Their horses raised dust that masked them, but the uniform was clear, as was the dress of the man leading them. Abu al-Hasan Ali, Sultan of Gharnatah, had returned from his expedition.

Just in time, Thomas thought.

He looked back towards Muhammed. The prince appeared as surprised as everyone else at the new arrival.

"See," Olaf said, "the Sultan comes. He asked for me to be here—something important, he said."

Something tugged at Thomas's sleeve and he glanced down to see Lubna had come to him.

"I found this," she said. "It's important."

He glanced at the paper in her hand, unable to read what it said.

"You came out here, into this, with a piece of paper?"

"It's important," she repeated.

Thomas looked away. The Sultan halted a hundred feet from his son, his troops fanning out to either side. Twenty men.

"You have to look at it!" Lubna said, waving the page in front of his face.

"Show your father." Thomas walked away, taking his time, moving in a long arc. He aimed to the left, planning to start with Muhammed, then the Sultan, finally Olaf. He was glad Jorge had disobeyed him and come down with Lubna. He had skills, and knowledge, that would prove invaluable.

He turned, seeking Jorge, found him standing beyond Olaf.

Thomas raised his arm, forgetting it was the one holding the sword. His gesture was greeted with a clatter as fifty men drew their own weapons.

"Come to me," Thomas called out.

Jorge looked at him as if he was mad.

Thomas beckoned him again, and the eunuch reluctantly started across the space between them. Beyond him Thomas saw Lubna talking animatedly with her father. She waved the paper at him as she had Thomas, but the general didn't read and her effort was once again wasted.

"I thought you wanted me to stay away." Jorge stopped beside him.

"I changed my mind. I need your humanity."

"You have plenty of that yourself. I think I'll drag Lubna back up the hillside. I felt safer up there. You need listen to what she has discovered."

Thomas grabbed Jorge's arm. "Stay with me, I need you now."

Something in his voice caused Jorge to stop pulling away.

"What can you need me for?"

"I'm going to walk in front of each of these men. I want you to study them. You said you would recognise the man again, now let's find out if that's true or not. And you read the signals on men's faces and in their bodies. Watch. Tell me who are the guilty."

"You're a fool to trust me in this."

"Then I'm a fool." Thomas turned away, started walking, not waiting to see if Jorge was with him or not. He had to do this regardless.

He focussed his attention on the first group. Faris al-Rashid, Valentin al-Kamul and Don Antonio Galbretti stood together, a conclave of conspiracy. Thomas expected a reaction, but although the men stared at him as he passed their faces showed either amusement or boredom.

As he approached Muhammed, a movement to one side distracted him, a familiar figure within the shadow of the tent.

Helena's white-blonde hair shone through the darkness, glowing brighter as she walked to the entrance and stood in sunlight. Her head was uncovered, a statement she was her own woman, beyond convention. She watched Thomas, her mouth quirking, but there was nothing of affection in her expression.

Has she hated me so much all this time?

"I'm sorry, Thomas." Jorge spoke softly beside him. So he had seen the truth as well.

Thomas turned to Muhammed, studying the young prince. His face showed its usual contempt for the world, but no recognition or fear.

Thomas strode past the Sultan's men, heading for the group of soldiers Olaf commanded.

"Stop," Jorge said.

Thomas turned. "What is it?"

"You weren't looking, but there is a man." Jorge indicated with a nod of his head. "There. Three to the right of Muhammed. He knows these robes. And..." The eunuch frowned. "...and I know him."

Thomas returned to stand in front of Muhammed's troops. They were dust-streaked from hunting. The Sultan spurred his horse and placed himself between Thomas and his son.

"Why are you dressed this way? Is it the latest fashion among Gharnatah's medical men?"

"I am dressed as an assassin," Thomas said, then softly to Jorge, "The tall man, thin? He has dark skin and an oiled beard?"

"He is our man. See him now?"

Thomas stepped closer, watching tightly held emotion move beneath the man's face. He scanned his companions, saw no-one else who reacted in the same way. There was a mixture of surprise, amusement, disdain and hatred, but only one man showed guilt. Thomas felt himself trembling, fought back a violent urge to attack the man immediately. Instead he turned to the Sultan.

"Malik, I know who the killer is."

"Are you sure of this?"

There was something too relaxed in the Sultan's voice.

"I'm certain."

The Sultan turned in his saddle. "Then point him out to me. Accuse the man and we will see what he has to say."

From the edge of his vision Thomas caught the soldier shift his feet.

"There—he is the one," Jorge said, then drew away, distancing himself from the scene.

Thomas raised his sword, ready to point at the man. The soldiers in front of him, to either side, raised their weapons in turn.

"Thomas!" It was Olaf, running across the ground. "Thomas, you have to listen to Lubna."

"Not now!" Thomas almost screamed. He thrust his arm backwards, the sword flashing in the sun. "This is our man. There!" He brought the sword around, pointing, the tip shaking with anger as he allowed rage to rise within him. It filled his entire being, pushing out the last traces of humanity.

The Sultan smiled as he saw who Thomas was pointing at. "And what do you say, Qasim?"

"I say this *ajami* will die soon, and in great agony."

"Do you deny his charge?"

"I admit I am a killer. It is who I am. But so is every other man on this field. This man…" He spat. "This man is nothing."

"Do you withdraw your allegation, Thomas Berrington?"

"I do not." His gaze remained locked on the assassin's.

"Then how do you propose we settle the matter?"

"Combat," said the man named Qasim. "I challenge the coward to trial by combat. If he kills me I am guilty. If I kill him he lies."

"What do you say, Thomas? Are you convinced enough in your beliefs to test them in this way?"

"He is the killer," Thomas said. "I accept the challenge."

The Sultan laughed and clapped his hands. "Trial by combat. So be it. Clear the field. Qasim, come out and show yourself." The Sultan twisted, taking in the groups arrayed across the hollow. He raised his voice. "Nobody interferes. This fight is between these two men. Clear the ground!"

FORTY

Qasim stepped from the line, tearing his heavy outer robes loose, discarding the turban marking him as a member of the palace guard. He drew his sword and unbuckled the belt holding it, stripping himself for battle.

Thomas stepped back. Back again. He jerked his head, the hood of the robe sliding away to reveal his face. He stopped, ready, a long forgotten rage surging through him. He recalled an old man in the mountains telling him tales of burning rock spewing from the ground. That is how his anger felt. Heated beyond containment.

Muhammed ran to his father, gripped the edge of his saddle and said something, but Thomas wasn't listening. His eyes tracked Qasim as the man stepped from the line of guards.

Qasim swung his sword loosely at his side, a steady surety in his eyes, and Thomas knew the man was convinced he was going to kill him. It was, after all, the most likely outcome.

Thomas walked backwards until he bumped against someone and stopped. Qasim continued coming, closing the distance. Without looking who was behind Thomas stepped to one side, but a hand grabbed at the flowing cloth of his robe, holding him back. When he looked down Lubna stood there, her face angry.

"You have to know about this!" she said.

"Not now." Olaf pulled her away. "Thomas doesn't have time. Don't distract him from what he must do. Come away now and I will see he is avenged. Here, take this." Olaf pressed something into Thomas's hand. He glanced down to discover a knife, its wicked blade honed to a razor edge. He recognised it. This was Olaf's own knife, the one he carried into every battle.

Thomas looked into Olaf's eyes with gratitude, recognising he had been wrong to suspect the man.

"I must tell Thomas—I know who is behind everything..." But Lubna's voice faded as she was dragged away from the killing ground. Thomas closed his ears as he turned inward, searching for emotions long buried, those he had hoped never to need again.

If I am to die, let it be because I wasn't good enough, not because I refused to try.

He should have been afraid, about to meet his own death. Perhaps it was madness, but he believed not. The grinning man pacing in front of him didn't know of Thomas's past. No-one knew of Thomas's past other than Jorge, and he didn't know everything. Thomas had buried the evil he did deep, but not so deep it wouldn't return when called on.

Flashes of memory seared across his vision. The first battlefield strewn with dead, both French and English. His flight and attempts to banish those memories, except they were of the kind impossible to purge. He delved deeper, remembering how to fight, how he used to be invincible. A demon with a strange accent and pale skin. He had been young then, and fighting came naturally. He hadn't lifted a sword in anger for over twenty years, but the muscle memory remained. Olaf had reminded him of that.

He swung his sword right, left, circled it in front of him in a pointless show of bravura.

Qasim smiled, his own sword still, a dagger in his left hand gripped by only thumb and two fingers.

Beyond him the Sultan and Muhammed were arguing.

Faris al-Rashid stood close to both, a smile on his face.

Helena stood to one side, between Valentin al-Kamul and Antonio Galbretti. One of them said something to her and Helena hit him, her slap louder than the murmur of conversation. Thomas looked around, saw men placing bets on the victor, and knew where the money would be going. He recalled the last time a circle such as this had formed, as the troops returned from Tajir. The memory felt years old but had been barely a week before. That fight had ended badly for both parties, and he knew today's outcome might end the same.

The Sultan turned away from Muhammed and rose in his saddle, waving a hand. His voice when it came was rich with authority.

"Let Allah decide!"

Even before the last word was out Qasim came fast, sword flashing. Thomas fell back, raising his own to deflect the blow. His arm stung from the force of it, and he retreated further.

Qasim grinned. "I liked your little friend, *qassab*. Liked her so much I fucked her before I killed her. She squealed like an animal, both times I stuck her."

The words were a lie. Thomas let them wash over him like water across a stone. He would remain and the water would pass, carrying his fear with it.

He stilled his mind, knowing rationality was as much an enemy as the man before him. The past flooded in to replace all thought. He stopped moving backwards and attacked, a swirling djinn in a cloak of dark fire.

It was Qasim's turn to fall back beneath the onslaught. He kicked dust at Thomas, but he came through it, blade scything down. Qasim blocked, blocked again, feinted and counter-attacked. For both of them nothing else existed. The nobles wagering on the outcome. The soldiers watching with dispassionate, professional interest. The women Thomas loved. He fought for another he had loved, his heart—too soft if he let it—turned to ice in his chest. They swung and ducked and growled. Qasim was fast, skilled. Thomas parried, attacked in turn, seeing the confidence leach from the man's eyes. For over a minute they clashed without respite.

Then they stopped, breathing fast. Thomas was gratified to see this was as hard on Qasim as it was on him. He wondered how much longer he could keep fighting at this pace. A thousand questions jostled in his mind and he dismissed them all. Now was too late to seek answers.

Thomas span, his robe billowing outward. He let Qasim thrust aimlessly through the cloth, heard the whisper of silk parting against the blade. For an instant fire burned along his side as a lucky thrust kissed his skin, then his sword flashed down.

Qasim raised his arm, for a moment his own blade catching in the swirling folds of silk before breaking loose. He barely countered the blow in time, and Thomas took the moment to punch his knife upwards into the man's side. The blow jarred his arm as the blade caught on a rib and he withdrew, his hand streaked with blood.

"You cut me," Qasim said, shock in his voice, as though such a thing had never happened before.

"Then we're all square." Thomas parted the tattered silk on one side to show his own wound. It wasn't serious, but Qasim didn't know that, all he would see was the blood running down Thomas's flank, and a glint of triumph sparked in his eyes.

"I've taken worse than this scratch. Call yourself a surgeon? Don't you know where a man's heart lies?"

"You have no heart." Thomas struck even as he spoke. Qasim parried, came again, and Thomas deflected a storm of blows. For a moment the sound of shouting came to him, and he realised most considered this an entertainment.

They fell back, circling, both wary now.

"Why did Muhammed put you up to this?" Thomas threw the name out wildly, half-rewarded when Qasim frowned.

"You have no clue."

"Al-Rashid has much to gain from the Sultan's dishonour."

Qasim spat, but Thomas knew some of Jorge's skills with people must have rubbed off on him because, for a moment, there had been a flicker of something on Qasim's face. Anyone else not looking so hard would have missed it.

Qasim came at him again, determined to finish the fight, his sword arcing down, knife arm slashing. Thomas scurried backwards, parrying, twisting, stumbling. His foot caught on a rock and one leg skidded from beneath him. He raised his right arm as Qasim's sword came at him, stumbled again, fell, knowing the fight was over.

Except Qasim didn't strike.

He stood over Thomas, legs spread either side of him, a grin across his face. His left heel trapped Thomas's hand which still held the sword.

"You think you know everything, don't you, you men of letters? Clever men like you. Well, you know nothing. Nothing at all. There is life and there is death and there is honour. Nothing else matters. Nothing."

"What do you know of honour?" Beneath the folds of his cloak Thomas straightened his left arm, praying the silk would mask any movement.

"I obey my masters. There is honour enough in that for me."

"Even when al-Rashid asks you to kill the innocent?"

"There are no innocents. And my master is not that perfumed clown. I answer to a greater power in this land." Qasim shifted position, searching for the perfect spot to strike. Thomas knew the man would take pride in the final blow. It would broadcast his skill to those watching.

Cries filtered through his fugue, soldiers calling out for Qasim to finish it, Lubna's voice cutting through them all, calling his name, her father's deeper bark.

Thomas kicked out and Qasim laughed, easily avoiding his foot, but he missed the sudden tug of Thomas's hand which released his sword arm. Qasim struck in an instant, the movement too fast to follow. Thomas's fist came up. The point of Qasim's sword entered through his palm, pinning his hand to the ground.

"I give you this, you fight well for an *ajami*. But I will still kill you. I will kill you slowly, like I killed your little friend." Qasim knelt, his knees on Thomas's upper arms, locking him to the ground. "She called your name at the end. It was so sweet. Whose name are you going to call, *qassab*?"

Thomas struggled, but he was pinned. He tried kicking with his leg again but the blow bounced from Qasim's back as though it was nothing.

"Stop this madness!" Olaf's voice boomed across the killing ground.

To be answered by the Sultan's. "Allah decides. This runs its course. No-one is to interfere. Do you hear me, Olaf Torvaldsson? *No-one is to interfere!*"

Qasim laid the point of his knife on Thomas's cheek and leaned in until his face was inches away. His body lay as close along Thomas's as a lover's.

"Look at me, surgeon, take good note of this face, because it's the last thing you will ever see. Carry it with you to whatever hell your people inhabit. I will take this eye first, and then the other. Finally I will cut out your heart while it still beats."

The man ran the tip of his knife across Thomas's cheek, opening it. His chest pressed to Thomas's. It was the moment he had been waiting for. Qasim's knees pinned his arms above the elbow, and Thomas believed, hoped, he was allowed enough movement. He raised his unpinned hand beneath the folds of silk. Yes, he thought, just enough freedom to do what was needed.

"You know what? You talk too much."

Thomas slipped his knife between Qasim's ribs, making no mistake this time, his aim cold and calculating. He watched the look of surprise on the Berber's dark face and twisted quickly to one side as the man's knife came down at his eyeball, felt it sear across his cheek again. Then the air left Qasim's body and blood gushed from his mouth in a final cough as he fell on top of Thomas.

It was Olaf who reached them first, tossing Qasim's body aside as though it weighed nothing, kneeling beside Thomas, patting his body, searching for wounds. When Thomas opened his eyes the old soldier sat back on his heels and made a sound that might be interpreted as relief.

Then Lubna was there, her fingers on his face. "Is it deep?"

"You tell me," Thomas said. "Olaf, pull this sword from my

hand. And thank you."

Olaf offered a smile and obliged.

Thomas bit back a scream, watched as blood spilled from the wound onto dry soil.

"My face will heal, Lubna, but my hand needs attention. Someone here will have bandage. Go find it, bind the wound tight." Thomas groaned as Olaf raised him to a sitting position.

"Can you walk?"

"With help."

"I will help him." It was Jorge, standing tall and strong, almost unrecognisable from the perfumed eunuch of a week before. His dark hair had grown half an inch on his skull, his cheeks were shadowed with dark stubble.

Olaf nodded and between them they raised Thomas to his feet. He swayed, not from any injury, but from the draining of the lust of battle. He was glad to feel it depart, glad to have held it within for so long.

Thomas lifted his head to find a circle of men still surrounding him and all strength left him. *Take me*, he thought, *but spare the others.*

The Sultan sat erect in his saddle, eyes cold.

Soldiers formed a solid wall between the small group in the centre and safety.

Olaf tugged Thomas forward. "He is the victor, Malik. Allah has decided."

"And now I must decide," Abu al-Hasan Ali said. "Was the fight fair? Did Thomas Berrington win by subterfuge? In fact, how could a lowly surgeon defeat one of my handpicked men? It's simply not possible." He turned in his saddle. "Did you drug him, Thomas? Or poison your blade?"

"Thomas won the fight fairly," Olaf said. He released his hold and stepped forward, seeming to double in size.

The Sultan looked around, making a judgement.

He chose wrong.

"I declare this combat void. Thomas Berrington cheated, and his life is forfeit."

"No, it is not." Muhammed pushed forward to stand beside his father's horse. "Thomas won. He must walk free."

"You dispute my judgement?"

"When you are wrong."

"Olaf—arrest my son. We will have two beheadings today." A tight smile crossed the Sultan's lips.

Muhammed made no move. Neither did Olaf.

The Sultan rose in his stirrups. "Arrest these traitors, all of them. Take them now!"

Lubna stepped forward, once more waving the sheet of paper. "There is only one guilty man here, and it is him!" She pointed directly at the Sultan. Around the edges of the circle some men drew their swords, others moved back as though to drift away.

"Are you all cowards?" the Sultan screamed, drawing his own sword. "If you cannot finish this then I will." He spurred his horse, coming directly at Thomas. Jorge stepped between him and the oncoming dervish, but Olaf pushed him aside like a reed, only to be bowled over by the onrushing beast.

The Sultan swung down at Thomas, who stepped to one side, the sword whistling past his ear, but he knew he couldn't avoid him for long. He was trapped inside the circle of men, with nowhere to hide. Too late, he now knew who had been behind everything.

So did Muhammed.

Around the circle soldiers drew their swords, forming an uncrossable barrier.

Olaf stepped close to the Sultan's horse, grabbing the reins in one hand, lifting the other to stop the blow that came down at him, a thousand battles honing his skills to an unmatched level. He gripped the Sultan's wrist and twisted, the sword clattering from his hand to the ground.

Muhammed strolled to the other side of his father's horse.

"It is over," he said.

FORTY-ONE

"I owe you an apology." Thomas sat on cushions while Lubna bandaged his hand. The wound was not as bad as it had first looked, but blood still welled from both sides where the sword had gone straight through.

Olaf knelt beside him, shaking his head. "You owe me nothing. You unmasked the killer. The whole of Gharnatah is grateful."

"He was a weapon, nothing more. The killer remains." Thomas stared at the old soldier. "I have something hard to ask of you, and you may refuse."

"Ask."

"Your loyalty is to the Sultan of Gharnatah, is it not?"

"He is my master."

"And if you know now it was him behind everything, what then?"

Olaf sat back. Here inside the royal tent Olaf looked out of place among the opulence.

"How sure are you? My daughter made the same claim, but I dismissed her ravings."

"It is the truth." Lubna spoke, kneeling on Thomas's other side, applying the last of the bandage. It was dark with blood, but she had tied it tight and soon the bleeding would slow. "I have proof. It's what I brought you, what I was trying to show Thomas before he insisted on fighting."

"I had no choice," Thomas said.

"There is always a choice."

"Not always, my sweet," Olaf said to his daughter. She scowled and leaned across Thomas.

"I need to look at your face." Her fingers touched, gentle, but

Thomas winced.

"I will have a scar, I think," he said.

"Like my sister."

He didn't want reminding of Helena. "Olaf, I want you to go to Muhammed, tell him what I have told you, tell him what Lubna knows. Take Jorge. I know Muhammed bears no love for him, but I believe he will accept his word as the truth. Lubna, tell us what your proof is before we take this risk."

"Tell me what?"

Thomas turned his head. Muhammed stood in the doorway. To his right was Faris al-Rashid. A little behind Helena waited, uncertainty on her face.

"Send the others away," Thomas said.

Muhammed surveyed the small group inside the tent. "Am I safe here?"

Olaf rose to his feet. "You are safe with me, prince, you know you are."

An expression of amusement crossed Muhammed's face. "You are my father's man, are you not?"

"I am the Sultan's man," Olaf said.

"And if my father is no longer Sultan?"

"I am the Sultan's man," Olaf repeated.

Muhammed entered the tent, waving his hand in dismissal to the others. Faris al-Rashid took Helena's arm and led her outside. "So tell me what proof you have. I can do nothing without proof."

"I have proof," Lubna said, getting to her feet.

Muhammed looked at her with open contempt. "You're a servant. No-one will believe a servant. I'm wasting my time here."

"Wait," Thomas said. "Lubna is Olaf's daughter. That must count for something."

"Olaf Torvaldsson's daughters don't have a sound reputation for honesty at the moment."

"That's as may be," Thomas said. "But tell me this, who did Helena come to tell her tales to? Was that you or your father?"

"It wasn't me."

"Show him the paper," Thomas said, hoping it was proof enough, unsure which of the pages they had studied might hold greater meaning than he had seen.

"Father." Lubna held out her hand and Olaf reached into his pocket, handed her a single sheet. She took it across to Muhammed and he studied it.

"A bill of sale?" He tossed the page aside. Lubna bent to retrieve it.

"A bill of sale for a special roll of cloth," Lubna said. "The cloth Thomas now wears."

"Let me see again."

Muhammed read more slowly, drew the page close to study the seal affixed to the bottom.

"This bill is in my name. I ordered no such cloth from this... this Spaniard."

"And the seal?" Lubna said. Thomas was proud of her. In the face of the second most powerful man in the kingdom she showed no fear.

"It's my father's seal. But it is known I use it at times. Our scribes conduct all such matters on our behalf, it is not unknown for the wrong seal to be used, everyone knows this."

"I went to Carlos Rodriguez and pressed him," Lubna said. "He didn't want to talk with a woman, but he knew who I was, and I think he spoke with me because of Thomas." She glanced at him, her face a mask. "He recalls this bill of sale because of what it concerns and how it came to him. He still has some of the silk in his workshop—"

"I knew I had seen it somewhere before," Jorge said.

Lubna waved him to silence. "He says it's the finest cloth he has ever seen, imported from the East. The bill of sale is in your name, prince, but it was your father who placed the order personally. Rodriguez remembers it well. It's not every day a merchant plays host to the Sultan of Gharnatah."

"When was this?"

"More than half a year ago, before last year's harvest. Your father wanted a special outfit made. Only one at first, with more to follow. Rodriguez made the robe—the one Thomas now wears."

"How did you come upon such a thing, surgeon?"

"In the tunnels."

"What tunnels? I know nothing of any tunnels."

"I will show you, but for now you must believe the tale Lubna tells. A girl I was extremely fond of died to bring me this robe. The man I have just killed recognised it at once, I saw it in his eyes. He is the one who murdered those girls, the one who murdered Safya. He would have killed all the Sultan's wives and anyone else who got in his way. On your father's orders."

Muhammed shook his head. "Why would he do such a thing?"

Thomas stared at the prince. "You know why. The whole of the palace knows why. Do you want your place usurped by the sons of the Greek woman?"

Muhammed waved the accusation away. "Talk. Nothing but talk."

"Then tell me how your father treats you. Does he speak with you as he always has, or does he cut you out from discussion? What does he say of the future? Does it include you?"

"My father is a busy man. He has no time to tell me everything he plans in his campaigns."

Thomas tried to sit up, failed. "Help me!"

Olaf offered a strong arm.

"Fetch Helena back," Thomas ordered, and Jorge left the tent. Muhammed read again the single sheet of paper that was their only physical evidence linking the killer's robe with the Sultan.

"That paper was in the possession of one of the palace's scribes. The same man who was first asked to investigate the killings." Thomas spoke as the ideas came to him, each slotting neatly into place. If this was a game of Mancala it would be perfect. "He must have recognised the importance of what it contained, may even have written it originally himself, for that was his job. I don't know who he went to with his suspicions, it wouldn't have been the Sultan himself, but someone wanted to protect your father and the man was dismissed. I consider him lucky not to have been killed immediately, although he was caught in the end."

Jorge returned, dragging a writhing Helena alongside. Her fists struck against his chest and shoulders, but they were no more than raindrops against a cliff.

"Who have you been so secretly visiting, my love?" Thomas asked, disdain dripping through his voice.

"I have visited with friends, you know I have."

"Who?"

"Friends in the harem."

"Have you seen her recently, Jorge, before this task dragged you from your duties?"

The eunuch shook his head, still holding Helena's wrist.

Muhammed moved suddenly and grasped her other arm, tugged her close. A knife appeared in his hand and he laid the edge against Helena's face.

"Do you want me to open you up again? Tell the truth."

"I have done nothing wrong!"

Muhammed flicked the tip of the blade and the scar running down Helena's face bloomed red. She screamed. Muhammed turned the knife to the other side of her face.

"Let's see how many men still want you when I've finished. Tell us now or I will peel the skin from you."

"Zoraya! I visited Zoraya."

"Why?"

"She is my friend. We are both strangers in this land and she recognises a kindred spirit. I am fond of her children, too."

Muhammed grinned. "Oh, I wager you are. Young men feeling the blood flowing in their loins for the first time. I expect you have many lessons you can teach them, the same as those you taught me." It was a wild accusation, but Thomas saw a flush rise along Helena's neck and knew there was truth to it.

Helena tugged away, breaking free. She got as far as the

entrance to the tent when she ran into a figure coming in.

"Oh, my love, help me, these men throw such accusations!"

Abu al-Hasan Ali pushed her to one side. "What's going on? What plot is taking place?"

"I know, father," Muhammed said. "I know everything."

Abu al-Hasan offered a dismissive glance. "You know little. I have tried to teach you much and you have pissed my lessons away. Thomas—tell me what this is all about."

Thomas leaned against Olaf.

"You are found out, Malik," Thomas said, and as he drew himself upright he saw the Sultan's gaze fall on the silk robe, and once more caught the same flash of recognition he had seen out on the field, the same flash that caused his blood to chill. "Your man is dead, and you are no longer Sultan of Gharnatah." Thomas glanced towards Muhammed, who nodded.

"You turn against me? You, an *ajami* I raised above all others? I abandon you. I abandon you all. My son, too. Olaf, come, we have work to do."

"I am no longer your man," Olaf said. "My loyalties lie with the Sultan."

"*I am the Sultan!*" Abu al-Hasan's voice was a scream.

"No longer, father." Muhammed straightened his shoulders. "You have betrayed this city for your own interests." He looked down at his hands, frowning. "I swear I will never love, for it weakens a man."

"Traitors, you are all traitors!" The Sultan turned and strode for the outside, but Olaf was faster, darting across the tent to catch him before he could show himself.

Thomas wondered what would have happened had Abu al-Hasan not been stopped, had he managed to command the men beyond; whether events would have turned out differently.

Thomas looked to Olaf. "Will your men follow you?"

Olaf nodded. "They will."

"Then Muhammed, go out with Olaf at your side and tell them your father is no longer Sultan. Olaf, make sure you back him up. They will follow you or not, prince, but the die is cast and cannot be taken back."

Thomas stumbled to the doorway and gripped Abu al-Hasan's arm as Olaf released his hold. Jorge came to join him and they pulled him inside. The man was strong, and Thomas weak, but Jorge was more than strong enough for the task alone.

From beyond the walls of the tent came a sudden commotion, the sound of clashing swords, shouts, screams as some men remained loyal to the end.

Abu al-Hasan smiled. "You will die in great pain for this betrayal, Thomas Berrington."

"I have been told that once already today, and the man who made that threat is dead himself."

"You would kill me, too?"

Thomas shook his head. "You know I would not."

"I considered you a friend."

"So you did. But the friendship of a Sultan is not as welcome a gift as you might think."

"And my other gift?" Abu al-Hasan gave a sly smile.

"Your other gift is tainted."

"She is skilled though, is she not? She will have shown you such sweet pleasures no-one else possibly could."

"Such is the way of all temptation," Thomas said. "Why did you have to kill them? I don't understand. You could have made Zoraya your preferred wife, even named her children as your heirs, all without murder being involved."

Abu al-Hasan made a noise of contempt. "You might be the best surgeon in Garnatah, but you don't understand this world at all if you think I would be allowed to do such a thing. People believe a Sultan rules them, but that's not true. We do the will of the people, or the people have us removed. A foreigner, a Greek woman, would not be accepted. Nor her children." The Sultan stared into Thomas's eyes, and he saw nothing there at all: no guilt, no shame, no sorrow. "I had no other choice."

"There is always a choice."

"Not one I was willing to accept." The Sultan took a step

closer, drawing himself up to his full height, but this time Thomas did not bend his knee, and looked down at him.

"Your man was out of control. You should have stopped him, reigned him in. Innocent girls were killed."

"Do you mean your little friend?"

Thomas held his anger hard in check. "And others. There was no need."

"There is always need. This is your fault," the Sultan said. "You *do* know that, don't you? If you had done what was expected of you when I asked you to find the killer, and failed, there would have been no more deaths than necessary."

This time it was Thomas took a step closer. They stood, almost touching. He could smell the Sultan's sweat—sweat like that of any other man, rank and sharp—and the scent of travel: dust and horse and leather. "You really don't know me at all, do you, if you expected me to fail. I trusted you. I wanted to serve."

"You speak of trust? To a Sultan? You are too innocent for this world, *ajami*."

"Oh, not so innocent," Thomas said. "That's where you made a mistake, because you don't know me. You're finished."

Abu al-Hasan smiled. "Do you think so?" He struck out, a blade all at once in his hand. Jorge tried to block the attack and was tossed aside, the old Sultan still a mighty warrior. He followed through, his knife embedding itself into Thomas's shoulder, and Lubna's screams followed him into oblivion.

FORTY-TWO

Thomas woke on a clean bed in a cool room. He lay for a long time listening to his own breathing, the scent of lemon and lime and lavender strong in the air, and knew he wasn't at home. Reluctant to make even an attempt at lifting his eyelids he waited. His chest ached on the opposite side to his wounded hand, which now seemed nothing in comparison, and gradually memory returned. He shivered even though it wasn't cold.

He heard a voice say, "He's awake," but it was distant. Then came the slap of sandals on a tiled floor and a cloth dampened his brow. He had no more excuses and opened his eyes.

Lubna leaned over him, her face concerned, her eyes scanning his body, and when they eventually rose and met his she smiled, a shy smile that said more than words could.

"Where am I?" Thomas's voice emerged cracked. Lubna helped him sit up, offered water. He sipped, felt a little better.

"The palace," she said. "I wanted to take you home but the Sultan insisted. The new Sultan, that is. He was here earlier, sat with you for an hour before leaving. There is much for him to do, but he has asked to be sent for as soon as you wake, as has Olaf. Yusuf is still here. He is fast asleep on a cot in the corner. He refused to leave you."

"Is he dead?" Thomas had no need to say who.

Lubna shook her head. "Banished."

"And your father?"

"Is still the Sultan's general. He simply has a new master."

"Who treated me?" Thomas asked. "You have fine skills, but my wound was beyond what I have managed to teach you."

"We had to fight them off. Every surgeon in Gharnatah

wanted the honour of repairing you."

Thomas smiled. "Then who? There are some I wouldn't want within a mile of me."

Lubna returned the smile, hers strained. "Al-Baitar."

"Then I will heal." He looked at Lubna. "I will heal, won't I?"

She nodded. "Al-Baitar says so, and he seems to know what he is doing. Not as good as you, but good enough."

"Yes. Good enough. You tried to tell me, didn't you?"

"It doesn't matter now," Lubna said. She laid her hand over his and he turned it to twine the fingers of his uninjured hand through hers. She leaned her slim body over his, making a show of checking his bandages. Her hair brushed his face and Thomas breathed in its scent.

"Helena?" he asked, and Lubna drew back quickly. "She is with the Sultan?"

Lubna shook her head and busied herself with meaningless work, tidying the low table beside his bed. He reached for her hand again, held it against his chest. Slowly she stilled and turned to him.

"Thomas!" Yusuf had woken, and whatever moment had been about to happen was dashed away as the boy ran across the room and almost knocked Lubna aside.

Thomas smiled, the young prince's excitement infectious.

"I did well, didn't I? I passed your message to Muhammed exactly as you asked. And he came. You have solved the killings, Thomas, you and my brother. He is grateful to you, he told me so. I know you haven't always liked him, but perhaps that can change now. He's a good brother and I love him dearly. He is not cold like father was. We three can be friends, can't we? What was it like to kill that man? My brother and the Vizier are planning to seal the tunnels. They didn't know they existed. Muhammed says they're a threat to the security of..."

Lubna smiled and rose. Thomas watched her walk across the room and wring the cloth out in a bowl of cool water. From outside the window the sound of swallows chattered and cried.

"...shall I do that now then, Thomas?"

"I'm sorry, my prince, do what?"

"Have you been listening to a word I've said? And don't call me prince. You always call me by my name."

"You're older now, it would no longer be appropriate." He didn't think he needed to mention that Yusuf was now next in line should an accident befall his brother.

"It's appropriate among friends. And I asked should I fetch Muhammed now? He insisted I call him as soon as you woke. And see, you are awake!" The boy grinned, stood, his body quivering. "Shall I?"

"As you wish, my prince."

After Yusuf had gone, Thomas called across the room to Lubna. "Where is Jorge?"

"I haven't seen him since he carried you here."

"Jorge carried me?"

"All the way from the hunting field. He insisted. He is strong."

"He would be stronger if he stopped eating and drinking so much."

"But then he wouldn't be Jorge."

"You like him," Thomas said.

"Yes, I like him," Lubna replied, seeming on the point of adding to her statement, then holding her words, if she had ever intended any and it was not simply Thomas's imagination.

"Perhaps he's returned to his former life."

"Perhaps. But if so it would take no time for him to walk along a few corridors and visit. That fat cook has been." Lubna looked at her hands. "She told me about your friend. The one that died."

"Prea."

"Was that her name?"

Thomas smiled. "She was smart, that one. Too smart to be a kitchen girl. And now her short life has been tossed aside. If I'd seen things sooner she'd still be alive. It's my fault she's dead."

Lubna's face changed, all humour leaving it. "Yes, it is. And you misjudged my father. I have to think on that. At the moment I can't find it in my heart to forgive you."

"I..." Thomas started to defend himself, stopped. She was right. He had misjudged Olaf. And he had been a fool not to see Helena's deceit. She had no doubt been working against him the whole time she shared his bed, and any last feelings he might have had for her were cast away in the wind. She didn't exist to him anymore. "You're right, I thought I was so clever. I believed too much in my own intellect and didn't see things that were right in front of me. I misjudged Muhammed, too."

"He saved us all," Lubna said. She rose and returned to the bedside, but didn't sit, didn't try to take his hand, and Thomas wondered if she ever would again. "He was strong on the hillside. A weaker man would have been swept aside. My father tells me the nobles were planning to put one of their own in the palace. Had Muhammed not been so determined it might be Faris al-Rashid commanding now."

"What is Tahir doing, and that grim cleric?"

"They are servants. They follow whoever leads. Now they must follow Muhammed. When his brother brings him you must thank him, Thomas."

"I have words to say to him, certainly."

There came the sound of footsteps from the corridor and Yusuf scrambled in, barely able to stay upright he entered so fast. Muhammed came more slowly, waving at his guards to remain outside.

"I would speak with Thomas Berrington alone," he said, an easy command in his voice. He wore the full regalia of a Sultan, his bearing that of someone used to giving orders, used to being obeyed.

"But I can stay?" Yusuf said, rocking from foot to foot beside Thomas's bed.

"Alone, my brother. I will tell you everything later, but Thomas and I have matters of state to discuss. Private matters." Muhammed flicked his hand. "Fetch me a chair," he said, to no-one, to everyone.

When a guard had brought a simple wooden chair and set

it beside the bed, Muhammed waved everyone away, waiting until it was only Thomas and himself left in the room.

Muhammed looked around. "I haven't been in this room for many years before today. This is where I recovered after I was wounded at Malaka, when they came across the sea at us."

"I remember, my prince."

Muhammed smiled. "I don't forget my debt to you, Thomas Berrington, even if I rarely show it. But now it seems I owe you an even greater debt than my father did. I owe you my position as Sultan."

"It's yours by right. I did nothing."

Muhammed finally sat in the chair and leaned forward, his face close to Thomas's, who smelled the fine oils sheening the prince's hair, the perfume on his skin. All false friendship departed his face, his dark eyes cold.

"You know I don't like you, but I will pretend because it is expected of me."

"Don't do so on my behalf, pr— Malik. I didn't welcome the friendship of your father, and I don't seek yours now."

"Oh, but you should. My father had many friends. Less so now he is banished, but no doubt some still remain. To them you are a wanted man. But with my patronage you remain protected. So tell me again you don't need a Sultan's friendship."

"I am a mere surgeon, Malik, and yours to command."

"Indeed you are. And surgeons don't question princes, even less so Sultans. It amuses me to keep you alive, you and that fool of a eunuch."

"The Sultan is generous."

"I believe I am. It serves my purpose to keep you on a leash. Just never forget, *ajami*, that I can have you killed any time I wish. More to the point, I know who your friends are. Olaf's ugly daughter, she will die first, and I would make you watch as my men take her over and over again, make you watch as we flay her skin to show the bone beneath. And then we will start on the eunuch. And his friends. I know everything, Thomas Berrington, everything. You are mine, and you will do as I command."

Thomas stared into Muhammed's eyes, his body tight with anger.

"You are unwell, my friend?" Muhammed leaned over, reaching out to close his hand over Thomas's shoulder. He squeezed hard.

Thomas bit down on his lip, refusing to scream, although the urge was almost impossible to suppress.

"I will heal, prince." Her could barely get the words out. "I exist to serve."

"Good." But Muhammed's pressure didn't ease, if anything it grew and the room began to fade to grey. "It doesn't please me to make these threats. Know that they are only made for the good of al-Andalus. We both love this land. We both want to see it survive and prosper. My father's approach has failed, battle after battle after battle, each time losing ground to the infidel. The Spanish have grown strong, but I have a rational approach, a pragmatic approach. And you will help me, I have decided." Finally he released his grip and sat back.

Sweat trickled down Thomas's face, beaded his skin beneath the sheet. He breathed rapidly, the fire in his shoulder almost all consuming.

"Tell me you agree." Muhammed leaned close, his voice little more than a whisper, the scent of cloves on his breath.

"I exist to serve, prince," Thomas repeated.

"Good." Muhammed sat back quickly, rose equally as fast, the chair toppling backwards behind him. "And as a reward I have decided Helena will return to your house and once more take up her duties." He smiled.

"A reward?" The sweat lay cold against Thomas's skin. "That is no reward—the woman is no longer welcome in my house."

"But that is where she will come, and you will take her back into your bed. Next to the other sister if you wish, it is your house, after all. I should have her killed for her treachery, but this punishment is so much sweeter. Tahir will visit you soon. He has sent the Spanish priest back to his masters, but he will return in a matter of months, and when he does Tahir will ask you to travel to Qurtuba with him, on a mission supposedly to aid the Spanish queen, but your real purpose will be otherwise. This time you will do as Tahir asks."

When Muhammed was gone Thomas lay on the cot and closed his eyes. The old Sultan had betrayed his trust and the new one was even worse. Perhaps it was time to slip away, to return to the land he had abandoned almost a lifetime ago.

A familiar sound reached him and he raised his head in time to see a section of the wall pivot out. Jorge peered through, extending one leg, grimacing as he squeezed through a gap too narrow to accommodate him. Although, watching him struggle, Thomas thought he looked slimmer than a week before.

"How did you manage to pass through these places, Thomas?"

"I had assistance." He didn't want reminding of Prea. "What were you doing in there?"

"Listening. Watching. I heard everything."

"Then you know I have no choice."

"You will go to Qurtuba?" Jorge pushed the panel shut behind him, came across, righted the chair and sat where Muhammed had. He studied Thomas, taking in the bandage to his shoulder, a second covering the wound at his waist. "Do you think you will you live long enough?"

Thomas smiled. He could always rely on Jorge for a tactless comment.

"I have overstayed my welcome in this city. It's time to move on."

"You can't do that." Jorge's voice took on a serious tone. "If you run away they have won, all of them. This city needs men of honour, men of science. You have to stay."

"With a woman I hate. At the beck and call of a man I don't respect."

"Then stay for me, and for Lubna. For the good men and women of this city."

"The city is lost," Thomas said.

"Not yet. Not if we have something to fight for."

Thomas closed his eyes again, wanting oblivion. He felt Jorge take his hand as he started to drift. And then, a moment later, a smaller hand closed gently around his on the other side, and someone sat on the foot of the cot.

"I think death would be less painful," Thomas murmured, opening his eyes to see Lubna and Yusuf with Jorge, knowing he couldn't abandon these three.

AFTERWORD

I need to make some comment regarding historic and cultural accuracy in The Red Hill. Although I have conducted extensive historical research—a list of some references follows—this is essentially a novel: a work of fiction. As such I made the decision that complete historical accuracy should not overrule the need for development of character and plot. All of the dates of rulers and main battles are as accurate as my research allows, but many names and characters are fictitious. In addition to this, some liberties have been taken with cultural issues. The Red Hill is written for a 21st Century audience, and many of the characters think from a 21st century perspective. Whilst this is no doubt lacking in historical accuracy, many sources indicate that the Moorish culture in Spain was one of the most enlightened and forward looking of the time, and so I would like to think that they would feel a sympathy with our modern day sensibilities. Should you disagree, my apologies, but as I have said, the story here takes precedence over complete historical or cultural accuracy.

I am not aware of any network of hidden tunnels present in the Alhambra palace, although there are rumours of some passageways which allowed the Sultan to visit his wives without being observed. The passages described in this book are a complete work of fiction, so please make no attempt to discover them, for they do not exist.

I would like to thank Esperanza and Richard Nother for their hospitality on my second visit to Gharnatah in 2012, the first being 40 years earlier, and a special thanks to the nameless Arab guide to al-Hamra whose knowledge and helpfulness added immensely to our tour of the palace.

* * *

384 | DAVID PENNY

The Red Hill is the first in a series which will take Thomas Berrington and the eunuch Jorge from the year 1482 to the fall of the Granada on January 1st 1492.

If you enjoyed this book then you can find out more about the tales of Thomas and Jorge on my website:

www.david-penny.com

You can also sign up to the mailing list there and be the first to hear of new releases and updates, as well as exclusive offers.

If you *really liked this book why not let others know by leaving a review on Amazon or Goodreads.*

REFERENCES

I am indebted to the John Rylands library in Manchester and to the kindness and helpfulness of their staff in finding me resources to start my research. Only subsequent to studying the original documents did I discover that many of them are also available through Amazon and other suppliers.

My main sources of research are listed below:

- History of the Moorish Empire in Europe by S.P. Scott publ. 1904
- The History of the Mohametan Empire in Spain by James Cavannah Murphy publ. 1816
- In Fair Granada (fiction) by E. Everett-Green publ. 1902
- Moorish Spain by Richard Fletcher publ. 1992
- Medieval Islamic Medicine by Peter E. Portman and Emilie Savage-Smith publ. 2007
- Sexuality in Islam by Abdelwahab Bouhdiba, translated from the French by Alan Sheridan, publ. 1925
- The Alhambra by Robert Irwin publ. 2005
- The House of Wisdom by Jonathon Lyons publ. 2009
- When the Moors ruled in Europe (DVD) from Channel 4, presented by Bettany Hughes, available through Acorn Media.

Lightning Source UK Ltd.
Milton Keynes UK
UKHW011457121020
371441UK00003B/463